ACCLAIM FOR ALEX RIDER:

"Explosive, thrilling, action-packed – meet Alex Rider."
Guardian

"Horowitz is pure class, stylish but action-packed ... being James Bond in miniature is way cooler than being a wizard." **Daily Mirror**

"Horowitz will grip you with suspense, daring and cheek – and that's just the first page! ... Prepare for action scenes as fast as a movie." **The Times**

"Anthony Horowitz is the lion of children's literature."
Michael Morpurgo

"Fast and furious." **Telegraph**

"The perfect hero ... genuine 21st century stuff."
Daily Telegraph

"Brings new meaning to the phrase 'action-packed'."
Sunday Times

"Every bored schoolboy's fantasy, only a thousand times funnier, slicker and more exciting ... genius."
Independent on Sunday

"Perfect escapism for all teenage boys." **The Times**

"Addictive, pacy novels."   ***Financial Times***

"Adults as well as kids will be hooked on the adventures of Alex Rider ... Harry Potter with attitude."   ***Daily Express***

"Meaty, thrilling and compelling." ***Irish Independent***

"This is the kind of book that's designed to grab the reader by the scruff of the neck, pull him into the page and not let go of him until he's well and truly hooked."   ***The Good Book Guide***

"If you are looking for a thrilling, exciting read, this is it."   ***Sunday Express***

"Crackling with suspense and daring, this is a fabulous story, showing that a bit of guts will take you a very long way."   ***Guardian***

"Will last for ever as one of the children's classics of our age."   ***The Times***

"The series that has re-invented the spy genre."
                    Independent

Titles by Anthony Horowitz

The Alex Rider series:
Stormbreaker
Point Blanc
Skeleton Key
Eagle Strike
Scorpia
Ark Angel
Snakehead
Crocodile Tears
Scorpia Rising
Russian Roulette
Never Say Die
Secret Weapon
Nightshade

The Power of Five (Book One): *Raven's Gate*
The Power of Five (Book Two): *Evil Star*
The Power of Five (Book Three): *Nightrise*
The Power of Five (Book Four): *Necropolis*
The Power of Five (Book Five): *Oblivion*

The Devil and His Boy
Granny
Groosham Grange
Return to Groosham Grange
The Switch
Scared to Death

The Diamond Brothers books:
The Falcon's Malteser
Public Enemy Number Two
South by South East
The French Confection
The Greek Who Stole Christmas
The Blurred Man
I Know What You Did Last Wednesday

ALEX RIDER
NIGHTSHADE

ANTHONY HOROWITZ

WALKER
BOOKS

To OF and BO'C with thanks.

First published 2020 by Walker Books Ltd
87 Vauxhall Walk, London SE11 5HJ

2 4 6 8 10 9 7 5 3 1

This book has been typeset in Officina Sans

Printed and bound by CPI Group (UK) Ltd, Croydon CRO 4YY

British Library Cataloguing in Publication Data:
a catalogue record for this book is available from the British Library

ISBN 978-1-4063-8929-6
ISBN 978-1-4063-9100-8

www.walker.co.uk

CONTENTS

PROLOGUE

The British Airways Airbus A318 had been kept in a holding pattern before it landed at Heathrow. Looking out of the window, Alex Rider watched the familiar landmarks slide beneath him for a third time. There was the River Thames, snaking its way past Slough and Maidenhead. Then Windsor Castle, built in the eleventh century and now home to the Queen, visible for miles around. In the distance, he could see the first high-rise apartments springing up around the edge of London.

He glanced at Jack Starbright who was dozing in the seat next to him. The two of them were on their way back from a long weekend in Amsterdam ... a treat they had promised themselves ever since they had returned from Smoke City, the industrial compound in Wales where Alex had come face to face with the Grimaldi brothers, the last two survivors of the criminal organization known as Scorpia. The Grimaldis had been planning the kidnap of the century, code named Steel Claw, and would have succeeded if Alex hadn't stumbled across their path. But it had been a close thing. Alex still woke at night remembering the huge steam train that had come blasting through the night, chasing him as he made for the single tunnel that provided the only means of escape.

So much had happened in the past few weeks. He had thought Jack was dead but discovered she was still alive. That in itself had changed everything for him, lifting a huge weight off his shoulders and giving him a fresh start. She had once been his housekeeper but she had become his closest friend and he had been unable to manage without her. At the same time, he had left America, picking up the pieces of his old life in London: his home, his friends. Jack had gone back to her studies – she hoped to become a lawyer – while Alex had gone back to school. As an added bonus, the two of them had suddenly found themselves with more money than they had ever known. They would be secure for life.

They had earned a weekend away together. It had been an opportunity to walk along the canals, to visit art galleries and coffee shops, to do some shopping, to relax and enjoy life. Above all, they had spent time together, laughing off everything that had happened. Even Mrs Jones, the head of MI6 Special Operations, had urged him to leave his adventures behind him and settle down to a more ordinary life. Alex was convinced that his time as a spy was all behind him now.

He was wrong.

The aircraft had just passed over Cookham, an attractive village on the banks of the River Thames, and if Alex had been able to see twenty thousand feet below, he would have watched for himself as a murder – which had been planned to the last detail several weeks before – was finally put into action.

The security officer sitting outside Clifford Hall on the edge of Cookham had noticed the plane circling and knew at once that it was flight BA 423 from Amsterdam. But then he knew the flight path of every plane that took off from or landed at Heathrow, just as he knew the names of everyone who lived in the village. He could even recognize them by their car number plates: the plumber in his white van, the local magistrate in her Volvo, the bank manager in his new Ford Fiesta. He was sitting in a folding chair next to the main gates with a newspaper in his lap. But he had not read a word of it. His job was to watch, to be ready, always to stay alert. And although he looked half-asleep, his hand was never very far away from the Glock 17 semi-automatic pistol which fitted snugly into the thumb release paddle holster clipped on to his belt, under his jacket. If necessary, he could load, take aim and fire with total accuracy in less than two seconds.

His name was Robert Spencer. He had been Second Lieutenant in Afghanistan until a roadside bomb had crippled him, ending his military career. He was now a senior officer in Protection Command, a highly specialized division of the London Metropolitan Police. His job was to look after the man who lived at Clifford Hall.

James Clifford – now Lord Clifford – had been a politician for more than forty years, but perhaps the most remarkable thing about him was that in all that time he had always been popular. He was a man who loved his country, who worked hard, who wanted to make a difference. He had been an extremely effective Home Secretary – in fact he had been so successful in his war on organized crime that when he retired, it was decided that he should be given round-the-clock protection … just in case. He had, after all, made plenty of enemies.

He was retired now and lived with his wife in the handsome country villa that his family had owned for generations. Clifford Hall had the look of a French château, with five bedrooms, a conservatory and a perfect lawn that led all the way to the river with a view of Lock Island on the other side of a narrow stretch of water. Second Lieutenant Spencer had been given a flat above the garage. There were CCTV cameras everywhere and, sitting in front of a bank of screens in his front room, he could see anyone who came near. Life in an English village is very much a matter of routine and after all the time he had spent in Cookham, he had most of the day pinned down to the minute. 8.10 a.m. – the newspapers delivered. 8.25 a.m. – the mail. 9.00 a.m. – Mrs Winters, the cleaning lady, arrives. 10.15 a.m. – Lady Clifford walks the dogs. And so on. There was almost no chance that anyone would seriously try to hurt Lord Clifford but, as Spencer knew from his time in the army, "almost" wasn't good enough. He took his job seriously. And he liked Lord Clifford. He wanted to keep the old man safe.

As the British Airways flight curved out of sight, he became aware of two figures approaching the gate and the short drive that led to the front door. His hand slid a few centimetres towards his gun, then stopped as he saw that the visitors were young girls, no more than twelve years old, dressed in the blue and red polo shirts that identified them as Girl Guides. One of them was carrying a wooden tray with a pile of chocolate muffins. They stopped in front of him.

"How can I help you, girls?" Spencer asked.

"Hello. My name is Amy and we're raising money for our local activity centre," the first of them replied. She had fair hair, framing a pretty face, with a scattering of freckles over her cheeks.

"We made them ourselves," the other said. She was a year or two younger, a black girl with glasses and hair tied back in pigtails. "I'm Jasmine," she added.

"They're fifty pence each."

"Or you can buy three for a pound."

Spencer smiled. "That's very kind of you, but I'm afraid I'm not into cakes." He patted his stomach. "I have to watch my weight."

"Would the people in the house like to buy some?" Jasmine, the girl with the pigtails, asked.

"I don't think so." Spencer shook his head. The truth was that he wouldn't allow anyone to pass through the gates unless they were expected; not even someone as innocent as a Girl Guide.

But then a voice called out behind him. "I'd love a chocolate muffin. I'll have it with my afternoon cup of tea."

Spencer turned round. The front door was open. As luck would have it, Lord Clifford had chosen that moment to come into the garden for a little fresh air. Spencer stood up as the man he was paid to protect arrived at the front gate. He was wearing a blue blazer and a straw hat to protect himself from the hot sun and he was supporting himself on a walking stick. He had suffered a heart attack earlier that summer and he still hadn't fully recovered his health. But he showed no sign of that as he stopped at the gate and smiled at the two new arrivals. "Do you live in Cookham?" he asked.

"No, sir. We live in Taplow."

Taplow was another village, further down the river.

"And you made these yourselves?"

"Yes, sir."

"I can bring a couple of muffins up for you, sir," Spencer said.

"No, no. That's all right, Robert." The old man fumbled in his pocket for loose change. "What did you two young ladies say you were collecting for?"

"It's for our activity centre," Amy repeated.

"We need to repaint our hut," Jasmine explained.

"And we're buying new equipment for the kitchen."

"Well, that's a very good cause." Lord Clifford drew out a shiny pound coin. "I only want one of your cakes, but you can keep the change."

"Thank you!" both the girls chorused.

One of them held up the tray. "You can help yourself to whichever one you want."

Lord Clifford licked his lips, then reached out and took the biggest muffin from the top of the pile. "It smells delicious!" he exclaimed.

He took a bite.

Fifteen minutes later, the plane touched down and taxied towards Terminal 5 before coming to a halt. Alex and Jack unbuckled their seat belts and reached up for their luggage, which included the great ball of Dutch cheese that Jack had insisted on buying in an Amsterdam market. Alex stuffed his exercise books into his backpack. He had school the next day and had been doing his homework during the flight.

At that same moment, Lord Clifford suffered the first seizure that would lead to a major heart attack, followed by death.

Nobody guessed that he had been murdered and that the muffin he had eaten had been made with flour, eggs, milk, butter, chocolate and sodium cyanide, a lethal poison that had begun to attack his heart and lungs the moment he had taken the first bite. Twenty-four hours later, the two Girl Guides had left the country. Protection Command made no further enquiries and so they did not realize that there was no activity centre in Taplow, no hut to repaint, no kitchen needing equipment.

The organization known as Nightshade had killed Lord Clifford for one simple reason. His death would give them the opportunity to launch a major terrorist attack on the city that was Alex's home. The attack would take place in exactly three weeks' time.

PART ONE: GENESIS

THE END OF ALEX

The steel-grey Jaguar XJ Sentinel swept round Trafalgar Square and continued through Whitehall. It was sleek and expensive with tinted windows that turned the single passenger sitting in the back into nothing more than a vague shadow. Had anyone checked the number plate, they would have discovered that it belonged to the chairman of a private bank in Liverpool Street.

The car had cost almost four hundred thousand pounds to manufacture and it was unique. It was kitted out with the very latest communications equipment, the windows were made of armoured glass, the interior was lined with titanium and there was a 15 millimetre steel plate underneath the floor. In the event of a chemical or biological attack, the car had its own oxygen system. The tyres could be shot out without slowing it down. An advanced weapons system including lightweight Javelin surface-to-air missiles was built into the bodywork.

The passenger, sitting with her legs crossed, did not work in a bank, although with her rather severe haircut, her midnight-blue suit and her gleaming black leather shoes she certainly looked like a business person. Her name was Mrs Jones and she was the Chief Executive of MI6 Special Operations – a division so secret that only half a dozen people in the country knew it existed. Today she was on her way to see one of those people and she had an uneasy feeling in her stomach. There was no actual reason for it. The summons, which had arrived by email, had been short and to the point.

Eleven o'clock. Tuesday morning.

But Mrs Jones had been a spy all her working life. Starting as a junior intelligence officer, she had risen up the ranks, finally replacing her boss, Alan Blunt, as department head. She had learned to trust her instincts and the moment she had received the message, she had known she was in trouble. What she didn't know was – why.

She glanced out of the window and saw the Houses of Parliament and Big Ben ahead of her. The time was seven minutes to eleven. The car turned left and passed underneath a stone archway, stopping outside a massive nineteenth-century building with row after row of arched windows and miniature balconies, columns and black wrought-iron railings. Everything – from the steps leading up to the main entrance to the statue of Queen Victoria on the roof – seemed to whisper how important the place was. Arriving here, you could not fail to be awed.

The building was the headquarters of the Foreign and Commonwealth Office, known as the FCO for short. This is the government department responsible for protecting British interests around the world. A large part of its responsibilities includes national security and counter-terrorism. It is in charge of both MI5 and MI6.

A young assistant was waiting for her at the front door. In fact he was ridiculously young – in his early twenties with fair hair slicked back and a face that had surely never been shaved. As Mrs Jones got out of the car, he watched her with watery eyes that seemed to cut her to the bone. He was wearing a made-to-measure suit that was a little tight on him, as if it had been made to measure for his younger brother. His shoes had been polished until they looked brand new.

"Good morning, Mrs Jones," he said. "Please will you come this way?"

He did not speak again. His job was simply to take her through security and on to the office of Dominic Royce, the Permanent Under-Secretary for Foreign Affairs and the single most powerful man in the building.

The head of the FCO is the Foreign Secretary. He is the man you will see on television, travelling around the world, talking to foreign leaders and the press. (So far only one woman has held the position.) But the Permanent Under-Secretary works behind the scenes. He is a civil servant, not a politician. He runs the department on a day-to-day basis and makes all the most important decisions. Dominic Royce had only joined the FCO a few weeks before. He was very much a cold fish with no close friends. When he walked into a room, people fell silent or, if they could, found an excuse to leave. It was said that the Foreign Secretary was terrified of him and that when he went to Downing Street, even the Prime Minister pretended to be out.

Mrs Jones thought of all this as she followed the young man across a spectacular entrance hall with columns and galleries stretching up to an iron and glass ceiling far above. They came to a grand staircase and suddenly their footsteps fell silent as they moved from bright coloured mosaic to soft carpet. They climbed two floors, then continued along a corridor to a double-height door at the end. They had passed a few people as they made their way but nobody had looked at them. In this building, everyone minded their own business.

They went in without knocking. A woman sat in an outer office with a desk, three telephones and a computer. "Mrs Jones," she said with the faintest flicker of a smile but no hint of enthusiasm. "Mr Royce is expecting you."

Outside, in the distance, Big Ben chimed eleven. Mrs Jones continued through.

Dominic Royce was sitting behind a desk so

enormous that it reduced him to the size of a school-boy. He was a small man anyway, thin with a long, narrow face, grey eyes and grey lips. His hair was very black, neatly combed back and a little greasy. He was wearing an old-fashioned pinstripe suit and round, wire-frame glasses that perched hesitantly on his up-turned nose. He was clean-shaven and from his looks Mrs Jones would have guessed that he was in his late forties. But there was no need to guess. She never went to a meeting without learning everything about everyone in the room and she knew that he was actually forty-three years old, educated at Eton and Cambridge, married with two sons who were also at Eton. He had inherited millions of pounds from his father who had inherited millions more from his. He owned several properties, including a flat in Pimlico and a huge country house with twenty acres of land just outside Salisbury. At the weekend, he liked to go shooting ... birds, rabbits, deer. Anything that moved.

He looked up as Mrs Jones came in but he didn't stand to shake her hand or anything like that. "Please sit down." He turned his attention back to the folder that he had been examining. Mrs Jones could see the words TOP SECRET in red on the cover.

In the silence that followed, she examined the office. She had been here before. The Permanent Under-Secretary before Dominic Royce had been an altogether different sort of man, loud and cheerful, happy to discuss business over tea and biscuits. Jaffa cakes had been his favourite. There were going to be no refreshments this time. The office was dark and severe with old wood panelling and leather-bound books on shelves. Two windows reached from floor to ceiling but very little light came in.

Royce laid the folder down and Mrs Jones saw a black-and-white photograph lying on top of the first page. She showed no emotion. She had been trained to give nothing away. But her throat tightened. Now she knew why she was here.

The picture, which had been taken more than a year ago, showed a very good-looking boy, dressed in a school uniform. He was gazing into the mid-distance, unaware that he was being snapped. Two strands of fair hair hung down, partly covering his eyes. He was pushing a bicycle, a Condor Junior Roadracer, and there was a backpack hanging off his shoulder.

"Tell me about Alex Rider." The Permanent Under-Secretary looked up from the file and challenged her with cold, unfriendly eyes.

"What is it you want to know?" Mrs Jones replied.

Royce blinked heavily, then looked at her as if she had deliberately insulted him. "Well, let's start with a simple question. Is it true that this boy works for you?"

"He used to work for the department. Yes, sir." Mrs Jones chose her words carefully. In fact several months had passed since Special Operations had last recruited Alex – sending him out as an under-cover agent to an international school in Cairo. That had brought him up against the criminal organization known as Scorpia and a secret hideout in the Western Desert. Not for the first time, it had almost got him killed.

"A schoolboy! He was fourteen years old!"

"That was what made him so effective. It's all there in the file. Because he was so young, nobody suspected him. He was the perfect secret weapon." She paused. The man sitting opposite her said nothing so she went on. "His uncle was an agent who also worked for our department. Ian Rider was unfortunately killed investigating that Stormbreaker business but it turned out that he had trained Alex—"

"Yes. I have read all this. Every last word of it!" The Permanent Under-Secretary's voice was thin and whiny and didn't change no matter how angry he became. He was angry now. "You had him train with the SAS in the Brecon Beacons."

"Alex passed with flying colours."

"I find that extremely hard to believe. But whether he was ready or not, you then sent him all over the world." He spread the file in front of him. All of Alex's missions were described in detail. "First Cornwall. Then the Point Blanc Academy in France, some island off the coast of America, Thailand, Australia ... you even blasted him into outer space!" He slammed the file shut. "Are you seriously telling me that the British government quite cheerfully went ahead and employed a child who wasn't even old enough to vote? That you took him out of school and endangered his life ... how many times?" He batted the answer away with his hand and continued without drawing a breath. "Do you have any idea how much embarrassment it would have caused if the wretched boy had managed to get himself killed? What do you think would have happened if anyone had found out?"

"We were very careful," Mrs Jones said. "And Alex was exceptionally gifted. Thanks to him—"

"I'm not interested," Royce cut in. "To be honest with you, I think you should be considering your position, Mrs Jones. You must have taken leave of your senses. I mean, what were you thinking of, recruiting him in the first place?"

In fact, it hadn't been Mrs Jones who had recruited Alex. That had been Alan Blunt's idea and she had actually been against it. But she wasn't going to tell Dominic Royce that. Whatever her differences with the man whose job she now occupied, she would never have taken sides against him. And there was something about Royce, his coldness and his arrogance, that disgusted her. She wasn't going to waste her time trying to make excuses.

She waited for him to continue.

"How many people know about Alex Rider and his involvement with MI6?" Royce asked.

"Very few." Mrs Jones considered. It was certainly the case that a great many people who had come up against Alex were now dead. Herod Sayle, Dr Grief, Colonel Sarov...

"Where is he now?" The question broke her train of thought.

"He's back at school."

"I want to get one thing absolutely straight, Mrs Jones. When I was shown the contents of this file, I found it almost impossible to believe. I've never heard of anything quite so ridiculous and downright dangerous." He lifted a finger. "Dangerous for us, I mean! Can we trust the boy not to talk? What happens if he tells his friends?"

"Alex is very discreet."

"Well, let me make it absolutely clear that you're to have nothing more to do with him. I never want to hear his name again. Do you understand me?"

"Yes."

"I presume he's signed the Official Secrets Act. If he says one word to anyone about this, we will make life very difficult for him and for everyone he knows. I want you to frighten the life out of him."

"Actually, Alex isn't very easily frightened."

"Just do it, Mrs Jones. This business with Alex Rider was a huge error of judgement on your behalf. You are not to have any further communication with him under any circumstances. Good morning!"

The last two words were a dismissal. Mrs Jones got to her feet.

Immediately, the door opened and the young man who had brought her to the office appeared. Presumably, the Permanent Under-Secretary had summoned him with a button concealed under his desk. Once again, he said nothing but stood there, pale and silent, like a ghost. As Mrs Jones walked back out of the Foreign and Commonwealth Office, he followed close behind, a half-smile on his face as if he had heard everything that had just been said. She ignored him, thinking about the conversation she'd just had.

As much as she disliked Dominic Royce, she had to admit that he had a point. It had been wrong to use Alex Rider even if he had been a quite extraordinary success. He was a schoolboy, not a spy, but that hadn't stopped MI6 tearing him away from his home and his friends, putting him in danger over and over again. How many times had he almost died? He had actually taken a bullet in the chest, right outside the office in Liverpool Street. Ever since Alan Blunt had first recruited Alex, Mrs Jones had seen just how much damage they had done to him. Although she had tried to persuade herself otherwise, she knew that Alex had no place in her world.

The Jaguar was waiting for Mrs Jones outside the Foreign Office with the engine already running. She got in and closed the door. She didn't need to tell the driver where to go. The car pulled away, heading back the way it had come.

So it was finally over. Dominic Royce was her boss and she couldn't argue with him. She could never use Alex Rider again.

Unless, of course, she went behind his back.

FLAMENGO PARK

It was one of the most dangerous cities in the world.

Rio de Janeiro may be famous for its fabulous beaches, its carnival, the huge statue of Christ the Redeemer standing on the summit of the Corcovado Mountain – but it is also home to violence and murder. Pickpocketing, kidnapping, bag snatching, car-jacking ... all of these are daily events and it's not uncommon to see dead bodies lying in the gutter. It's hardly surprising. There are over one thousand slums – or *favelas* – in the city. Overcrowded, polluted and full of disease, they are a breeding ground for organized crime. Ordinary people live their lives between the drug lords on the one side and the police and the army on the other with armed militias patrolling the streets, killing anyone who gets in their way. In Rio de Janeiro it's possible to download an app that will tell you where the nearest shoot-out has occurred. It's at least one way to stay safe.

John Crawley was thinking about this as he left

the British Consulate in the Praia do Flamengo in the fashionable area of Rio close to Guanabara Bay. It was still early in the morning – Brazil is four hours behind the UK – but the sun was already shining and in the distance he could see the dark blue water of the Atlantic Ocean. The Consulate itself was a smart building on a corner, seven storeys high with a roof garden and a Union Jack fluttering over the main entrance. It would have been easy to mistake it for an expensive hotel and he had indeed just spent the night there. But as he crossed the four lanes of traffic and headed into the park opposite, all his senses were alert. He was not carrying a gun. He wondered if that was wise.

It was unusual for Crawley to find himself so far away from Liverpool Street and the offices of MI6 where he was both a deputy to Mrs Jones and one of her closest colleagues. To look at, he was one of the last people you would expect to be a spy. Although he was only in his thirties, he had the thinning hair and the blotchy skin of a much older man. He was dressed like a tourist with a striped jacket, sunglasses and a straw hat, and looked as if he had just come off a cruise ship. In fact, Crawley cultivated his appearance quite deliberately. He wanted the enemy to think that he was nothing more than an office manager, responsible for paperwork. They would be completely surprised when he killed them.

He was here to meet one of his agents, a man called Pablo. That wasn't his real name, of course.

He was Mario in Italy, Jean-Paul in France and Samir in Beirut. He had a different passport for every country he visited and no two passport photographs were quite the same. His hair could be dark or fair. He could be thin or fat, old or young. He was a deep-cover field operative who took extreme care to stay invisible. That was what had kept him alive.

But now he was in danger. Shortly after he had arrived in Rio, his cover had been blown and there had been two attempts to kill him. He had spent the last week in hiding but had managed to send an emergency signal to MI6 requesting immediate assistance. Pablo had vital information but he needed protection. There was nobody in Rio de Janeiro he could trust. He wanted someone he knew to meet him and to bring him in from the cold.

Crawley had recruited him. It was Crawley who had sent him on his current mission. Pablo knew him and would recognize him. The two men had agreed a meeting place: 8.00 a.m. in Flamengo Park. That was where Crawley was heading now.

Halfway across the road, Crawley glanced to the right and saw the Sugar Loaf Mountain, another Rio landmark, rising up in the distance. There was still very little traffic. At the weekends, the road could be jammed with drivers making their way to the beach. The perfect lawns and many palm trees of Flamengo Park were in front of him and he quickened his pace, already looking around him for any unexpected movement, anything that might suggest a trap.

Apart from Mrs Jones, nobody knew that Crawley was in Rio. He was travelling with a fake passport. He was certain that he hadn't been followed from the Consulate. But he was still being careful. Pablo was one of his best agents and yet he was scared. That made him scared too.

He stepped off the concrete and felt the grass under his feet. He had left the city behind him and was quickly being swallowed up by the park. There was nobody around him but that was hardly a surprise at this early hour. A single jogger ran past and clambered up the slope of a hill, disappearing into a cluster of palm trees at the top. Crawley followed him more slowly. He reached the trees and saw the sea straight ahead of him with about a dozen sailing boats moored next to each other on either side of a wooden jetty. This was the Marina da Glória. Crawley had only visited Rio once and that had been a while ago but he had spent several hours on Google Earth, taking a virtual tour of the city. He knew that there was a modern art museum close by and that if he continued along the coast, he would come to a small, domestic airport. He knew the name of every street for a mile around.

He quickly found what he was searching for. What looked like a sports arena sat between the road and the marina, with two concrete circles cut into the grass forming the shape of a figure of eight. A wider track ran all the way round it and the whole thing was enclosed in a low blue fence. This was the *Pistas de*

Aeromodelismo – the model aeroplane track – a place which had been specially built for Brazilian kids who gathered every weekend to fly their radio-controlled planes. Crawley glanced at his watch. He had arrived, deliberately, ten minutes early. Apart from two children – a boy and a girl who must have got up early and who were leaning over a model plane, putting it through its final checks – the track was empty. There was no sign of Pablo but Crawley was certain that he would be somewhere near by, watching. Only when he was sure that the area was completely safe would he show himself.

Crawley walked into the middle of the figure of eight and stood there, waiting.

It was a perfect place for a meeting like this, both private and yet out in the open. The park stretched out for about two hundred metres in every direction, with nowhere to hide, nowhere a sniper could take aim without being seen. The arena was completely flat and so large that Crawley would get plenty of warning if anyone approached. The sea was a short distance away, providing a natural barrier. To the north he could see a modern archway, poking up above the bushes. He had never visited it but knew that it was a monument to Brazilian soldiers killed in the Second World War. A concrete bridge stretched over the road behind him. He wondered which direction Pablo would come from. Would he show up at all? Crawley hadn't heard from him for forty-eight hours and it was always possible that he was already dead.

Several minutes passed. The sun was getting warmer as it rose into the sky. Crawley could feel it beating down on his shoulders and he was glad he had decided to wear a hat. The children had moved their plane to the centre of the track and, even at this distance, Crawley recognized the model: a Supermarine Spitfire. It was incredible how the old warplane was still an icon all over the world. He heard them start up the engine. A real Spitfire has a deep, throaty roar but the model was more like an angry wasp. Now the children were fighting for the remote control, arguing who was going to fly it first.

A figure appeared, coming through the trees, walking towards Crawley with the sea behind him. It was Pablo. When Crawley had shaken hands with him and wished him luck in his office in Liverpool Street, the agent had been wearing a suit. He had been relaxed, sure of himself. Now he was dressed in torn jeans and a dirty T-shirt with the single word BUMBU, a make of Brazilian rum, printed on the front. His hair was long and matted, and he had an untidy beard. His skin had been burned dark brown by the Brazilian sun. If Crawley had not been expecting him, he might not have known who it was.

It took Pablo a long time to cross the arena. His entire body language was defensive, his shoulders hunched and his head twisting from side to side as if he expected to be attacked at any time. He glanced at the two children and hesitated as if even they might be a threat. But they were ignoring him, still fighting for control of the plane. Carefully, he checked there was no one else around. Then he continued forward.

As he drew closer, Crawley saw that he had been wounded. There was a bandage tightly wrapped around his left arm. Blood had seeped through, drying and turning brown. He looked as if he hadn't eaten for days. Finally, he reached the centre of the track and stood opposite Crawley. Behind them, the boy and the girl had come to an agreement. The girl stood back while the boy pushed a miniature joystick on his remote control. The buzzing of the engine became louder and more insistent as the Spitfire raced down the track and, with a brief wobble, launched itself into the air.

"How are you, Pablo?" Crawley asked.

"I'm glad to see you." If anyone had been close by, they would have been surprised to hear the words, spoken in an upper-class English accent. Pablo was twenty-seven years old. It hadn't been that long since he had been studying politics and economics at Oxford University.

"We got your message. It's unlike you to sound so ... nervous."

Pablo tried to smile but he was obviously in pain. More than that – he was afraid and he couldn't completely hide it. "You have no idea!" he muttered. "These people ... I've never come across anyone like them. You want the truth? They make Scorpia look like a vicar's tea party." He shook his head. "You were

right to send me here, Mr Crawley. What they're plan‚
ning ... it's going to happen in London and it's going
to be soon. That's why I had to see you ... to warn
you!"

He was about to go on but just then the model
Spitfire crossed the sun, casting a shadow over the
two men. They were both trained to react to the
slightest movement. Crawford saw Pablo reach behind
him and guessed that he had a gun tucked into the
waistband of his trousers. He himself lifted a hand,
shielding his eyes from the glare. He watched the
Spitfire tear past. That was the sound it was making
now. It seemed to be ripping the sky in half.

"What happened to your arm?" Crawley asked.

Pablo touched the bandage as if he had forgotten
it was there. He winced. "There were three of them,
waiting for me outside a bar in São Paulo." Suddenly
he was angry. "There's been a leak, Mr Crawley. They
knew who I was. They knew I was there."

"That's impossible." Crawley was aware of the
seconds ticking away. The longer they were out in
the open, the more dangerous it was. He wanted to
find out what Pablo knew and to arrange his safe
passage out of Brazil. "I sent you here and I report
directly to Mrs Jones. Your mission was code red.
You really think either of us talked to anyone else?"

"I'm telling you ... they were waiting for me,"
Pablo insisted.

"Who were they?"

"Local gangsters. Hired hands." Pablo shrugged.

"You don't need to worry about them. They've retired."

So Pablo had managed to kill all three of them. But he had been hurt in the process.

"We need to get to the Consulate," Crawley said. "And then we're going to get you home."

"Yes. But first, I have to tell you..."

Crawley was aware of the Spitfire before he saw it. It was louder than before, which meant that it was closer. What were the two children doing? They had brought it swooping down ... so low it was going to hit them. Suddenly it was in his vision, a dark shape, nothing more. He saw it shoot past between him and Pablo, the wings outstretched. There was a spark of light, the sun reflecting off something silver. Pablo shouted and twisted round and there was a spray of crimson that seemed to come from nowhere, splashing over Crawley's shirt. Pablo fell onto his knees. The Spitfire span out of control and crashed to the ground. The boy had dropped the remote control. Both children had turned and were running away.

It took Crawley a few seconds to work out what had happened. Pablo had a terrible wound in his throat. He had been stabbed. But it was the Spitfire that had done it. One of its wings wasn't a wing at all. It was a knife, razor-sharp and the child – was it really a child? – had expertly guided it out of the sky, using its own speed and momentum to strike the killer blow. Pablo was finished. There was no doubt of it. As Crawley knelt beside him, he tried to speak but no words came out.

"Don't try and talk," Crawley said. "I'm getting help."

Crawley's hand was already in his pocket, squeezing the button on the transmitter that he had brought with him. As the two assassins sprinted to the edge of the park, half a dozen agents appeared from different angles, running towards the model aeroplane track. They worked for ABIN – the intelligence service of Brazil. Their job had been to provide back-up for the MI6 men, staying out of sight unless they were needed. They were most definitely needed now.

For a moment they were confused. They saw Crawley kneeling beside the man he had come to meet. Mysteriously, that man had been badly injured. There was nobody in sight apart from two kids who seemed to be empty-handed.

"Stop them!" Crawley shouted and pointed at the same time.

It was already too late. There was a scooter, a little Vespa 300, parked behind a bush, out of sight. The girl was sitting in the front and started it up while the boy got on behind her. Neither of them bothered with helmets and seconds later they were away, bouncing over the grass and onto the narrow road that curved all the way round the Marina da Glória. But they hadn't got away yet. Crawley heard the growl of engines and looked round as two more ABIN agents appeared, both of them riding bright red Honda motorbikes, cutting across the park. These were the machines used by the Brazilian police and

43

with their 500cc engines they were much more powerful than the scooter they were following. It would take them thirty seconds, maybe less, to catch up.

But the children had the advantage of the distance. They had already passed the war memorial and, as they sped forward, the boy reached into his pocket, took something out and hurled it behind him. There was a soft explosion and a great curtain of black smoke seemed to spring up across the road, blocking them from sight. The agents pursuing them were forced to slow down. Then, they heard another sound: a soft humming that rose in pitch and very quickly became a high-pitched whine. Half a mile away, in the park, Crawley heard the sound and knew instantly what it was. A helicopter was preparing to take off.

It was a bright red, single-engine Bell 407. It had been parked close to the edge of the airport, beside the fence that separated the main runway from the perimeter road. Later on, it would be discovered that it had been there for forty-eight hours, supposedly with engine trouble. The helicopter was registered to a hospital in Salvador. Of course, they had never heard of it.

The Vespa pulled up. The girl leapt off and ran the short distance to the fence with the boy right behind her. The two red Hondas were roaring towards them. The fence was less than three metres high but it was topped with loops of razor wire and there was no way they would be able to climb over. They didn't need to. Someone had already cut a hole big enough for them to pass through and even as the two agents drew up, they were peeling back the wire as if it were a trapdoor. Meanwhile, the helicopter was ready to take off, the blades spinning so fast they had become invisible, whipping up a cloud of sand and dust.

The girl was through. The boy followed. The first of the two ABIN agents drew a gun but he was half-blinded by the dust. The helicopter pilot, no more than a blur behind the glass, leaned forward and opened the cockpit door. The engine was screaming now. The helicopter was rocking slightly, ready to leave the ground. The ABIN agent shouted out a warning in Portuguese.

They would have both made it. But at the last moment, the boy was unlucky. The back of his T-shirt got snagged on the fence where the wire had been cut and suddenly he was like a fish squirming on a hook. The girl hesitated. The agent saw that he had an opportunity and leapt forward, covering the ground between the edge of the road and the fence, throwing himself onto the boy. The pilot shouted something and the girl turned and ran. She lunged into the cockpit and instantly, with the door still open, the Bell 407 twisted into the air and then soared away, over the sea.

The two agents grabbed the boy and handcuffed him before he could make a move. He was screaming at them, swearing, his face contorted with anger.

Neither of the men could quite believe what they were seeing. The boy had short hair and ears that stuck out. He was wearing round, plastic-framed glasses. He was only a teenager.

Meanwhile, in the park, an ambulance had finally arrived. Crawley was still kneeling beside Pablo and looked up as it drew to a halt, wondering if it had come in time.

It hadn't.

Pablo's eyes flickered open. He grabbed hold of Crawley's arm. With the last of his strength, he uttered a single word. "Nightshade."

And then he died.

THE BIG SKULL

It was a horrible room. The walls, the floor and the ceiling were all made of concrete, raw and unpainted. The door was a slab of iron with no handle on the inside. There were no windows. The light came from a neon tube that hung crookedly, buzzing and flickering as it cast out a hard, white glare. The room was in the basement and although it was a warm afternoon, down here the air was chilly and damp.

The boy from Flamengo Park had been here for nine hours. He was sitting on a wooden chair on one side of a wooden table; both pieces of furniture were bolted to the ground. The boy was handcuffed, the chain fastened to the table. So far he had not spoken a word. He had been given a glass of water and a sandwich but he hadn't touched them. Some of the police officers who had seen him were beginning to wonder if there hadn't been some sort of mistake. It was impossible to believe that he could have been involved in a murder. From the look of him, even stealing from a sweet shop would have been beyond him.

He was small for his age, slim and muscular. It would have been easy to imagine him as a dancer or an athlete. He had dark hair, cut very neatly in a style that was almost military, as if he was about to go back to school. He was now dressed in a pale grey tracksuit that had been provided for him. He had been allowed to keep his glasses but everything else had been taken away for analysis. He had been wearing short trousers and a polo shirt, the sort of clothes that might have been chosen for him by a mother or father wanting him to look smart. His trainers were expensive, made by Adidas and not available in Brazil. In fact, the police had decided that the boy was almost certainly European. Although he had evidently been out in the sun, he was still too pale to be Brazilian. He had been given a complete physical examination and the police doctor had noted that he was in perfect physical shape apart from a curving scar underneath his right ear which had long since healed.

After his arrest, the boy, who still had no name, had been handed over to the Special Operations Battalion of the Brazilian police. BOPE is also known as "the big skull" because of the logo – a skull impaled by a dagger – which appears on their uniforms and vehicles. BOPE is one of the toughest police units in the world. They carry a huge range of weapons, from assault rifles and semi-automatic pistols to general-purpose machine guns ... they need them in their constant fight against the violent drug gangs that infest the city. They work out of an ugly, square building in the south of Rio de Janeiro. It's reached by a single track that leads to a yard filled with burnt-out motor vehicles and piles of broken-down crates and tyres. It wasn't just the room that was horrible. The whole place was.

The boy was being recorded and observed. A microphone was concealed under the table and there was a camera behind the neon tube. In another room, one level up on the ground floor, two men were watching him on a TV monitor. One of them was John Crawley. The other, dressed in a loose-fitting camouflage jacket and trousers, was an older man with a tangle of greying hair, a hawk-like nose and dark, watchful eyes. His name was Lieutenant Carlos Oliviera and he was the senior commander of BOPE.

"Nine hours and not a single word," he was saying. He spoke excellent English. "I had one of my best interrogators in the room with him. We tried to be nice to him. We tried threats. We put the fear of God into him ... and nothing!"

"What language did you speak?" Crawley asked.

"English, French and Portuguese ... but there's not a flicker of interest. We've had the clothes that he was wearing examined and they came from Athens so we tried Greek. That didn't work either."

"So you don't know who he is or where he came from?"

"We've taken fingerprints and DNA samples. They've gone to every police force on the planet.

But you know how it is, my friend. It's going to take time to get a result, even if he does turn up on somebody's database."

"We may not have time." Crawley was thinking of the last words spoken by Pablo before he died. An organization called Nightshade. They were planning something hideous in London. It was clearly going to happen soon. That was why it had been so important for them to kill Pablo before he could speak.

"What else can we do?" Lieutenant Oliviera asked.

"I want to take him back to London."

"Are you serious?"

"Pablo was my agent. I recruited him. He worked for MI6. And it looks like the UK is under threat."

Lieutenant Oliviera liked Crawley and he had also met Crawley's boss when he was in London. Mrs Jones. A tough, intelligent woman. He wanted to help them – but he had his orders. "This is all true," he said. "But I'm sorry. What you ask is out of the question. The crime was committed on Brazilian soil and therefore it is a matter for the Brazilian authorities. BOPE will handle this." He shrugged. "We're much more likely to get results. We're used to having kids in our cells. The filthy gangs use children to carry money and drugs ... they call them *avioes*, little aeroplanes. If this boy refuses to talk, we'll rough him up a little and see where that gets us. You *gringos* are too soft-hearted. You wouldn't know where to begin!"

And then the boy spoke.

"I want to go to the toilet."

They heard him on the television screen and turned to watch. He had spoken in English. He sounded on the edge of tears.

Oliviera thought for a moment, then picked up a radio transmitter and flicked it on. "Take him to the toilet," he ordered. Crawley looked at him, alarmed. "He can't hurt anyone," Oliviera explained.

"He's just cut a man's throat with a radio-controlled plane," Crawley reminded him, adding: "I thought you said we were the ones who were too soft-hearted!"

It was too late. Oliviera's command had been relayed to a guard outside the room. Watching the monitor, they saw the door open and the man – dressed in the black BOPE uniform – walk in.

The guard's name was Fabian and he had only been with BOPE for a few months. Although he was not married himself, he had several nieces and nephews. Perhaps that was why he felt sorry for the *gringo* boy who had been brought in. He looked so young and innocent! As Fabian approached the table, he saw that the boy had been crying. Both sides of his face were streaked with tears.

"Don't worry," he said, in heavily accented English. "I am here to take you to the toilet." He leaned down to unlock the handcuffs.

"Thank you," the boy whispered. The moment his hands were released, he brought them up to the side of his head, as if he were in pain.

"What is it?" Fabian asked.

He never found out.

When the boy had been arrested, his clothes had been taken and he had been made to shower but nobody had noticed the flesh-coloured stud that he wore in his left ear: a tiny plastic ball on top of a metal pin. The moment he was free, the boy had pulled it out and, even as Fabian leaned over him, he had plunged it into the man's neck. The pin was actually a syringe. Squeezing the ball had released the contents which would later be identified as carfentanil, one of the most dangerous drugs in the world. Carfentanil is used to tranquillize large animals and it is ten thousand times stronger than morphine. Just one milligram will knock out a five-thousand-kilogram elephant. Fabian was dead before he could realize that he had made two mistakes.

He had come in on his own. And he hadn't locked the door.

The boy covered the distance to the door with astonishing speed. He knew that he was being watched and that the alarm would be raised in the next few seconds. He had also seen that the guard he had just killed hadn't been carrying a gun. That was unlucky but he didn't let it bother him. There were plenty of guns in the building. He would get one soon enough.

He opened the door and at the same moment, sirens went off throughout the compound, a high-pitched scream that was so loud it was deafening.

The alarm actually helped the boy. There were two more guards standing outside the room. They were waiting to escort him to the toilet but now they froze, thrown off-balance by the sudden explosion of sound, unsure what it meant. They saw the door swing open and a figure in a grey tracksuit emerge like some small demon out of a bad dream. Before they could even begin to take defensive action, he was onto them.

The boy was small but he was incredibly strong. His first strike, a spinning back punch, put all his body weight behind his fist, smashing into the first guard's face, lifting him clean off the floor and slamming him into the opposite wall. The second guard was armed. He had a Taurus PT92 semi-automatic pistol in a holster tucked into his waistband and he was already scrambling for it as his colleague crumpled to the ground. The boy seemed to be in no hurry to attack him. The gun came free – but that was what he had been waiting for. He swung round a second time, the flat of his foot shooting up diagonally in an axe kick straight into the guard's shoulder, causing him to cry out and drop the gun. For a moment the two of them gazed at each other. Then, even though his whole arm was tingling and he was barely able to move his hand, the guard threw himself onto the boy, pinning him to the ground.

The ear stud hadn't been the boy's only concealed weapon. As the guard launched his attack, he had whipped off his spectacles as if to see more clearly and now he was clenching them in his fist. The two plastic arms of his glasses, the parts that hooped behind his ears, contained very slender blades, made from surgical steel, sharpened to a vicious point, and when the boy stabbed forward, the point of the weapon easily broke through the thin plastic casing and plunged into the side of the guard's neck. The guard felt no pain. There was a brief flash of brilliant white light, the final punctuation mark in his life.

Three more men came pounding round the corner and this time there was going to be no element of surprise. The scene told its own story. Somehow the boy had got out of his cell. Fabian was dead. Two more men were down, one of them with a pool of blood still spreading around his head. The boy was there in front of them. He had to be taken out immediately. All three of them had pistols. They took aim.

"*Fique onde está!*" one of them shouted. A warning. "Stay where you are!"

It was another mistake. The BOPE officers were used to dealing with drug dealers and gang members who were violent and often psychotic. They were criminals who would kill without a moment's hesitation – but they were still smart enough to obey the rules of the game. When three men pointed guns at them, they stopped. They knew when the odds were hopeless and didn't want to die themselves.

The boy didn't care. He threw himself onto the

ground, his hand reaching out for the Taurus PT92. Perhaps he had gambled on the fact that, despite everything, the three men would be reluctant to open fire. If so, he was right. They had been too slow. As a fan of bullets spread above his head, ricocheting off the walls and turning the brickwork into dust, he twisted round and fired six times. His bullets found their targets. The men jerked and fell onto each other in a miniature dance of death. The boy sprang to his feet ... quite literally. It was an extraordinary judo move, using his shoulders and the arch of his back to flip himself up. The Taurus held seventeen rounds. The boy had used six of them. But even without doing the arithmetic, he knew he had eleven shots left. He had been trained to know instantly how many bullets there were in a gun, simply from its weight.

Leaving a tangle of bodies behind him – just one man remained alive, groaning – he continued down the corridor. The strange thing was that he didn't act as if he was in any danger. He hardly seemed to be aware that he was trapped in the basement of a heavily fortified police building, surrounded by armed men who were now actively searching for him and that even if he did break out into the open air, he would find himself fenced in and trapped. From the way he behaved, and even with the siren still screaming and the gun dangling from his hand, he really could have been going for a stroll, perhaps looking for the toilet.

He came to a staircase. An armed policeman dressed entirely in black with Kevlar vest and helmet was coming down towards him. The policeman reached for his gun but he was too slow. The boy shot him in both his legs, waited until he fell and then stepped over him. Another CCTV camera recorded what had happened. There was something particularly nightmarish about the images – which were black and white, slightly out of focus, captured from a single point of view. They looked as if they had come out of an old silent horror film.

Oliviera had been watching all this on the monitor on his desk, waiting for his men to control the situation but seeing the last policemen fall, he knew he had to take action himself. He opened a drawer in his desk and pulled out a gun. "Wait here," he said.

"I'm coming with you." Crawley got to his feet. He had no weapon himself but that didn't matter to a man who had once trained in seven different martial arts.

"I don't believe this. This is insanity! It's never happened before."

Crawley remembered the last words of the agent before he had been killed in Flamengo Park. *"These people ... I've never come across anyone like them."* The police chief had said almost the same thing.

They left the office and found themselves in a wide corridor, brightly lit. Unlike the basement, this one had windows looking out onto the yard in front of the building. Crawley knew that the boy had no chance of leaving the complex. He wondered what he was trying to achieve.

Oliviera signalled – with the alarm, it would have been difficult to hear what he said – and the two men began to move down the corridor. And that was when, quite suddenly and with no warning, the boy stepped out in front of them. He had reached the top of the stairs and found them quite by chance. He didn't know who they were. Nor did he care. Quite casually, he lifted his gun and fired. Oliviera cried out and fell backwards.

The boy took another two steps forward so that now he was standing right in front of Crawley. For what seemed like a long time, nothing happened. Carefully, the boy took aim. Crawley knew he was finished. The boy was only a teenager, but he showed no emotion at all. His eyes were two empty holes. Little circles of death. His finger tightened on the trigger.

"Who are you?" Crawley whispered. "Where did you come from?"

And then, before the boy could answer, another policeman appeared behind him, carrying a rifle. The boy became aware of him, but too late. The policeman used his weapon like a club, crashing the stock into the back of his neck. The boy fired – but his bullet went wild, smashing a window. He fell. The policeman was left, staring at Crawley.

"Thank you," Crawley said. Then, again, in Portuguese: *"Obrigado."*

"Are you just going to leave me sitting here?"

The voice came from behind him and Crawley turned to see Lieutenant Oliviera struggling to his feet. He had been hit in the shoulder and his jacket was covered in blood, his right arm hanging limp. His face had lost much of its colour. He looked down at the unconscious boy with disgust and rapped out some commands to the soldier who had knocked him out. "Take him to a cell. Handcuffs. Leg-cuffs. No one is to go in under any circumstances. No food, no drink, no toilet breaks ... nothing!"

Ignoring Crawley, he turned and staggered back into his office. There was a bottle of rum in a cupboard. He took it out, using one arm, poured himself a glass and threw it back in one. Then, remembering his guest, he poured two more glasses. They drank together.

An hour later, they knew the worst.

Five men had been killed. Another two had been seriously injured. Oliviera himself had been lucky. The bullet in his shoulder had missed the artery but it had done severe damage to the nerve bundle that controlled all the movement in his arm and it would be weeks before he was able to return to work. Worse than that, though, his pride had taken a direct hit. He had been attacked in his own headquarters. He had lost five good men. And the enemy had been a boy in short trousers!

Perhaps that was why he made the decision.

"You can take him," he told Crawley as the para-medics arrived to lead him out to the ambulance. "He's not a child. He's a devil. Take him back to London. I never want to see the little swine again!"

THE BOY FROM BRAZIL

The Great Western train from Exeter to London had arrived twenty minutes late, its wheels grinding and its carriages giving one last shudder as if it was glad that the ordeal of the journey was finally over. That was certainly true of the passengers. As soon as the doors opened, they came pouring out, quickly spreading over the platform and disappearing with their brightly coloured backpacks, prams and wheeled suitcases towards the barriers.

The last two people to leave the train were different. They walked slowly and seemed unsure of themselves. They were a husband and wife. Although they were both in their early fifties, they looked older, with grey hair and slightly stooped shoulders. They were wealthy. That much was obvious from their clothes, their expensive suitcase and the fact that they had travelled first class. The man was wearing a jacket, jeans and open-neck shirt. The woman had a skirt and jacket with a single pearl necklace. They were not speaking to each other.

The station was busy but somehow they were completely alone.

As they moved down the platform, a young man approached them. He was smartly dressed in a dark suit and tie but looked ill at ease, as if he was a little out of his depth. "Sir Christopher?" he asked.

"That's right."

"I was sent to meet you and Lady Grey. Can I take that for you?" He reached out for the suitcase. "I have a car waiting for you outside."

"You're with MI6?"

"Yes, sir. I work directly for Mr Crawley. Would you like to check into your hotel or would you prefer to meet him straight away?"

Sir Christopher glanced at his wife. She nodded. "We'll go straight to wherever he is, I think."

"Whatever you say, sir. Actually, Mr Crawley is at Paddington Green. It's only a few minutes away."

"I'm sorry?" Susan Grey frowned. "Paddington Green is a police station."

"That's right, ma'am."

"Is that where the boy is being held?"

"I'm sure Mr Crawley will explain everything." The man didn't want to give too much away. "I'll let him know we're on the way."

If the Greys had been nervous when they arrived, they were even more so now. They both knew that Paddington Green was no ordinary police station. It was a maximum security building with sixteen cells located below ground level, specially designed for the most dangerous terrorists who would be brought here for interrogation.

There was a car with a chauffeur waiting for them outside. The young man opened the door for the new arrivals, stowed their case in the boot and then sat in the front. They didn't speak again as they drove off, joining the traffic which was moving at a crawl. In fact, it might have been faster to walk, although the Greys, sitting together in the back seat, seemed in no particular hurry to arrive. Lady Grey, in particular, barely looked out of the window, clinging on to her husband's arm.

They pulled in outside an ugly, old-fashioned building. The front was made up of double-height windows with blue and frosted glass making it impossible to see inside. It was surrounded by a wide concrete pavement with a couple of trees that looked lonely and out of place. A four-lane flyover rose up opposite, carrying a constant stream of traffic in and out of London. The entire area was contaminated by dust and noise and the smell of petrol.

The MI6 man jumped out to escort the Greys, leaving their suitcase behind. As he led them to the front door, they were watched by one of the many security cameras around the building and the door was buzzed open the moment they approached. John Crawley was waiting for them on the other side, sitting on a metal chair that seemed to have been deliberately designed to offer no comfort at all. He had left the tourist clothes he had worn in Rio.

Now he was dressed in an old-fashioned suit with a striped tie that might belong to a club. The reception area was plain and empty. A few officers in the uniforms of the Metropolitan Police walked past.

"Sir Christopher, Lady Grey! I'm John Crawley. Welcome to London. Did you have a pleasant journey?"

"Not really." Sir Christopher was a military man. He had been commissioned into the Royal Engineers and had risen to become Lieutenant General, working with the multinational force in Iraq. He had been given a DSO – a Distinguished Service Order – and a gold bar for gallantry, and when he had retired from the army, he had been knighted. He was a man with a short temper. He wouldn't hesitate to speak his mind. "To be honest with you, I'd quite like to know what's going on. You told me you had news about Freddy. What exactly do you mean and why have you brought us here?"

"Shall we talk inside?" Crawley was unfazed. He gestured at an open door, leading into an interview room.

"Very well."

The young man had already gone back to the car. The three of them walked into a blank, square room with no windows, a table and three chairs. They sat down.

"Who exactly are you?" Sir Christopher asked.

"I told you..."

"You told me your name. Nothing more. You don't look like a policeman – and nor did the young man who met us at the station. I know you're with the intelligence service but in what capacity?"

Crawley gave him a thin smile. "I'm a sort of general manager."

"So what is it you want to tell us about our son?"

Crawley hesitated. "This is very difficult, Sir Christopher. Your son, Frederick, died in a boating accident, ten years ago."

"That's what we've always believed. Yes. That's what we've had to live with."

"I wonder if you would mind telling me exactly what happened?"

"Don't you already know?" Sir Christopher frowned. "There was an inquest, Mr Crawley. I'm sure you've read the official report."

"Of course. But I'd still like to hear it from you."

Sir Christopher hesitated and his wife stepped in, wanting to get it over with. "Freddy was almost five years old," she said. "He was our only child. It was the end of August, ten years ago. My husband was home on leave and we went on a family holiday ... to Instow in Devonshire. We had a nanny, a lovely girl called Jenny, and she came with us. She would look after Freddy during the day so that we could have some time alone."

"It happened on the third day of the holiday." Sir Christopher took over. "Jenny asked us if she could take Freddy out in a boat on the River Torridge. She wanted to hire a dinghy with an outboard motor and we agreed. Well, we trusted her completely.

She'd been sailing all her life, Freddy was wearing a life jacket and there weren't any waves. The weather was perfect. Believe me, Mr Crawley, my wife and I have wondered about that decision a thousand times and of course if we could go back in time, we wouldn't have let him out of our sight."

He paused for a moment. His face showed no emotion.

"They left at eleven o'clock and they were meant to be gone for an hour. But lunchtime came and there was no sign of them. I went down to the Marine Parade, which was where they had rented the dinghy, and the man there said they hadn't got back yet. That was what set off the alarm bells and we called the coastguard at once." He paused a second time and his wife reached out, taking his hand. "It wasn't long until they found the boat," he went on. "Somehow it had upturned. The nanny hadn't been wearing a life jacket and she had drowned. Her body was found washed up near the sand dunes. There was no sign of Freddy. The coastguard brought in frogmen and they searched the entire river but without success. Although there weren't any waves, there had been a strong current and it was assumed that he had been swept out to sea. They asked for witnesses but nobody had seen anything. The inquest took place a few weeks later. The verdict was accidental death."

"We didn't have any more children," Lady Grey said. "But I've never believed that Freddy was dead." She went on quickly before her husband could interrupt.

"A mother always knows. And somehow, I've felt it in my heart that Instow wasn't the end of the story, that one day he would come back to us." She looked at Crawley beseechingly. "Is that what you're saying? Is Freddy here?"

"You've found him?" Sir Christopher was staring at Crawley in disbelief.

"We've found ... someone," Crawley replied, choosing his words carefully. "We're holding a young person downstairs but so far he's refused to give us his name. However, we ran his photograph through facial recognition software and someone had the idea of comparing it against children who had gone missing in the past fifteen years, and we got a match with your son. We've also looked at NHS records. He has a very unusual blood type – AB negative – the same as you, Lady Grey. His hair and eye colour match too."

"How long has he been here?"

"He was flown into the country only yesterday. We picked him up in Rio de Janeiro—"

"Rio de Janeiro?" This time it was Susan Grey who had cut in. "That's insane!"

"There's a great deal about this business that is hard to explain, Lady Grey. We've asked you to come up to London because we hope you can identify him. That would at least be a start."

Lady Grey had gone very pale. Her hands were clutching the edge of the table. "I want to see him now," she said.

"I'll take you down in a moment," Crawley replied.

"But I have to warn you first. You have to prepare yourselves. I'm afraid this may not be a pleasant experience."

"Has he been hurt?"

"No. It's not that, Lady Grey." Crawley seemed unsure how to continue. "In fact, it's quite the opposite. The boy that we are holding in custody is responsible for the deaths of five people."

"How is that possible?"

"I'd prefer not to go into details at this stage. But what I'm saying is that you may find his appearance and general manner distressing. We've been forced to restrain him and he's barely spoken a word since his arrest. He said nothing at all on the plane that brought him here and he has remained silent."

"None of this makes any sense," Sir Christopher said. "A five-year-old boy disappears in Devonshire. He turns up, ten years later, in Brazil. And you're asking me to believe that he killed five people?"

"There's no doubt about it. I was there."

Sir Christopher stood up. He had made his decision. "I think we should see him."

Crawley nodded. "I'll take you down now."

They left the interview room. Security cameras watched them as they crossed the reception area and came to a steel-plated door which had to be opened electronically to let them pass. There was a loud buzz and then a click as the lock was released. On the other side, a solid flight of stairs led down to a metal gate with two armed policemen who examined Crawley's pass before letting the group continue. Down here, everything was silent. No daylight was allowed to intrude and the brick walls and arched ceiling closed in on them from all sides, as if they were being buried alive. They passed a number of doors with tiny observation hatches and single numbers, stencilled in black ink. Two more policemen were on duty, standing with their Heckler & Koch machine guns, slanted down.

At last they stopped outside Cell Seven. The Greys – Lady Grey in particular – had become increasingly uneasy. Crawley turned to them. "I'm afraid you cannot touch him," he said. "I must ask you to keep at least three steps away. If you do believe him to be your son, you'll want to embrace him or hold on to him, but under no circumstances can you do that." He nodded at the nearest policeman, who unlocked the door using a magnetic swipe key. "I should also warn you that he may not recognize you," Crawley added. It was a last thought. "You need to be prepared for that too."

They went in.

The cell was very similar to the interrogation room in Rio. Once again the boy was sitting at a table, wearing a tracksuit – this one dark blue. In addition, he had been strapped into a leather harness that pinned his arms to his sides at the elbow. His feet were chained to the floor. There was a tray of food in front of him with a plastic knife and fork. So far he had eaten none of it.

The boy looked up. There was perhaps a flicker of recognition as he noticed Crawley but he didn't even seem to register the other two visitors. Sir Christopher and his wife hovered by the door, neither of them speaking. It was Crawley who broke the silence.

"I've brought two people to see you," he said to the boy. "Do you know who they are?"

Nothing from the boy.

"They've come all the way from Exeter to be with you today," Crawley went on. "That's where you used to live. Aren't you going to say hello?"

"Freddy?" Lady Grey had uttered the single word. She sounded shocked, puzzled, sad. It was impossible to tell what she was thinking.

Very slowly, the boy turned to examine her. At that moment, Crawley was sure he had made a mistake. If this was Freddy Grey, he certainly didn't look anything like his parents. He might have the same colour eyes as Lady Grey, the same shaped face as Sir Christopher – but he was a world apart from either of them. The truth was, he didn't really look human at all.

"I don't know who you are. Leave me alone."

"I want to talk to you."

"I don't want to talk to you. Go away."

Lady Grey let out a muffled sound that might have been a sob. Her husband took hold of her. Crawley saw there was nothing more to add and led them back out into the corridor.

"I'm sorry..." he began, once they were outside.

To his astonishment, Lady Grey was smiling. Her entire face had come alive and she seemed ten years younger than the woman who had got off the train. She glanced at her husband, who nodded, agreeing with what she was going to say. "It's a miracle!" she exclaimed. "I don't know what's happened to him but it's Freddy ... I'm absolutely certain of it. Instow was a lie. He didn't die there. You've found our son, Mr Crawley. He's alive!"

V FOR VENOMOUS

The meeting took place on the twelfth floor of the building in Liverpool Street. There were six people sitting in the black leather chairs around a conference table that stretched almost from wall to wall with another dozen chairs empty. Mrs Jones was at the centre with Crawley next to her. On his other side, a fair-haired woman sat, listening intently to every word that was spoken. This was Samantha Redwing, the chief science officer at MI6. She would normally be there to deal with issues that demanded technical knowledge: cyberterrorism, weapons development, national defence. It was said that Samantha had more brainpower than an advanced search engine and, from the moment Mrs Jones had taken over as head of Special Operations, she had come increasingly to rely on her.

The three agents were sitting opposite two men from the Foreign Office. One was Dominic Royce, the Permanent Under-Secretary for Foreign Affairs. The other was the young assistant who had greeted Mrs

Jones when she had last been summoned to a meeting. He was sitting next to his master and hadn't yet spoken. In fact he had barely moved. With his pale skin, fair hair and almost colourless eyes, he had all the presence of a hologram and Mrs Jones wondered why he was even there.

The sixth person in the room was a smartly dressed, serious-looking woman with a laptop open in front of her. She was Mrs Jones's secretary, Mary Makepeace, and as the others spoke, her fingers tapped quietly at the keys, never missing a word.

Right now, Crawley was talking.

"His parents confirmed that the boy was their son, Frederick Grey," he was saying. "The DNA samples we took proved – one hundred per cent – that they were right. They are, of course, extremely bewildered and upset. It now seems that the boy was deliberately kidnapped in Instow and that his nanny was murdered."

"So where has he been for the last ten years?" Dominic Royce demanded.

"We have no idea. Frederick has been trained to withstand all interrogation techniques. We've threatened him and we've offered to help him. We've tried sleep deprivation and white noise. We gave him a chocolate milkshake laced with the truth drug, sodium pentothal, but it had absolutely no effect. The Brazilians wanted to try more ... painful methods but I doubt that they would have worked either."

"Have his parents spoken to him again?"

"He doesn't recognize them. He refuses to acknowledge that they are his parents." Crawley shook his head. "Frederick Grey has been turned into a killing machine, nothing more nor less. In Rio de Janeiro, he assassinated one of my best agents and then went on to take out another seven men at BOPE headquarters. Let's not forget we're talking about some of the toughest and most highly trained police officers in the world. Five dead and two badly injured! He would have killed me too if he hadn't been knocked out at the last minute and, looking into his eyes, I can tell you ... I've seen friendlier sharks!"

"What was your man doing in Rio in the first place?" the Permanent Under-Secretary asked.

"It was in the report I sent you," Mrs Jones replied. "He was following a lead we'd received concerning an organization that has recently become active all over the world and which we believe to be a danger to the United Kingdom. They call themselves Nightshade."

"And what exactly have Nightshade been up to?"

"It's hard to be sure, but we think they were behind the bombing last year in Istanbul. They've been involved in assassinations in Moscow, Riyadh and Beijing. They were also behind the kidnapping of Paul Saba, the Vatican banker in Rome. A ransom of two million euros was delivered but they killed him anyway. They're efficient. They're ruthless. And they don't obey any rules."

Royce sniffed, his nostrils briefly widening like

two dark tunnels. "So there's another terrorist group at large," he said. "But if they're not actually threatening us, why should it be any concern of ours?"

"Actually, they're not terrorists." It was Samantha Redwing who had interrupted. "Nightshade have no beliefs, nothing they wish to achieve. They are, if you like, subcontractors. They work *for* different terrorist groups. They will kill anyone and destroy anything and all they want in return is a great deal of money. I would say this makes them even more dangerous than the people who employ them. They're making a living out of death."

"They also work for criminals," Mrs Jones continued. "They were in Rio de Janeiro because they had been hired by one of the biggest drug gangs in Brazil, the Third Command – or *Terceiro Comando*, in Portuguese. Third Command had decided to get rid of their main rivals and so they called in Nightshade to do the work for them. You may have seen the newspapers. Thirty-seven deaths in the past two weeks! Whole families massacred. As a result, Third Command now have control of ninety per cent of the cocaine being smuggled out of Brazil. It's a worldwide market worth billions of pounds so that's not a bad result!"

"That's all very interesting, Mrs Jones. But, again, I don't see that this is any business of ours."

"It wouldn't be," Mrs Jones agreed. "Except this time Nightshade weren't paid for their work ... at least, not in cash. We heard a rumour that, in return for the killings, Third Command were going to provide them with a canister containing a nerve agent called VX which had been smuggled out of North Korea."

"VX is a weapon of mass destruction," Samantha Redwing said. "It was actually discovered in England and is banned all over the world. It's one of the most deadly chemicals in existence. It's yellow and oily – it looks a bit like cooking oil – but you only have to get a tiny amount on your skin and it will kill you immediately. The V stands for Venomous. It's horrible stuff."

For the first time, Dominic Royce looked concerned. "Are you suggesting that Nightshade are planning to use VX against us?" he asked.

"We sent an agent to Rio to find out," Crawley said. "He was an extremely capable man but somehow he was compromised. He was killed in front of my eyes." Crawley drew a breath. "However, he managed to confirm our worst fears in the last moments of his life. He told me quite clearly that the target was London."

"But why would Nightshade want to attack London?"

"Because somebody has paid them to do exactly that." The answer was simple. Crawley didn't need to add anything more.

"It's a great shame your agent wasn't more careful," Royce remarked. "Getting himself killed like that. And you too, Crawley! Letting it happen! You should have done something!"

Nobody in the room had any answer to that. The secretary's finger pattered lightly over the keys, then fell still.

"London is a very large city," Royce remarked. "Assuming they manage to get this VX into the country – and I suppose that won't be too difficult – do you have any idea what the actual target might be?"

"This is a busy time of year," Samantha Redwing said. "Parliament will be sitting again at the start of the month. There's a state visit by the President of France, a memorial service at St Paul's Cathedral, a major art fair in Regent's Park, Remembrance Sunday is coming up soon ... the target could be any one of them."

"We're raising the terrorist threat level to severe," Mrs Jones said.

"And what are you going to do about this boy, Frederick Grey? Surely there must be some way to get information out of him."

"We'll keep trying." Mrs Jones couldn't help remembering her last meeting with the civil servant. At the Foreign Office, Dominic Royce had expressed horror at the fact that MI6 has used a fifteen-year-old agent and had forbidden them to do so again, and yet here they were, confronted by a fifteen-year-old terrorist. Wisely, she kept her thoughts to herself.

"Well, I want to be kept informed of all developments. And to that end, I'm going to ask my personal assistant to stay here and work out of your office." Royce gestured at the young man who had come with him and who was still sitting with his lips tightly sealed. "His name is Owen Andrews and he will liaise between Special Operations and the Foreign Office. What you know, I want to know. Do you have any problem with that?"

"None at all." Mrs Jones opened a small plastic box of peppermints and slid one into her mouth. At the laptop, Mary Makepeace could see how angry she was. MI6 Special Operations was, as its name made clear, special. It was a secret and very close organization. It did not welcome outsiders.

"Good!" The Permanent Under-Secretary got to his feet. But before he left, he had a final thought. "What happened to the other child at the park?" he asked. "There was a boy and a girl. But she got away."

"She was taken out by helicopter," Crawley said.

"Did you trace the helicopter?"

"We tried, of course. But it had a false registration. It landed at the airport at Curitiba and half an hour later it exploded in flames. They must have left some sort of device in it ... to get rid of any evidence."

"Do you have a description of the girl? Surely someone has a photograph."

Crawley hesitated for a moment before he answered and at that moment Mary Makepeace knew that whatever he said next would not be true. "We've asked for CCTV footage from Flamengo Park and the surrounding area," he replied. "We're also looking for witnesses ... anyone who saw the scooter as it made its way to the domestic airport in Rio. So far, we've drawn a blank."

Royce turned to his assistant. "You'll let me know if something comes in," he said.

"Of course, sir." Andrews spoke for the first time.

"All right. It seems to me that Special Operations has made a complete hash of this so far but it's early days and at least we have the boy. I'll be waiting for your next report."

Dominic Royce stood up and left the room.

A few minutes later, Crawley came into Mrs Jones's office. She had taken over the room where Alan Blunt had once worked and it sometimes seemed to Crawley that his ghost was still there, watching over her shoulder, whispering into her ear. In the past few weeks, Mrs Jones had become withdrawn, more lost in thought. She was now in charge of the safety and security of the entire country and the responsibility was weighing down on her.

She looked up as he came in. "Sit down, John." She waited as he drew up a chair. "Who's looking after that young man from the Foreign Office?"

"Redwing is keeping an eye on him," Crawley said.

They both knew what that meant. She would make sure that Andrews found out as little as possible. The department was very careful with its secrets. That was why Crawley was here now.

"I have something you might like to see," he said,

producing a large, white envelope. "Royce asked about the girl in Brazil."

"The one who escaped in the Bell helicopter."

"Yes. I don't know if you want to share this information with Mr Royce, but it turns out that a tourist managed to get a snap of her just as she broke into the airport. He was out walking with his wife and saw the helicopter, the police cars and all the rest of it and took a few shots with his iPhone. There's only one good one and I've had it blown up and digitally enhanced."

"Can we get an ID?"

"We're already onto it." Crawley passed the envelope across.

Mrs Jones opened it and took out a colour photograph that had been taken from across the road right next to the domestic airport in Rio. The image had been caught just as she pushed her way through the hole in the perimeter fence. The helicopter was on the other side, in the right-hand corner of the image. The girl had stopped to look back to check that the boy – Frederick Grey – was behind her and that was when the photograph had been taken. It showed dark brown eyes, a small nose, black hair cut in a fringe and reaching down to the shoulders. The girl looked the same age as the boy, about fifteen.

Mrs Jones stared at the image and then, to Crawley's astonishment, something very strange happened. He saw her visibly start. Her eyes widened and she let out something that sounded like a gasp. A moment later, she stood up and, still clutching the photo-graph, went over to the window. She stood there for a long time with her back to the room. Crawley waited for her to speak.

"You don't need to ID her," Mrs Jones said, still not turning around. "I know who she is."

Crawley stayed silent, waiting. At last, Mrs Jones went back to her desk and Crawley knew that some-thing in the room had changed, that it would never be the same again. When she next spoke, her voice was low, determined. This was her skill. In just a few moments she had assessed the information, made her calculations and knew what she was going to do.

"We can't keep Frederick Grey at Paddington Green," she said. "It's too dangerous and it's not in our control. I want him sent to our facility in Gibraltar."

"All right. I'll see to it."

"There's something else." She raised a hand before Crawley could move. "This is to go no further, John. Nobody else is to know and there'll be all hell to pay if anyone finds out. But we need Alex Rider. No one else can do this. We need him like we've never needed him before."

"All right," Crawley said. "Let's get him."

ENGINE TROUBLE

Alex Rider had settled back into school.

The best thing about Brookland was that nobody was trying to kill him. Mr Donovan, who taught maths, might take a stab at him with a linear equation or Mr Nash might bore him to death, droning on about the origins of the Korean War with his flat, slow-paced delivery. But none of the teachers wanted to take over the world. None of them had attempted to assassinate the Prime Minister or create a famine in Africa or drop a space station on the Pentagon. It made a difference from some of the people Alex had met in his time with MI6.

It often occurred to him that nobody would believe a word he said if he did tell them where he had been over the past months ... the long line of near-death missions that had more or less been forced on him by MI6. He was just glad it was over. He had never asked to be a spy. He just wanted to catch up with his work, pass his GCSEs and get on with his life.

He had said as much to Tom Harris, his best friend at Brookland and the only person in the school who knew the truth about him. Tom had been with Alex in Venice when he had infiltrated the criminal organization known as Scorpia ... in fact, he couldn't have done it without Tom's help. The shared secret had brought them closer together and Alex knew a lot about Tom's private life too; the fact that his parents had recently split up and that life at home was difficult to say the least. Tom had sworn that as soon as he was sixteen he was going to leave home and live in Italy with his brother, Jerry, who worked there. He had even started learning Italian, listening through earphones to dialogue which he had downloaded on his mobile.

The two boys were walking together to art class, the last lesson of the day. This was a Thursday, four days since Alex had got back.

"What are you doing this weekend?" Tom asked.

"I've got to work." Alex grimaced. The moment he had got back to Brookland, he had been told he would be getting double homework for the rest of the term.

"There's a party on Saturday night."

"Whose party?"

"Ed's."

Ed was Edward Channon, a boy who had just arrived at the school from America. His parents had a large house in Chelsea and they were going to be away for the weekend.

"*Forse possiamo incontrare ragazze,*" Tom went on, speaking almost to himself.

"What does that mean?" Alex asked.

Tom blushed. "Nothing!"

The door of the art class was ahead of them but before they could go in, they found their way blocked by Mrs Desmond, who was usually stationed behind the window of the reception area at the main entrance to the school. She was an unsmiling, elderly woman whose main job was to issue passes to anyone who wanted to visit but who always seemed reluctant to do so.

"Rider!" she exclaimed. She never used first names.

"Yes, Mrs Desmond?"

"You are aware that the school day ends at a quarter to four? You've only just got back so I'm a little surprised that you're so anxious to leave."

"I'm sorry?" Alex had absolutely no idea what she was talking about.

"I just had your driver in reception ... he was asking when the last class would finish. I told him he'd come an hour too soon and now he's waiting outside."

Mrs Desmond continued on her way. The school was on the edge of Chelsea, a wealthy part of London, and she clearly didn't approve of parents sending drivers to pick up their precious children.

Alex was baffled. He had come to school, as always, on his bicycle. Jack certainly wouldn't have sent a car. It had to be some sort of mistake.

Why would a driver come looking for him?

He followed Tom into the art room and for the next fifteen or twenty minutes he tried to work on the scene he was supposed to be painting. They had been given the subject of "Home", which could mean the house where they lived or the country they were born or anything that the word suggested. Alex glanced at Tom's work, which was huge, painted on six sheets of paper. It showed a terraced house, on fire, with blood coming out of the windows, an axe buried in a wall and an atomic explosion happening in the back garden. There were times when Alex worried about his friend.

Alex had started drawing a picture of the King's Road in Chelsea but he couldn't concentrate on what he was doing. He kept on thinking about what Mrs Desmond had just told him. A man had come into the school, a driver. He had asked for Alex. But who was he? All sorts of alarm bells were going off in Alex's mind. There had been two occasions when he had been attacked at Brookland. He had very nearly died on the roof of the science block while it burned down around him. And a sniper had taken a shot at him in the middle of a maths lesson. Could it be happening a third time? Alex had only been back in England a few days and he had really wanted to believe that his adventures were over. But he had been in danger so many times that he had developed a sense for it and right now he couldn't shake off the feeling that something was wrong.

Casually, he picked up his drawing pad and went over to the window as if he needed natural light to show him what he was doing. The art teacher was leaning over an easel, talking to one of the other students, and didn't see him. He looked outside. Yes. There it was. It had to be the one ... a silver car, parked on the other side of the road, opposite the main gate, with two men sitting in the front seats, gazing silently out of the windscreen. With all the fuss about security, there was now only one entrance to Brookland and so only one way out. The car was parked in exactly the right place so that it would be impossible for Alex to leave without being seen.

Suddenly, Alex was angry. He didn't have any idea who the two men were but one thing was certain: they didn't belong here. They were part of the life that Alex was determined to leave behind. What were they planning? To shoot him? To kidnap him? That had happened before too. There were any number of people who could have sent them here. They might even work for Scorpia – or what was left of it. Well, Alex was fed up being mucked around. Whoever they were, he was going to teach them a lesson.

But how? Alex thought for a moment. In a way it was lucky that he was at school. He wasn't on his own and he was surrounded by things that might be useful to him. There were chemicals in the science block, various pieces of equipment in the gym. Where were the javelins kept? No. That was too extreme. What else was there?

Alex looked around him, past the pictures on the wall, the papier mâché sculptures, the jars filled with brushes and pencils. His eyes fell on a row of plastic bags full of powder paint. An idea began to form. Was it possible? Yes – but he would need help.

He went back to his table. Tom was opposite him, carefully adding a hanged man to the front porch of his house. "Reception area," Alex whispered. "Two minutes from now."

Tom didn't show any surprise or puzzlement. He nodded quietly.

First of all, Alex found a ball of string and cut off about two metres. Moving quickly, he took a sheet of paper and folded it in half, closing the edges and taping them shut so that it made a container. Making sure nobody was looking, he went over to the powder paints and, using the container as a scoop, filled it to the brim. For no particular reason, he had chosen the colour black. At that moment, the art teacher looked up from the canvas, noticing him for the first time. Alex lowered his hand, concealing what he was holding. He smiled at her. "Excuse me, Miss. I need the toilet."

"That's all right, Alex. Don't be long."

Still keeping the powder hidden, Alex left the room and went back downstairs. It was strange padding through the silent school with everyone tucked away in their classrooms for the last lesson and he hoped he wouldn't bump into any stray members of the staff. He passed the school kitchen and glanced through the porthole windows set in the two swing doors. There was nobody there. Alex thought of the two men waiting for him in the car outside. The anger inside him stirred a second time. Quickly, he pushed open the kitchen door and went in.

A few minutes later, Tom joined him on the edge of the reception area. Alex didn't ask what excuse he'd given to leave the art class but, knowing Tom, he might simply have tiptoed out. The two of them crept forward, being careful to keep out of sight of the office window where Mrs Desmond would have once again taken her place. Fortunately, this was the end of the day. There were no visitors coming into the school. She was at the back of the office, talking on the phone. They reached the main door. Quickly, Alex described the men in the silver car and explained what he wanted Tom to do.

Tom's eyes widened. "Are they dangerous?" he asked.

"I don't know," Alex said. "But for some reason they're waiting for me and I want to get rid of them."

"Are you going to kill them?"

"No!" Alex was shocked.

"I don't mind. But my mum probably wouldn't like it if I got arrested as an accessory to murder, and she's mad enough at the moment anyway."

Tom pressed the release button on the front door and slipped outside. Nobody saw him as he crossed the yard and went out through the main gate, wedging a ball of paper into the lock to prevent it from closing properly. A few cars were drawing up, parents arriving early to pick up their kids, but most of the children who went to Brookland walked, cycled or took the bus. Tom crossed the road and went straight up to the car, a Volkswagen Passat Estate. He knocked on the window. The man in the passenger seat rolled it down. The other man looked towards him.

"Yes?" Both men were in their thirties, blank-faced, dressed in cheap suits with white shirts and knitted ties.

"Are you looking for Alex Rider?"

"Who are you?"

"I'm Tom. I'm his best mate. He said if you wanted to talk to him, he's in the yard." Tom jerked his thumb.

"Why didn't he come himself?"

"He's on detention. He has to pick up litter."

The men glanced at each other, unsure. It seemed odd that anyone should have detention duties during class – but at the same time the skinny boy with bright blue eyes who had approached them seemed completely innocent.

"I'll take you over to him, if you like," Tom said.

"Fine. All right." The men got out and followed the boy through the main gate. They would only be gone for a minute or two but they still made sure to lock the car door.

From behind the front doors, Alex watched Tom and the men disappear round the side of the school.

He waited until they were out of sight, then hurried out. He kept low, more afraid that he would be spotted by a teacher looking out of one of the classroom windows than by any of the parents arriving at the school, and he was relieved when he skidded to a halt next to the Volkswagen without being noticed. He reached up and tried to open the passenger door. He wasn't surprised to find it had been locked.

But that was no problem. It was something that Ian Rider had shown him when he was about eleven years old. To the young Alex, it had been nothing more than a game. He could not have imagined that he was being trained for a future he would never have chosen for himself.

Taking the string, he tied a reef knot in the middle. This was like a miniature hangman's noose and would tighten when he pulled the ends. Then he slipped the string over the corner of the car door and eased it through the narrow gap between the door and the frame. Now the noose was inside the car, on the other side of the glass, and by manipulating both ends, Alex was able to lower it so that it travelled down towards the little stub that locked and unlocked the door.

It took him longer than he had thought it would. The first time he tried, the noose missed and he was beginning to sweat. Tom wouldn't be able to distract the two men for ever. The moment they realized they had been tricked, they would return to the car. The art teacher would be wondering where he was. And it couldn't be too long before lessons finished for the day.

Forcing himself not to panic, he focused on the little loop of string on the other side of the window. There! On the second attempt, it slipped over the door lock. Alex pulled the two ends of the string and the loop tightened around the plastic stub. Alex jerked upwards and there was a click as the door unlocked. He glanced towards the corner where the two men had disappeared. There was still no sign of them. He opened the car door.

He knew exactly what he was going to do.

Thirty minutes later, the bell went for the end of the final lesson and almost at once the stillness in the building was shattered by the sounds of slamming desks and opening doors, footsteps on rubber flooring and the babble of nine hundred voices. Boys and girls, all dressed in the same uniform, appeared from every direction, a flood of grey and blue that cascaded down the stairs, surged through the corridors and rushed towards the main entrance.

Alex Rider was somewhere among them. The two men in the Volkswagen were sitting upright, gazing out of the window, waiting to catch sight of him. They knew what he looked like. They would spot him immediately, even in this sea of different faces. They were a little annoyed. Alex hadn't been in the school yard when they had gone round. The boy who had taken them there had been mystified. "I'm really sorry! He was here a minute ago." He had stayed with them as they tried to find him but without success. Eventually, they had given up and gone back to the car.

Right now they were silent and tense, determined not to miss Alex for a second time.

"That's him!" The man in the passenger seat pointed.

Alex had appeared all too suddenly, weaving through the gates on his Raleigh Pioneer 160 bicycle. He veered into the road and for a moment he was right next to the car, almost as if he meant to crash into it. Then he was away, speeding down the road and disappearing into the distance. Despite everything, the two men had been taken by surprise. The driver snapped out a swear word, then leaned forward and turned on the engine.

It was something he would regret.

The Volkswagen Passat, like all modern cars, has a sophisticated climate-control system that allows air – heated, chilled or street temperature – to circulate inside the car. The air comes in through demister vents in front of the main window as well as through a grille set in the bonnet. There's a filter behind the glove box and this ensures that the air-stream doesn't carry any dust, dirt or pollen into the cabin.

Sneaking out of the school with a container of paint powder, Alex had known that he had to bypass the Volkswagen's filter, which was why he had asked

Tom to distract the two men and lead them away from the car. The moment they had gone, he had opened the door and had set to work. Using a spoon from the kitchen and, working as quickly as he could, he had tipped paint powder into the vents that ran along the dashboard on either side of the steering wheel. Now he realized why he had chosen the colour black. The powder was invisible, disappearing into the shadows behind the dashboard and, presumably, coming to rest on the filters behind. Alex had got rid of about half the container that way. He had spilled some of it in the process but the car had black carpets too so he had finished by upending the container, spreading the rest across the floor. Finally, he had turned the two manual dials that controlled the air current. The one on the far right showed its direction. He had changed it so that the air would come in at both floor and face level. The one in the middle determined the power. Alex had cranked it up to six – the maximum.

The moment the driver started the car, the powerful climate-control fans began to turn and, instantly, the black paint powder exploded into the cabin through the vents, more powder being blasted off the carpet, completely engulfing the two men. To anyone standing outside the Volkswagen, it was as if day had somehow become night, the driver and the passenger disappearing in a dense, swirling cloud that completely filled the interior, pressing against the windows. For the two men inside, it was much,

much worse. They were blinded. Their eyes were on fire. They couldn't breathe. Even as they cried out, they were swallowing black paint.

Alex hadn't just taken a spoon from the kitchen. He had noticed a box of black pepper on one of the surfaces and, unable to resist the temptation, he had added that to the mix as well. It was the pepper as much as the paint that was attacking the men. In just seconds, he had turned the interior of the luxury car into a torture chamber.

Somehow the driver managed to get the door open and fell out into the street, coughing and gasping, followed by his passenger. There were still dozens of students and teachers pouring out of Brookland and they stared in astonishment at the two unfortunate men who were now lying on each side of the car, coughing uncontrollably. Meanwhile, Alex had cycled all the way round the school and had now rejoined Tom Harris at the gate as if they had just left, the two boys looking as surprised as everyone else.

Miss Bedfordshire was also on her way home and came over to them.

"I don't suppose you'd know anything about this, Alex?" she asked.

"No," Alex replied. He examined the two men with their black-smudged shirts, black-smudged faces and hair. One of them had staggered to his feet. He was weeping black tears. "It looks like they've had engine trouble."

"Better get home," Tom said.

With Alex pushing his bike and Tom walking beside him, the two friends set off together. They didn't look back.

SPY STORY

Alex didn't go straight home. He'd agreed to spend an hour doing physics homework at Tom's house. Somehow having two of them in the same room made it easier. But as the time approached five o'clock, Alex noticed his friend glancing more frequently at the clock and knew that it was time to go. Tom's mother was on her way back and he didn't want Alex there when she arrived. Alex put the finishing touches to his velocity-time graph, then folded his book away and left, cycling the fifteen-minute journey back to his own house in the quiet, tree-lined street between the King's Road and the river. It was just after quarter past and the evening was beginning to draw in when he finally pedalled down the road and pulled in outside his own house.

There were no other cars in sight as he climbed off the bike ... certainly no silver Volkswagens. He wondered if he should tell Jack about what had happened at Brookland. Even as he walked up to the front door, he knew he had no choice. They had promised each other that there would never be any more secrets between them. And if someone was seriously looking for him, it was very likely they would soon turn up again.

Alex took out his key, opened the front door and went in. He had taken two steps into the hallway when someone stepped out in front of him. Alex recognized him instantly. His hands, his face, his clothes were all covered in patches of black paint. He had tried to wash the colour out of his hair but he had only partly succeeded. He was a mess.

"I've been waiting for you," the man said.

At that same moment, the second man loomed up behind him. He must have been hiding somewhere outside. Alex was sandwiched between them. He didn't dare turn round but saw the first man give a nod and heard the coffin lid sound as the front door of the house swung shut.

Two men. One in front of him, one behind, possibly armed.

Alex was already measuring distances, examining his surroundings. A lamp with an electric flex. A vase of flowers. A bicycle pump on a table. Even the simplest household object could become a weapon if you knew how to use it. His mind was racing. The men had been waiting for him at school and when that had failed, they had come here. But who were they and what did they want? And where was Jack? That thought worried him more than anything.

Without showing it, Alex had already tensed for action. The three of them were in a narrow corridor but that was to his advantage. If either of the two men had guns, they wouldn't be able to fire them without the risk of hitting the other. Alex transferred his weight to one leg, preparing to spin round and...

"Alex! How are you?"

To Alex's shock, Mrs Jones had appeared, walking out of the living room ... *his* living room. She looked completely relaxed, as if it was normal for her to be here.

"Where's Jack?" Alex demanded.

"She's in the kitchen, making tea." Mrs Jones glanced at the two men. "You don't need to look so threatening, Burton. He's not going to hurt you."

"Yes, ma'am." The man unbuttoned his jacket and tried to relax. Alex was pleased to see a trickle of black paint appear under his nostril and worm its way past his lip.

Mrs Jones had seen it too. "I sent a car to pick you up from school, Alex. I thought you might like a lift. I didn't expect a declaration of war."

"They should have said who they were," Alex replied.

"From what I hear, you didn't give them a chance."

Then Jack came out of the kitchen. She was safe and well but Alex could see at once that she wasn't happy having any of these people in the house.

"What's going on?" he asked.

"Mrs Jones wants to talk to you," Jack said, with a scowl.

"You two wait outside. I won't be long."

Mrs Jones had given the order and the two agents obeyed. Once they had gone, she turned back to Alex. "I apologize for the misunderstanding," she said. "I wanted to talk to you and I sent them round to the school. I should have warned you they were coming."

"It wouldn't have made any difference," Alex said. "I still didn't want to see them."

"I can understand that."

"The last time we met, you said you weren't going to use me any more."

"I said it would be your choice. Something has happened, something very serious. It could affect you and all your friends. That's why I'm here now. I need your help."

"I agreed Mrs Jones could talk to you," Jack cut in. "But only if you want to listen. And any time you want her to leave, you only have to say."

Alex didn't want to hear what she had to say but it was already too late. She had suggested that he and his friends might be in danger. And at least he would have Jack with him. "Five minutes," he said.

They went into the living room. Sure enough, Jack had put out three mugs of tea and some biscuits, even though that wasn't really her job. The two of them had agreed that she was no longer going to think of herself as a housekeeper or Alex's nanny or anything like that. She had applied to go back to law school and would be out most of the day, and studying in the evenings. Jack was Alex's legal guardian but she wasn't going to look after him any more. From now on, they would look after each other.

Mrs Jones got quickly to the point.

"I shouldn't be here," she said. "You might like to know that my superiors take a dim view of your past involvement with MI6." She was thinking of Dominic Royce but didn't actually name him.

"They could at least be grateful," Jack muttered.

"They are. But they're also scared of what would happen if your activities became public. I'm risking my neck coming to you, Alex – but I can't think of any other way. The whole of London is in great danger. I don't want to scare you, but we know something is going to happen, although we don't know where and when. You're the only person who can find out."

"Why me?"

"I'll tell you."

Mrs Jones explained what had happened in Rio de Janeiro; the meeting between Pablo and Crawley, the fifteen-year-old killer and the girl on the scooter. She told him about the VX nerve agent that Nightshade had acquired. She described what had happened at the BOPE complex and Sir Christopher and Lady Grey's subsequent visit to London.

"Where is this boy, Frederick Grey, now?" Jack asked.

"He's in Gibraltar. We have a maximum security facility high up on the Rock." Mrs Jones paused. "It's where we sent Julius Grief."

There was a brief silence. It didn't take Alex very long to work things out. "You want to send me in there," he said.

It had been obvious from the moment Gibraltar was mentioned.

Julius Grief had been a prisoner there and he looked identical to Alex. He had actually been given advanced plastic surgery to make him look that way. Julius was a clone, manufactured by Dr Hugo Grief in the Point Blanc Academy in the French Alps. And he was dead because Alex had shot him in a street on the edge of Cairo. It was the only time Alex had ever fired a gun in anger but he'd had no choice. He had saved his own life.

"You want me to pretend to be him," he added.

"Exactly. Before Freddy arrived, there were just six other prisoners in Gibraltar. They all know Julius Grief – he was with them until he escaped – but none of them know that he's dead. You could go in there and tell them that you've been recaptured. You're exactly the same age as Freddy and it wouldn't be difficult for the two of you to become friends. All we want is information. Where is Nightshade and what are they planning to do with the VX? If you could persuade him to tell you that, you could be saving countless lives."

"Wait a minute!" Jack cut in. "You're saying that

you've managed to arrest a kid who's an insane criminal. You've put him in a prison with six other insane criminals and you want Alex to pretend to be an insane criminal and move in with them. Well, you know what I think of that idea? It's insane!"

Mrs Jones turned to Alex. "What do you say, Alex?"

Alex thought for a few moments, then shook his head. "I'm sorry, Mrs Jones. I agree with Jack. Even if I could get away with it and persuade everyone that I was Julius Grief, this other kid, Freddy, might not want to talk to me. You said he didn't even talk to his own parents."

He sighed.

"Anyway, it's more than that. I've only just got back to school. I like being with all my friends again. I've only been there a week and here you are already knocking on my door. I'm sorry. Get someone else to do your dirty work for you. I've had enough."

Mrs Jones nodded but she didn't stand up. Something had come into her eyes that Alex had never seen before. She was a powerful woman in charge of a major department of the Secret Service. But for the first time she looked almost afraid. "There is something else," she said. "I said that this was a question of national security but that's only partially true. I have a personal involvement. It's quite a long story but if you'll allow me, I'd like to tell it."

Alex and Jack glanced at each other. "Go on," Alex said.

"I haven't told anyone else this," Mrs Jones said. "Nobody knows. But there hasn't been a day in my life when I haven't thought of it. It feels very strange to be telling you now. But, funnily enough, you're part of the story, Alex. Do you remember that time when you came to my flat, when you were sent by Scorpia to kill me? Well, I'll come to that in a minute but I suppose I'd better begin at the beginning."

She took a deep breath. And then she began.

"Very few people choose to go into the secret service. It may surprise you, but you weren't the only one who stumbled into the world of spies without meaning to. When I was your age, I wanted to be a relief worker. I had this idea that I'd travel around the world and help people caught up in famine and floods and other natural disasters. My father was a diplomat so I had experience of living in other countries ... like India and Turkey.

"I was mainly educated in England. The diplomatic service paid for me to go to a private school in Cheltenham and after that I went to Cambridge, where I got a first-class degree in politics and Arabic studies. I suppose what happened next should have been obvious. I was planning to spend a few years writing a doctorate on climate change and its effects on developing nations when I got an invitation to lunch from a professor I knew slightly. He spent a long time quizzing me about my work, my political views, my private life ... and then he said he had a job opportunity that might interest me. There were some people in London who wanted to meet me. I knew straight away what he was talking about. He wanted me to become a spy.

"I was interviewed at MI6 headquarters in Lambeth, just round the corner from Waterloo Station. That was before they moved to the building by the River Thames – you may have seen it in one of those James Bond films. Anyway, I was offered a job and I decided almost immediately to accept. Even then it was clear to me that although the country wasn't at war, there were plenty of people around the world who wanted to do us harm. You've met quite a few of them! I wanted to help protect us.

"I was never a field agent. I started as an operational officer and although I think my work was useful, it wasn't at all exciting. I spent a lot of time reading foreign publications. It helped that I was fluent in four languages. I had to look at intercepts ... which is to say, letters written by people to each other and transcripts of their telephone calls. Emails began in the nineties and that soon became a very large part of my work. I did very well though. I had an eye for detail and I was able to connect things, and quite quickly I began to rise up the ladder.

"Around this time, Alex, I fell in love. It's something I never talk about, but when I was in my late twenties, I met a young writer called Hans Mayer who was living in London. He had been born in

Berlin but his parents had died and he had moved to England where he had been brought up by an aunt. He was a very handsome man, incredibly intelligent, someone you could talk to all night. I was introduced to him by someone at a party and we hit it off straight away. It was amazing how many things we had in common. We liked the same films, the same music, the same food. You have to remember that I was in a very lonely job. I couldn't tell anyone what I did. I often worked long hours. Hans came into my life and swept me off my feet. We started going out together. Then he moved into my flat. After just eighteen months, we got married."

"You didn't take his name," Jack said.

"No. I decided to keep my maiden name of Jones. As I think I may have told you, my parents gave me a very unfortunate first name – Tulip. It's actually Lâle in Turkish, which sounds much nicer, and I think that's what they had in mind but somehow it got translated and I'm stuck with it. Anyway, the secret service was quite old-fashioned about married women. They knew me as Mrs Jones and that was how I stayed.

"I'm going to move forward quickly now. Over the next few years, two things happened. The first is that I was approached by a man called Alan Blunt to work in a new division of MI6 – Special Operations. He was going to head it up and I would be his deputy, so this was a major promotion.

"I had two children with Hans. The first was a boy.

I called him William. Two years later, he was followed by a baby sister, Sofia." Her dark eyes settled on Alex. "I think you saw their photograph when you came to my flat."

Alex remembered the framed picture, sitting on a shelf in the empty room in Clerkenwell. He had assumed that the two children were Mrs Jones's niece and nephew. He had never thought of her as a mother. She was too cold, too absorbed in her work. But it seemed he had been wrong.

"It wasn't easy, living in two worlds," Mrs Jones said. It was as if she had read his mind. "Having children, being a parent, buying nappies and preparing bottles and all the rest of it, trying to be normal. And at the same time, doing the work I did, knowing so many secrets, every day reading about things that would make your hair stand on end. Sometimes, at the weekend, sitting in the park with William and Sofia, I would look at the other mothers and I would wonder what they would say if they knew the truth about me. And my own children too! One day, they would ask me what I did when I went to work. What would I tell them? Would I have to lie?

"Hans made everything possible for me. I've told you he was a writer. He wrote about politics and economics ... books and newspaper articles. Most of the time, he worked from home and although I was earning enough money to afford a nanny, he'd stand in for me when I was working late. He did most of the cooking. He was the one who read to the children at night. Nothing was too much trouble for him. And although, of course, he knew the truth about my job, he never asked me for any details. That was another reason why I loved him. I wasn't allowed to talk about my work but he completely understood that. He never got angry or upset. He understood that there was a whole part of me that he could never come near.

"I can't tell you how happy we were together. We were soulmates. The children adored him. I simply couldn't believe how lucky I was to have found him.

"And then Alan Blunt told me the truth.

"I'll never forget the day he called me into his office, where he was waiting with two grim-faced men I'd never seen before. It was a Tuesday morning. It was raining. Alan was quite cold-blooded about it. He didn't waste any words and he never showed me the slightest bit of sympathy. Hans Mayer was not a writer. He was not a journalist. His parents were still alive and he didn't have an aunt. He wasn't even German. He was a Russian agent, what we call a deep-cover spy. I had only been a junior operative at the time, but someone in Russian intelligence had decided that one day I might be useful to them and Hans had been deliberately introduced to me – to become my friend, to get to know me, to marry me.

"Does the idea shock you? Do you find it hard to believe that a man would deliberately introduce himself to a woman, live with her and have children with her, simply to spy on her?"

Alex tried to think what it must have been like for her. His own family had lied to him, but this was in so many ways even worse. He shook his head.

"Well, that's the world I inhabit," Mrs Jones went on. "And it's not shocking at all. I knew things that Russian intelligence wanted to know and as I became more senior, the more valuable I became. Who could be closer to me, who could know me better than my husband, the father of my children? Alan Blunt told me that Special Operations had become aware of a security leak, that they knew that the Russians had been stealing secret information, but that it had taken them more than a year to find the source.

"I was the source. Even as he had been smiling at me, living with me, being close to me, Hans had been listening to my phone calls, accessing my computer, following me, filming me. Do you have any idea what I felt when Alan told me that? It was a hammer blow. I couldn't believe it. At least, I couldn't believe all of it. Hans was a spy. He was an enemy of my country. But all the time we had spent together, all the things he had said, they couldn't all be a lie. I can see him even now as I tell you this. He was a perfect dad. I refused to accept that he hadn't loved me, that all of it – the entire marriage – had been pretence.

"I asked Alan Blunt what would happen next

and he told me, well, bluntly. I was not being held responsible. My career would not be damaged. But Hans would be arrested later that day. There would be no lawyers, no publicity. He would simply disappear. He might end up in our facility in Gibraltar but there were plenty of other places where he could be questioned at length. MI6 wanted to know how much he had found out, who he worked for. It might be possible to 'turn' him, which is to say to make him work for us. I had no doubt that he would be treated very roughly. Alan Blunt assumed that I would be happy to know that he was going to suffer for what he had done.

"He was wrong. I'm still ashamed about what happened next and, as you'll hear, I was about to make the biggest mistake of my life. But despite everything, I still loved Hans. I remembered all the wonderful times we'd had together. He was the father of my children! I couldn't bear the thought of him being dragged off to jail, disappearing for ever into the darkness. You have to remember, I was quite young. I wasn't as hard then as I am now. I've had to learn..."

Mrs Jones stopped and Alex realized she had reached the climax of her story. It was possible that she had never told anyone what she was about to tell them now.

"I did something stupid," she said. "But I couldn't stop myself. I didn't want him to be hurt or punished or anything like that. What was the point?

The damage had already been done. I just wanted him to leave. And so, after I left Alan's office, I made a telephone call. I used a phone that couldn't be traced to me and I kept the message short. I just said that I knew the truth about him and my bosses knew it too. I warned him that he was going to be arrested. Then I hung up. He hadn't argued or tried to pretend he was innocent. He hadn't apologized for deceiving me. He hadn't said anything.

"Those were the last words I spoke to him. After I rang off, I destroyed the phone. I knew that I had betrayed the service and that I would get into terrible trouble if anyone found out, but I didn't care. All that mattered to me was that he should get away."

"And did he?" Jack asked. She had been completely absorbed by the story.

"Oh yes." Mrs Jones nodded.

There was another long silence.

"Alan Blunt knew that Hans had been warned but he never found out who made the call. Maybe he suspected me. I don't know. Anyway, Hans disappeared before anyone could reach him. A deep-cover agent like him would have been prepared for the worst. He would have had a false passport, a stash of money, a handler he could call in case of emergency. From the day he met me, he would have known of a secret route out of the country, a way to get himself quickly back to Russia ... a private plane, perhaps. Or a boat waiting at the coast. He simply vanished into thin air. I knew I would never see him again.

"What worried me most, though, was what I was going to tell the children. How could I make them understand that the father they loved had abandoned them? I was feeling sick as I drove round to the school to pick them up that day. I didn't want to lie to them but I knew there was no way I could tell them the truth."

Mrs Jones took out a small box of peppermints and slipped one into her mouth.

"The children weren't there," she said, bleakly. "The headteacher told me that Hans had come round just after midday. That would have been about an hour after I called him. He had explained that there was an emergency and he had taken William and Sofia out of school. They had left with him in a car. Do you understand what I'm telling you? He had taken them with him. That was how much he cared about me! I had quite possibly saved his life. I had betrayed everything I believed in for him. And he had repaid me by stealing my children."

Mrs Jones was very calm. There was no emotion in her voice. Alex glanced at Jack and saw the horror in her eyes.

"We put out a general alert," Mrs Jones went on. "Every airport, every railway station, every port, every road. But of course it was much too late. By the time I left the school – in shock – Hans was probably halfway to Russia, and William and Sofia were with him.

"Since then, not a day has gone by that I haven't searched for them. I am, of course, in a position of power. I have contacts all over the world. But it's as if all three of them never existed. I have nobody but myself to blame for what happened, but I have had to resign myself to the fact that I have lost my children and that I will never see them again."

She fell silent. Jack was staring at her. Alex wasn't sure what to say.

"Why have you told us all this?" he asked, eventually.

"It's the reason why I'm here," Mrs Jones replied. "Of course I'm concerned about any threat to London and I'm desperately sorry that our agent was killed in Rio de Janeiro. But as I said at the start, this is also very personal for me, Alex, and it's why I've broken my own promise to myself and come here to ask you for help.

"I have always assumed that William and Sofia were somewhere in Russia and that Hans was bringing them up, presumably under another name. I tried to imagine them in their new life and I've always hoped they were happy. William is sixteen now. Sofia is fourteen. I often wonder if they ever think of me or even remember who I am and of course I have done everything I can to find them again. The strange thing is that the Russians have always denied that Hans ever left England. They've told me that he is dead. How else would it be possible to disappear so completely in an age when all of us are being watched and listened to all the time? Sometimes, I've woken up in the middle of the night and thought that maybe my children are dead too. Perhaps the plane that was carrying them crashed. Or maybe the Russians decided they had no use for them and killed them.

"That is what I have lived with for the last ten years. I am the mother who lost her children and never saw them again. At least, that's what I thought until the day before yesterday."

Mrs Jones took out a photograph and slid it onto the table in front of Jack and Alex. It was the picture that Crawley had shown her, taken outside the airport in Rio de Janeiro just after Pablo had been killed. It showed the girl who had driven the scooter, breaking through the fence.

"This is my daughter," she said. "Just like Frederick Grey who was missing believed dead, she's turned up again. She was in Rio de Janeiro. For reasons that I can't begin to imagine, she helped Freddy murder our agent. She's working for Nightshade."

Jack stared at the photograph. She could see the similarity. The girl in the picture looked like a younger version of the woman sitting opposite her. Even so, she had to ask. "Are you sure?"

"I'm a hundred per cent certain." Mrs Jones turned to Alex and there was something in her face that he had never seen before. "Only you can help me," she said. "Only you can get close to Frederick Grey. And that's why I've come here. Help me find Nightshade.

Help me stop whatever it is they're planning. But above all, help me find my children. They're alive. I'm sure of it. Nightshade has them. And only you can get them back."

THE HOUSE OF DOLLS

"Are you sure about this?" Jack asked.

"No. Not really." They had stopped at a red traffic light and Alex looked out of the car window, at the London streets moving slowly past. It was a bright sunny day. He saw a woman pushing a pram, a black cab pulling in to pick up a young family, a man walking a dog. Everything looked normal – but how would it be after an attack by a deadly nerve agent? He couldn't bring himself to think about it.

"There is no one else," he said, at length. "I look like Julius Grief. I can go into the prison and get the information out of Freddy Grey. If I refuse, and the attack happens, how will I ever live with myself?"

Jack nodded. "What about Mrs Jones ... William and Sofia?"

"I feel sorry for her. She made one mistake and it ruined her life. Maybe that's what made her so ... tough." Alex sighed. "If I find her children, maybe that will be the end of it. Maybe, after that, she'll leave me alone."

The lights changed and they moved off again. They turned into a narrow street and Alex noticed the great bulk of the British Museum on his left. He had been there a couple of times on school trips. He was puzzled. He had thought they were on their way to the MI6 offices in Liverpool Street.

Jack had noticed the same thing. "Where are you taking us?" she demanded.

The driver was a young man, dressed casually in jeans and a sweatshirt. He didn't look round. "We're almost there," he said.

"That's great. But where is there?"

By way of an answer, the driver pulled in and parked in front of a small shop that could have come straight out of Charles Dickens with iron railings and a single window bulging out of the front. An old teddy bear sat behind the glass, looking utterly miserable as it gazed at the modern world. Two steps led up to a black door with a sign reading THE HOUSE OF DOLLS and beneath it the single word, CLOSED. As they got out of the car, Alex noticed an electronic keypad next to the door. It was slightly odd, out of place on such an old-fashioned building. He watched as the driver punched in a code: 753159. The six digits formed the shape of a letter X and Alex wondered if they had been chosen on purpose, to make them easier to remember. There was an electronic buzzing sound and the door opened.

They went in and found themselves in a rectangular space surrounded by about a hundred dolls, teddy bears, puppets and stuffed animals, sitting on shelves or dangling on strings, staring at them with shiny glass eyes. A row of antique doll's houses stretched along a raised counter, forming what was almost a street with a miniature castle at one end and at the other an old train set, complete with a station platform and two steam locomotives frozen in time. The whole shop was dark and silent. There was something very creepy about the toys and Alex realized that the children who had once played with them must have all died long ago. He was already wishing he hadn't come.

Jack was evidently feeling the same. "Are you serious?" she muttered as the driver closed the door.

"It is a bit creepy," the driver admitted. "But follow me..."

He went over to a shelf and reached out as if he had decided to take one of the dolls for himself. He had chosen a clown with orange hair and a painted face, sitting with its legs dangling over the edge. Carefully, he turned the head to one side. Alex heard a click and at once the entire section, complete with all the different toys, sank into the floor, revealing a passageway behind.

"This way," he said.

Alex and Jack followed him into a much more modern hallway, thickly carpeted with steel-grey walls and a CCTV blinking at them from above. There were no windows but black glass panels stretched from floor to ceiling on either side and Alex had no doubt they were being scanned for concealed weapons as they went. There was a door ahead of them. As they approached, it slid silently open to reveal John Crawley waiting for them, dressed in a suit and a striped tie.

"Hello, Alex," he said. "I'm very pleased to see you again."

"Hello, Mr Crawley."

"Where's Mrs Jones?" Jack demanded.

Crawley looked uncomfortable. "I'm afraid she's not here. Thank you, Miles. You can wait in the car." The driver turned round and went back the way he had come. "Shall we get started?"

Crawley took them back through the doorway and into a long, narrow conference room with a glass table, eight chairs, and French windows looking out into a garden with rose bushes in full bloom and a fountain sparkling in the sunlight. A coffee machine, drinks and biscuits stood at one end of the table but Alex was more interested in the metal box, about the size of a small book, that had been placed right in the middle. It had a tangle of wires, a series of what looked like miniature antennas and a green light flashing behind a glass panel on the side.

"What's that?" Alex asked.

"It's a portable RF inhibitor," Crawley explained. "Battery-operated so it's completely self-contained. It'll jam every radio frequency, any triangulation or surveillance system, Bluetooth ... and any sort of trigger mechanism for a remote-controlled explosive device. It works in an area of up to sixty metres. Obviously, it means you won't be able to make or receive any calls while you're here but at least we can be sure that nobody is listening in. Or trying to blow us up!"

"Why are you so worried?" Jack asked. "And what is this place anyway?"

"It's an MI6 safe house." Crawley poured coffee for Jack and slid a can of Coke towards Alex. "We use it for agents visiting London ... also for witnesses who need protection. There are half a dozen bedrooms, a kitchen and a nuclear bunker. That's in the basement."

"Nice garden." Jack was looking out through the window. She stopped and frowned. "But how come you've got roses blooming in the middle of October?"

Crawley smiled. "Well spotted," he said. He went over to the wall and pressed a button. The garden vanished. In its place, the window was now looking over the edge of a lake with a sailing boat gliding past. "It's a hologram," he explained. "The trouble with having windows that look out is that they allow people to look in, which is too much of a security risk. But it's depressing to stare at a blank wall all day, so Smithers had the system put in before he left." He pressed the button a second time and the garden reappeared. "He also supplied the jamming equipment," Crawley went on. "I must say, I do miss him!"

"So why aren't we in Liverpool Street?"

Crawley sat down. "This is an unofficial operation, Alex," he said. "The truth is that apart from Mrs Jones and myself, nobody knows that you're involved and we want to keep it that way. It's important you understand this from the start. Once you take on the identity of Julius Grief and enter our Gibraltar facility, you'll be on your own. Only one other person will know the truth about you and she'll be your one point of contact if anything goes wrong. I'll introduce you to her shortly." He pointed at the jamming machine. "That's why I had this installed. An agent of mine was killed in Rio, which means that there was a leak. Somebody knew about him. So right now I'm not in the mood to trust anyone."

"What about the driver who brought us here?"

"Miles? Actually, he's my nephew. He's my private assistant – I trust him completely." Crawley poured himself a coffee. "Now, if you're still up for this, shall we begin?"

Mrs Jones had told Alex that, as well as Freddy, there were six prisoners being held in Gibraltar. When he arrived on the peninsula, and if he was going to be convincing as Julius Grief, he would need to know everything about them, to pretend that he had met them already. Crawley had their photographs and personal details on his laptop and turned the screen round so that Alex could see.

Six faces. Four men and two women. Different ages, different ethnicities. Crawley took Alex through them one by one, giving him their names and a quick rundown of what each of them had done.

"Derek and Claire Miller. Not husband and wife. Brother and sister. They belonged to an extreme right-wing terrorist group, the Dark Angels. They came within minutes of exploding a nuclear device in Washington, DC."

Alex examined the image of a man and a woman, in their thirties, both of them dressed in Nazi uniforms, holding hands. "Tell me this was taken at a fancy-dress party," he said.

"No. They always dressed that way." Crawley moved on to another image. "This is Henry Mellish. He spied for the Russians. And Jayne Chumley. She spied for anyone who would pay her. Both of them extremely dangerous, personally responsible for the deaths of at least fifty agents all over Europe. Ali Blasim – he's the oldest man in the Gibraltar compound – started life working in a torture chamber in Iraq. Later on, he joined the weapons inspectors searching for nuclear missiles. The only trouble was, when he found them, he stole them and sold them to the highest bidders, including the Millers. Finally, Mr Someone. We don't know his real name so that's what we call him. He's a freelance assassin, one of the best in the business. He claims to have killed his parents when he was twelve years old. By the time he was fifteen, he had turned professional."

Mr Someone was a good-looking Caribbean man with grizzled hair and a thin moustache. His eyes, staring out of the photograph, managed to be intelligent, good-humoured and very dangerous.

"I have ten pages on each one of them, Alex, and you're not leaving here until you've learned them off by heart. You've got to know everything about these people. What they did and what they think about it. What they eat. Where they come from. Their nicknames. What annoys them and what makes them laugh. Julius Grief spent months with them and got to know them inside out. You have to remember that they're being kept in Gibraltar because they're too dangerous to go anywhere else. If they even suspect there's something wrong, they'll kill you without even thinking about it."

"You're not making this mission sound very attractive," Jack growled.

"I'm just being honest with you, Jack. If Alex wants to back out, I'll understand that. But I'm not going to send him in under false pretences."

"What else have you got for me?" Alex asked.

Crawley tapped a button and a diagram appeared on the screen: a compound consisting of half a dozen buildings with pathways and gardens, surrounded by a wall. "I'm going to take you on a virtual tour of the Gibraltar facility," he went on. "When you arrive, you're going to have to find your way to the library, the dining room, the cells, the governor's villa ... with no hesitation. You're meant to have lived there, so you're going to need to know every minute of the day's routine. What time you eat lunch. Where you pick up your knife and fork ... plastic, of course.

When you're allowed to talk. How you address the guards. I'm not saying you can't misbehave. On the contrary, they'll expect that. But you have to understand all the rules before you can break them.

"And that's another thing. You won't like this, Alex, but you're going to have to get inside Julius Grief's head. It's not enough that you look like him. You have to talk like him, think like him and behave like him too. We'll give you a complete rundown of his time in custody. There are things you need to know – like when he got into a fight with Henry Mellish, for example. Mellish won't have forgotten that and he may challenge you."

"How long do I have once I get there?" Alex asked.

"You're going to have to move fast. We have to assume that Nightshade has taken possession of the VX nerve agent supplied to them in Rio. We don't know when they're going to strike but it's going to be soon. Pablo told me that before he was killed."

"Didn't he manage to tell you anything else?" Jack asked. "I mean, do you really have no idea what Nightshade have in mind?"

"No. It all happened too quickly." Crawley shook his head. He turned to Alex. "You have to get close to this other boy, Frederick Grey. Somehow you have to get the information out of him. Who are Nightshade? Where are they based? What are they planning? As soon as you've found that out, you tell us and we get you out of there."

"How will Alex communicate with you?" As Jack

spoke she couldn't keep the worry out of her voice.

"Do I get gadgets?" Alex asked. He was already imagining a hidden transmitter.

"I'm afraid not. When you enter the compound, everything you own will be taken from you and thoroughly examined. You'll be strip-searched. It won't be very pleasant. Anything that we gave you would be found. But you will, as I said, have a contact and you can reach us through her." He paused. "Her name is Dr Rosemary Flint. She's a psychiatrist who was working at Gibraltar while Julius was there. How would you feel about meeting her now? I thought you might like the opportunity to play at being Julius."

"How about some time to prepare?" Alex countered.

"Relax, Alex. You remember Julius Grief. You're identical to him. Let's see how this works."

There was a telephone on the table, with a wire trailing to the floor. With the jammer still turned on, a mobile phone wouldn't have worked. Crawley dialled a number and spoke briefly. "Could you ask her to come in?" He put the phone down. "Dr Flint will be able to help you." He went on. "She spent weeks talking to Julius and she knows more about the workings of his mind than anyone."

"And you've told her about your crazy scheme?" Jack asked.

Crawley shook his head. "As a matter of fact, I haven't. She's agreed to help Special Operations but we haven't yet told her what we're doing. She only arrived in London this morning and she was brought straight here." He turned to Alex. "If you can fool Dr Flint, you can probably fool anyone."

Alex had already been trying to put himself into Julius Grief's head, to change his personality to suit the other boy. He nodded his head. "All right," he said.

A minute later, the door opened and a smartly dressed woman walked purposefully into the room. With her brown hair cut in a straight line across her forehead and glasses that were a little too large for her face, she was clearly someone who treated life seriously. She wasn't smiling. She was wearing a blue and grey suit and carrying a leather brief-case. Clearly she also took her career seriously.

"Good morning," she said, addressing Crawley. She glanced at Jack, then noticed Alex, sitting at the table. At once, she changed. Alex saw her falter and step back. Her lip trembled. There was real fear in her eyes. "You..." she began.

"Good morning, Dr Flint," Alex said.

The woman took hold of a chair, almost as if it were a weapon she could use to defend herself. "What is *he do*ing here?" she demanded.

"Please sit down, Dr Flint. I've been looking forward to seeing you again."

Alex was shocked how easy it was to become Julius Grief. He remembered the other boy from the time they had been together in Egypt: he would never be able to get the memories out of his head. Alex had never met anyone quite so cold, so eaten up by hatred. He was careful to keep any emotion out of his voice. He kept his eyes fixed on the psychiatrist.

"It's very nice to see you, Dr Flint," he went on. "How are you?"

"No! I heard you were dead...!"

"I'm sorry to disappoint you."

The psychiatrist had gone pale, as if she were about to faint. Her eyes were wide open, her face frozen in disbelief. Alex knew that he had gone too far and quickly held up his hands in a sign of surrender. At the same moment, Crawley stepped in.

"This isn't Julius," he explained.

"What...?"

"This is Alex Rider, the boy Julius was meant to replace. We're sending him to Gibraltar and we need your help."

"You're Alex?" Dr Flint was staring at Alex in disbelief.

"Yes."

Dr Flint sat down. "I don't believe it!" she exclaimed. "You look exactly like him."

"Actually, he looked exactly like me," Alex said. "He was the one who had surgery. Dr Grief turned him into a perfect copy of me."

"You even sound like him. It's extraordinary." She turned to Crawley. "What exactly is this all about?"

"I'm sorry, Dr Flint," Crawley began. "I didn't mean to scare you – but it was important to know that Alex could pass as Julius."

"You've certainly established that much. But why? What are you trying to do?"

Quickly, Crawley explained what was being planned and why it was necessary. The psychiatrist nodded a couple of times but listened in silence. "Once Alex is inside the prison, we're going to need you to watch over him," Crawley continued. "You'll be the only person who knows his real identity. As soon as he has the information we need, he'll come to you. You'll contact us and we'll arrange for him to be returned to the UK. We're hoping this won't take too long."

"Half-term only lasts a week," Jack muttered, sourly.

"A week is all we need. Maybe ten days at the most. We want Alex back in school as soon as possible."

"And the idea is that he gets close to this other boy ... Frederick Grey? Becomes his friend?"

"That's right."

Dr Flint looked very unhappy. She turned to Alex. "Do you have any idea what you're letting yourself in for?" she said. She answered her own question before he could speak. "I've spent time with all the inmates at the Gibraltar compound and they're not just dangerous. They're really quite sick. As for the new prisoner, Frederick Grey, I've been introduced to him and I've read the psychiatric reports. He's barely spoken a word since he was arrested. Clearly something has happened to him while he's been with Nightshade. What makes you think you can get him to talk to you?"

Alex shrugged. "I don't know. This wasn't my idea!"

"They'll be sharing a cell," Crawley said. "They're more or less exactly the same age. If Frederick is going to talk to anyone, he'll talk to Alex and we can arrange things so that they become friends."

There was a long silence. Alex wondered if the psychiatrist was going to walk out of the room, refusing to take any part in what was suggested. He wouldn't have blamed her. He was tempted to do the same himself. But finally, she nodded. "What do you want me to do?" she asked.

Crawley leaned forward, pleased. "To start with, you need to tell Alex everything you can about Julius Grief. He may look and sound like Julius but that's not enough. He has to become him."

"Where is Julius? What happened to him?"

Alex didn't want to answer that. He glanced down at the floor, as if he hadn't heard.

"Julius died," Crawley said. "You were right about that. But nobody in the prison knows. As far as they're concerned, we'll simply say he's been recaptured."

"What else?"

"We've given Alex details of all the other prisoners. You can help him learn about them. And you can tell him what to expect when he arrives."

"I will help you," Dr Flint said. "But I want you to know, right from the start, that I think this is a crazy idea. These prisoners ... the Millers, Jayne Chumley, all of them! You have no idea how dangerous they are. If they even begin to suspect this boy isn't who he says he is..." She glanced at Alex and fell silent.

"I don't believe this is happening," Jack muttered. "I thought we'd put all this behind us."

"We have no choice," Crawley said. "But we're going to be very careful. One week in and out. We'll do everything we can to make sure Alex is safe. Nothing is going to go wrong."

But it was already going wrong.

At MI6 Special Operations in Liverpool Street, Owen Andrews was dialling a number on his mobile phone. Nobody had spoken to him from the moment he had arrived. He had been given an office at the very back of the building, next to the toilets. But that didn't bother him. The Permanent Under-Secretary at the Foreign and Commonwealth Office wanted to know everything that went on in the building ... and it was his assistant's job to make sure that happened. He wasn't here to make friends.

And only that morning, he had overheard a conversation in the corridor. A man called Burton had been complaining about something that had happened outside a school in Chelsea. He had been sent to pick up some kid but had ended up with black paint all over his face.

"I could have been blinded!" he was whining. "He put black pepper in with the paint powder. I complained to Mrs Jones but she just seemed to think the whole thing was funny. She said I should have been more careful."

"So who was the kid?" his friend asked.

"I don't know. His name was Alex Rider and she went to see him at his home. I thought I was just giving him a lift. I didn't expect him to try and kill me!"

Alex Rider.

Andrews knew that name. He had helped draw up the report that his boss had been reading when Mrs Jones came to the Foreign Office. She wasn't allowed to employ him. She wasn't even meant to be talking to him. So what was she doing visiting him at his home?

The telephone rang three times before it was answered.

"Yes?" The voice at the other end sounded distant, bored.

"Good morning, sir. This is Owen Andrews."

"Ah yes, Owen! What have you got for me?"

"I think it's something you need to know, sir. It's about Alex Rider. It seems that he's back."

PART TWO: EXODUS

BACK TO JAIL

There were times when Alex found it almost impossible to believe what was happening to him ... when he had to struggle to work out if it was real or some sort of dream. This was certainly one of them.

He should have been home for half-term. He had promised to go round to Tom Harris's house to work on Deadmaster, a computer game Tom was trying to develop. Instead, he was sitting in the back of a Lockheed C-130 Hercules transport plane, thirty-five thousand feet above the Mediterranean, wearing a flimsy orange jumpsuit and strapped into a low metal seat which was itself bolted to the floor. Both his wrists and his ankles were chained. He was resting against a length of coarse red webbing which rose above his head. Two men sat opposite him, watching him with eyes that were cold and curious.

He had spent the last twenty-four hours immersed in the character of Julius Grief, acting like him, talking like him, helped by a reluctant Dr Flint.

"What you are doing is very dangerous," she had

133

warned him. "It's easy enough to change your personality, to become evil. The trouble is, it stays with you. And it damages you."

But Alex had no choice. If he was going to convince the other prisoners, and Freddy in particular, he couldn't pretend to be Julius. He had to be Julius. They were two very different things.

It was time to put his hard work to the test.

He glanced at one of the guards. "I don't suppose there's any chance of a cup of coffee and a Kit Kat?" he called out. "I have to say, the service on this airline is pretty rubbish. Next time, I think I'll go with easyJet."

The men ignored him. Alex half-smiled to himself. They had already dismissed him as a juvenile delinquent, not even worth talking to. He sat back, silently, focusing on what lay ahead.

Get the information. Get out. Get back to school. That was the plan and Alex turned it over and over in his mind. He had felt sorry for Mrs Jones and he had volunteered for this, but that didn't mean he had to like it. He couldn't wait for it to be over.

The plane droned on through the darkness. Alex finally managed to nod off but it felt as if only minutes had passed before he was woken up by the change of pressure in his ears which told him they were coming in to land. There was still nothing to see and the jolt of the wheels hitting the runway took him by surprise. There was the roar of reverse thrust. The plane slowed down and came to a halt.

The guards stood up, flexing their muscles.

"You don't speak, Julius. You do as you're told. We have Tasers and we'll use them if you even try to step out of line. Do you understand?"

How would Julius have answered? Would he have tried another joke? No. He wouldn't have wanted to give them an excuse to hurt him. Alex smiled, his face filled with contempt. *I am Julius Grief*, he thought. *The living replica of Dr Hugo Grief. I am more than human and you are nothing.*

Think like Julius.

Act like Julius.

Be Julius.

The door was yanked open and the grey light of early morning spilled into the hold. Alex was pulled to his feet and led down a flight of steps. He glimpsed a wide expanse of tarmac, more armed guards and, in the distance, a looming shadow that he knew was the Rock of Gibraltar. Somewhere, high above, a maximum security prison – known only to a handful of intelligence officers – was waiting for him. A black prison van had been parked next to the Hercules, its back doors open. With his hands and feet still chained together, Alex shuffled forward. He felt a hand push him, hard, in the back.

"Good to have you back, Julius," a voice said.

"I won't be staying long," Alex replied, automatically.

Three men climbed into the van with him and the doors were slammed shut. A moment later, they moved off slowly – but Alex's mind was already racing ahead. It suddenly occurred to him that Crawley had made a serious mistake. Alex had been briefed on the other prisoners in the Gibraltar facility. He knew about the governor and the governor's new wife, Dolores. The two of them had got married just a few months ago. He had met the psychiatrist, Dr Flint. But Crawley had forgotten that there were still a few guards at the prison who had been close to Julius Grief too. One of them had just addressed him but Alex had no idea which one it was. He was going to have to be very careful until he had worked out who exactly he was supposed to know.

For the next fifteen minutes, Alex was bumped up and down and thrown from side to side as the van made its way round a series of hairpin bends, following the road as it climbed uphill. The guards said nothing but their eyes never left him. The van slowed and stopped, then started again. This happened three times. Checkpoints? Alex pressed his head against the side of the metal box but apart from one voice, calling out in Spanish, he heard nothing.

Finally, they stopped and this time the engine was turned off. Alex guessed that they must be inside the prison. They had arrived.

The sun had begun to rise by the time the van was unlocked and he was allowed out. Alex saw shafts of pink in an otherwise grey sky, a few clouds, a distant flock of birds wheeling around. He climbed down and found himself standing on a stretch of ground surrounded by walls, an electrified fence with razor wire and automatic gates that were already sliding shut. He had been shown photographs of the prison but it still took him by surprise with its tidy lawns, vegetable gardens and low brick buildings. It almost looked like a holiday camp, although he reminded himself that any holiday here would last years or even decades. The van had parked in front of a three-storey villa – the only building in the compound that was actually higher than the walls. This was the governor's home. Alex recognized it at once.

"The governor is waiting to see you."

Alex allowed himself to be led along a gravel path and up to the front door of the house. A metal detector had recently been installed around the entrance and Alex knew exactly why it was there. Julius Grief had escaped from the prison, using a gun that had been smuggled in for him. He had used it to hold Dr Flint hostage, walking out of the governor's house with the muzzle pressed against her head. Well, that would never happen again. No prisoner could carry anything metal in or out of the door and as if to prove it, the machine began to blare as Alex passed through, alerted by his handcuffs and ankle chains.

But on the other side, everything was peaceful. The governor was British and it showed in his taste: thick carpets, antique furniture, pictures of the English countryside and, on a central table, a vase of roses. There was a half-open door straight ahead of him.

"You go through there."

A single guard had come in with Alex but he stood where he was, allowing Alex to continue on his own. He became aware of a clock, ticking loudly, as he shuffled forward. Otherwise, the house was silent. It could only have been about six o'clock in the morning. He didn't knock. He pushed the door open and went in.

The governor was sitting behind his desk. He was a scowling bulldog of a man with grey hair cut short and a face that was beginning to sag in middle age. Alex had read his file and knew that his name was Frank Sheriff and that he had been in the Royal Navy for twenty years before being sent here. What he had not been prepared for, though, was the look of sheer hatred that came over the man as Alex entered the room.

"Julius Grief!" The governor rasped out the name as if he had difficulty forcing it through his throat.

"Good morning, Governor." Alex spoke carefully. He knew he was in trouble and didn't want to make things worse.

The governor looked surprised. He clearly hadn't expected such politeness but his eyes were still as hard as stone. "Sit down!" he snapped.

The room was an office and it was modern, with a glass table, metal filing cabinets, a few shelves with books in English and Spanish. There were windows on either side. One looked out onto the main compound, where a sprinkler had just sprung into life, spraying one of the lawns. The other was facing the perimeter wall, which rose just a few metres from the side of the house, blocking the light.

Alex sat down. The governor examined him in silence for a long minute, then began to speak.

"I didn't expect to see you back," he said. "Nor did I want to. I've always found you a bit creepy if you want the truth, Grief. You weren't born. You were manufactured. I suppose there are some who would call you a scientific miracle ... a clone. But that's not how I see you. To me, you're just a freak. You should never have been created in the first place. All the inmates here are unpleasant in their own way but, for me, you're the worst of the lot."

The governor had been sitting in a modern office chair, one that swivelled on wheels. Now he stood up, pushing it away. Slowly, he walked round the table and perched on the corner so that he was closer to Alex. He was not a tall man but he was stocky and muscular. He spoke quietly, as if he was afraid of being overheard.

"There's something I want you to understand," he said. "When you escaped from this facility, you caused us a great deal of inconvenience. We wasted hours going through a complete review of security and then reporting back to London. We put in new procedures and spent hundreds of thousands of pounds on new technology. But you did something worse than all of those things." He leaned forward, his nose almost touching Alex's face. Alex could feel the man's breath on his cheek. "You made me look like a fool. I was about to be promoted, to move out of this bloody place. Bigger and better things! That didn't happen. London blamed me for what happened, so here I still am."

Alex knew he had to say something – and he had to say it in the character of Julius Grief.

"I'm so sorry!" He spoke in a falsetto, his voice mocking.

The governor's hand lashed out, slapping him across the face. Alex was taken by surprise and propelled backwards on the chair, crashing down onto his shoulders. If the floor hadn't been carpeted, he might have been badly hurt, but even so the breath was knocked out of him and every bone in his body jarred. And then Frank Sheriff was on top of him, his hands around Alex's throat, squeezing so hard that he couldn't breathe.

"You listen to me, you little worm," he hissed. "Things have changed. The last time you were here, we treated you with kid gloves. We were too easy on you. But I'm going to tell my guards that if you step out of line, if you make any more of those funny jokes of yours, they can do anything they like to you and I'll simply look the other way."

"You ... strangling me!" Alex could barely speak. He could smell the governor's breath – cigarette smoke and coffee.

"Nobody cares if you live or die, Grief. Get that into your head. There are prisoners here who can't wait to see you again. Henry Mellish for one. And the Millers. There are old scores they want to settle and we're not going to stand in their way."

Alex really thought the governor was going to kill him there and then. But suddenly Sheriff let go of his throat and grabbed hold of the back of the chair, pulling him upright again. Alex slumped forward, the room briefly swimming in front of him. The governor walked away from him, taking his place behind his table.

"I shouldn't have done that." The governor wiped the back of his hand across his forehead. He was breathing heavily. "You provoked me and I let myself get carried away. It's the last time it will happen. I won't see you again, Grief. I'll let others deal with you." He smiled grimly. "But maybe, just maybe, I'll come to your funeral."

He pressed a button on his desk and a moment later the door opened and the guard who had brought Alex in reappeared.

The governor glanced up briefly. "Get him out of here," he said.

"Do you want him in solitary confinement, *señor*?"

The question horrified Alex. It was something he hadn't considered. If he was thrown into solitary, he might not get close to Freddy for months.

But the governor had come to a decision. "No, Diego. He's here for the rest of his life. We can save those pleasures for later. Just get him out of my sight."

"Let's go, Diego!" Alex mocked.

Diego grabbed hold of Alex by the back of his neck and dragged him, painfully, to his feet. Before he could react, he found himself being pushed at speed across the hallway and back out into the garden, the shackles cutting into his ankles. He hesitated briefly as he stepped outside and Diego punched him, hard, in the back. So that was a good start. He had antagonized the governor and at least one of the guards – and this was before he had even met the other prisoners.

It was still early in the morning and nobody was up. Alex knew that breakfast was served at seven with the day's various activities – gardening, reading, workshops, exercise – beginning an hour later. Life inside the Gibraltar prison had been carefully designed to keep the prisoners manageable. There were also punishments. The governor had already talked about solitary confinement and Alex had seen images of the three cells where unruly inmates would be locked up deep underground.

But that wasn't where he was heading now. Diego prodded him towards a modern, low-rise building made of wood and brick. Just the bars on the windows revealed its true purpose. Alex had already counted six CCTV cameras and two more watched him as he was led down a narrow corridor and along to a door at the end. Only now did Diego unlock the handcuffs and ankle chains, all the time making sure his hand was never far away from the Glock 17 semi-automatic pistol in a holster at his side. Alex was fairly sure he would be shot down if he so much as coughed.

"You're sharing a room," Diego said. He had learned his English in America. It was obvious from his accent. "I'm sure you two guys are going to get along just fine."

"I thought I got a single room," Alex complained.

"Well, think again, toerag."

The door opened electronically, responding to a key-card that Diego had taken from his pocket. Alex wondered how they stopped the cards falling into the prisoners' hands. Not that breaking out of the accommodation block would have done any good. There was the wall and the electrified fence to consider – along with the two sliding gates manned around the clock which provided the only way out.

The door was open. Alex was pushed inside.

It took him a moment or two to get used to the dim light. The room was surprisingly spacious with a set of bunk beds, two desks, a wall-mounted television and a second door leading into a bathroom. There were no pictures on the walls, no carpet, no curtains. The light – not yet turned on – was contained behind a wire grille and the window was barred. Otherwise, it looked comfortable enough.

Then Alex saw that there was a boy lying on the lower bunk.

Freddy Grey was watching him with clear blue eyes that gave nothing away. It was possible that Alex had woken him up, coming into the room, but from the look of him, he might never have been asleep.

"Hello," Alex said. "I'm Julius. Who are you?"

The boy said nothing.

The door slammed shut and Alex heard an electronic buzz as the lock engaged. The two of them were alone.

DOING TIME

Alex watched as Freddy Grey uncurled himself and sat up, throwing back the thin blanket that had covered him. He was naked apart from a pair of shorts and, examining him from the door, Alex had to fight back a sense of unease. The boy didn't look dangerous. He was the same age as Alex and quite a few centimetres shorter. The muscles in his chest and arms were well defined but he still had the appearance of a lost child. And yet there was something unquestionably lethal about him. He had been held by the toughest police force in Brazil and had gone on to kill five men, one after another. Alex had read the file. He had shown no hesitation, no remorse. And now the two of them were in a cell together and the door was locked. If Alex had been thrown into a cage with a man-eating tiger, he would have felt about as comfortable.

He took a step forward, grateful that he could walk freely, without shackles. The boy's eyes never left him. Suddenly, Alex was angry with himself.

He wasn't Alex Rider. He was Julius Grief. His new cell mate might be a ruthless killer. He might be as mad as a hatter. But Julius was madder. He wouldn't have worried if he was going to get killed. Alex remembered him the last time the two of them had met in the fort at Siwa, Julius giggling and capering as Alex was tortured. This was the boy he was supposed to be. He wasn't afraid of anything.

"I asked you your name," he snarled. "Why don't you tell me? Or are you going to sit there like a dummy in a shop window. Is that what you are? A dummy?" Alex went up to Freddy and clapped his hands right in front of his face. "Hey, dummy! Can you hear me?"

Somewhere deep inside him, a voice was whispering that he was committing suicide, but he ignored it. He cast his eyes around the room.

"OK, dummy. Let's get a few things straight. This is my room now and we do things my way. If you don't want to talk to me, that's fine. I've got nothing to say to you either. But maybe, just maybe, it'll occur to you that we're on the same side. It's those losers out there who have locked us up. MI6. The military. The British government. You and I should take them on together. Maybe we can even escape. I've been here before. I already busted out once. I know a few things that might help you."

Had Alex imagined it or had there been a slight gleam in Freddy's eye when he had said the word "escape"? Otherwise, he was expressionless. And he still hadn't uttered a word.

146

Alex gave up for the moment. At least he had broken the ice – and Freddy hadn't killed him yet.

"All right. Suit yourself. Maybe I've got time for half an hour's sleep before breakfast. I hope the food's not as bad as I remember."

A short wooden ladder led up to the top bunk. Alex climbed up and rolled onto his back. Freddy Grey sat where he was and he was still sitting there half an hour later when the light in the cell flicked on and a buzz announced that the door had opened once again.

The dining hall was simply furnished with a single long table in the middle and windows along one side, looking out towards the governor's villa. There was a serving hatch at the far end opening into a kitchen where a scowling chef, in grubby whites, stood over a tin tray of greasy fried eggs. The prisoners ate together here and the room was also used for meetings, card games and chess. With the shutters drawn, it became a makeshift cinema and films were shown once a month.

Alex was the last to arrive for breakfast and as he entered, the room fell silent and heads turned in his direction. Only Freddy Grey, sitting at the end nearest to him, continued eating a square of toast and sipping tea, as if he was unaware of anything around him. Alex forced a smile onto his face and slouched into the room, avoiding eye contact with anyone at the table. He felt like an actor walking onto the stage. And right now, the other prisoners were his audience.

He reached the serving hatch, picked up a plate and accepted an egg and a slice of fried bread. The cook handed him a mug of lukewarm tea. He had already noted that all the cutlery was plastic and that the knife was so flimsy it would barely cut through the egg. The prisoners weren't allowed anywhere near anything that might be used as a weapon – not even a kettle – and he knew that if he tried to climb through the hatch, the chef would hit a panic button which would bring a steel shutter crashing down in less than a second. Taking his food, he walked back to the table and sat down opposite Freddy Grey. That was why he was here. The two of them had to become friends – and fast.

Alex had changed his clothes before he had left the cell. There were no uniforms in the Gibraltar facility: the prisoners wore what they liked. He and Freddy, of course, had nothing of their own and so they had ended up identically dressed in jeans and black sweatshirts which had been provided by the prison authorities. The jeans were too loose and the sweatshirt was too tight but at least they looked better than the orange jumpsuit he had worn on the plane. And maybe it was a good thing that they were dressed the same. It might actually help bring them together.

Alex poked the plastic fork into his egg and watched as the yolk oozed onto the plate. He had no appetite at all. Opposite him, Freddy nibbled his dry toast as if he was actually enjoying it.

"Hello, my dear Julius. How very delightful and unexpected to see you again. I could hardly believe my ears when I heard you were coming. But then you always were full of surprises."

The speaker was on Alex's left; a dark-skinned man in his sixties, slim, with a moustache and greying hair. He was wearing a loose-fitting T-shirt, shorts and sandals. Alex recognized him at once and knew that he came from Kingston, Jamaica, that he had a wife and nine children and that even they did not know his real name. He was a professional assassin and he loved his work so much he had offered his clients a special deal: three deaths for the price of two.

"How are you, Mr Someone?" Alex asked.

"All the better for seeing you. I would say 'welcome back' – but I'm not sure it's appropriate."

"I won't be here long," Alex said.

"That may be true – but not, alas, in the way you mean. I can think of at least one gentleman at this table who would like to say goodbye to you. Permanently."

Alex looked past him at Henry Mellish, the Russian spy. He was round-faced and boyish with thick, black spectacles. He was dressed, bizarrely, in a suit and bow tie. Crawley had already warned Alex that Mellish and Julius had got into some sort of fight – although he didn't know what about. Mellish was staring at

Alex now, his face flushed with hatred. He was holding his plastic knife as if he could actually use it as a weapon.

"I think it's fair to say that our friend Henry isn't too happy," Mr Someone continued. "Those names you called him. I did warn you to be careful."

"Maybe you can kill him for me," Alex suggested. Wasn't that the sort of thing Julius would say?

Mr Someone chuckled. "You could never afford me, Julius. Anyway, with great regret I have to tell you that I've retired. You'll have to deal with this one yourself."

Alex turned his attention back to the boy sitting opposite him. He didn't need to get involved with anyone else in the room. *One week,* he told himself. *Get the information Crawley wants and you're out of here.*

"So what do you think of the food here, Freddy?" he asked.

It was a stupid enough question but Alex was deliberately being more pleasant than he had been in the cell. He had established that he was in command. Now it was time to be friends.

It didn't work. Still holding his piece of toast, Freddy paused, then looked up and suddenly Alex found himself looking at a pair of eyes that drilled right into him. Crawley had seen exactly the same thing in the BOPE offices in Rio. Alex knew that he was looking at his own death – but he didn't know why.

Then the boy spoke to him for the first time.

"How did you know my name is Freddy?" he asked.

Alex froze. He was furious with himself. It was such an obvious mistake and it could have made him the target of a cold-blooded killer. And the worst of it was, he couldn't think of an answer. His mouth had gone dry. He didn't know what to say.

It was Mr Someone who came to his rescue. He had overheard the conversation and leaned across the table. "You can relax," he said. "In this place, everyone knows everything about everyone. There are no secrets here. Why should there be?" He smiled. "We're a family. We aren't going anywhere. You should get used to the fact that we're here for ever!"

Still the boy's dreadful eyes would not let him go. Alex saw Freddy making his calculations. Was he going to launch an attack, right now, simply because he was suspicious? Everything had come to a standstill. Nobody else in the room was saying anything, as if they were waiting to see what was going to happen. Then Freddy nodded and looked away. It was as though the sound had been turned up on a television set. Everything returned to normal.

It had been a close call. Alex picked up his mug of tea, forcing himself to keep his hand from shaking. He would have to be more careful in future. Another slip up and he would be dead.

The day continued. Time barely existed in the Gibraltar prison. Prisoners weren't allowed watches and no clocks or calendars hung on the walls but even so, Alex was horribly aware of every minute as it went past. All too soon, Nightshade was intending to attack London somehow. There weren't many minutes left.

The activities had finished for the morning. In the summer months, the prisoners were encouraged to grow their own vegetables in the gardens near the governor's villa but this was October, too late for sowing or digging. Alex noticed the two terrorists, Derek and Claire Miller, walking arm in arm around the compound, identically dressed in brown shirts, trousers and black leather boots. They had obviously been forbidden to wear military uniforms but that didn't stop them behaving like soldiers on parade. Ali Blasim, who had once sold nuclear weapons, had dozed off in the morning sun. He was the oldest person in the prison, in his eighties, and looked completely harmless. But then, Alex reminded himself, so does a crocodile when it's asleep.

He had seen Freddy going into the library and after about half an hour, followed him inside. He didn't want to look too keen. The library was small but it was modern and surprisingly well stocked. Freddy was sitting cross-legged on a beanbag, reading a book of Greek myths. Alex noticed an image of the wooden horse of Troy on the cover and made a mental note. According to the Brazilian police, the clothes that Freddy had been wearing when he was arrested had been bought in Greece. Was his choice of reading a coincidence or was it a clue as to where Nightshade might be found?

There was a woman sitting behind a desk close to the entrance, looking as if she were a professional librarian – although Alex knew at once she wasn't. Her name was Jayne Chumley and she was a spy, a traitor responsible for the deaths of many British agents. To Alex, she looked slightly mad with staring eyes, frizzy blonde hair and oversized front teeth ... two white tombstones in the graveyard of her face.

"So what are you doing here?" she asked, seeing him. She had the voice of a headmistress in an expensive girls' school.

"I got caught," Alex muttered, sourly.

"I know that, darling. I meant ... what are you doing in the library? You never used to like books."

Freddy was listening to every word. Alex knew he had to see this through and pressed on, playing the part.

"I was looking for a horror story," he said. He leered at her. "And looks like I found one. When did they make you the librarian?"

"When they fired Carlos." Alex had already been told the name of the librarian who had worked in the prison at the time of Julius's escape. "They thought he was responsible for your breaking out of here."

"Why would they think that?"

It was one question too many. He shouldn't have asked. But already it was too late.

"Because the gun you used was smuggled into the library. They found the book with the hollowed-out pages." She frowned. "Or had you forgotten?"

"Of course I hadn't forgotten." Alex was aware of Freddy, looking up from his book. Inside, Alex was raging. He had been told that Julius had a gun, but not how it had been concealed. It was another lethal mistake. He shrugged. "Carlos had nothing to do with it. He didn't know anything."

"Well, thanks to you, we don't have a librarian so I have to do it." Chumley didn't seem suspicious. She opened a book and date-stamped it. "Do you want something to read?"

"Yeah. I'll have a travel guide."

"You're not going anywhere."

"Wait and see..."

Alex had hoped that Freddy might engage him in conversation if he came into the library. But the other boy had returned to his Greek myths, flicking the pages, seemingly unaware that there was anyone else in the room.

He said nothing at lunch either and by the time he left the dining hall, Alex was beginning to think that Crawley's scheme was a complete waste of time. Walking across the compound towards the wood and metalwork shop, he thought of Jack and Tom and wished that he was with them. And that was when it struck him. He had allowed Mrs Jones and Crawley to talk him into this but there was actually no easy way for him to get out of it. If he went to the governor or to any of the guards and told them that he wasn't actually Julius Grief, they would simply laugh at him. The only person who knew who he was was Dr Rosemary Flint but he hadn't even glimpsed her yet. What if she didn't show up? What if she was ill? MI6 had no idea what was going on and he had no way of communicating with them. Anything could happen to him and they would only hear about it when it was too late.

"So you're back!"

Deep in thought, Alex hadn't noticed that his way was blocked by a scowling, portly figure who was now blinking at him through heavy, plastic glasses.

"Get out of the way, Henry," Alex said. He couldn't show that he was afraid of Henry Mellish. It was a lesson he'd learned in the schoolyard. If you show the bully you're scared of them, it just makes them worse.

But Mellish stood his ground. "I always hoped they'd find you," he rasped. He licked his lips with a moist, pink tongue. "I always hoped they'd send you back."

"Miss me, did you?"

"Oh yes." Suddenly Henry was very close to him. "All I wanted was to be your friend. Your special friend. I liked you. But you were horrible to me. You lied about me and you let everyone know." He looked around him as if he had remembered all the hidden microphones. He couldn't threaten Alex without being overheard. "I'll make you sorry!" he whispered and reeled away.

Alex stood where he was for a moment, then continued into the workshop. It was only the beginning of the afternoon and he was wondering just how much worse the day could get.

It was compulsory for the prisoners to do one activity every afternoon. The workshop was a large space and with all the tools lying around – chisels, screwdrivers, even saws – security here was at its tightest. Every piece of equipment was fastened with a short length of chain so that it couldn't be taken or used in a fight. There were three guards on duty all the time and CCTV cameras watched what was happening from every angle. Alex wondered why the prison needed a facility like this but guessed that the prisoners would go mad if they had nothing to do. Or madder than they already were.

The Millers were here, working on a wooden model of a thermonuclear missile. Ali Blasim was patiently carving a *dhow* – a little Arab sailing ship – out of wood. Freddy was sitting at a workbench, gazing out of the window. Taking a deep breath, Alex went over to him.

"Mind if I sit next to you?"

Freddy turned and looked at him but didn't speak.

"Look," Alex went on, "we're sharing a cell. Maybe we didn't get off to a great start this morning but we might as well be friends. We're stuck in this bloody place."

"Leave me alone." The words were quietly spoken but Alex could feel the menace behind them. What

Freddy really meant was: "Leave me alone. Or else..."

This wasn't the right time to start an argument. "All right," Alex muttered. "Whatever you say."

Alex turned away, wondering what he was going to do to occupy himself for the next hour. The question was answered by one of the guards who was holding a half-finished model of a submarine, made out of metal. Alex stared at it blankly.

"I thought you'd like this, Julius," the guard said. He was English, not Spanish. And he was smiling, pleased with himself.

"What?" For a couple of seconds, Alex wasn't sure how to respond. Then he realized. As unlikely as it seemed, Julius Grief must have been building a model submarine out of metal before he had escaped. He hadn't finished it. The guard was offering him a chance to do just that.

"I kept it for you!" The guard was mocking him, reminding him how quickly he had been caught.

"Great!" Alex took it, showing no enthusiasm at all. In fact, the model was just another problem to add to all the others he had faced that day. Crawley should have warned him. Alex might be the spitting image of Julius. He even talked like him. But he had never done any metalwork in his life. He didn't know how to use a grinder, a lathe or anything like it. He examined the submarine. It was crudely put together with the periscope sticking out at an angle and the rudder barely hanging on. Something had come loose inside and was rattling about. It was obvious that Julius had only been working on the thing because he had to.

With a sigh, Alex carried it over to a free work-space. *One week,* he told himself. He picked up a file, dragging the chain towards him, and began to scrape it against one of the fins. Every time he came here, he could pretend to work without actually doing anything. He glanced across the room at Freddy, still staring blankly out of the window. One more week and he would tell Dr Flint he was ready to go home.

Dinner was served early evening. Alex had already learned that everything in the prison was done to the minute. It was as if the whole complex was a huge clock and the guards and the prisoners, really not so different from each other, simply parts of the mechanism. He had only been here for a day but already he understood what it meant by "doing time".

Once again, he found himself sitting opposite Freddy and, as before, Freddy ignored him. The meal that night, slopped onto the plates by the miserable chef, had been described as paella but looked more like porridge; a mess of overcooked rice with a few pieces of white meat and an evil-smelling sauce. Alex picked up his plastic fork and ate a mouthful. The paella was warm but that was the best that could be said about it. It tasted vile.

Further down the table, Derek and Claire Miller were having a heated discussion ... in German. They never spoke their own language after six o'clock.

Jayne Chumley was reading a book. Ali Blassim was half-asleep. Mr Someone was tucking into his dinner as if he had wandered into a local restaurant and was expecting someone to come along with a dessert menu. And Henry Mellish was watching him, utterly motionless, but his eyes alive with hatred and menace.

He was waiting for something to happen!

As Alex lifted his fork a second time, he was suddenly alert. Mellish wanted to hurt him. But how could he, surrounded by all these people and with the cameras watching every movement? Alex hesitated and it was then that something glinted, reflecting the light. He looked down and saw a tiny sliver of metal in his food. He had been about to swallow it. Carefully, he laid the fork down, then used his fingers to separate the grains of rice. The metal was part of a razor blade. It was less than a centimetre long but that would have been enough to do terrible damage. Alex imagined the metal shard travelling down the inside of his throat. Suddenly he felt sick.

Alex had no doubt that Mellish was responsible. The two of them had been standing together at the serving hatch, and as Alex had taken his plate, Mellish had knocked into him and apologized. Of course the apology had been fake. Alex had wondered about it at the time. Now he understood. Mellish had used the moment to slip the fragment into his food.

What would he try next and when would it happen? It was only now, at the end of day one, that Alex recognized how much danger he was in. He looked across the table. Freddy was watching him. He had seen what had just happened but showed no interest at all. Alex was surrounded by seven of the most dangerous and unpredictable people on the planet.

It was just a question of which one would kill him first.

He was glad, an hour later, to be back in his cell. At least the door was securely locked and until the wake-up call the following morning he only had one other prisoner to worry about. Freddy was in the bunk below him, lying on his side, watching a Disney cartoon on the television. All the TV content was controlled by the prison authorities. There was no news, no current affairs; just light entertainment programmes – singing, dancing, cooking, baking – and films which had been carefully chosen to contain no sex or violence. The television blinked off at ten o'clock, followed by the lights, half an hour later.

It was never completely dark inside the cell. There were spotlights on all night, all over the compound, and some of the glare spilled in through the barred window. Lying on his back, Alex saw Freddy roll off his bunk and kneel on the floor. What was going on now? Exercises before bed?

The answer was the last thing Alex would have expected. Freddy Grey had clasped his hands in front of his face. He was saying his prayers. Alex could hear some of the words.

"Oh Great Master, Creator of the universe, protect me in this, my hour of need. Although I am far from your guiding light, I am close to you and your voice is in me. I ask you to lead me as you have always done. I promise to obey your every command and to act without hesitation, no matter what you ask..."

Freddy went on like this for the next three or four minutes. Looking down from where he lay, Alex could see the boy's naked shoulders and the back of his neck. And there, caught in the electric light, was the scar, shaped like a comma, curving round, following the jawline underneath his ear. It had been mentioned in Freddy's medical report, sent through by the Brazilian police. They had assumed that the boy had been involved in some sort of accident but, examining him now, Alex came to a different conclusion. It made him feel queasy but there was something about the scar that was too neat, too precise. He would have said it had been made deliberately.

The prayer finished with the words "for ever and all eternity". Then Freddy got back into bed and, although Alex could no longer see him, he was fairly sure that his cell mate was asleep in seconds. He did not sleep well himself and when the morning finally came, he found himself exhausted, troubled and wishing he was far away.

THE DEAD SPOT

"This isn't working. I want to go home."

"Calm down, Alex. Let's take this one step at a time..."

Alex was sitting on a sofa in the living room of the governor's house with Dr Rosemary Flint opposite him. It was the first time he had seen the psychiatrist since he had arrived in Gibraltar. As the two youngest people in the facility, he and Freddy Grey were meant to meet her twice a week and she had insisted that the sessions should take place inside the villa as they had before. It provided a more homely feeling, she explained. It would help them relax.

She was perched on a chair with her oversized glasses halfway down her nose and a notebook open on her lap. If anyone happened to come in, it would look as if she was interrogating her new patient, trying to work out what was on his mind. Even so, Alex was on edge. He looked around him. "Are we safe here?" he asked. "How do you know no one's listening?"

"These sessions are held in the strictest confidence," Dr Flint said. "Nobody's allowed to record anything. And yes, we're perfectly safe. There's a guard outside the door but he won't come in unless I call him. After Julius escaped, they put in a whole lot of new security measures. Every door in the house is kept locked ... so you can't get into the kitchen or the bedrooms upstairs. There's a panic button hidden right here." She pointed to the arm of her chair. "And you must have seen the new metal detector when you came in."

Alex was glad to be here. It was an opportunity for him to be himself. He was constantly on edge with the other prisoners, thinking like Julius Grief, acting like Julius Grief, in fear of the next mistake that might blow his cover. Then there was Henry Mellish, who had already tried to hurt him once and who might make a second attempt at any time. And finally, of course, there was Freddy himself, the most dangerous of them all.

They had been locked up together for four days and three nights and in all that time Freddy had still barely spoken a word – apart from the lengthy prayers that he never missed before he went to sleep. Alex wondered how someone who had cold-bloodedly killed at least five people could possibly be religious, but there was no doubt that Freddy was sincere. Alex had tried to ask him what sort of church he belonged to – but only once. Freddy had again turned on him with that dreadful, icy stare and he had known immediately that he had strayed into forbidden territory and that if he continued he would be the one needing prayers.

He didn't want to quit. Alex wasn't someone who gave up easily. But he had decided that Crawley's plan wasn't going to work. He hadn't made any progress and he doubted that he would, even if he stayed here for another six months. Quite soon half-term would be over and he wanted to get back to Brookland. He had promised himself an ordinary life. A schoolboy, not a spy and definitely not a high-security prisoner! And so he had come to his decision. It was time for Dr Flint to make the phone call that would get him out of here.

"You know I was against this idea the moment I heard it," the psychiatrist said. "I was worried about you and even though you've done a brilliant job – you look and behave exactly like Julius Grief—"

"That's not true. I wasn't given enough time to prepare and I've already made mistakes."

"You've done brilliantly, Alex." The psychiatrist examined him carefully. "Look, if you want me to call MI6 and get you out of here, of course I will. But before we do that, I was hoping you might be able to do something for me."

"What?" Alex felt his heart sink. It was funny how everyone – Crawley, Mrs Jones and now Dr Flint – forgot about his safety when they thought they could use him.

"I've had two sessions with Frederick Grey and,

I'll be honest with you, they were completely unsuc-
cessful. Most of the time he just ignored me. Talking
to him is like talking to a brick wall. It was as if
I wasn't even in the room. I had to remind myself
that he's only fifteen years old ... basically just
a child."

"I don't think I can help you," Alex said. "He
won't talk to me either."

"He may not have done so yet, but there's a differ-
ence. You're close to him ... physically close, I mean.
You're there when he goes to bed and when he wakes
up, two moments when he may be at his weakest.
What you told me about the prayers, for example.
That's a fascinating insight."

Dr Flint closed her notebook and set it on the
table beside her.

"Frederick Grey has been brainwashed," she went
on. "I thought that must have been what had happened when the case was handed to me and I'm
certain of it now that I've met him. He wasn't even
five years old when he was kidnapped and since then
he has been turned into this ... machine. The prayers
may be a part of it. I don't know. But I'm convinced
that he isn't responsible for his actions ... for what
he has become. In a way, he's a victim in all this.
He didn't choose to be what he is."

She paused, deep in thought.

"But this is what you've got to understand, Alex.
When you brainwash someone, it's as if you've built
a series of blocks inside their head. It's a delicate

structure. Pull out one of those blocks and the whole thing comes tumbling down. That's how I think you can help me."

"What do you want me to do?"

By way of an answer, Dr Flint reached down into her briefcase and took out a stuffed toy. It was a monkey, dressed in blue pyjamas. It was clearly very old. The years had worn out its fur, leaving bald patches, and its arms and legs were hanging limply.

"I got this from Freddy's mother," she explained. "It belonged to Freddy before he disappeared. He left it in Instow. He had it from the age of two." She handed the monkey across. "Its name is Benjamin," she added.

"You think I can use this to unlock his memory?" Alex asked.

"Something like that. Yes."

Alex turned the monkey over in his hands. It gazed up at him with blank, button eyes. "Mr Crawley told me that Freddy doesn't even remember his own parents," he said. "What makes you think a stuffed toy will be any different?"

"There are two reasons," Dr Flint replied. "Although you may not know it, babies and very young children have excellent memories. In fact, aged three, your brain is already ninety per cent as large as it will be when you're an adult. That's why your first memories – the early wiring – are so important. Freddy will have had a strong emotional bond with

Benjamin. It's just possible the sight of it will bring down some of those blocks."

"And the second reason?"

"Whoever kidnapped him must have been watching him for some time. They will have known about his parents. They knew where he lived and where he went to school. But they almost certainly didn't know about this toy. So when they brainwashed him, they won't have been able to remove it from his mind. Do you see? Benjamin is a direct link with the boy he used to be." She sighed. "I know it's a lot to ask, Alex, especially as it may mean staying a little longer, but will you give it a try? You could pretend that the monkey is yours and have it on your bed … that sort of thing. At the end of the day, I want to help Freddy. With you on my side, maybe I can."

Yes. Unless I get killed first.

That was what Alex was thinking as the guard led him out of the villa at the end of the session. Carrying the monkey but being careful to keep it out of sight, he went straight back to his cell and placed it on his bunk, then thought better of it and hid it under the pillow. He would produce it once he was alone with Freddy.

It was four o'clock by now – the session with Dr Flint had lasted exactly one hour – and he had nothing to do until dinner. He decided to go to the gym. He had seen Freddy silently exercising, doing squats and press-ups and lifting weights until he was bathed in sweat. The boy seemed to have no pain barrier. If he was there, Alex would join him. If not, it wouldn't hurt to stretch a few muscles himself.

He passed a guard who was standing at the entrance and took the stairs down to the changing room, a narrow, stuffy room with thick concrete walls and a line of metal lockers. Alex had been supplied with an exercise kit when he had arrived – the prisoners were encouraged to keep themselves fit – and was about to get changed when he saw that he was not alone. A man was sitting in the far corner, hidden in the shadows.

"Well, hello there, Julius," Mr Someone said. He was pulling on a black polo shirt and Alex noticed an AK-47 machine gun tattooed on his chest. He had finished his exercise but he had been waiting for Alex.

"Mr Someone..." Alex muttered. The assassin seemed completely friendly but still Alex felt the hairs on the back of his neck begin to prickle. He was alone in a basement with a man who had started killing before he was in his teens. And he wanted something. Alex wondered if he would be able to supply it.

"I was rather hoping you were going to come down here," Mr Someone said. "I wanted to have a word with you."

"What about?" Alex opened his locker and pulled out his kit, signalling that he didn't really care what Mr Someone had to say.

"I thought we could continue that rather interesting discussion we were having before you produced that gun and walked out of here. That wasn't very thoughtful of you, Julius, my dear boy. I thought we had an agreement."

Alex froze for a moment. Mr Someone was referring to a conversation that he knew nothing about. Certainly it hadn't been mentioned in any of the files that Crawley had shown him. He shrugged. "I didn't agree anything," he said. "Anyway, that was a while ago. I've forgotten what we were saying and right now I haven't got time. I want to go to the gym."

But Mr Someone hadn't finished. Suddenly he had slithered forward so that he was inches away from Alex, his eyes like two black beads, blinking at him. He might have been in his sixties but he had the energy and strength of a much younger man. "Have you really forgotten our escape plan?" he whispered. "The plan we were working on before you took off." He squinted, the thin line of his moustache twitching above his lip. "I have to say, I'm surprised. That's not the sort of thing I'd have thought anyone would forget."

"I changed my mind," Alex said.

"Well, if I were you, I'd change it again. Unless, of course, you don't mind leaving here feet first in a box."

Alex stared at the other man, uncertain, waiting for him to continue.

Mr Someone smiled. "It seems to me that you don't have a great deal of choice," he said. "You see, our friend Mr Mellish is very disappointed that you didn't swallow that little treat he'd prepared for you the other day. Fillet of razor blade, I think it was! So, from what I hear, he's going to follow it up with something quite a bit nastier. And next time, you're not going to be able to stop him."

"I can deal with Mellish," Alex said, clamping down on the fear that he could feel rising inside him.

"I'm not so sure. You had one lucky escape but next time..." Mr Someone smiled. "The answer's simple. You need to get out of here and you need to take me with you. That's what we always agreed."

Alex didn't know what to say. The situation was completely out of his control. A conversation he'd never had. An escape plan he knew nothing about. A professional assassin breathing down his neck. Alex could feel the walls closing in on him.

"We can't talk about this here," he muttered. "They'll hear us!"

Mr Someone cocked his head as if he didn't believe what he had just heard. "But this is the dead spot," he said.

It meant nothing to Alex. "Let's talk about it later," he pleaded.

"No. Let's talk about it now." Mr Someone's hand slammed against Alex's chest, knocking the breath out of him and pinning him against the locker. "Nobody can hear us down here, Julius. No cameras – it's too dark. And these walls are solid concrete. No microphones. We worked that out together. Or have you forgotten that too?"

Alex tried to move but it was impossible. Mr Someone looked completely relaxed but his arm could have been made of steel and now Alex remembered something from his file. He had killed several of his victims using just his fists.

"I have to tell you, my friend, there's something about you that doesn't add up. You look like you and you sound like you but if it didn't sound crazy, I'd say you aren't you. Something's changed." Alex squirmed. He could almost feel the truth being drawn out of him. "You still haven't told me what happened after you got out of here. Or how you got caught and brought back."

"There's not much to tell," Alex insisted, playing for time. His mouth was dry. "I was hiding out in a place called Siwa, in Egypt. I had friends who were looking after me. They were the ones who sent in the gun. But then MI6 found us." He rubbed his head as if he was dazed. "There was a fight and I got hurt. I was hit in the head – I don't remember things so well."

"What about the plan?"

"I haven't forgotten the plan."

"And you'll take me with you?"

"Of course."

"All right. So tell me. Where is it? After you finished making it, where did you put it?"

It was another question that Alex couldn't answer. And there was every chance that Mr Someone would kill him there and then if he didn't. The assassin knew he was being tricked. He just couldn't see how.

"Please..." he began.

But then the door banged open and the guard who had been standing outside appeared. Alex was relieved to see him. The guard had become suspicious.

Mr Someone took one last look at Alex. "We'll pick this up later, Jules. I think you need a chance to clear your thoughts, particularly after that accident of yours. Getting hit in the head! That's very unfortunate."

Alex could tell from his tone of voice that he didn't believe a word of it. Mr Someone left the locker room and climbed the stairs.

Quickly, Alex got changed and went up to the gym. Freddy wasn't there and he was glad. He needed to be on his own. There was an ancient running machine standing against one of the walls and he turned it up as high as it would go and began to run, his feet pounding out a steady rhythm. He was thinking furiously. He shouldn't have agreed to help Dr Flint and now it was too late. The psychiatrist lived outside the prison compound and he wouldn't see her for another few days. Freddy was still ignoring him. Mellish wanted to kill him. Mr Someone had begun to suspect him.

The rubber track whirred and span beneath his feet. Alex was running at full speed, the breath rasping in his throat. But at the same time, he knew it didn't matter how fast he went. He was stuck in a maximum security prison, surrounded by killers and maniacs, with no plan and almost no time. The machine was telling him what he already knew. He was going nowhere.

CELL MATES

Freddy Grey was already in the cell when Alex got there. He was lying flat on the lower bunk with his head resting on the pillow, and although the television was on, showing an old episode of *Star Trek* dubbed into Spanish, he wasn't watching it. He wasn't doing anything. Stretched out in a T-shirt and boxer shorts with his schoolboy haircut and his eyes far away, he looked more like a robot than a human being – and one that had been switched off.

Alex remembered what Dr Flint had said: that Freddy must have been brainwashed and, looking at him now, Alex was ready to believe it. As far as he knew, Freddy had not yet spoken to anyone in the complex. He had made no friends and ignored any threats that had come his way. Jayne Chumley had tried to start a conversation but she had given up, and although Henry Mellish had quickly moved in, he had soon been scared away. All the other prisoners just thought he was creepy.

It was quite possible that Freddy would be kept

in Gibraltar well into his twenties and then his thirties ... perhaps for the rest of his life. But he didn't seem to care. Alex shuddered. Nightshade had done this to him. They had taken a five-year-old boy and snatched him away from his family. And then, somehow, they had turned him into this. A monster.

Had they done the same to William and Sofia, the two children taken from Mrs Jones? It seemed very likely. William might no longer be alive but, ten years later, Sofia had been identified. Even if Mrs Jones did get her back, she would be nothing like the daughter she had lost.

But that wasn't Alex's problem. His job was to find Nightshade and, hopefully, Mrs Jones's missing children. And the key to that might be right here, in the room with him now.

Casually, he walked over to the bunk and drew out the monkey which he had hidden under his pillow. It was ridiculous, really. He hadn't had a stuffed toy with him in bed since he was seven or eight, but now here he was, pretending that it meant something to him. He carried it over to his desk, making sure that Freddy was able to see it. There was no reaction at all from the other boy. For a moment, Alex held it, the legs dangling. What should he do with it now? He had an idea. Quite deliberately, he set it on a chair so that it was facing the television, in plain sight.

Nothing from Freddy. On the screen, Spock was trying to explain something to a Klingon, speaking with a voice that didn't belong to him.

Alex sat at the desk, leaving Benjamin to watch the show. Still Freddy ignored him. After a few moments, Alex had to accept that Dr Flint's plan had failed and there was nothing more he could do. He was sorry. It wasn't just that he had let down Mrs Jones. He realized now that over the past few days, despite himself, there was a part of him that wanted to help Freddy too. It wasn't Freddy's fault that he had been kidnapped and if Alex had been able to get through to him, he might have been able to find out where Nightshade was located. He could have prevented the attack on London. He could have found the other children.

But it wasn't going to happen that way.

So what next? Somehow survive the next couple of days and then see Dr Flint at the governor's villa. She would arrange everything. He would leave the same day.

"What's that?"

The two words came from the other side of the room and took Alex completely by surprise. Freddy had asked him a question! It was the first time he had spoken to Alex since they had sat opposite each other in the dining hall and there had been no tension, no sense of menace in the enquiry. Very briefly, he had sounded like an ordinary boy. He had turned onto his side and he was looking at the monkey, still perched on the chair.

"It's nothing." Alex chose his words carefully. He didn't want to sound too eager. If he tried too hard he might drive Freddy back into his shell.

"Where did you get it?"

"Dr Flint gave it to me." Alex shrugged. "I used to have it when I was a kid and she thought it might help me with my anger issues. At least, that's what she said." He waited for something more and when it didn't come, he added: "Its name is Benjamin."

Freddy hadn't moved. He was still lying on his side, his slender body forming a letter "S" on the bunk. But there was a faint glimmer in his eyes that hadn't been there before. He couldn't stop staring at the stuffed toy.

Alex decided to press on.

"I took it everywhere with me," he said. "When we went on holiday ... we used to go to this place in Devon called Instow. Benjamin would come with me. He used to sit on the beach and watch me build sandcastles. And we'd watch TV together too. Isn't that stupid? But I was only five years old. I didn't know any better."

"I don't think that's stupid." Freddy frowned. There was just a tiny crease in his forehead but it was the first emotion that Alex had seen. "Did your mother give him to you?" he asked.

Now Alex had to be careful. He didn't know how much Freddy knew about Julius Grief. He might have heard the other prisoners talking. He couldn't move too far away from the truth. "I never knew my mother," he said. "My dad brought me up in a place called Point Blanc – in France."

"Did he go with you on holiday?"

"No. I had a nanny. A woman called Jenny." Alex was deliberately stirring up old memories, hoping that one of them would provide a breakthrough. He remembered what Dr Flint had said. There might be a small part of Freddy's brain – childhood memories – that Nightshade had been unable to reach. Was it possible that Benjamin was somehow unlocking them? Certainly, Alex knew he was never going to get a better chance than this.

Freddy twisted his legs round and sat up. His eyes were fixed on the monkey and Alex could see that he was confused, trying to make sense of whatever was going on in his head. "Can I have him?" he asked.

"Sure." Alex picked up the monkey as if it meant nothing to him and handed it across. "If you ask me, Dr Flint is pathetic," he went on. "What does she think? That I'm going to fall into line just because I've got him back? Well, she's wasting her time. I'm fifteen years old. I don't go to bed with a cuddly toy any more. And I don't need bedtime stories either."

Freddy was still holding the monkey, gazing at it as if he was expecting it to speak to him. And in a way, Alex realized, it was.

He grabbed the moment.

"Look – I'm really sorry," he said, "talking to you the way I did when I first arrived, calling you a dummy and all the rest of it. I was angry. I'd been arrested and brought back to this dump. I couldn't believe it. And I wasn't too happy about sharing a cell either. The last time I was here, at least I had a single room! So maybe I was a bit out of order. I'm sorry. But you don't seem too bad and maybe the two of us..." His voice trailed away. "Well, it's us against everyone else. What do you say?"

To Alex's dismay, Freddy didn't reply. He seemed to have retreated into himself once again and Alex was left wondering if he could have handled it better. Freddy put the monkey back on the chair and Alex noted that at least he hadn't thrown it there. It still meant something to him. He had even positioned it so that it could watch the TV. But he said nothing more, returning to his bunk and lying with his back to Alex.

Thirty minutes later, the television flicked off, followed by the lights. Alex climbed into the top bunk, wondering how much progress he had made and whether he would see any difference when the sun rose the next day. He got the answer a few minutes later when Freddy went on his knees to mutter the words that Nightshade must have taught him and which he thought of as a prayer.

"Oh Great Master, Creator of the universe, protect me in this, my hour of need. Although I am far from your guiding light, I am close to you and your voice is in me.

"And I pray to you also to reach out to my friend, Julius Grief, and show him your wisdom and your way. Let him become one of your followers so that together we can destroy our enemies and obey your commands for ever and all eternity."

Together.

It was the word Alex had been waiting for. Perhaps, after all, this was going to work.

THE KEY

Freddy didn't speak to him the next morning; not while they were getting dressed and not at breakfast either. When Alex left the cell, Benjamin was still sitting in the chair, gazing at a blank TV.

There were now two people that Alex had to avoid at the breakfast table. Mr Someone had been interrupted before they had finished their conversation but he watched Alex darkly over his Spanish omelette, his eyes never leaving him as he spooned the rubbery, yellow egg into his mouth. And two places away, Henry Mellish sat twitching and sending him malevolent smiles to remind Alex that they would be meeting again soon. It reminded Alex of the terror he had felt when he was eleven years old, at his first day at school, how he had sat in assembly with several hundred boys, nearly all of them older than himself – but of course this was much worse. Not everyone at Brookland had become his friend but none of them had wanted to kill him either.

Worse still, it seemed that the guards had it in for

him too. Carrying his tray back to the serving hatch, Alex didn't see the booted foot stretched out in front of him and the next thing he knew, he had been sent flying, his plastic tray, plate and cutlery clattering to the floor. He looked up and saw Diego scowling over him. This was the guard who had escorted him out of the villa. Diego had threatened to hurt him then. It seemed that he had only been waiting for the opportunity.

Alex collected his things and got to his feet. "What did you do that for?" he demanded.

"I did nothing," Diego replied. "You clumsy!"

"And you a moron," Alex snarled. The last thing he needed was to make another enemy but he was aware of the other prisoners watching and knew that it was expected of him.

Diego smiled unpleasantly. "You insult me. Very good! Solitary confinement for two months. We begin when the governor gets back. And when you alone, then you see what happen."

Great! The governor had been called to London for a few days but now he had something he could really look forward to: being thrown into the darkness and emptiness of the punishment block, sitting on his own day and night. Alex had been warned about what went on in the Gibraltar facility. Nobody knew they were there. So there was nobody to care how they were treated.

He had borrowed a book out of the library and spent the rest of the morning out in the sun, reading.

The book was an old Philip Pullman with a cracked spine and loose pages but he was glad to escape into a world of daemons, hot-air balloons and warrior bears. Then, after lunch, he did another session in the metal workshop and it was there that, once again, everything changed.

He was still working on the submarine that Julius had left behind. It was strange but he had found that he was actually quite keen on trying to improve it. At least it gave him something to do. He had decided to repair the rudder and straighten the periscope. When he got out of the prison, he would leave it behind as a souvenir – of himself and of Julius Grief. It would be the only decent thing that Julius had done in his entire life.

He rolled it in his hands and heard once again the rattle that came from inside. What had broken? He turned the submarine upside down, noticing for the first time what looked like a crack continuing in an unbroken circle all the way round the metal shell. He hadn't seen it before because the whole thing was so scratched and disfigured but now that he examined it more closely, he would have said that it had been made deliberately. It wasn't a crack. It was a groove.

Moving slowly, not drawing any attention to himself, he looked around him. The Millers were painting. Ali Blasim was carving his boat. Jayne Chumley was working on a pair of wooden earrings. A bored guard was sitting on a stool by the door and as usual there were security cameras everywhere. Alex took the submarine in both hands and, keeping it close to his lap, slightly out of sight beneath the level of the counter, twisted. Nothing happened. He tried again, harder, and this time he felt movement in the palms of his hands. The hull was unscrewing!

It had been brilliantly done. Alex had to hand it to Julius. He had manufactured an almost invisible thread with a great deal of skill, which was completely at odds with the rest of the submarine. It made complete sense. His father, Dr Hugo Grief, would have insisted that Julius was an expert in everything he did and that included metalwork. Julius didn't want to draw attention to himself so he had made the submarine look as amateurish as possible. But, in fact, he had turned it into a safety deposit box – and he had hidden something inside!

The whole thing had come apart in Alex's hands. He tilted the two pieces towards each other. The inside was hollow but nothing came out. For a brief second, he was disappointed but the rattle was still there and he looked more carefully. There was something, concealed behind a metal shelf. Alex reached in with his finger and felt a blunt edge, an object a few centimetres long. Gently, he prised it free. The single hinge that had been holding it in place snapped and something slid into his hand. He looked down.

It was a key.

Alex stared at it for what felt like a long time. It was exactly the same shape as the key that he used to open his own front door back in London, slim with a series of peak and troughs like a miniature mountain range. Julius had clearly manufactured it. How? Alex remembered Mr Someone challenging him in the changing room under the gymnasium. *"Tell me. Where is it? After you finished making it, where did you put it?"* At the time, the words had made no sense but this must have been what he was referring to. Mr Someone knew about Julius's secret plan to escape. He must have helped him. Somehow the two of them had stolen a key from one of the guards and made a copy.

Alex came to a decision. He took another quick look around, then palmed the key and, pretending to scratch his leg, slipped it into his pocket. He had no intention of escaping. That was the one thing he didn't need to do. But the key might be useful in other ways.

He screwed the submarine together again and went back to work. His mind was racing. There must be hundreds of locks scattered throughout the prison: not just doors but cupboards, drawers, lockers, windows, handcuffs and so on. And now he had a key.

But a key to what?

Alex still had no answer to that question several hours later, by which time night had fallen and dinner had been cleared away. It was a Saturday – not that it was easy to tell, as every day inside the prison was much the same. But this was the one evening in the month when the dining room was turned into a cinema. The chairs were arranged in front of a screen. The shutters on the windows were closed, blocking out the searchlights so that the film could be projected without interruption.

The films themselves were downloaded, carefully chosen by the governor to keep the prisoners quiet as much as to entertain them and everyone was encouraged to attend. They should do things together, as a group. It would help to ease the tensions between them. At least, that was the idea. Tonight the film was *The Martian* which had an astronaut getting stuck on the red planet and, with his life being threatened in all sorts of ways, trying to survive. Sitting in the dark, surrounded by people who were completely alien to him, Alex had an idea of how he felt.

He watched as the main character stumbled around in a dust storm and got knocked out. His rocket took off without him. He was stranded. But Alex couldn't focus on the film.

The key. He couldn't get it out of his mind. Julius Grief had stolen a key and made a duplicate. He and Mr Someone had been planning to escape. But how could a single key help them?

Alex thought about all the different doors he'd had to pass through in the course of a single day: his cell, the dining hall, the library, the gymnasium. Some of them – the library, for example – were left open. Only the kitchen and the metalwork shop were secured at all times but they had electronic locks. The key wouldn't work. Thinking about it, Alex realized that, on its own, the key would be useless. Whatever it might open, the prison was surrounded by a wall and an electric fence. To get in and out, everyone had to pass through a holding area with sliding doors at each end. One closed and only then the other opened. And there were guards and security cameras everywhere. The simple truth was that no single door opened onto the outside world.

So the key had to be part of a wider plan. Julius would have used it to gain access somewhere or to get hold of something that could help him escape. But where? And what?

On the screen, the astronaut had returned to his base and was trying to grow food using his own body waste as fertilizer. Despite everything, Alex found himself being drawn into the story and he was actually beginning to enjoy it when he felt something slip over his head and suddenly he was fighting for his life.

There was some sort of cord around his neck, strangling him. It had been tightened so quickly that he had no time to cry out. He could feel it biting into his flesh, closing his windpipe. He had been breathing normally. There wasn't a lot of air in his lungs. Taken by surprise, he knew that unless he did something quickly, in the next few seconds, he would die.

He kicked out with one leg, trying to force his

chair to topple over backwards. But whoever was behind him had been expecting that. They were holding the noose with one hand while the other had wound around his chest, squeezing him in a hideous embrace. In the darkness, nobody could see what was happening – or if they could, they didn't care. Julius Grief had never been popular. What would it matter to them if he lived or died?

Alex brought up his hands, clawing behind him, trying to reach the person who was attacking him. He found only thin air. He tried to get his fingers under the cord. But it was too tight. It was made of plastic. He could feel it gouging into his neck. There was nothing he could do. In front of him, it seemed that the film had gone out of focus but he knew that it wasn't the fault of the projector. There was no oxygen reaching his brain and he was losing his vision. His heart was pounding, his lungs screaming. He tried stamping his feet on the floor to get the attention of the guard but Alex was wearing rubber-soled trainers and the music in the film had risen, drowning out any sound.

He was getting weaker. His whole body was shutting down. The darkness was closing in on him and it was permanent.

And then someone whispered something in his ear.

"Goodbye, Julius." It was Henry Mellish of course. He had chosen the seat directly behind him and, like a fool, Alex had taken his place without giving it a second thought. He tried one last time to reach behind him but his hands would no longer obey his commands.

He was going to die. And his killer didn't even know who he really was.

But then Henry cried out. Not loudly. It was simply as if he had made an "Oooh!" of surprise. The cord fell away and Alex found that he could breathe. His throat was on fire and sucking air into his lungs was like drawing a saw across his chest. But the cord – now he realized it was a piece of electric flex – was still looped over his shoulders and with a shiver of disgust Alex pulled it away. He breathed a second time, then a third. On the screen, the astronaut had mended a lunar rover and set off to explore.

For the next few minutes, Alex didn't move, waiting for his strength to return. He no longer had any interest in the story being played out on the screen in front of him and he didn't want to look behind him, afraid of what he would see. His legs were trembling and he knew that he had had a very close escape. At last, moving slowly, he turned round.

Henry Mellish was sitting, sprawled out in his seat, his glasses crooked and blood streaming down his face. He had been hit, once, very hard. His nose was broken and he was unconscious. How could that have happened? Alex looked through the shadows to the person sitting next to Mellish. It was Freddy Grey. The image on the screen changed and Alex saw him clearly in the reflected light. Freddy smiled. Alex wanted to smile back but he sat there in blank-faced astonishment, aware that the other boy had just saved his life.

The next hour passed very slowly. Matt Damon was rescued and returned to Earth. The lights were turned on and suddenly the room was full of excited guards all shouting questions as Henry was discovered unconscious. Freddy had already walked away. Alex followed him. Half an hour later, just as they were getting into bed, they heard an ambulance arrive at the prison gates and guessed that Mellish was being taken to hospital.

"Thank you," Alex said. He was lying on his back, his throat still sore, the ridges in his neck so deep that when he ran his fingers over them, he could still feel them.

"That's all right, Julius." The voice came from below, drifting up from the lower bunk. "I've been praying for you and you're one of us now."

"That's great, Freddy. Thanks."

"Freddy is not my name. You can call me that when we're with the others. But when it's just the two of us, you have to call me Number Nine."

"If that's what you want. Of course."

"And maybe one day you will become Number Twenty-Six."

Freddy didn't say any more and a short while later he was asleep. But Alex lay where he was, unable to close his eyes. Mrs Jones was aware of three children who had been kidnapped. Freddy Grey was one of them. Her own children, William and Sofia, were two more. But, according to what Freddy had just told him, it seemed there were actually twenty-five of them hiding somewhere in the world. A small army!

What had he got himself into? Alex had hidden Julius's key in the metal frame of his bed but now he fished it out. Holding it tightly in his fist, he closed his eyes and tried to sleep.

NO WAY OUT

They met the next morning in the changing room under the gymnasium: the dead spot. It was the first time they had spoken that day. Once again, Freddy had got dressed silently, perhaps because he was aware of the microphones listening in. They had sat apart at breakfast, surrounded by just five other prisoners. Henry Mellish had been taken to the Royal Naval Hospital in Gibraltar and wouldn't be back for a few days. He had told the guards that he had fallen asleep during the film and slipped out of his chair. It was the same rule in every prison in the world. No matter what happened, you never squealed.

From the moment Freddy had arrived, Alex could tell that he was more relaxed. He wasn't smiling. He wasn't normal in any way. But nor did he give Alex the impression that he might strike out at any time and put him in the bed next to Henry.

"I need your help," he said. He was speaking in a low voice and made no mention of what had happened in the dining hall the night before.

"Sure." Alex waited for him to continue.

"Your parents are dead." It was a statement, not a question.

"My father's dead. I told you. I never met my mother."

"But if you got out of here a second time, you'd have nowhere to go."

"That's right." Alex was beginning to get nervous, wondering where this conversation was going. "But there is no way out of here," he said.

"You're wrong." Freddy was sitting on one of the benches. He was wearing gym shorts and a vest that made him look more harmless and childlike than ever. The scar on his neck stood out, dark mauve against his pale skin. "I have a plan," he went on.

"Tell me!" Alex had to pretend he was interested even though it was the last thing he wanted to hear. He needed information – nothing more. Where had Freddy come from? Where were the missing children being held?"

"They think this prison is secure but it isn't," Freddy went on. "There are weapons in the metal-work shop. They must be crazy to have a place like that. There's one guard inside, one guard outside. I'll take care of the one inside. I'll get a chisel or a screwdriver. It must be possible to snap the chain. And then I stab him in the throat."

"What about the cameras?"

"There are four cameras pointing into the room. But they're trained on the prisoners. None of them are looking at the guard. You call to whoever's outside and tell him that his friend is ill. Then, when he comes in, I kill him."

Alex swallowed. Two deaths and Freddy hadn't even begun.

"That gives us two guns. They carry SIG Sauer 9mm Lugers: double-action, hammer-trigger with a fifteen-round magazine. With the element of surprise, we can kill every single person in this compound, including the other prisoners, before they realize what's happening."

Alex faked a smile. "Great. And what then?"

"Through the gates, down the hill and out of Gibraltar by boat."

Presumably, he'd kill the boat owner too.

Alex pretended to consider, buying time to collect his thoughts. Whatever happened, he couldn't allow Freddy to go through with his insane scheme. He was going to turn the prison into a bloodbath.

"It sounds a bit messy to me, Fr—I mean, Number Nine," he said. "Yeah, I'd love to get rid of some of the guards. But why don't we ask some of the prisoners to come on our side? Mr Someone would be useful..."

"I don't trust him. I don't trust any of them."

"I suppose you're right." Alex was still desperately trying to find something to say. "If we get out of Gibraltar, where exactly do we go?" he asked.

"Don't worry, Julius. We'll look after you."

"We?"

"Nightshade." It was the first time Freddy had mentioned the word and Alex seized on it.

"Who are Nightshade?"

"I can't explain. They're my family. They've been talking to me while I've been in here. I listen to them every night. Soon, you'll meet them."

How was that even possible? What did it mean? Alex assumed it must be part of his brainwashing. "I'd like that," he said. "But where are they?"

"You'll see. I'll take you to them."

Freddy was getting agitated. Alex could see it in his eyes and didn't dare push him any further.

"OK," he said. "So when are we going to bust out of here? When do we kill everyone?"

Freddy nodded slowly. He had worked that out too.

"Tomorrow," he said.

In London, the weather had finally changed.

It had been raining for at least a week, spoiling everyone's half-term, but now, just as the schools were preparing to go back, the sun had come bursting out from behind the clouds and suddenly it was summer again. People were back in their shirt-sleeves, queuing up at any bars or cafés that had tables outside. And all the vehicles making their way towards Piccadilly Circus were fresh and gleaming as if they had just emerged from a very large car wash.

The grass was still wet underfoot as Owen Andrews came out of Green Park station and turned into the park itself. He was dressed in the same suit that he had worn when he met Mrs Jones at the Foreign Office and he was far too hot. It was pinching him all over and, if he raised his arms, he would show off sweat patches that had managed to seep through the material. As he walked, he glanced at his watch for the tenth or eleventh time. It was three minutes to one. He quickened his pace, cursing the fact that the tube from Liverpool Street had been so slow. He was going to be late and, knowing the sort of man he worked for, the thought quite terrified him.

The Permanent Under-Secretary for Foreign Affairs, Dominic Royce, was sitting on a bench, his briefcase on his lap, eating a smoked salmon sandwich. There were a few pigeons pecking around his feet but he hadn't given them so much as a crumb. If he wasn't having lunch with another civil servant or a politician, he liked coming out here on his own. The park was only a short walk from his office and it did him good, getting away from his desk with all its paperwork. Also, it was hard to know who might be listening inside the Foreign Office. There were some conversations he preferred to have undisturbed.

He looked up as he saw Owen hurrying towards him. Big Ben struck the hour at exactly the same time. He smiled to himself – but without moving his lips or showing any emotion at all. As the echo of the clock died away, Andrews stood in front of him, waiting to be invited to speak. He knew never to open a conversation. Speak when you're spoken to. That was the rule.

Royce finished the last corner of his sandwich, chewing it slowly. "Good afternoon, Owen," he said, at last.

"Good afternoon, sir."

"Have you had lunch yet?"

"No, sir."

Royce nodded as if in sympathy and finished eating his sandwich. There were two quarters left in the packet but he didn't offer one to his assistant. Meanwhile, Owen stood in silence, wishing that he could get out of the sun. He burned very easily. Even now he could feel the skin on the back of his neck going red. But Royce was in no hurry, He took out a napkin and touched it against his lips. Finally, he looked up.

"So what can you tell me about our friends at MI6?" he asked.

"Not very much, I'm afraid, sir. They're doing everything they can to keep me out of the way. They don't let me attend their meetings. I don't really like them, if I can be honest with you. They're very stuck up."

"I didn't send you there to make friends, Owen. I sent you there to keep an eye on them. Have they made any progress in this business with Nightshade?"

"No, sir. They don't seem to be doing very much about it. It's almost as if they're waiting for something to happen and until it does they don't really care."

Royce scowled. "So we have a terrorist organization planning an outrage in London and the very people whose job it is to stop it are simply sitting there, twiddling their thumbs?"

"That's what it looks like, sir."

"And what about the boy from Rio? Have they spoken to him again? Have they interrogated him?"

"No, sir. He's in Gibraltar." Royce looked up, surprised, and Owen went on quickly. "They have a special facility there. He was taken in a Lockheed Hercules. I managed to intercept a message sent by the pilot."

"I know about the facility," Royce muttered. "I just didn't know they'd sent him there. I can't imagine what Mrs Jones thinks she's playing at. Frederick Grey is her only connection to Nightshade. You'd have thought she'd be making his life very uncomfortable, trying to get answers from him."

Owen Andrews stood silently with his neck on fire. He'd have to get his mother to rub some cream on it when he got home. But he had nothing else to say and waited for his master either to ask him something else or to dismiss him.

"What about Alex Rider?" Royce asked, at length. "Did you manage to find out why Mrs Jones wanted him?"

"No, sir." Owen hated having to admit defeat. "I tried to talk to the driver, Burton, who was sent to pick him up, but he wouldn't say anything."

"Is Rider working for Special Operations?"

"I haven't seen him in the building – but he's not at home either. I telephoned the woman who looks after him. She has rather a stupid name. It's Jack Starbright. I pretended to be from his school and asked if I could speak to him. She said that he had gone to stay with friends in the Lake District. But I'm not sure she was telling the truth."

"Why is that?"

"I looked in his file and he doesn't have any friends in the Lake District. I also checked her telephone records. She hasn't phoned Alex at all in the last week and she hasn't called the Lake District either. You'd have thought if he was away, she'd have wanted to speak to him."

"So where is he?"

"He could be anywhere. I also called his best friend … a boy called Tom Harris. But he hung up on me."

"You've done very well, Owen. I knew I could rely on you."

Dominic Royce folded up the packet and put the last sandwiches back into his briefcase. He got to his feet. "Here's the thing," he said. "I have very little confidence in MI6 Special Operations. I'm not convinced that they're taking this business with Nightshade quite seriously enough and I wonder if

I can trust them them to keep London safe.

"I gave Mrs Jones strict instructions not to go anywhere near this child and if I find that she has disobeyed me, it will only confirm my doubts over her judgement. We have a major threat hanging over us, Owen, and I will not allow the city I love to be harmed because of her shortcomings. Do I make myself clear?"

"Absolutely, sir."

"You'd better get back to Liverpool Street. Keep your ear to the ground. Call me if there are any developments at all. And Owen..."

The assistant had turned away, about to leave, but now he stopped and turned back again.

"Yes, sir?"

"You should get your neck looked at. It's quite a nasty colour."

There was nothing more to be said. The two of them went their separate ways.

He had run three miles on the treadmill. He had lifted weights. He had stretched and exercised until his muscles were crying out, unable to take any more. Finally, Alex had showered and changed and now he was walking back to his cell, desperate to be on his own. He needed to work out what he was going to do.

He could somehow get a message to Dr Flint and tell her what Freddy was planning. She would warn the governor and the guards would take immediate action. Freddy would be isolated, locked up in solitary confinement and never allowed near the metalwork shop again. That seemed to be the only option. Alex had no interest in the other prisoners. Mr Someone, Jayne Chumley, the Millers, Mellish, Ali Blasim … they all deserved to be here. But that didn't mean they deserved to die. The same was true of the guards. None of them had treated him very well but at the end of the day they were only doing their job. They would have wives and children. Alex had to protect them.

But if he came forward, what would happen next? It would be the end of his mission. MI6 would never find out about Nightshade. Mrs Jones would have lost her children. And what of Jack and Tom and all his friends? He was here because Nightshade was planning a terrorist attack on London and he had to stop it. He remembered what Mrs Jones had said to him. *"The whole of London is in great danger … we don't know where and when. You're the only person who can find out."*

She had hoped that Freddy would tell him more about Nightshade. That had been the plan – but so far Freddy had refused to say a word and probably never would. But instead he had been offered an opportunity. *"They're my family. They've been talking to me while I've been in here."* If Alex wanted to find Nightshade, he had to go with him. They had to escape together.

But, if they did, every guard and every prisoner

in the compound would die.

There was no way out of the situation. Whatever Alex decided, people were going to get killed.

Unless...

He had the key in his trouser pocket and he came to a halt, reaching down and feeling it through the fabric. He didn't dare take it out in case he was seen. Julius Grief had also been planning to escape and he had manufactured a key to help him do just that. But what did it open?

Alex looked around him – at the main entrance with the guards checking a delivery van as it waited on the other side of the sliding gate. He turned to the library, the dining hall, the governor's villa. Briefly, he thought back to his first session with Dr Flint. There was something she had told him about the villa and he knew it was important but what was it? Even so, he found himself examining the front door with its metal detector, the windows and curtains, the flower beds. It occurred to him that it was the only building in the complex that was higher than the perimeter wall. He looked up at the roof with its chimneys and red tiles, slanting down towards the trees on the other side. Even if he could get up there, it would be impossible to jump over the wall. It was too far away.

He remembered meeting the governor in his office, the glass table, the furniture and the windows on either side. At that moment, what Dr Flint had said came back to him. And that was when he realized that there might be a way out after all. He just had to engineer things. He had to change the prison rules, persuade Freddy that he could be trusted and hope that he wasn't shot before or after he had broken his neck.

Apart from that, it would be easy.

OVER THE WALL

The following afternoon, Alex and Freddy Grey entered the villa together. This was a completely new departure and had only been allowed following a heated argument between Dr Flint and the governor – who had just got back from London. As far as he was concerned, it was bad enough having one of these young killers in his living quarters but having them both at once struck him as an unnecessary security risk.

But Dr Flint had insisted. "I'm not getting anywhere with them on their own. They won't talk to me. It's as if I'm not even in the room."

"What makes you think it'll be any different with two of them?"

"They'll feel stronger. There will be two of them and just one of me. That will make them more confident. I'm hoping I'll be able to spark a conversation between them."

"I'm concerned that you'll be putting yourself in danger."

"I don't think so, Governor. Both the boys have to come through your metal detector so there's no chance either of them will be armed. One of your guards will be sitting outside the room the whole time and I have that new panic button right next to me. I think we should give it a try."

"Well, it's your lookout."

In fact, the governor had no real choice in the matter. He had been told from the start that Freddy Grey had important information relating to a possible terrorist incident and that it was Dr Flint's job to draw it out of him. He couldn't be seen to be standing in the way. Even so, he ordered both boys to be thoroughly searched before they went in. And all the doors in the house would be locked while they were there.

What he didn't know was that it was Alex himself who had suggested the double session. For his plan to work, Alex needed Freddy and himself to be inside the house and, the day before, he had persuaded the psychiatrist to help him. Alex had come to a decision. Freddy was never going to tell him what Nightshade were planning so he had to find them for himself. And the only way to do that was to agree to Freddy taking him to them. As much as he hated the idea, they had to escape together. And if they did it his way, nobody would get killed.

"Tell Mrs Jones I'll contact her as soon as I can," Alex had said. "And if I can't reach her, I'll call Jack."

Still Dr Flint tried to plead with him. "This is

madness, Alex. Everyone thinks you're Julius Grief. If you try to escape from here, they'll shoot at you. And it'll be real bullets."

"Then let's just hope they miss."

Alex and Freddy arrived late in the afternoon. There were two guards waiting at the door and before they were allowed to go through, the boys were stripped down to their underwear and searched. They hadn't been allowed to carry anything. All their clothes were passed one piece at a time through the metal detector … shirts, trousers, shoes. At one point, the machine burst into life, bleeping loudly, and at once the guards had their guns out, expecting trouble. But it was only the buckle of Alex's belt that had set it off. Another guard glanced at it, then handed it back to Alex. He and Freddy got dressed again. They were shown into the front living room, where Dr Flint was waiting for them. One of the guards took up a position outside. So far, everything had gone according to plan.

"Good afternoon, boys," Dr Flint began. "How are you both feeling today?"

Alex glanced at Freddy, who was sitting silently, his face as blank as ever. Freddy – or Number Nine if that was what he wanted to be called – wasn't happy. He'd come up with a plan of his own and he would have preferred to stick to it. It had taken all of Alex's powers of persuasion – an hour in the locker room – to get him to change his mind.

"We're OK," Alex said, answering Dr Flint's question.

"Freddy?"

Nothing from the other boy.

"I thought it might be helpful to you if the three of us talked together," Dr Flint continued. "I want you to understand that, really, I'm on your side. My job is to help you look at all the choices you've made and all the things you've done and to decide if this really is the life you want for yourselves. It's not too late to change! But if you—"

"Excuse me, Doctor," Alex interrupted. "I'm quite thirsty. Could I have a glass of water?"

"I'm sorry, Alex. Nobody can leave the room until the session is over. You know that's the rules."

"But there's a bottle of water right behind you."

Dr Flint turned to look and that was when Alex pounced. In a second, he was on his feet rushing towards her and by the time she realized what was happening, it was too late. He had seized hold of her, clamping his hand over her mouth.

At least, that was what it would look like to Freddy. In fact, he had warned her exactly what he was going to do. The two of them had discussed it carefully. The most important thing to Alex was that nobody should get hurt.

Freddy was also out of his seat. He went over to the door.

"Call the guard in," Alex whispered to Dr Flint. She did nothing, so he spoke a second time, loud enough for Freddy to hear. "Do what I tell you or I'll break your neck. Call him into the room!"

Dr Flint looked terrified. She might be a good actress but Alex knew her fear was genuine. There was no going back now. If things went wrong, all three of them might find themselves caught in a hail of bullets.

Alex took his hand off her mouth but still kept a grip on her neck.

"Guard!" She called out the word but not loudly enough to be heard through the door. Alex shook her, staring into her eyes. "Diego!" she tried a second time. "Can you come in, please?"

Diego had been on duty the day Alex had first come to the villa. It was his bad luck that he was here again now. Dr Flint had called him – but she hadn't pressed the panic button. As far as he was concerned, that meant there was nothing to worry about. Perhaps the English woman simply wanted the two little creeps taken back to their cell and if so, he would be happy to oblige. He opened the door and came in.

He only saw the trap when it was too late. One boy – Julius Grief – was kneeling beside the psychiatrist, holding on to her. There was no sign of the other one. Then something moved in the corner of his vision. Freddy had stepped out of his hiding place beside the door. Diego tried to react, reaching for his gun, but it was already far too late. Something – a fist – pounded into the side of his head. He was unconscious before he knew he had been hit.

Freddy reached down and grabbed hold of the gun, drawing it out of the guard's holster. He turned it on Dr Flint. This was what Alex had most feared. If Freddy had his way, anyone who came near him would be killed, starting with the psychiatrist. Alex stepped in front of her, shielding her with his own body. "No shooting!" he urged. "We've got surprise on our side. Do this my way and we'll be out of here before they even know we've gone."

Freddy hesitated, then nodded. Alex reached out for a table lamp and, with a single jerk, tore out the flex. He used it to tie Dr Flint's hands behind her. She had been wearing a scarf and he pulled it free, then forced it into her mouth, turning it into a gag. Diego was lying still and before Alex could stop him, Freddy hit him a second time, using the handle of the gun. Well, it was too late to worry about that now. Diego would be unconscious for a while and he would wake up with a bad headache – but at least he would still be alive.

So far, so good. They had a gun. Nobody knew that anything was wrong. Diego and Dr Flint were both out of action. The governor and his wife weren't in the compound ... they had gone shopping in Gibraltar. Alex and Freddy were alone in the house.

What next?

Alex took off his belt and laid it flat on the table. On the way in, the guards had assumed that it was the buckle that had set off the metal detector but they hadn't noticed that there was something else concealed in a fold of the leather. It was the key that Alex had found inside the submarine. Now he drew it out and examined it nervously. This was the moment of truth.

Dr Flint had told him that every room in the governor's villa was locked. That was what he had been trying to remember. Assuming that all the locks were the same, these must be the doors that the key opened! What other plan could Julius have had in mind? Get access to the roof. Use the roof to get over the wall. There was no other way.

And if he was wrong?

Freddy was a fanatic. He was completely unpredictable. If he thought Alex had deceived him, he would probably shoot him there and then. And then the guards would shoot Freddy. They would both die and nothing would have been achieved. Alex realized that he had just taken, in every sense, the gamble of his life.

It was time to find out. Dr Flint was sitting, securely tied and gagged, staring at him furiously. Diego was lying still on the carpet. Neither of them was going anywhere. Alex nodded at Freddy and, taking the key, led the way out of the room. The two boys crossed the silent hallway and came to a closed door: the governor's office. Alex's eyes were drawn to a round metal disc – a lock about halfway up. This was it. He inserted the key and felt his heart skip a beat when it refused to turn. It didn't fit! Next to him, Freddy made no sound but Alex saw the gun rising slowly, coming up behind his head. He wiggled the key and tried again. It was a copy, roughly made. He shouldn't have expected it to work at once.

With a flood of relief, he felt the key turn and the tumblers click. The door opened. He had been right.

But the hardest part still lay ahead.

They entered the office and almost at once everything went wrong. The scream of the alarm was so sudden and so loud that it seemed to tear the very air into shreds. How had it happened? Perhaps entering the room had activated a sensor or, more likely, there was a camera somewhere in the house and someone had seen them as they appeared in the hall. Anyway, that didn't matter now. They had lost the element of surprise. They had perhaps seconds until every guard in the prison piled into the house.

Alex was frozen, uncertain, but this was the moment when Freddy Grey took over. He didn't even look worried, as if he had been expecting this all along. Slowly, quite purposefully, he walked over to the office window and, using the gun, smashed one of the panes of glass. Then he took aim and fired off three shots, the noise of the explosions almost lost in the endless wail of the alarms. Alex didn't know if he had hit anyone but there was a brief pause and he heard shouting from outside. Then, two seconds later, both of the windows shattered and the curtains leapt up, dancing crazily as the guards returned fire. He saw Freddy dive for cover and did the same. He had only just acted in time. When he looked up, the wall where he had been standing was pockmarked with bullet holes.

His first thought was that Freddy had lost his mind and that he would get both of them killed. But as he got to his feet, he decided that shooting out of the window had been a smart move. The guards had known they were moving through the house. That was why the alarms had gone off. Freddy had reminded them that he had Diego's gun and that he was prepared to use it – so nobody was going to break into the villa any time soon. What he had done was to buy them time. There was still a chance they could get out of here.

Alex had come into the office for a reason. He remembered the chair that the governor had been sitting in – modern, with castors ... basically four wheels. That was what he needed now. He got to his feet and, being careful not to put himself in the line of fire, grabbed hold of the chair and wheeled it out into the hall. He felt safer here. There were two narrow windows on either side of the front door but solid walls everywhere else. Freddy had followed him out.

"Are you sure this is going to work?" he asked.

Alex nodded. This was certainly no time for an argument.

Like a lot of office furniture, the chair had originally been delivered in sections that slotted together and it took Alex just a few moments to remove the back and the arms, leaving only the wide leather seat with the wheels below. As Alex straightened up, Freddy stepped forward, lifted the gun and fired off two more bullets. For a terrible moment, Alex thought he had been aiming at him but then he turned and saw silhouettes framed in the windows on either side of the front door. A couple of the guards had been about to break in. Freddy had fired through the glass and the men had fled.

Quite suddenly everything fell silent. Someone must have decided that there was no need for the alarms any more and had turned them off. To Alex, the silence was even more unnerving. He could imagine the guards circling the house, taking up their positions, preparing for an assault – and, sure enough, a moment later, he heard a voice, echoing across the compound as someone called to them through a megaphone.

"Come out with your hands up or we will come in. You cannot escape. Surrender now or we will kill you."

Across the hallway, Freddy grinned. It was as if the thought of being shot to death genuinely amused him.

"Let's move," Alex said.

He grabbed hold of what was left of the office chair and began to carry it upstairs. It weighed less without its back and arms and he could manage it easily. He still had no idea if he was going to find what he was looking for and even if he did, he hadn't worked out the angles, the distances. He was just hoping that Julius Grief had done the work for him. Julius had manufactured the key. He must have believed it was actually worth the effort.

They came to the first landing. The doors were locked here too but to Alex's immense relief the same key opened them just as he had thought. The first led into the governor's bedroom with a king-sized bed covered in a pink duvet. Next to it there was a bathroom, then a guest bedroom, then a laundry room.

"You have one minute!" The same voice echoed from outside. "Give yourselves up or we're coming in."

Alex ignored it. He found the door he was looking for at the very end of the corridor. It opened onto a short corridor with a narrow flight of stairs leading up to the second floor. Carrying the chair, Alex clambered up and found himself walking through a series of empty storage rooms, some of them with slanted ceilings that followed the line of the roof. Alex was sweating. He could feel his shirt sticking to his shoulders and back. The welts on his neck had gone down a little but they were still hurting.

"There has to be a trapdoor!" he said.

"It's here." Freddy had already found it but from the tone of his voice he was in no hurry, as if he was enjoying wandering around the governor's villa in what might be the final moments of his life.

"Then open it!"

The trapdoor was in a ceiling high above them, with a handle clearly visible but far out of their reach. Looking around him, Alex saw a pole with a hooked end, propped up in a corner. He snatched it and threw it to Freddy who used it to reach up and catch hold of the handle. Freddy pulled. The trap-door swung downwards, releasing a flight of metal steps, a ladder that unfolded all the way down to the carpet. Looking up, they could see the dark shadows of an attic.

"Thirty seconds!" the voice warned.

Freddy had already begun climbing the ladder with the gun tucked into the waistband of his trousers. Alex pushed the office chair over to him and, holding it awkwardly between them, the two boys carried it up into a narrow, uneven space packed with old trunks and boxes. There was a single window in front of them and as Alex went over to it, a cobweb brushed against him, depositing itself over his face.

The window wasn't locked. Alex pushed it open and climbed out. Freddy passed him the office chair and followed.

They found themselves on a small, lead-lined plat-form, hidden from the ground below, with a chimney towering over them and two red-tiled roofs, one on either side. The roofs were shaped liked two ticks in an exercise book. They sloped down steeply, then rose for just a couple of metres at the end. One of them faced the compound, but the other reached out towards the electrified fence and the wall that stood next to it. Alex worked out the distances. The edge of the roof finished at least five metres away from the double barrier. Much too far to jump. But if he could get over the fence and the wall, he might have a chance. There was a small wood made up of pine trees on the other side and the nearest of them had several branches stretching out towards him.

Reach the branches and they could climb down. They would be on the outside of the prison, away from the guards. But they would need extra propulsion to get over the two barriers. If they hit the wall, they would electrocute themselves first.

Far below, somewhere in the house, Alex heard the crash of breaking wood. The guards had charged the front door. They were in!

Freddy knew what they were going to do and the idea delighted him. He had manipulated the chair so that it was at the top of one of the roofs – a rocket on a launch pad. Kneeling down, he lowered his body so that his stomach was on the seat. There was hardly any space left for Alex but he somehow managed to do the same so that they were now lying next to each other, one arm around each other's shoulders, the other holding tight to the chair.

There were shouts, echoing up from the hallway. The stamp of heavy boots on the main staircase.

Alex and Freddy pushed off, using their feet, their arms stretched out in front of them, their legs behind. The office chair shot down the slope of the roof, carrying them with it. At the last moment, the guards who had stayed outside caught sight of them and at once the roof exploded, the tiles shattered by gunfire, red dust filling the air. They were moving incredibly fast. Alex was terrified that he was going to lose his balance, that the chair would topple over. But then the wheels reached the last section of the roof which sloped upwards and, as if they were on a ski-jump, they were shot back up into the air. Their own momentum carried them forward, over the top of the fence and over the wall. A stray bullet hit one of the wheels. Alex felt the chair jerk and heard the sound of the ricochet. Now they were falling clear, outside the prison. The pine trees had become a green blur, a tunnel of leaves and branches. Alex reached out, his hands protecting his eyes. He felt a thousand pine needles stabbing into his flesh. Freddy was no longer next to him. The chair had also gone. A tree trunk smashed into his shoulder spinning him round and he cried out, wondering if he had broken his arm. But he could still move his fingers. He used them to grab hold of a branch. He couldn't see. His whole body was in pain. It was as if the trees had decided to come together and beat him up.

And then it was over. He was about twenty metres above the ground, halfway up or halfway down one of the pine trees, clinging on to it with both hands. He was covered in so many needles that he knew he must look like a green hedgehog or sea urchin. He could feel blood trickling from a wound in his forehead. He blinked, shedding more pine needles from his eyelids, grateful that none of them seemed to have entered his eyes.

"Julius? Are you coming?"

It took him a few seconds to work out that he was Julius and that Freddy was calling up to him from below. The other boy had already climbed down. Still dazed, Alex examined the tree that had stopped his fall. He was spreadeagled in the middle of it, like a kite caught in the wind. He took a deep breath. There were enough branches to climb down. Moving as quickly as he could, he lowered himself, finally joining Freddy at ground level. He had never been more grateful to have soft earth beneath his feet. Vaguely, he wondered what had happened to the office chair. There was no sign of it.

"Where now?" he asked. He had got them out of the prison but that was it. Alex was completely exhausted. He had no more ideas.

"Follow me," Freddy said.

Behind them, the wail of the alarm broke the silence once again. Although they weren't to know it, two helicopters were taking off from Gibraltar. Half a dozen armed guards had assembled in front of the prison gates while a whole convoy of jeeps and military vehicles were on their way up the hill. The border with Spain had been closed immediately and Royal Navy boats were already patrolling the water that surrounded the peninsula on the other three sides.

The net was closing in. Alex and Freddy might be out, but they had nowhere to go.

DOWNHILL ALL THE WAY

The Rock of Gibraltar rises more than four hundred metres above the Spanish mainland. From the top, there are views over two continents: Europe in one direction, Africa in the other. Much of it has been given over to a nature reserve, the home of the famous Barbary apes. It's a steep, unfriendly landscape with patches of rubble, huge boulders, tangles of wild plants. Asphalt tracks lead up to military installations that are hidden behind fences and gates. Underground there are networks of caves and tunnels, souvenirs from different wars.

The prison had been built here for a reason – and not just because it happened to be British territory. Even if a prisoner broke out, they still had to get down and that was almost impossible. On one side, the ground simply fell away with a vertical rock face plunging towards the sea. On the other, a single road zigzagged all the way down to Gibraltar Harbour and the main town but it had been blocked the moment the alarm was raised.

Stay on the road and you would be picked up in minutes. Leave it and you would probably end up breaking your neck.

Standing outside the prison in the growing darkness, plucking pine needles out of his hair, Alex was all too aware of the challenge ahead. The town of Gibraltar was so far below that he might as well have been in a plane. He could just make out cranes, warehouses and a long, concrete jetty next to the sea and, further away, the twinkling lights that came from dozens of oil tankers and container ships lying at anchor. He had already decided that the road was out of the question. To get to the bottom, they would have to clamber down a hillside that was covered in trees and gorse bushes with bare patches where a soldier or a policeman with a rifle could easily pick them off.

"We need to get started," Freddy said.

Alex nodded. "I know."

Freddy patted his belt and frowned. "I lost the gun."

"That's annoying." Secretly, Alex was delighted. "Do you want to look for it?"

The answer came from the prison just behind them. The gates had opened and the guards were pouring out. Alex heard voices, shouting in a babble of English and Spanish. At least there weren't any dogs, although he suspected there would be some of those on the way too. There was no time to waste. Without another word, they threw themselves into the woodland, ducking behind the pine trees, leaving the prison behind.

The darkness helped them. When Alex glanced back over his shoulder, the wall was already invisible, lost in the gloom. He saw the beam of a torch stabbing uselessly in the trees. Over to the east, a helicopter was sweeping the landscape, a single beam of brilliant light cutting through the branches. The sound of the blades shuddered in the night air. Somewhere, a police whistle shrieked out. A car roared past. The guards had seen them propel themselves off the roof of the villa but they had no idea which direction they had taken. Nobody knew where they were now.

But the darkness was also an enemy. As he made his way down, Alex could feel the ground sloping beneath his feet but he couldn't see it and was almost sent flying as his foot caught in a root. A branch whipped into his face and he would have cried out if he wasn't afraid of being heard. He was moving faster and faster, carried by his own momentum, and only when it was too late did he realize he was out of control. He stretched his hands out in front of him, trying to slow himself down. It didn't work. He had broken out of the treeline and now he was running on loose scree and gravel. A second later, he tripped and found himself somersaulting forward, his feet in the air, at the mercy of the hill and whatever lay ahead. He just had time to bring up his arms and cover his face. And then he was rolling down the slope, his back and his shoulders repeatedly stabbed, his whole body a spinning ball of pain.

He had no idea how long this went on for. It might only have been a few seconds but when he finally stopped he felt as if he had been in a major traffic accident. He was covered in scratches. There was dirt in his mouth. At least he didn't seem to have broken or twisted any bones. He was grateful for that – but he wondered how much longer he could go on. Brushing himself down, he got back to his feet. A moment later he heard feet slithering down the hill and then Freddy was at his side.

"Are you OK, Julius?"

"I think so."

"We need to take it carefully from here. There's a road just in front of us. Once we cross it, there's a track..."

"Right."

Freddy was already on his way. Alex set off after him but even in all the pain and confusion, a question was pressing on his mind. How on earth could Freddy have got the information to say what he had just said? He would have been driven from the airport to the prison in a closed van just like Alex. He might have visited Gibraltar before but even so, there was no way he could know the hillside in such detail. It was pitch-dark now. They couldn't see anything. And yet he had spoken as if he was holding a map and this was the middle of the day.

And, impossibly, he was right!

They came to a wall with a road on the other side. They dropped back just as a jeep came roaring past, its headlights glaring. For a moment Alex saw Freddy, his pale face illuminated in the reflected glow, staring excitedly into the distance. It was as if he was possessed. Certainly, he didn't look nervous. To him, the escape was nothing more than a game and he knew that he was on the winning side. He was enjoying himself. Watching him, Alex got the sense that it was the first time he had been fully alive.

They waited until the jeep had gone, its red tail lights disappearing round the corner, then quickly climbed down and slipped across the road. Looking further down the hill, Alex saw a barrier and a group of armed soldiers, little more than ghostly shapes. He was hurting all over and there was a large part of him that was tempted to finish it now, to walk down the hill and hand himself in. This wasn't what he had volunteered for! But he had made a promise to himself. He was going to find Nightshade – and that meant sticking with Freddy. Anyway, there was always a chance that if he showed his face, he would simply be gunned down.

There was another path on the other side of the road, just as Freddy had said. It twisted through the trees, then emerged onto a wide slope covered in more loose rubble. Alex tried to pace himself, keeping up with Freddy without losing his footing a second time. Black shapes loomed up ahead of him, the remains of concrete blockhouses, left over

223

from the Second World War. Another car drove along the road they had just left and Alex heard it hooting as it approached the barrier. Suddenly there were voices everywhere, travelling easily through the cold night air. The whole side of the hill was echoing with orders being shouted, questions being asked. A single gunshot tore through the sky. Someone must have fired at a goat or maybe a monkey, thinking it was them. Alex swallowed hard. He and Freddy had turned themselves into moving targets ... wanted, dead or alive.

Another helicopter buzzed overhead, this one rising towards the peak. And then came the sound that Alex most feared. Barking. They had brought out dogs! He froze, trying to work out how close the animals might be. Would they be able to pick up a scent? He cursed the fact that the weather was dry. Rain might have helped conceal them, even if it had turned the hill into a mudslide.

Freddy was next to him. "Don't rest! Not yet. We have to keep moving."

A rest was the last thing on Alex's mind – but it did make him wonder. Where would they go when they made it to the bottom? Where would they hide? Perhaps Freddy had more information on his magic map. He opened his mouth to speak but right then someone shouted and there was a volley of shots, coming from behind and above them. They had been seen!

With the bullets whistling past, inches over their

heads, they had no choice. Freddy and Alex broke into a run, sprawling, tumbling, hurtling down the hill. They came to a fence. Alex didn't see it until it was almost too late and crashed into it, squirming like a fish in a net. He pulled himself free.

Freddy was staring at the fence, perplexed, as if he hadn't expected it. Now he had a simple choice. Left or right. But he seemed undecided. Alex saw him close his eyes and heard him whisper, "Which way?"

Was Freddy talking to him? No. He had forgotten that Alex was even there and a moment later he answered his own question. "Left! There's a gate..."

"Are you sure?" Alex had no idea what was going on. But Freddy had already started and a minute later they came to an opening in the fence, a gate half-hanging off its hinges. Without pausing, they went into a field, strewn with boulders. Alex felt his ears pop. They had descended hundreds of metres in just a few minutes. They must be getting close to the bottom. Someone shouted something in Spanish – a command, a warning – but they ignored it. More trees. Alex was glad to put anything between him and the guards closing in behind him. He still thought it was hopeless. He was close to exhaustion and once they reached the town they would be horribly conspicuous. Two fifteen-year-olds in torn clothes, scratched and filthy. They had no money. There was no way off the peninsula. How had he got himself into this?

They came to a low wall made out of different

shaped blocks of stone. They hauled themselves over it and dropped down. Alex could hardly believe it when his feet landed on concrete. He was on a pavement, next to a road. On the other side, he saw a single-storey, cream-coloured house. It had the same red tiles as the governor's villa. A window was open and he could see a lounge and a television showing some sort of chat show. He heard voices in Spanish and music. A couple of cars and a bus drove past. The two boys shrank back against the wall, trying to hide in its shadow.

"Where now?" Alex asked.

Somehow he knew that Freddy would have the answer. And he was right. "There are footpaths. On the other side."

Sure enough, a walkway twisted between the houses and took them through parkland – gentler and less overgrown – with the main town over to their right. Alex was glad that they weren't going too close to the shops. They would all be closed by now but there would still be plenty of people out in the streets and it would only take one passing police car for the whole adventure to be over. A concrete path and a flight of stone steps led them down and, as before, Alex got the impression that Freddy knew exactly where they were going, that somehow this had all been planned.

They emerged into another main road, this one busier, with commuters on their way home from work.

"We're going to have to split up," Freddy said.

"They're looking for two of us. We've got more chance on our own. Meet at the cinema."

"What cinema...?" Alex began. But Freddy was already on his way, hurrying towards a roundabout and an intersection where the traffic was at its heaviest. Alex noticed a man standing still, watching them, wearing a peaked hat with one arm folded across his chest. No. It wasn't a man. It was a statue. Horatio Nelson, for heaven's sake!

He waited a minute, catching his breath, then followed. He had to admit that Freddy was right. The call would have gone out that two boys had escaped, last seen heading – fast – downhill. They stood less chance of being seen if they separated. But a cinema? Alex was certainly in no mood for a film.

He came to it almost at once, standing on a corner facing the Rock with the sea behind it. It was called the Queen's Cinema – the name was mounted in green on the front wall in letters that looked as if they had been scribbled by hand – and it had clearly been shut down long ago, abandoned on the side of the busy intersection like an unwanted dog. It was an ugly concrete block with cracked paint and boarded-up windows. There was a panel beside the main door with the single word: TODAY. This would have been where the programme was displayed but it was empty.

How had Freddy known it was here? And how did he plan to get in?

And a third question – where was he? The other boy seemed to have vanished and for a horrible moment, Alex thought he might have abandoned him. How would he explain that one to MI6? That he had not only failed to get any information out of Freddy Grey but that he had actually helped him to escape! Alex checked that there were no police cars in sight, then hurried across the road. A few drivers noticed him but he hoped that his description hadn't been put out on the radio. Since the prison was supposed to be top secret, it was surely unlikely that they had told the public there had been an escape.

The front door of the cinema was locked and chained. Looking through the window, Alex saw a foyer strewn with rubbish. He went round to where an alleyway ran down the side of the building, away from the main road. About halfway down he came to a door which should have been bolted but which had recently been forced open. Even in the darkness, Alex could make out the smashed lock and the freshly splintered wood. Freddy must have done it – but how was that possible when he had come down the hill with nothing in his hands?

Feeling ever more mystified, Alex went in, stepping from one degree of darkness to another. Now he really couldn't see anything. He was following a corridor. He could feel carpet – thin and sodden – under his feet. A soft green glow was coming from around a corner. He continued towards it, through two swing doors which had been hooked open.

Freddy was waiting in the main auditorium. He was sitting on a stage in front of about three hundred empty seats with a giant screen behind him. Two curtains hung in tatters, one on either side. The electricity hadn't been disconnected. The light was coming from the emergency exit signs which he must have switched on. The old cinema would have been ghostly enough but the green light made it more so. There was more rubbish piled up in the aisles. The whole place smelled of damp and rotting fabric.

Freddy reached into his jacket and took something out. It was Benjamin, the stuffed monkey that Alex had given him in the cell. He had rescued it before he left and must have been carrying it with him all the time. Now he set it down beside him as if he were a performer, a ventriloquist, and this was his prop. "Guess what film they're showing, Julius," he called out. He didn't seem to have a mark on him. He had made it down the hill without falling once.

"I don't know," Alex replied. He was hurting and he was exhausted. He could have fallen asleep on his feet.

"*The Great Escape!*" he exclaimed. He began to laugh, manipulating Benjamin so that he seemed to be laughing too.

Alex sat down heavily on one of the chairs and closed his eyes, wondering how he had ever got himself into this nightmare and, more to the point, how he could find the way out.

LA MÁQUINA

It could have been morning. It could have been the middle of the night. Alex hadn't worn a watch in the prison and without windows there was no way of seeing if the sun had yet risen. All he knew was that he had a headache, his neck felt as if someone had tied a knot in it, and he was alone.

He had fallen asleep in the abandoned cinema, lying on the floor with a seat cushion as a pillow. He opened his eyes to the sight of the stuffed monkey sitting on the edge of the stage, lit by the same dull green light, rows of empty chairs and no sign of Freddy. Once again, Alex worried that he had been left behind, but even as he sat up and tried to get some feeling back into his arms and legs, he heard a door bang open and Freddy appeared, looking completely relaxed, carrying a plastic supermarket bag.

"Wake up, sleepyhead!" he announced, cheerfully.

"Where have you been?" Alex asked.

"Shopping!" Freddy upturned the bag and a whole load of things fell out: two clean T-shirts, sandwiches, biscuits, a six-pack of Coke and a bunch of grapes wrapped in two pages torn out of an out-of-date copy of the *Daily Mail*.

"I thought you didn't have any money," Alex said.

"I didn't."

Alex thought about that. Freddy must have stolen it all. He just hoped nobody had been hurt.

"Don't worry!" Freddy said. "Nobody saw me. I was very careful. I don't want anyone to know we're in town." He picked up a packet of sandwiches and threw it to Alex, who caught them. Ham and cheese. "I also talked to my family."

"Brilliant. Did you get a phone?"

Freddy hesitated. "Yes."

"Can I use it? There are people I'd like to call."

"It was out of battery, Julius. I left it behind." It was obvious Freddy was lying. He continued quickly. "It doesn't matter. They're on their way … they're sending people to help us. We're safe here. We're just going to have to wait until it gets dark again."

There were all sorts of questions going through Alex's mind but for the moment he stayed silent. He suddenly realized how hungry he was. He broke open the packet and took out a sandwich. He ate it in three mouthfuls, then drank half a can of Coke.

"So listen to me, Freddy … I mean, Number Nine. You've got to tell me a bit more about this family of yours," he said. "You said they'd look after me, which is great – but I'd like to know where I'm going."

"We'll start in Tangier," Freddy replied. "That's only

fifty kilometres across the Strait of Gibraltar."

"And then?"

Freddy frowned. "I'm not allowed to tell you, Julius. You have to trust me. My family are very happy that you helped to get me out of prison and they want to meet you. But I can't tell you where they are. You'll have to wait and see."

"OK." Alex considered. "But we've got the whole day together. You could at least tell me who you are and what you did to wind up getting arrested. I don't even know that. And why don't you use your name? Why are you just a number?"

Freddy had finished his sandwich. He tore open the biscuits. "I'm just one of twenty-five," he said.

"Nightshade."

"Yes. We are all orphans. Our parents didn't want us and put us in a boat in the ocean. We sailed for a hundred days until we were found by the Teachers who took us into their home. The British police called me Freddy and they showed me a man and a woman who pretended to be my parents but I know that's all a lie. We are numbers because we have no identity outside the group. We don't make any choices. The Teachers tell us what we have to do and we obey them."

"And what's that? What do you have to do?"

"We have to make the world a better place."

"By killing people?"

Freddy nodded. "Sometimes. There was a man in Rio de Janeiro that I was sent to kill. He was a spy and he was evil. Unfortunately, I got caught when I was running away and that's how I ended up in prison with you. The Teachers are angry with me because I was already in training for Leap of Faith."

"Leap of Faith? What's that?"

"My next mission. After I got caught, I prayed for forgiveness and maybe that's why you were sent to me. I really hope they're going to let you join us, Julius."

"Yeah. Number Twenty-Six. That's me."

It was all madness. The Teachers, the fight against evil, the Leap of Faith, the prayers. Freddy talked a little more but then he'd decided he'd had enough and closed his eyes and suddenly he was asleep. He was sitting cross-legged with his hands resting on his thighs. Alex realized it must be a technique he had been taught, the ability to switch off in an instant. He finished his Coke and lay back on the floor, gathering his strength, aware of the monkey watching him with blank eyes.

Sitting in her office on the sixteenth floor of the building in Liverpool Street, Mrs Jones read the document that had just been handed to her, then went through it a second time. She had been away the evening before, at an old factory in South East London, watching the Special Air Service take part in an anti-terrorist exercise. There had been hostages, blank ammunition, training grenades and smoke bombs. Apparently, a dozen local residents had called the police, mistaking what was happening for the real thing.

"This happened yesterday," she said.

Crawley nodded. "I tried to contact you but there was a security blackout where you were. No messages in, no messages out."

"You should have reached me at home."

"By then, it was too late. There was nothing you could have done, so why give you a sleepless night?"

Mrs Jones stared at the sheet of paper as if she might find some secret message between the lines. It wasn't there. "What happened?" she demanded. "This was never part of the plan. Alex was sent in to get information, not to organize an escape. And certainly not to take part in it! What does he think he's doing?"

"I imagine he's trying to help you," Crawley suggested, gently.

"Me?"

"You told him, didn't you?" Crawley was one of the very few people in MI6 who knew the truth. "You told him about your children."

Mrs Jones thought about what Crawley had just said and when she replied, there was anger in her eyes. "Alex doesn't owe me anything," she said.

"I've spoken to Dr Flint. Freddy Grey wasn't talking ... not to her, not to anyone. Then Alex managed to break through. Freddy still wouldn't tell him anything about Nightshade but he'd worked out a plan to get out of the prison. A lot of people would have been killed. Alex persuaded him to do it his way."

"With no casualties."

"That's right. One guard concussed, another shot in the arm. Once again, Alex has done a remarkable job. If Freddy takes him to Nightshade, there's every chance that he'll be able to get a message to us and then we can move in and extract him."

"Do we have any idea where he is now?"

"I'm afraid not. The two of them have vanished into thin air. It's incredible. The police and the military are combing the peninsula and the Spanish are helping too. The border is closed. But there's no sign of them." Crawley paused. "They must have had outside help."

Mrs Jones looked up at him. "That's impossible. We didn't take any chances after what happened in Rio de Janeiro. Freddy Grey went into that prison without a stitch of his original clothing and no possessions. He was strip-searched. There was no way he could have communicated with the outside world."

"Then maybe he's just very lucky."

They both knew there was no such thing as luck – not in the world they inhabited. Everything happened for a reason.

Mrs Jones laid the document down. "Who else knows about this?" she asked.

"The Duty Officer took the message when it came in last night. She decrypted it and sent it to me. Obviously, the authorities in Gibraltar are involved and Freddy Grey's description has been circulated. But we've managed to keep Alex's name out of it ... and by that I mean Julius Grief too." He coughed. "I did consider letting people know that he's one of ours."

"You were right not to. It's too risky. If Nightshade learned the truth, he'd be killed instantly."

"Exactly. He stands a better chance if we keep him out of the picture altogether and focus on the other boy."

"Thank you, John." It was unusual for Mrs Jones to use first names in this room. "Only three people in London know about this. You, me and the Duty Officer. Let's make sure we keep it that way."

But just down the corridor, in a small office next to the men's toilets, Owen Andrews was looking at a report on his computer screen.

"...a breakout from the HMS Secure Unit in Gibraltar reported at 18.30 hours. Prisoner XF 242837 Frederick Grey now missing in the company of a second inmate [name withheld]. Two officers injured, not critical. Blanket land/sea search continues..."

He was puzzled.

It seemed incredible that the prison authorities – and MI6 Special Operations – should have allowed Freddy Grey to escape. He was the one link with the terrorist event being planned by Nightshade in London and to lose him now was a catastrophic failure on their part. But who was the prisoner who had escaped with him and why had his (or her) name been removed from the report? That made no sense at all.

Unless MI6 was hiding something.

Owen Andrews had no friends. He still lived with his parents and he didn't even like them very much. All that mattered to him was his career and it was this that made him so useful to Dominic Royce. He had been told to find out what was going on in Special Operations and right now he was certain that they were lying. Mrs Jones was holed up in that office of hers just down the corridor and Owen had seen Crawley going in. It seemed to him that her deputy was looking distinctly worried.

He stared at the computer screen in front of him. It really shouldn't be too hard to hack into Crawley's private account. After all, he was inside MI6, inside the firewall. He had already made quite a bit of progress, running a scan of all the ports in Crawley's operating system, selecting the ones that were least protected. Very soon, he would start work on the passwords.

Through the wall, Owen heard the sound of gurgling water as a toilet was flushed. Ignoring it, he reached out over his keyboard and began to type.

It had been the longest day of Alex's life. He had been stuck in the empty cinema with only a few pages from an old newspaper to read. He'd found a crossword and done half of it, having to visualize the answers as he had no pen with which to fill them in. There was no point trying to talk to Freddy, who seemed to have switched off.

After that, Alex rested, dozed, daydreamed. He would have liked to have gone outside if only to see if the sun had begun to set, but once again Freddy dissuaded him. It was too dangerous. That much, at least, was true. Alex could imagine that the whole area of Gibraltar was being searched. The Rock itself was riddled with caves and old buildings. Then there was the main town, the area around the airport, the various bays. With a bit of luck, the security forces wouldn't come in here though. As far as they were concerned, the cinema was meant to be locked up.

That led Alex to ask himself again – how had Freddy managed to break in through the side door? The wood was thick and the lock was solid. Surely it would have demanded a crowbar or an axe but Freddy had neither. For that matter, how had he even known the cinema was here? He glanced at the other boy who was sitting in a chair as if there was actually a film being projected onto the blank screen. He shivered. None of this made any sense.

"They're here," Freddy said, suddenly.

"Who?" Alex listened but he couldn't hear anything.

"La Máquina."

Alex thought he must be mistaken but a second later there was the thud of a door opening and as he got to his feet, two men came into the auditorium, both of them dressed in jeans and dirty T-shirts. They were Spanish, dark-skinned. One had a shaven skull and an earring. The other was heavier, older with greasy black hair and suspicious eyes. He was the one who spoke first.

"You are Number Nine?"

Freddy nodded. Alex noted that the man had not used his prison name.

"And the other?"

"I'm Julius Grief," Alex said.

The man ignored him. He was talking only to Freddy. "We are to leave him behind," he said. "Our instructions are to take only you."

Alex felt his heart sink. So after all that, the escape, the chase down the hill and the long wait in this horrible place, he wasn't going anywhere! He was about to argue when Freddy took a step forward. "No," he said.

The two men looked at him in disbelief.

"He's my friend," Freddy went on. "He was the one who got me out of the prison. He wants to join us. I'm not going to leave him behind."

The shaven-headed man spoke for the first time. "You make big mistake," he said. His English was much worse than his friend's. "There no room for two."

"It's both of us or it's neither of us," Freddy insisted. He reached out and took the stuffed monkey. "All three of us," he added.

There was a long silence. Then the first man shrugged. "All right. But your people will pay double. They will not be pleased."

"Who are these men?" Alex took a step forward, standing between Freddy and the two Spaniards.

He wanted to show them that he wasn't scared. "How do we even know we can trust them?"

"They're from La Máquina," Freddy explained. "It means 'The Machine'. They're part of a gang. They run drugs between Tangier and Spain." He smiled. "Except tonight they're going to run us! I told you. Fifty kilometres across the Strait of Gibraltar. They've been paid to get us out of here."

"And you arranged all this by phone?"

Freddy hesitated briefly. "That's right. We can trust them. This is their business."

"Great. I just hope it's not going to be too rough. I get seasick."

Freddy grinned at that. But the two men weren't amused. "Come now," the shaven-headed man said. "We move quickly. No police or soldiers near." He pointed. "This is Matías. I am Sebastián. You do everything we tell you. No more argue."

"Whatever you try to say..." Alex muttered.

The four of them hurried out of the cinema, taking the door into the alleyway. As they emerged into the open air, Alex saw that it was dark once again, just as it had been when they arrived, with traffic rushing past in both directions. With a bit of luck, they wouldn't be noticed. He and Freddy were both wearing new T-shirts and now there were four of them. Two kids going out for dinner with their dads. Alex hoped that was what any passing driver would think.

They crossed the road and continued downhill past an office block and a brightly lit Italian restaurant – MAMMA MIA – on the other. Glancing back, Alex could see the immense bulk of the Rock towering over them and imagined the governor, scowling inside his secret prison, waiting to hear from the dozens of policemen and soldiers who would still be searching through the undergrowth. His bare arms were covered in cuts and he could feel the breeze, actually hurting him as it brushed against his skin. Freddy briefly rested a hand on his shoulder and that hurt too but he smiled. If it wasn't for his new friend, he'd have been left behind.

The sea was right in front of them. They crossed a second road – wider, emptier – and came to what looked like a holiday village with a white archway over the entrance and a gate. A sign read: QUEENSWAY QUAY. Alex was sure that there would be guards here but either La Máquina had paid them or scared them off. Nobody noticed them as they slipped through.

There was a marina on the other side. Alex saw boats of every size and description moored together in the square of water formed by a line of shops, with restaurants on one side and concrete jetties on the other three. There were sailing boats, motor boats, cruisers, catamarans, all of them bobbing up and down with their masts creaking and tinkling in the darkness. He saw at once which one belonged to the gang.

It was an ugly grey RIB, a rigid inflatable boat about twelve metres long with a deep-V hull designed to cut through waves. It had been moored between two speedboats, sitting there like a beached whale. It was powered by three massive outboard engines mounted behind a single mast which rose up with a white radar dish mounted on the top. There were four seats in the middle and a fifth behind the steering wheel, which was attached to a console with a glass window to protect the skipper from the spray. A third man was standing on the jetty, holding a rope, waiting for them. Alex was amazed that nobody had noticed them. They were surrounded by pleasure boats but even at a glance it was obvious that the RIB had nothing to do with pleasure at all.

"Get in!" Matiás hissed. "And be careful not to step on the tarpaulin."

Alex felt a hand shoving into the small of his back and was almost propelled into the water. Somehow, he stumbled into one of the seats, resting against the side of the RIB, which was made of something soft – rubber or neoprene perhaps. Meanwhile, the man with the rope was arguing in Spanish. He had clearly been expecting one passenger and wanted to know why there were two. Sebastián snapped something at him and all three men climbed on board.

A moment later, they were backing out, the water churning around them. Alex was sitting next to Freddy. Sebastián and Matiás were behind. The third man was steering – and he clearly knew what he was doing. Alex could feel the vibration of the propellers. They were still on low power but the RIB seemed almost to glide over the surface of the water and when the skipper pushed down on the throttle, it leapt forward, the nose rising, the engines growling. Sebastián reached down and produced a bottle of some sort of spirit – rum or tequila. He took a swig, laughed, then passed it to Matiás.

They were already moving fast but Alex guessed the engines weren't even at a tenth of their full power. Expertly, the skipper steered them to a gap between the concrete walkways. They passed under a bridge. Now they were in open water, leaving the lights of Gibraltar behind. Alex shivered. It was almost the end of October and although they were in the Mediterranean, he could feel the first touches of winter in the wind. How long would it take them to reach Tangier? The RIB had three engines, each one with three hundred horsepower. Working together, they would easily be capable of thirty knots – about thirty-five miles per hour. If they continued at full speed, they should be there in no more than about fifteen minutes.

But the skipper clearly didn't want to draw attention to himself. He was carefully controlling the throttle. Any boat speeding at this time of night had to be up to no good and the more noise he made, the more likely they were to be spotted. Better to cruise gently with just a soft rumble carrying them forward. Nobody was speaking. Matiás held out the bottle for Freddy, who shook his head.

"I'm not allowed alcohol," he said.

Matiás shrugged and took another swig himself. He didn't offer any to Alex.

It had all been ridiculously easy. Alex was almost embarrassed that a British Overseas Territory, jammed with officers and personnel from the army, air force, navy and police, should have allowed a bunch of criminals to slip through the net without a single alarm bell being rung. There was a large part of him that wanted them to be caught. After all, if the boat was seized, the drug smugglers would be arrested and Freddy would be taken back to jail. It would be the end of the adventure for him but nobody would be able to say that it was his fault. In a few days, he would be back at Brookland, putting all this behind him.

But it wasn't going to happen. Alex stared at the horizon, invisible in the black emptiness of the sea. They were slipping away into an immense darkness. Nobody had seen them leave.

The thought was no sooner in his head than he was proved wrong.

It came, looming up from nowhere. It had picked them up almost at once and had been quietly tracking them. A spotlight cut through the darkness at the same time as the roar of an engine announced itself – and twisting round, Alex was just able to make out the shape of a high-speed interceptor vessel marked in the colours of the Royal Gibraltar Police. He had to smile. With the word POLICE on the side and the blue-yellow chessboard along the edge, it looked like a marine version of the police cars that patrolled the streets of Chelsea. And it was closing on them with deadly speed. Alex could make out four figures on board – three men and a woman – and guessed they would all be armed.

"Pull over!" The amplified voice belonged to the captain and echoed across the water. "Cut your engines and stay where you are. You will receive no further warning."

There was a brief pause, then the three men from La Máquina acted as one. The driver slammed his hand down on the throttle, making the engines howl and sending the RIB hurtling forward. Sebastián knelt down and began to fumble under the tarpaulin. Matiás waved a finger in front of Alex's face. "Stay where you are!" he shouted. "No move!" Still holding the bottle, he stood up and staggered back towards the wheel.

The captain of the interceptor had seen what they were doing. She rapped out an order and a second later there was a burst of gunfire, a warning shot that passed inches over their heads. Still the RIB didn't slow down and the next burst came almost at once, hammering into the wheelhouse and smashing the bottle in Matiás's hand. Matiás yelled out and dropped the pieces. Alex and Freddy crouched low, feeling the bullets fly past, knowing that they were quite literally sitting targets but that there was nothing they could do. The interceptor vessel was catching up with them. Its engines were more powerful than theirs. The spotlights were slicing through the darkness, pinning them down. It seemed to be doubling in size with every second.

Then Sebastián stood up, propping himself against the radar mast for balance. Alex saw that he had retrieved something from underneath the tarpaulin. It was a weapon of some sort, about one metre long, made of wood and metal. He had slipped a strap over his shoulder and he had the stock pressed into his chest. With a sense of disbelief that made his head spin, Alex recognized what the weapon was.

Sebastián was about to fire a Russian-made RPG-7 anti-tank rocket-propelled grenade launcher at the interceptor vessel coming up behind them. A small gunpowder charge would launch the grenade but then, after ten metres, a rocket motor would ignite, propelling the deadly missile across the water at 295 metres per second. If it hit the boat, it would kill everyone on board. The explosion would be seen for miles.

Alex knew he had to do something. He couldn't just sit there and watch British policemen and women being murdered. But he was trapped in his seat, surrounded by gangsters. He couldn't move. The RIB was rushing at full speed across the surface of the sea. He could feel the spray hammering into him. Freddy was next to him, his eyes wide, something like a grin on his face. Sebastián was still aiming. The skipper was gripping the wheel with both hands, his teeth showing in a snarl of determination.

What to do without giving himself away?

It had to be now.

Alex looked down and saw part of the bottle that Matiás had been holding before the first gunfire had shattered it. The neck and a jagged blade of glass were lying on the floor right beside him. Hoping he wouldn't be seen in the darkness and the spray of the water, Alex reached down and picked it up. He saw Sebastián's finger tighten on the trigger of the grenade launcher. The interceptor vessel was so close that it would be impossible to miss. There was another burst of gunfire and Alex used that moment to slash sideways, driving the point of the broken bottle into the side of the RIB.

There was a bang as the air-filled fabric exploded. Alex felt it shred beneath his hand, like an oversized party balloon. The whole RIB veered to the right. At exactly that moment, Sebastián fired. But he had been knocked off balance. The grenade shot forward and ignited, then soared past the interceptor vessel, missing it by inches. Alex wondered how much damage he had done. The RIB wasn't going to sink. It had been designed with separate air compartments to stay buoyant in the event of a puncture. Even so, the shock of the blast had sent the whole vessel into a spin-out. The skipper was shouting, fighting with the wheel. The RIB was out of control, spinning on the surface of the water like a crazy fairground ride. Alex couldn't see anything. The night was whirling around him.

Somehow, the skipper managed to stop them

capsizing. Alex felt himself being thrown against Freddy but then the RIB was upright, ploughing forward in a straight line. The darkness swallowed them up. Twisting round, he saw that the interceptor vessel had dropped back. The captain had seen the grenade go past and had known how close they had come to destruction. They weren't equipped to face such weapon power. They had no choice but to let them go.

Nobody said anything for the next few minutes, not until the Gibraltar Police vessel was out of sight. Suddenly they were alone in the ocean with the Rock swallowed up behind them and a few tiny lights twinkling ahead. It was Matiás who spoke first. He knelt down and examined the torn skin of the RIB. Alex wished now that he had dropped the broken bottle into the sea. Instead, it was lying there, on the floor of the RIB, the evidence of what he had done.

"What happened?" Matiás demanded.

"What do you mean?" Alex asked. "They were shooting at us! They hit the side of the RIB!"

"It was a lucky shot..." Matiás was suspicious. The damage to the rib didn't look as if it had been made by a bullet, but then again, he knew nothing about Alex. Why should an escaping prisoner have wanted to get himself caught? He turned to Freddy. "Did you see what happened?"

Freddy shrugged. "No. It was like Julius said. They were shooting at us. We got hit."

Matiás was about to say something more but then

Sebastián called to him. Alex looked up and saw a blaze of lights in front of them: a busy harbour, houses squeezed together in narrow streets rising up the hillside, roofs and minarets – all of them beneath a crescent moon and a confusion of stars.

Beside him, Freddy laughed and clapped his hands.

They were in Tangier, on the coast of Africa.

They had arrived.

PART THREE: NUMBERS

KIDS IN CRISIS

Crete is the largest and the most populated of all the Greek islands, covering one hundred and sixty miles from east to west. Every year, more than two million tourists fly into the airports at Heraklion and Chania. Some have come for the beaches and perfect weather, some for the historical sites, some for the bars and tavernas – but they're all looking for a good time. The Greeks are always welcoming. Prices are cheap.

At the very east of the island is a beach called Vai. It's famous for its palm forest and tropical sand, and people will cross the island to spend the day there. But the area around Vai is less well known. There are very few buildings scattered across the land-scape and, apart from the occasional watermelon or pineapple stand, the roads seem to be deserted. There are several military camps in the area. Greece and Turkey have waged four wars against each other and although there hasn't been any actual fight-ing for a long time, the two countries are still at each other's throats. Every Greek has to spend one year in the armed services. Turkish ships and planes are constantly monitored. The camps are closely guarded and it is forbidden to enter them. In the past, tourists have been arrested simply for taking photographs.

The military base at Kavos Bay had once been an important outpost, on the edge of the Aegean Sea, with the Turkish mainland – and the enemy – just two hundred and fifty miles away. It was at the end of a rough track that climbed steeply into the hills with warning signs in Greek and English – PRIVATE ROAD CLOSED TO TRAFFIC. If a tourist or a local farmer were to ignore the sign and keep driving, they would come to a tall fence with a locked gate. If they managed to get through that, a second fence would block their way a quarter of a mile later and this time there would be a soldier waiting for them, dressed in khaki and carrying a gun.

All of this was strange because the base at Kavos Bay hadn't belonged to the Greek army for twenty years. It had been closed down and then sold to a charity called Kids' Crisis Relief. It was now home to a number of children – boys and girls from all over Europe – who had lost their parents in different war zones and who might have starved if they hadn't been brought here and looked after. The children never left the complex. It was believed that many of them were traumatized. They needed round-the-clock care. The charity asked the local people to leave them alone, to allow the sunshine, the silence and the smell of the pine and eucalyptus trees to help with the healing process.

Cretans have learned, over the years, not to ask too many questions. They keep themselves to themselves. Even so, some of them were puzzled by the activity at the Kavos Bay camp. Why, for example, was there a full-length airstrip? Planes and helicopters were often seen landing or taking off, and it was said that some of the poor children had even taken up parachuting! There were rumours that as well as a school, a hospital and two accommodation blocks, the charity had also constructed an army-style assault course. Gunshots had been heard at night, echoing down the hillside.

Two years before, a fisherman – Yannis Hordakis – had sneaked into the compound with his brother. The two of them were going to take photographs and sell them to a newspaper in Athens. That was the plan. Yannis had never been seen again. His brother George had caused a mass panic when his body was washed up on Vai beach. It looked as if he had been mauled by a shark ... even though there have never been any shark attacks in the Aegean.

After that, nobody had gone near the place again.

Kids' Crisis Relief was a real charity. It had registered offices in Geneva and could show a comfortable amount – but not too much money – in the bank, with accounts in apple-pie order. It raised money all over the world with collection tins outside stations, advertisements in the newspapers and even celebrity concerts in London and New York. There were elderly ladies who cheerfully sold pins and badges and vicars who passed around the collection plate to help them. Had they driven to Crete and entered the camp, they might have been surprised by what they saw.

To begin with, it was very large. It had been built on a plateau, a quarter of a mile in diameter, with steeply rising hills on all sides forming a natural barrier against the outside world. The slopes were inhabited by goats, and every evening the silence was broken by the sound of their bleating or by the chime of the bells they wore around their necks. A clump of olive trees disguised the entrance to a narrow gorge – a crack in the earth that dated back to prehistoric times – which ran down all the way to the sea. The airstrip, with a pair of gleaming silver hangars, stretched the full length of the compound. Any plane taking off would have to climb rapidly to avoid the side of the hills.

More than a dozen buildings had been constructed close to one another, forming what was effectively a village with its own little square. There was even a Greek taverna with a name, Mistral – a wind which often blows in Crete – above the front door. Everything was made of stone, painted white against the glare of the summer sun, and there were two dormitories – one for boys, one for girls – that were made of wood. Solar panels had been set in the roofs and in addition, two wind turbines were constantly turning at the very edge of the property, above the sea. A natural spring provided fresh water and there was enough land to grow vegetables and to raise sheep and chickens. The goats provided milk and cheese. Kavos Bay needed no help from outside. It could survive on its own.

The most impressive building stood some distance from the main village, at the end of a road that ran dead straight between two rows of cedar trees. It was made almost entirely of white marble, shaped like a Greek temple with massive columns and wide steps leading up to the main entrance. This was the only way in and it was guarded by two oversized statues, winged angels on plinths, one with its arms spread in welcome, the other more threatening with a sword and shield. A line taken from a prayer, written in gold, ran all the way across the front of the building: FOR EVER AND ALL ETERNITY. At midday, the sunlight would hit the letters and they would glimmer so brilliantly that they could be seen a mile away.

The building – it was actually known as the Temple – might have been designed to look ancient but it was easy to see that it was brand new. Behind the columns, the front doors were electronic and connected to a fingerprint scanner set in a block of stone. Long, narrow windows had been constructed at intervals with one-way glass so that nobody could look in. There was a cluster of sophisticated satellite dishes and aerials as well as water tanks and air-conditioning units on the roof. Nobody was expected to walk here in the hot Greek sunshine. Instead, driverless electric buggies made the journey from the village and back again, whirring almost silently up and down the road.

This was the home of the Teachers. At least, that was what they called themselves. There were four of them and they were, in fact, the executive committee of Nightshade.

It was six o'clock in the evening, the same day that Alex had left Tangier, and two men and two women had gathered in the conference room on the ground floor. They were sitting around a table that was a single block of wood, taken from a one-thousand-year-old tree that had once grown on that very spot. The Teachers had chopped it down when they constructed the Temple. The walls of the room were grey stone. There were no pictures and no ornaments. The air conditioning had been turned up so high that it was almost like sitting in a fridge.

The Teachers were all dressed identically in grey shirts buttoned up to the neck, loose-fitting grey robes and sandals. They looked a bit like monks ... though New Age ones. Each one of them wore a gold disc around their neck, decorated with a half moon and the shadow of a star. They were drinking small cups of green tea.

They did not use surnames. They always referred to each other as "Brother" or "Sister".

"Shall we begin?" The speaker was sitting at the

head of the table. He was about fifty years old – all the Teachers were a similar age and they were all American. The speaker was completely bald with a round head that seemed to be melting. His neck and his cheeks hung down in loose folds and his lips were so thick that they bulged out beneath his nose. His name was Brother Lamar and he was the founder and Chief Executive of Nightshade.

"I want to start with an update on Number Nine," he continued. "We've got him back and I suppose we can be glad for that. But the question is – can we keep him? Is he still any use to us or has he been compromised?"

"In my view, he's performed well." The woman sitting next to him, Sister Jeanne, had the look of a matron in a private clinic. She was well built with chestnut hair which she had spent hours styling but it still looked fake. Her skin was beginning to wither and all the colour in her face – on her lips, her cheeks, her eyelids – had come out of a bottle.

"I've had a long talk with Number Nine since his return," she went on. "I don't think it was his fault he was captured in Rio. Number Six saw what happened and she told me it was pure bad luck. He was held by the Brazilian police and he did pretty well. Five men killed and two more injured! It's too bad he was unable to escape.

"After that, he was held by the British secret service but he told them nothing. Brother Mike has obviously had success with the advanced interrogation techniques." She nodded at the man opposite her. "He didn't give them zip!"

"The Brits sent him to Gibraltar and, as you'll remember, we did discuss whether we should use our communications system to instruct him to commit suicide. It's lucky we didn't. He was there only for a few weeks before he managed to escape and, with help from a local gang – La Máquina – he was taken off the peninsula and over to Tangier. We flew him home from there."

"What did we pay La Máquina?" Brother Lamar asked.

"The fee was a hundred thousand euros." Sister Jeanne sniffed. "Unfortunately, this was doubled as two people, not one, escaped."

"That's right! And what about this second kid?" It was the other woman who had asked the question. Sister Krysten had long white hair that swept down over her shoulders and a thin, angular face with a nose like a kitchen knife. She wore glasses and dangling silver earrings that swung every time she moved her head.

"His name is Julius Grief," Sister Jeanne replied, glancing at her notes. "He has an interesting bio. He was actually cloned by his father, Dr Hugo Grief, and given extensive plastic surgery. He has something in common with the Numbers in that his whole life has been devoted to a single purpose and he has pursued it ruthlessly, without hesitation."

"Are you saying he could join us?"

"I don't know, Brother Lamar. My feeling is that we might be able to use him. We should discuss it in due course. But before that, there is a much more serious matter to consider and that is the fact that Number Nine disobeyed orders."

There was a brief pause as the four people around the table took this in. It had never happened before. It was actually unthinkable.

"He disobeyed?" Sister Krysten's earrings shuddered as she repeated the words.

"Number Nine was told to leave Julius Grief behind. He refused. During his debrief, he told me that Julius had helped him. He described him as his friend."

Brother Lamar shook his head angrily. "Numbers don't have friends," he intoned. "They know that's one of the first rules. They do as they're told. They help each other. If necessary, they give their lives. But friendship is not part of the equation."

The fourth member of the group leaned forward. Brother Mike was African American with round glasses and a face that, from the look of it, had never learned to smile. His hair was close-shaven, his eyes endlessly suspicious. There was something very precise about the way he spoke. Each word was measured before it emerged. "Number Nine has clearly been compromised," he said. "He should be killed. Why have we not done this already?"

"Because we need him," Brother Lamar snapped back. "I'm sorry, Brother Mike. Number Nine is perfect for Leap of Faith ... and right now that's less than a week away. Any change at this stage could be bad for morale. I'm sure you'll agree."

"I'm not so sure. I've been training Number Seven to take his place."

"Number Seven's smart. But the truth is, when it comes to Leap of Faith, there's not a single one of them who's as accurate as Number Nine. He's just got a feeling for it. He flies like a bird! Added to which, he and Number Six work well together ... they proved that in Rio. I think it would be a mistake to replace him."

"I agree," Sister Krysten said.

"Well, then. Let's at least kill this other boy ... Julius Grief," Brother Mike insisted. "Whatever Sister Jeanne may say, we don't need him. It's too late to make changes to our plans now."

"Again, I disagree," Brother Lamar said. He picked up his teacup between a pudgy finger and thumb and sipped. "Let's face the facts. Number Nine feels he owes something to this Grief character. If we kill him now, it might throw him off his stride. I vote we let things settle down a bit. We have this week's training before we hit London. Let's go with the flow."

"And then kill him?"

"I'm sure we can find a way to use him to our advantage." Brother Lamar put down his cup. "You never know. He may even fit in with our little family. He's an orphan. He's resourceful. He's not afraid to kill."

"Where is he now?"

"He's waiting outside."

"Then let's bring him in."

Brother Lamar pressed a button on the table and a moment later the door opened and a guard came in. "Get the boy!" Lamar instructed, speaking in Greek.

Alex Rider was waiting in a shadowy anteroom on the other side of a solid door, sitting on a sofa. The room had thick, stone walls and no window. He hadn't changed since he left Tangier and he had begun to shiver in the chill of the air conditioning. He was handcuffed and that didn't make him feel any better either. He had no idea what was going to happen to him.

It had been almost twenty-four hours since he had found himself in Tangier. Alex thought back to the moment they had arrived.

Matiás had examined the RIB as soon as they had moored and Alex had followed his eyes as they travelled from the broken bottle to the gash in the side. The drug smuggler was certain that they hadn't been hit by gunfire and could well have accused Alex of sabotage ... except that there seemed to be no motive for it. Why would he have wanted to be recaptured? In the end, Matiás had stayed silent. He was going to be well paid for the night's work and they had got away. That was all that mattered.

Alex had seen nothing of the old city of Tangier. It was dark and there was a van waiting for them right next to the harbour. He and Freddy were bundled into the back and the next minute they were rattling along the coast with two dusty windows giving almost no view at all. They spent the rest of the night in a farmhouse surrounded by fields, with no other lights anywhere near. At least they were well fed. A woman had served up a healthy meal of chicken tagine with couscous, flatbread, salad and fruit.

They left the next morning. The same driver took them to the Ibn Battouta Airport, which was outside the city with a single runway stretching out towards the sea. There was a private plane waiting for them – a twin-propeller Beechcraft King Air C90 with room for up to seven passengers and two crew. The pilot, in a white, short-sleeved shirt and sunglasses that blanked out his eyes, didn't turn round as they climbed in. Nor did he speak throughout the entire journey. Alex gazed out of the window, trying to work out where he was going. Was he being taken further away from home? They were heading east. That was about all he could say.

They flew for several hours. Alex did the maths. Suppose they were doing 350 miles per hour. That would suggest a journey of around 1,400 miles. So where would they land? It could be Egypt. No. Too far. Looking out of the window, he saw a landmass that might be Sicily. So they were passing south of Italy. Alex tried to visualize the world map that he had seen a hundred times in geography class at Brookland. What was the nearest landmass to Italy, heading east? Greece! That had to be the answer. That was where Freddy's clothes had come from and it had also been the subject of his book in the prison library.

The moment they landed, he knew he was right. The private airstrip was bordered by olive and pine trees, both native to Greece, and the intensely blue sea and brilliant sunlight couldn't have belonged to anywhere else. Even the smell took him back to holidays he'd enjoyed long ago.

As soon as the door of the plane was opened, things took a turn for the worse. Two guards – Greeks in military gear – appeared and whisked Freddy away. Alex saw him being driven towards what looked like a purpose-built village in an electric cart. Another guard grabbed hold of Alex and before he could protest, his hands had been cuffed and he was frog-marched into the nearest hangar, pushed down onto the concrete floor and told to wait. He had sat there for the entire afternoon, surrounded by oil drums and the smell of aviation fuel. Somewhere in the distance, he could hear Greek music being played on a radio. By the time the sun began to set, he was seriously worried. He remembered that Matiás hadn't wanted to bring him in the first place. Perhaps Nightshade had decided they could do without him after all.

At last he had been put in a second cart and taken round the village and on to a great white temple that pretended it had come from ancient Greece but actually reminded him of Las Vegas. He had been led through the sliding doors – noticing the fingerprint scanner – and brought into a waiting room where he had spent another hour.

And now, finally, the door opened and the guard was pushing him into the next chamber. As he was led to an empty chair, Alex took in the great slab of wood that made up the conference table and the four people sitting there with their little cups of green tea and their strange robes. A fat man, a woman with too much make-up, Mrs White Hair and an undertaker.

Definitely a creepy quartet.

Just looking at them somehow made his skin crawl but at the same time, he had to hold back a sense of excitement. He had done it! He had made it to the very heart of Nightshade and if he could get the information back to MI6, he would have succeeded against all the odds. There were just a few problems. He knew nothing. He had no exact idea where he was. He hadn't seen Freddy Grey for several hours. Nor had he met any of the other "Numbers" if that was what they wanted to be called. Once again, he was a prisoner and if there was any way of getting a message out of this place, he hadn't yet seen it.

The bald man was the first to speak. "Julius Grief," he said. "I am Brother Lamar. This is Sister Krysten, Sister Jeanne and Brother Mike. We are known as the Teachers and we want to welcome you to Nightshade."

Alex held up his wrists, showing the metal cuffs

and the chain between them. "These don't make me feel very welcome," he said.

"Yes. We like to play things safe around here."

"And where is here, out of interest?" Alex sniffed. "Smells a bit like Greece to me."

The Teachers exchanged a look. He had impressed them.

"It seems you should be thanking me, not locking me up," Alex continued. He tried to sound as if he meant business. "If it wasn't for me, Number Nine would still be in Gibraltar."

"We know that and we're grateful to you," Sister Krysten said. She poured herself some more tea, although she didn't offer him any. "Why don't you tell us what you want from us, Julius? Do you want to stay here – or maybe there's some place you'd rather go?"

Alex felt all the eyes on him, examining him minutely. He shrugged. "I don't have anywhere else to go," he said. "My father is dead. You probably know that. MI6 killed him. I don't have any friends ... except for Number Nine. He and I got along OK. I'd like to stay here. Maybe I can even be useful to you."

"How do you think you can be useful to us?" Sister Jeanne asked. She sounded reasonable enough but there was an edge to her voice that was razor-sharp.

Alex knew he was walking on the thinnest of ice. He had to persuade these people that he was a vicious criminal who might be worth keeping on.

If he annoyed them or if they decided he was useless to them, they would get rid of him without a second thought. "Number Nine told me he killed people for you," he explained. "I can do that. He said I could be Number Twenty-Six. Why not? What do you pay? I've got nothing else to do."

The four Teachers leaned towards each other and whispered a few words. Then they turned back to Alex.

"It's possible we might let you stay here, but you would have to obey our rules," Brother Lamar said. "You would have no further contact with the outside world; not with friends or family."

"I don't have friends or family."

"You would have to pray with us. How do we know we can trust you?"

"Because I'm not a fool," Alex said. "You've got some kind of religion thing going here. I can live with that. Right now the whole world is searching for me and I've got nowhere else to go. You look after me and I'll play along with whatever you say. I reckon we could get on fine."

There was another quick consultation.

Brother Lamar nodded. "Your job will be to support Number Nine and to help him with his work," he said. "He's getting himself ready for a mission of great importance. But let's get one thing straight, Julius. You can't ask him any questions. You can't leave this place. You must say nothing to the other kids about the outside world. They're not interested anyway. They don't read the newspapers. We don't have TV."

"Sounds like a lot of laughs," Alex growled.

"He's not taking it seriously!" Brother Mike hissed. "Let me shoot him now. We don't need him!"

"Relax!" Alex turned to the African American with the glasses and the funeral-parlour face. "I don't know what you people want," he said. "But whatever it is, I want to be part of it. I want to be part of Nightshade."

"Shall we vote?" Sister Krysten asked.

She raised her hand. Two more hands followed. Finally, slowly, Brother Mike agreed. The decision had been made.

Sister Krysten got up and walked round to Alex. She had produced a key and unlocked the cuffs. Alex felt his hands fall free and gratefully rubbed his wrists.

"We'll be watching you," Brother Lamar warned him. "Every minute, every day. You don't let us down, maybe things will work out OK. You think you can handle that? Just remember – you're part of Nightshade. From this moment on, you do everything our way."

"Fine. Sure. So where do we start?"

"We must introduce you to the family. We'll do that now." Brother Lamar got to his feet and smiled. "In our church."

VOICES

Unlike the Temple, the village church was genuinely old … it had been built at least two hundred years ago. Once, it would have been used by the soldiers stationed at Kavos Bay and it was in the Greek style: pure white with a blue dome, small, arched windows and thick walls to keep out the heat. Even so, Alex noticed that it had been adapted for the special demands of Nightshade. The cross on top of the dome had been removed and the bell tower that soared up behind was also bare. Once, the walls inside would have been covered in richly coloured images: God, the Virgin Mary, various saints. But they had all been painted over. The pews and the pulpit were still there but there was no obvious altar – just a table covered in a white cloth in front of a circular window and five chairs, four of them occupied by the Teachers, who were sitting down, facing the congregation.

Organ music was playing through hidden speakers as Alex walked forward. What was left of the evening sunlight was slanting in through the windows – if there had ever been any stained glass, that had gone too – but there were candles, flickering in glass jars, arranged on every surface. The congregation had already arrived and Alex saw them turn to examine him as he came in. Here, then, were the twenty-five children who had been recruited by Nightshade! No. There were only twenty-three of them. Alex had made the headcount quickly. Two were missing. He wondered what had happened to them. Perhaps they were away, on another mission.

The children who were here varied in age from about twelve to sixteen or seventeen. Was Sofia here? Was William? Alex searched for them but it was hard to make them out in the fading light and the children were all identically dressed in grey trousers, dark blue jackets, mauve shirts. Shades of night. He could tell at a glance that they had been assembled from many different parts of the world: Asia, the Middle East, Scandinavia, South America. Their faces were neither friendly nor unfriendly. They were simply curious. Two of the youngest were sitting together, a fair-haired girl with freckles and, next to her, a black girl with pigtails. They whispered to each other as he went past. Only Number Nine, sitting at the front, turned round and gave him the smallest nod of recognition. It was hard for Alex to think of him as Freddy Grey. In his uniform, surrounded by the other members of Nightshade, he had lost what little identity he'd ever had.

Sister Krysten had got to her feet. She called out to Alex. "Welcome, Julius Grief!"

"Welcome, Julius Grief!" the rest of the congregation echoed the three words. It was impossible to say if they meant what they were saying or not. They had been trained not to give anything away.

Sister Krysten gestured to the fifth chair. Feeling very self-conscious and unsure how to behave, Alex sat down so that he was now facing everyone else.

"Julius will be joining us for the next few weeks and maybe longer," Sister Krysten explained, her deep voice ringing out through the church. "It is thanks to him that Number Nine has come back to us and we are truly thankful. He has not yet earned the right to become a Number, like you. You must all call him Julius. But maybe one day, if he proves himself worthy, he'll join us and he will be Number Twenty-Six."

This announcement was greeted with silence.

"Julius is an Outsider," she went on. "He has come here by accident and we cannot think of him as a Follower. So although he will work with us, train with us, live with us, sleep with us, he is not yet one of us and you must all remember that. Do not ask him about the world he has come from and do not tell him anything of ours. If he asks questions – and although I have great faith in him, he may still become curious – direct him to the Teachers. That is why we are here. To educate, to inform and to support you in your work."

She smiled.

"Shall we sing our daily hymn?"

The Teachers and the congregation rose and not wanting to be the odd one out, Alex did the same. The organ music changed and the entire assembly joined in together.

Our lives do not belong to us.
You speak and we rejoice.
You never will do wrong to us.
We live to hear your voice.

We do what you have taught us.
We know we have no choice.
We are your sons and daughters
And live to hear your voice.

It was just so weird. Alex had never heard the tune before. It sounded like a hymn but the words made his skin crawl. To be religious was one thing but to have no choice, to do everything you were told ... what sort of religion was that? And there was something else. Everyone in the assembly was singing as if they really meant it. Nobody was yawning or fidgeting or daydreaming, which is what would have happened at Brookland. Alex remembered Freddy praying before he went to sleep every night. There was no doubt that these kids believed what they were singing. It seemed clear it was everything for them.

The hymn finished. Sister Krysten sat down and Brother Lamar took her place.

NIGHTSHADE

"OK," he said. "We have a busy week, as you all know. These are the last few days before Leap of Faith. We all have to remember that what we're planning in London is going to make the whole world a better place. We're relying on you, as we always do. So work hard. Fight hard. Be your best. I want you to show our new friend, Julius, what you're capable of."

He raised a hand and everyone stood up.

"Oh Great Master, Creator of the universe," he intoned. "We thank you for bringing us together and watching over us. We will be with you for ever and all eternity."

"For ever and all eternity," the congregation muttered.

And that was it. The service – if that was what it had been – was over and everyone stood up and left quietly together. Alex noticed that Freddy was holding back, waiting, and went over to him.

"I'm so glad you're being allowed to stay here," Freddy said. "I thought the Teachers were going to ask me to kill you, which would have been a shame."

"I wouldn't have been too happy about it either," Alex said.

"Do you want supper?"

Alex hadn't eaten since he'd flown out of Tangier. "I'm starving," he said.

"Come with me."

As they left the church, Alex noticed two grave-stones standing next to each other, surrounded by rough grass and gravel. He hadn't seen them as he went in but now he read the inscriptions. Whoever had been buried here had no names. They were just numbers: Fourteen and Twenty-One. So that was why he had only been able to count up to twenty-three in the church.

"What happened?" he asked.

"Oh. They died." To Freddy the answer was obvious.

"How?"

"It was an accident. In training." He didn't seem at all put out. Two young people had been killed but to Freddy it meant nothing.

They walked into the village and came to the taverna which was on one side of the main square with a dozen tables laid outside beneath a sprawl of purple flowers and dark green leaves which formed a roof over them. The sun was below the horizon by now and someone had turned on fairy lights, which glowed in the twilight. Alex could smell roast lamb and garlic wafting out of the kitchen. His uncle, Ian Rider, had taken him on a tour of the Greek islands when he was nine years old and he couldn't help being reminded of it. It was as if nothing had changed. Except, of course, that he was now working for MI6, he was using a false name, his new best friend was a psychotic killer and he had less than a week to stop London from being destroyed.

Freddy showed him to a table that was already half-full. "This is Number Six," he said. "And these are Number Seven, Eleven and Twenty-Two..."

"Nice to meet you, Julius." It was Number Eleven who had spoken, a fair-haired boy the same age and build as Alex.

All of them were smiling, friendly – and yet there was something unworldly about them, as if they had been told what to say and were only rehearsing the lines.

Almost at once the food arrived. Every table had one young person designated to serve. Looking into the taverna, Alex noticed an old man, dressed in black with a white apron: the chef. The food was delicious and there was plenty of it. Greek *mezes* including aubergine, fried cheese, grilled mushrooms and smoked pork followed by steaming chunks of lamb served with roast potatoes and the wild green leaf known as xorta, boiled with olive oil and lemon.

Already, Alex was working out a few things about Kavos Bay.

The children – or Numbers or whatever they wanted to call themselves – were not prisoners. They seemed quite happy to be here, chatting and laughing over their meal as if there was nothing unusual about the situation. The guards weren't here to watch over them or to stop them leaving. They weren't even called guards. To the children they were Primes and there was also another level of staff – technicians and scientists – who were known as Cardinals. Prime numbers, cardinal numbers ... it made some sort of sense.

There might be a fence running around the compound but its job was to stop people coming in, not to stop anyone leaving. Nobody wanted to leave. That was the truth of it. They had been brought here from many countries but this was now their world. They did not think of themselves as prisoners.

So what was it that made them so weird? Perhaps it was the uniforms, which seemed out of place in this forgotten corner of Greece. But it was more the Numbers themselves. They were all in perfect health, completely fit, not a gram overweight. They were somehow too neat. And the fact that they were so comfortable with each other was odd too. They didn't seem to exist as twenty-three individuals: they were one unit, a cult. If Alex asked for an opinion, he felt sure that every single one of them would agree. He listened to them talking now. There were no arguments, no raised voices. It was as if they had a single mind.

Alex was hungry and, despite everything, he ate heartily, while listening to the conversation around him. That was another thing: everyone spoke perfect English. They weren't supposed to ask about the world outside, but they all wanted to hear about Freddy's captivity. As he talked about his time in Gibraltar, it became clear to Alex that Freddy had never visited the peninsula before – and that he had only seen the slopes of the Rock and the town once he had escaped from the prison. So how had he known which paths to take? How had he found the abandoned cinema? Alex couldn't work it out.

There was a girl next to Freddy and Alex was quite

sure that she had chosen her place at the table deliberately, that she wanted to be close to him. When he was describing how he had flown over the wall, crashing through the trees, she reached out and took hold of his arm. When she saw his plate was empty, she offered him more to eat. Were they more than friends? He was certainly getting that impression.

He looked at her more closely – and quite suddenly he realized that he knew her. He couldn't believe that she had been sitting at the same table throughout the meal, that she had been introduced to him and that he hadn't recognized her immediately. Perhaps he had been too hungry to think straight. But of course he knew who she was. The black hair, the dark intelligence in her eyes, the shape of her neck ... she was the spitting image of her mother. He would have known who she was even if he hadn't been shown her photograph.

Number Six was Sofia Jones. Mrs Jones's missing daughter.

He realized that he also knew the boy sitting on her other side. He had barely spoken, seemingly deep in thought, but he had the same dark hair as her and the same shaped mouth. And then there was his number. She was Six. He was Seven. Just one apart. It couldn't be a coincidence. Alex tried to visualize the framed photograph he had once seen in Mrs Jones's flat: the two children together.

Yes. He was sure of it.

The boy was William Jones, Sofia's brother.

He had found them!

"What's the matter?" Number Seven asked. He had noticed Alex staring at him and there was a coldness in his voice.

"Nothing." Alex sounded innocent.

"You were looking at me."

"I was just wondering if the two of you were related." He pointed at Sofia. "You look very similar."

He had been probing for information. Were they brother and sister? Did they even know if they were? But he had made a mistake. Number Seven had been suspicious before but now he was positively hostile. "What are you doing here?" he demanded. Before Alex could answer, he went on: "We've never had any Outsiders before. But suddenly you're sitting here, asking questions about us and we don't know anything about you."

"He's OK," Freddy cut in. "Julius looked after me. He's my friend."

"That's easy enough for you to say, Nine. But you were stupid enough to get caught when you were in Rio. Maybe you're being stupid trusting him."

"That's enough!" Sofia cut in. "I was with him in Rio and I saw what happened. It wasn't his fault. The Teachers have told us that Julius is welcome. Are you arguing with them?"

William lowered his eyes. "No," he muttered.

"They'll punish you if they hear what you said."

"I shall pray for forgiveness." William was still looking down. His voice was low.

Sofia turned to Alex. "It's difficult for us. We don't ever see new people. But I'll answer your question. Seven and I are related. We all are. We're one family. We live with each other and we'd die for each other. That's all you need to know."

"Thank you," Alex said.

At least he had learned something. If Number Six had been in Rio, then she was, definitely, who he thought she was. And yet she had no memory of her mother. She had no knowledge of her brother.

How could that be? What had they done to her?

At half past eight, the bell in the church tower sounded once and immediately everyone stopped talking, got to their feet and carried their empty plates and glasses through to the kitchen. Freddy put an arm over Alex's shoulder. "I'll show you where you're sleeping," he said.

The boys' dormitory was behind the church, a long barrack-like building with fourteen single beds facing each other in two lines of seven. The beds were all the same with a metal frame, one pillow and a thin blanket. They were each separated by a low table on one side and a cupboard on the other. There was a bathroom at the far end with half a dozen showers, toilet cubicles and sinks. The windows were covered in mosquito netting and three large fans turned slowly overhead.

Freddy showed Alex to a bed next to the entrance. "You can have this one," he said. "It's where Number Twenty-One used to sleep."

Alex remembered the number that he had seen on the gravestone. "He's the one who died," he said.

"Yes." Freddy still sounded completely matter-of-fact.

"I'm sorry." Alex looked down at the empty bed, trying not to imagine the boy who had once occupied it.

"Don't be sorry. Our lives don't belong to us so we can't complain if they're taken away."

Those were the words that Alex remembered when, half an hour later, the lights blinked out and he found himself lying in the darkness, surrounded by thirteen other boys who seemed to have fallen asleep at once. He found it less easy. So much had happened in one day – beginning with a flight that had brought him ... where? He still had no clear idea where he was. And then there had been the Teachers, the church, the other children, William and Sofia.

It must have been almost midnight when he heard it. There was a voice – several voices – coming from somewhere close by. At first, he thought he was asleep and dreaming but he knew that he hadn't yet closed his eyes. Was he imagining it? The voices were in the air, all around him and yet at the same time far away. He wasn't sure what language they were speaking in. He couldn't make out what they were saying but he thought he heard his own name – Julius – whispered in his ear. Nobody else in the room was moving. He alone was awake.

Alex remembered the hymn that everyone had sung in the church. *"We live to hear your voice."* He turned over and pulled the pillow over his head. It didn't help. The voices stayed with him, following him into a troubled sleep.

HAND TO HAND

Alex had never been anywhere quite like Kavos Bay.

He thought of the Point Blanc Academy in the French Alps – the school where Dr Grief had been looking after some of the richest children in the world and where Alex had himself spent a week, pretending to be the son of a supermarket billionaire. But that had been different. It only had six students – and they most definitely hadn't wanted to be there. Lessons had included classical music and poetry but, as Alex had discovered, it wasn't really a school at all.

And then there was Malagosto, the island just across the lagoon from Venice, used by Scorpia to train its agents. Here Alex had been given classes in poison, unarmed combat and the techniques used by the Ninja warriors of Japan. The difference was that Alex had been the only teenager there, training alongside soldiers, mercenaries and secret agents. They were people who would kill for a living. It was the profession they had chosen. It wasn't their entire life.

The young people who had been recruited by Nightshade knew almost nothing outside Kavos Bay – just as Brother Lamar had told him. They didn't read the news. They didn't watch football, listen to music or play computer games. They didn't choose the clothes they wore or the food they ate. They didn't tell jokes. They never disobeyed an order. Alex was quite sure that if they'd been told to jump off a cliff or put their hand in a fire, they wouldn't have thought twice. It wasn't surprising that they knew each other as numbers because that was what they had become.

How had it been done? Left to himself, Alex had been able to put together the information that Mrs Jones and Dr Flint had told him along with what he had seen.

They had stolen children from their parents when they were four or five years old. That was true of Sofia and William Jones, who had somehow been spirited away from their Russian father to become Number Six and Number Seven. It was also true of Freddy Grey, Number Nine, who had supposedly died in a boat accident in Devonshire. It was interesting that Freddy's father had been a senior officer in the British army. Sofia and William's mother had been a spy. Alex was willing to bet that Nightshade had deliberately targeted the children of parents who were physically active; involved in army, intelligence ... even crime. It meant that the children would have the right genes. They were ready to be reshaped.

From the moment they had been torn away from their old lives, they had been brainwashed. Dr Flint had been right. The fake religion was a large part of it. He remembered the lines from the hymn. *"We do what you have taught us. We know we have no choice."* Alex had read about cults in America and other parts of the world and he knew there were extremists in all religions who twisted everything that was good and turned their disciples against the rest of society. That was what had happened here. Freddy Grey had been sent to Rio to kill a man he had never met and he had done it because his "Teachers" had said the man was "evil". It was as simple as that. Nobody at Kavos Bay questioned anything they were told. Why should they when they had been told the same thing for their whole life?

The voices in the dormitory had to be part of it. The morning after he had first heard them, Alex had carefully searched for the speakers that he knew must be hidden in the walls or the floor. He found nothing. Next, he examined the beds themselves, wondering if there might be wires and microphones concealed in the metal frames. Once again he drew a blank. In the end, he wondered if he had simply imagined the whispers in the darkness. Perhaps he had fallen asleep and they had been part of some weird dream. He listened out for them but he didn't hear them again.

Alex was in an impossible situation. He was surrounded by people who would kill him if they knew who he really was but he couldn't think of them as his enemies. There was a part of him that actually liked Freddy and felt sorry for him. He remembered the moment when he had produced the stuffed monkey and had seen, just for a second, the child that Freddy must once have been. As a direct result of that, Freddy had saved his life during the film screening and he had remained close to Alex from the moment they had landed. It was Freddy who, over breakfast, had mentioned Vai, which was the part of Crete where they were – he must have over-heard the name from one of the Primes, although he would have been unable to point to it on a map. Even so, he had given away too much information and William Jones had given him an angry look. Freddy didn't care. As far as he was concerned, Alex was already part of the family.

William had been hostile to Alex from the start and nothing had changed. He was still suspicious. He was almost daring Alex to take him on in a fight – but Alex had no intention of doing that. He wished there was some way he could get through to William, to tell him who he really was. He wondered if he could start with Sofia. She certainly seemed more relaxed than her brother. In fact, he wanted to do the same for all the Numbers. But he knew it was impossible. He couldn't alter what had been done to them. His job was to get out of here and to call in MI6.

And he had to do it before London was attacked.

Another day had passed since he had arrived and

Alex had tried to join in the lessons and the various activities as if he actually wanted to be there and was unaware of the terrible danger drawing closer by the minute. He had to admit that the twenty-three students had been trained to a standard that left him far behind. In the morning, there were language lessons: French, Russian, Greek, Mandarin. They spoke each one of them fluently. From the classroom they went to the assault course, the gym or the shooting range. Alex watched them working out with revolvers, rifles, knives … a dozen different weapons. They were also experts in hand-to-hand combat. In Rio de Janeiro, Freddy Grey had shown himself to be, quite simply, lethal. This was where he had learned his skills.

Brother Mike was in charge of the physical training, watching the students with unforgiving eyes. On the first day, he had put them through the assault course, timing them as they hauled themselves over immense walls, crawled through the narrowest of pipes and dragged themselves under nets, all in the full heat of the midday sun. He had quietly whispered to the girl who came last and although Alex couldn't hear what he said, he watched her burst into tears. It had only taken her six minutes to complete the course. Alex came in thirty seconds later and Brother Mike had gazed at him with contempt.

The white-haired woman, Sister Krysten, headed most of the classroom sessions, including languages, maths and science. It was hard to be sure but Alex suspected that everyone at Kavos Bay was already well past A-level standard in every subject they studied. It didn't stop there. A small hospital stood on the northern edge of the village and the children had been given enough medical training to be able to perform minor operations on each other; stitching up wounds that might have been made by gunshots or knives.

Finally, there were the special programmes. Before Freddy and Sofia had been sent to Rio, they had spent hours learning how to fly radio-controlled planes until they could manoeuvre them through a gap that was centimetres wide. Nothing had been left to chance. Now Freddy and William, along with five other children, were being put through a parachute course. It was the only clue Alex had as to what was being planned for London. Whatever the target, they were going to reach it by air.

What most struck Alex was that everyone seemed to be enjoying what they were doing. Nobody ever complained. Nor were they ever afraid. Their lives didn't belong to them, so what did it matter if they lost them? He thought of the two gravestones outside the church and his blood ran cold.

He was also becoming increasingly nervous. As far as he could see, there was no way he was going to be able to slip out of the compound. It wasn't just a question of getting through the fence or past the guards. Everyone was watching him all the time. He was hardly ever alone. He never saw anyone using a mobile phone. He had come to the conclusion that if he wanted to get a message out, he would have to find a way into the Temple. The massive satellite dishes on the roof suggested there had to be some very sophisticated communications equipment somewhere inside. It was also where the Teachers had their offices. If Alex wanted to know what they were planning, this was where he had to begin.

But the doors were controlled by an electronic fingerprint scanner and only the four Teachers and one or two of the guards had access. The windows were sealed into the walls and didn't even open a crack. There was no way up onto the roof. Even if Alex managed to separate himself from the rest of the group, he would never find a way in. There were no deliveries, no boxes he could hide in. Somehow he had to trick the fingerprint scanner. He remembered the duplicate key that Julius Grief had made for himself in Gibraltar. Slowly a thought began to form in his mind. Perhaps he could do something similar here.

He started with the kitchen. That was the easy part. Nobody noticed when he picked up a sachet of white sugar and slipped it into his pocket. And then, that same day, there was a lesson in the hospital – a demonstration by one of the Cardinals who had trained as a doctor. He had shown the students how to close a wound with a red-hot knife. Much to Freddy's amusement, Alex had pretended he felt faint. He had used the moment to steal what he needed from a hospital bin.

Now he was waiting for the right moment to put his plan into operation. Curiously, it was William Jones who finally gave it to him.

Alex had always known that trouble would catch up with him. When he had been presented to the Teachers, Brother Mike could hardly have expressed himself more clearly. And William had never forgotten his argument with Alex on that first evening at Mistral – nor the fact that Sofia had stuck up for him. The Numbers were forbidden to fight with each other or to take sides – but Alex wasn't yet a Number. He could feel William circling around him, desperate to prove that he was the biggest wolf in the pack, waiting to take him down.

Finally, the time came. It was the second morning and they were all in the gym. Brother Mike was there too, taking them through advanced techniques of karate. This was a martial art that Alex knew well. Ian Rider had started taking him to classes when he was six years old and by the time he was thirteen, he had become a first grade *Dan* with a black belt to show for it. Even so, he knew that he was nowhere near the standard of the Nightshade students. He had learned karate so that he could defend himself. They had learned it in order to kill.

The gymnasium was a large space with a high ceiling, air conditioning and rubber mats spaced evenly across the floor. The students had been divided into pairs for the practice bouts and Alex found himself facing Number Eleven – the fair-haired boy who had sat at the table with him on his first night. Although nobody talked about the mission in London, Alex knew that Number Eleven had been getting extra parachute training and wondered whether he was going to be sent as part of the team for Operation Leap of Faith.

For the next thirty minutes, Alex went through a series of defensive moves – blocks and counter-attacks – trying to prevent Number Eleven causing him too much harm. Number Eleven wasn't holding back and if any of his blows had landed, Alex knew he would have been badly injured. Looking around him, he saw several of the fighters go down, knocked off their feet or doubling up in pain. Meanwhile, Brother Mike walked between the mats, nodding his head and occasionally offering advice. It didn't matter how hard they'd been hit. Alex saw one girl sitting with blood pouring from her nose but Brother Mike didn't even glance her way. He didn't care. Nobody was allowed to stop.

At last the session drew to a close. Standing there, panting in his *keikogi* – the white, loose-fitting prac-tice uniform he had been given – Alex knew he had been lucky. Number Eleven was faster and stronger than he was but, for some reason, had decided to go easy on him.

Perhaps Brother Mike had noticed this.

"I want to finish the class with a *kumite*," he said. It was a karate term meaning "grappling hands", a contest between two fighters. "Why don't we ask our new recruit to show us what he can do?"

Alex had been sitting cross-legged, like everyone else. Now he jumped up quickly as if he was excited by the idea of a demonstration bout, although inside, his stomach was shrinking. It was obvious that Brother Mike was hoping he would get hurt. And the fact was, he had to be hurt if his plan was going to work.

"Who is going to take on Julius?" Brother Mike asked.

"I will!"

Number Seven, William Jones, had raised his hand and the Teacher nodded, pleased, like this was what he had been hoping for. Suddenly Alex found himself face to face with the other boy and again he had to fight back a sense of disbelief. Mrs Jones had sent him here to find her son. He had done that. And now the son could be about to kill him ... because they both knew that no one was going to complain if he went down with a broken neck. Even so, Alex was glad things had worked out this way. He had prepared for exactly this opportunity. Quietly, he slipped his hand into his trouser pocket while William moved into position opposite him.

The two boys looked each other in the eyes. William was sixteen – a year older than Alex. He was very muscular, with solid shoulders and a thick neck. Examining him, Alex noticed – for the first time – that he had a scar just like Freddy, under his ear. What was that about? Had all the Numbers been hurt in some way? Was that part of their training?

Alex put the thought to one side. All that mattered for the next few minutes was to survive.

"Hajime!" Brother Mike rapped out the single word which was the call to begin.

William launched himself without hesitation and in the next few seconds, Alex had to defend himself against a flurry of kicks and punches, any one of which could have crippled him. It was as if, after ten years with Nightshade, some inner fury had been released and William was blaming Alex for everything that had been done to him. Alex wondered if he had unlocked something deep in Number Seven's memory when he had suggested he was Sofia's brother. As a result, William was being torn apart inside and this was his way of dealing with it. He was utterly cold, ruthless. This was no longer an exercise. It was sheer murder.

Alex used every technique he knew to keep William at bay, twisting from side to side and countering every strike. Out of the corner of his eye, he saw Sofia watching him. She could see what was happening and she was worried. As always, Freddy had taken his place on the mat right next to her and he was puzzled too. Nobody in the gym was making any sound, aware that they were watching a fight to the death. Only Brother Mike padded round, barefooted, the electric lights reflecting in his circular glasses and a faint smile on his lips.

William grunted and launched a roundhouse punch that Alex actually felt as it lashed past his face. It left the other boy exposed. Alex could have countered with a knife-hand into the throat which would have finished it there and then. But that wasn't part of his plan. As much as he wanted the fight to be over, he could still use it. He just had to survive a few more moments and then time things so that, hopefully, it would all work out the way he wanted.

The moment came. William had tried a front jab which Alex had blocked and suddenly they were locked together, shoulder touching shoulder, their heads inches apart. Glancing down, Alex saw William's left fist piling towards him. It would be easy enough to twist sideways but Alex did nothing. They were still very close. William didn't have the momentum to hurt him too much. Gritting his teeth, Alex let the fist land then gasped out in pain and collapsed, pitching forward onto the floor. To everyone watching, it seemed as if he had been badly hurt and it was true that he would have a bruise to show for it the next day. But in fact he had ridden the blow and even as he hit the floor he knew that no serious damage had been done. Now it was just a matter of pretending. With William standing over him, he writhed on the mat, holding his side as if several of his ribs had been broken.

"*Yame!*" Brother Mike had no choice but to call out the instruction meaning that the fight was over, at the same time signalling with a raised hand.

Only William knew that something was wrong, that Alex was faking his injury. He hadn't hit him that hard, certainly not enough to send him sprawling. Even so, he stepped back obediently while the Teacher stood between them.

"You did well, Number Seven," he began. "A good display of *kizami-zuki* in the opening encounter and some fast footwork." He glanced down at Alex who was still groaning on the mat. "This boy was clumsy and over-confident. He deserved to be hurt more."

The words were a dismissal. The other children got up and began to leave the gym. Alex rolled onto his side and reached up, grabbing hold of Brother Mike's hand. The Teacher was taken by surprise and reluctantly pulled him to his feet.

"Thank you," Alex said.

"Take a shower," Brother Mike replied. "You are dirty and you smell." Wiping his hand on the side of his trousers, he walked away.

Alex watched him go. He was still short of breath. The flesh on the side of his stomach was smarting. But he had got what he wanted.

It was a latex glove. That was what he had taken from the hospital. He had prepared it long before the fight began, sitting on his own in the dormitory. First he had torn open the sachet of sugar and mixed it with water. Then he had coated the outside of the glove to make it sticky. He had finished the process by drying it in the sun.

He had been waiting for a chance to shake hands with any one of the Teachers and when the fight had been announced, he had known that Brother

Mike was going to be the one. He had been wearing the glove throughout the fight. It was flesh-coloured and practically invisible. Even if someone had noticed it, they would have had no idea what Alex intended to do.

Once he was alone, he peeled it off carefully. The water-sugar solution had dried and, holding the latex glove up to the light, he could see a clear impression of the Teacher's fingerprints, printed on to the back.

He had the key that would open the main door to the Temple.

Now all he had to do was find a time when he was alone.

THE TEMPLE

The martial arts class that morning was followed by two lessons in the classroom – French and then physics.

In fact, Alex spoke fluent French, along with Spanish and German. He could even manage a few sentences in Italian and Japanese. This was all thanks to his uncle, Ian Rider, who had looked after him after his parents had died. What Alex had thought of as holidays had secretly been training sessions. Mountain climbing, map-reading, diving, skiing, judo, karate ... all these activities had been presented to him as entertainments when in fact they had been preparing him for a life he would never have chosen and didn't even want. Alex had dreamed of becoming a footballer, not a spy. But Ian Rider had had other ideas and, although he had himself been killed, it looked as if he had won.

Watching the Numbers translating an article from a French magazine, it occurred to Alex that perhaps he wasn't so very different from them. They had been brainwashed to become killers. Although they didn't see it that way, they'd never had a choice. MI6 might think of themselves as "the good guys". It was true they were protecting the country. But at the end of the day, their methods were hardly any better than Nightshade. They had taken over Alex's life without asking him and it sometimes seemed that he would never escape them.

He had used the French lesson to scour the magazine for anything that might tell him what was happening in London. But Sister Krysten, who was in charge of the lesson, had chosen it carefully. It contained no news at all – just articles about theatre and fashion. Alex remembered what Brother Lamar had told him. Newspapers weren't allowed at Kavos Bay. As far as possible, the Numbers were kept insulated from the outside world.

Physics was more interesting ... but not in a good way. At Brookland, Alex might have been learning about atomic structure or electricity. At Kavos Bay, the lesson focused on IEDs – improvised explosive devices: how to make them, where to place them and what sort of blast waves to expect. This lesson was led by Brother Lamar, using photographs taken in Syria and Iraq. As he discussed the horrific injuries caused by the roadside weapons, Alex felt sick. All he wanted to do was to break out of here, to get back to London, to put an end to this nightmare.

The Numbers showed no emotion at all. They listened carefully and took notes. Some of them asked questions. There were no bells at Kavos Bay. When the clock showed one o'clock, they closed their books, got up quietly and went for lunch.

As a reward for their hard work, the Teachers had decided that the students could have lunch on the beach. Packets with *tiropita* – Greek cheese pies – fruit and salad had been prepared along with bottles of water, and together they all made their way through the olive grove and down the twisting, rocky path that cut its way through the hillside. A beach and the brilliant blue water of the Aegean were waiting for them less than a mile away but as he walked with the others, Alex was gripping the side of his stomach where William had struck him.

"What's wrong?" Sofia, William's sister, had been walking beside him and she had noticed him stop.

"Nothing." Alex gritted his teeth. "I'm just bruised where your brother hit me."

"He's not my brother!"

"You said you were all family." Alex knew exactly what he was doing. If he had managed to win over Freddy with a memory from his childhood, maybe he could do the same with Sofia. "That means you're all brothers and sisters," he added.

"I suppose so." Sofia looked doubtful but that was good. None of these kids ever doubted anything.

He decided to press a little further. "Do you really have no memory of your parents?" he asked.

Sofia stiffened. "My parents didn't want me," she said. "They put me in a boat and sent me away." It was exactly the same answer that Alex had heard from Freddy in Gibraltar.

"How do you know that?"

"The Teachers told me."

"But how did the Teachers know?"

Sofia was becoming more and more uncomfortable. "They know everything," she replied, shortly. "And you shouldn't be saying these things, Julius. You'll get into trouble."

"They can't hear us." Alex looked around him. The gorge had opened up with a wide shingle beach in front of them. But there were no buildings in sight and nobody was close to them just then. "We're on our own," he added.

"No." She shook her head. "They hear everything."

Sofia quickened her pace to join the others but Alex stayed where he was, cupping his hand against his ribs. After a few steps, Sofia turned round. "Aren't you coming?" she asked.

"I'm not feeling well," Alex replied. "I'm going back to bed."

"Do you want me to come with you?" Sofia looked worried. Despite everything, and unlike her brother, she seemed to like him.

"No. I'll be OK."

"You should talk to Sister Jeanne. She looks after us when we're hurt."

"Although sometimes we have to operate on each other," Freddy added. He had just caught up with them and casually took hold of Sofia's hand.

"Nice of you to offer but I think I'll pass on that one, Number Nine, thanks all the same." Alex handed over his paper bag. "Here, you can have my lunch."

"I don't want it."

"Then give it to the fish. I'm sure they love *tiropita*."

Alex turned round and walked back the way he had come, still clutching his side as if he was in pain. It was only when he turned the corner and knew that he was out of sight that he straightened up and began to move more quickly. There was something else he had learned about Nightshade and he knew it would work to his advantage. The Primes were lazy. No strangers ever came to Kavos Bay and none of the Numbers wanted to leave, so although the Primes carried rifles and might look dangerous, most of the time they were actually half asleep. As he came out of the olive trees and skirted round the side of the assault course, he was confident that he hadn't been seen.

The Temple lay ahead of him. He paused briefly, taking in the satellite dishes, craning their necks up into the empty sky, the blacked-out windows, the electronic sliding doors and those golden letters: FOR EVER AND ALL ETERNITY. If he could get his hands on a radio transmitter or a computer that didn't need a password, he could send out a Mayday signal that would bring every intelligence agency in the world to Greece and it would be all over for Nightshade. For ever indeed. But first he had to get in.

An electric buggy whirred past with no driver and

no passengers either. Alex ran forward and jumped in, crouching in the back. It would take him all the way to the entrance and if there did happen to be anyone watching, he wouldn't be seen. As he travelled, he drew the latex glove out of his pocket, carefully unfolded it, then put it on. Brother Mike's fingerprints were still imprinted in the sugar solution that covered the surface.

He just hoped it would work. Vaguely, he remembered that when Apple had launched one of their most recent iPhones, there had been security issues with the fingerprint sensor. Tom Harris had once shown him a YouTube film that proved it was possible to make a fingerprint key using Play-Doh and dentist's paste. That was what had given him the idea. The buggy slowed down and stopped, presumably controlled by some sort of signal coming from the roof. Alex jumped out, quickly making his way up the front steps between the columns. It was always possible that someone might glance out of a window. If anyone asked him what he was doing, he would use his injury as an excuse.

A bead of sweat trickled down the side of his face. It was intensely hot in the afternoon sun. Thousands of cicadas were sawing all around him as if they knew what he was planning and wanted to warn the Teachers. He went over to the stone block with the fingerprint scanner. There was nobody around. He reached out with the latex glove and touched the glass screen.

There was a hiss and the front door slid open. Alex looked inside. The entrance hall – with its marble floor and bare concrete walls – was empty. He slipped through the door, which immediately closed behind him.

For a moment he stood quite still, listening out for any movement. Because of the triple-height ceilings and lack of carpets, any sound would travel very easily but, apart from the faint hum of the air conditioning, everything was silent. He knew that the conference room where he had met the Teachers was over to the right. Ahead of him he saw a passageway and a flight of metal stairs, leading up to the next floor. Where was he most likely to find the offices and communications rooms?

He decided to start at the top, then work his way back down. First, he peeled off the glove and put it in his pocket – there was always a chance he would need it again – then crept up the stairs, his rubber-soled trainers making no sound. The upper floor of the Temple was very different from what he had seen so far. It was much more modern, white, with lower ceilings and strip lighting. If the ground floor had been designed to impress, this area was more serious and workmanlike. It reminded him of a hospital or perhaps a hi-tech office. Once again, Nightshade had shown that they weren't careful enough when it came to security. The entrance of the building had been locked and none of the Numbers would have dreamed of coming here. So they hadn't installed

CCTV cameras. There was nobody standing guard.

Alex made his way along a corridor with doors on either side. The first opened into a kitchen and dining room. The second was locked. But the third was more interesting. Turning the handle, Alex found himself looking into what looked like an operations room with several tables and work surfaces covered with sheets of paper as well as various maps and diagrams pinned to the walls.

Still everything was silent. Alex went inside.

A photograph of London dominated one of the walls. It had been taken with a wide-angle camera and showed the River Thames with the Millennium Bridge stretching across, the Tate Modern on one side, St Paul's on the other. Alex recognized the London Eye, the Houses of Parliament, Waterloo Station. Any one of them could have been Nightshade's target.

There was another series of shots, in black and white, taken inside a building. One showed a very narrow staircase spiralling up between two stone walls. The next showed a metal ladder reaching up towards a half-size door. A third had been taken outside: a curving balustrade the London sky beyond. It was an old building, certainly. And a large one. But what was it?

He came to a newspaper article, torn out of the *Financial Times*. He could tell because the paper was pink, not white. It reported the death of someone called Lord Clifford and showed a photograph of an elderly man wearing a blazer and a hat. The headline read: A NATION GRIEVES. The name – Clifford – was familiar to Alex but he couldn't remember where he'd heard it. And what did the death of an old man (a heart attack, the newspaper said) possibly have to do with Nightshade?

The next wall was given over to a set of diagrams with wavy lines and different shades of colour imposed onto a map with various times and dates underneath. Alex recognized London again. He knew he was looking at weather information: air mass and wind patterns. Nightshade had been keeping a close eye on the London sky and this must tie in with the parachute training.

London was the target and the jump was going to happen there. That must be the plan. But Alex wondered how it could possibly work. If the security services were on full alert, all the air spaces would be closed. No private planes or helicopters would be allowed to fly over the city so a jump would be impossible.

The last photographs showed close shots of the roofs of different buildings. Alex didn't recognize any of them, although one was certainly unusual. It looked half-finished, open to the elements. It was almost as if someone had cut part of it away. He was sure he ought to know what it was and he was annoyed that he couldn't name it.

That was what was so frustrating. Alex was certain that if he could make sense of all the evidence around him, he would know exactly what Nightshade were planning. It was happening soon. That much he knew already. But it was as if he was looking at an enormous jigsaw puzzle with no idea of what picture it was supposed to create and he didn't have the time to work it out.

He broke away and hurried over to the nearest computer, sitting on a table. If it was connected to the internet, he could use it to send a message and MI6 would work everything out when they got here. He tapped the mouse and the screen lit up, challenging him for a password. It was hardly surprising but still Alex sighed. The password could be anything. He tried NIGHTSHADE, then LEAPOFFAITH, then BROTHERMIKE but none of them worked and he didn't dare risk entering more words at random in case he set off an alert. How long had he been here? The lunch break was only an hour and soon everyone would be returning for the last three lessons of the afternoon. He had to keep moving.

There was nothing more to be found in the room. Alex checked there was no one around, then continued on his way. The next two rooms were empty offices – no computers, no phones – and turning a corner he came to a set of heavy-duty doors blocking the corridor. There was another fingerprint scanner set in the wall and once again he brought out the latex glove with Brother Mike's fingerprints. He was almost surprised that it worked a second time. He heard a hiss of compressed air as the doors swung inwards. He hurried forward, noticing at once that the air was even cooler in this section and that it was quite possibly purified too. Everything was spotlessly clean. The lights were kept low. There were no windows anywhere.

He came to a wide, rectangular chamber that was thickly carpeted, with three chairs facing a bank of machinery that mainly consisted of switches, dials and microphones and audio mixers, all of them connected to sophisticated computers. It reminded Alex of a recording studio. All that was missing was a space for singers or musicians to perform. He ran his eye along the audio mixers and realized that they were labelled from one to twenty-five, with fourteen and twenty-one missing.

One for every Number at Kavos Bay. Alex thought about the whispering sounds he had heard on the first night in the dormitory. Had they originated here?

He moved on. The walls were now covered in white tiles, the floor with some sort of plastic. A little further along, he arrived at an open door that led into a locker room with benches, showers and toilets. Why would anyone need to change here? He saw the answer immediately. Hanging opposite him, two of them: a pair of orange suits made out of reinforced nylon with bulky hoods fitted with transparent visors and sophisticated air filters. Two pairs of green plastic boots stood on the floor.

They were hazmat suits – short for hazardous materials – also known as decontamination suits.

They were what you would wear if you were handling a deadly nerve agent. VX, for example.

Alex knew he would find a laboratory near by and, sure enough, there it was at the very end. Even if he'd been able to, he wouldn't have dared go in but this time there was no fingerprint scanner. Instead an illuminated sign above a steel door spelled out a series of warnings in red letters:

EXTREME DANGER.
ABSOLUTELY NO ADMISSION
WITHOUT AUTHORIZATION.
PROTECTIVE CLOTHING TO
BE WORN AT ALL TIMES.

Briefly, his hand rested on the metal handle, although he had no intention of going in. The VX was almost certainly on the other side and he didn't want to go anywhere near it. Anyway, there could be any number of technicians – Cardinals – working silently on the other side. Drawing a deep breath, he retraced his steps and went back downstairs.

Part of him was disappointed. He might have located the VX. He had found lots of clues as to how it was going to be used, but no real answers. Worse than that, he hadn't come across a phone or a computer that might have connected him to the outside world. He was running out of time. The agent who had died in Rio had said the attack was going to happen very soon. The Numbers were in the final phases of their training programme. During the church service, Brother Lamar had talked about "the last few days".

What were his options? He could try to escape from the training camp. If he took the path down to the beach at night, he might be able to swim round to Vai. He could try to sabotage Nightshade from within. Perhaps he could persuade Freddy and Sofia that he was on their side and turn them against the Teachers. Using the latex glove, he could get into the Temple any time he liked. He could blow the whole place up.

He had returned to the entrance hall with the glass doors in front of him and was about to head out when he heard voices coming from the conference room. While he had been upstairs, the four Teachers must have arrived and they were meeting together. Alex was desperate to get out, to find safety with the other Numbers, but it was too good an opportunity to miss. Moving silently, he hurried into the anteroom where he had waited on the day of his arrival. The door to the conference room was open. He didn't dare look round in case he was seen but he could hear the conversation quite clearly.

"...The weather conditions are going to be perfect." It was Brother Mike speaking. "We will have the windsock in place at sixteen hundred hours..."

"Not before?" Sister Jeanne asked.

"We don't want to put up anything that will draw

attention to ourselves. I have my doubts that we need it at all. But certainly it's best to leave it until the last minute."

"And who is going to make the jump?" Brother Lamar asked.

"We're very lucky that Number Nine has been returned to us," Brother Mike continued. "No one is more reliable than him. During the summer training sessions he made fourteen jumps in many different atmospheric conditions and didn't miss the target once."

"What about Number Seven?"

"He will go too ... as backup. Number Six will approach the target on the coach. Nobody will look at her twice. She will make her way past the Ornamental Gallery and let the others in."

"What about the evacuation plans?" Sister Krysten asked.

"Exactly as we agreed. We have a police helicopter on standby. There will be a great deal of panic and confusion after the attack and that's when we'll move in. We'll be able to airlift all three of the Numbers to safety."

"Excellent." Brother Lamar seemed to have lit a cigar. Alex heard him puffing away and smelled the smoke wafting through the door. It was interesting that none of the Teachers had smoked when he – or any of the Numbers – were present. "And I have good news," he continued. "I spoke to the Doctor in London this morning. He's paid the final instalment of our fee and it'll show up in our Geneva bank account any time now. Twenty million American dollars! As you guys know, this is our most ambitious operation so far. And this payment only represents a fraction of the money we're going to make. The London stock market will collapse following Leap of Faith. The pound will plunge on the international markets. Because we know what's going to happen, we'll use the information to make ourselves millions more."

"When is the final training session?" Sister Jeanne asked.

"Tomorrow morning. I thought we might put Julius Grief up in the plane. Let's see how he reacts when we tell him to jump from thirteen thousand feet..."

"He may refuse," Sister Krysten said.

"In a way, I hope he does. If the Numbers see he's scared, maybe they'll think a little less of him."

"I hope he accepts!" Brother Mike spat out the last word like a snake. "And if he does, I'll be the one who packs his parachute."

Sister Krysten laughed briefly. "You really don't like him, do you, Mike?"

Not "Brother Mike". That was interesting too. As Alex had suspected from the start, the whole religious thing was just a front. They ignored it when they were on their own.

"I don't trust him," Mike said. "There's something about him that doesn't ring true. I still think it's a mistake having him here."

"Relax!" Brother Lamar muttered. "The only reason

that he's here is because Number Nine likes him and right now we need to keep Number Nine focused on what he's doing. I still think we can use him – but if not, once Leap of Faith is over, we can get rid of him. I'll tell you what, Mike ... you can see to it yourself. Maybe we can get the other kids to hunt him down ... use him as live bait in the woods. Or we could have a public execution. We haven't had one of those for a while."

"Thank you, Lamar. It'll be a pleasure."

Alex was already on his way out.

So the operation in London – Leap of Faith – had been paid for by someone who called himself "the Doctor". It involved a coach, an ornamental gallery (whatever that was) and a parachute jump. Thirdly, it was going to be huge, producing a shock wave that might actually bankrupt the country.

Alex still didn't know what Leap of Faith was. He didn't know when it was going to happen. He had no idea how to stop it. As far as he could see, there was no way of getting any help.

And the only thing that was certain was that when it was all over, he was going to be killed.

"How are you feeling?" Freddy asked him when they met, about twenty minutes later. The other boy was tanned and relaxed, water dripping from his hair.

Somehow, Alex managed to force a smile onto his face. "Couldn't be better." he said. He had never felt worse.

ROGUE OPERATION

"So where is he?" Jack Starbright demanded.

She was sitting in the conference room at Liverpool Street, inside MI6 Special Operations. Mrs Jones and John Crawley were opposite her on the other side of the table. *Them and us*, Jack thought. With a rectangle of polished walnut making sure they didn't get too close. Jack had dressed smartly for the meeting and wished now that she hadn't. The dark jacket and skirt, her red hair tied back with a band, the lack of any jewellery ... it had all been intended to make her look serious but she didn't feel herself. Here she was, sitting politely with the cup of tea that someone had brought her, when what she really wanted to do was get up and scream at these people.

"It's not easy to explain, Ms Starbright," Crawley began.

"Oh please! Call me Jack!" She smiled at them. "After all, we've known each other quite a while now. You tried to get me deported once. Thanks to you, my boss got killed. And the person closest to me in the world has nearly died twenty times." She leaned forward. "Don't mess around with me, Mr Crawley. You said Alex would be away just for a week or ten days at most. But half-term's over and I've heard nothing from you. I don't know where he is. I don't know if he's even dead or alive."

"We're fairly sure he's alive," Mrs Jones said.

"Well, that's terrific!"

"We just don't know where he is."

Jack took a deep breath, trying not to lose her temper. "How is that possible?" she demanded. "You told me he was going to be locked up in some sort of top-secret prison, that he was going to be looked after. All he had to do was make friends with this other kid, get some information, and then you'd send him home." She pointed a finger accusingly. "The only reason he agreed to go was because of that story you told him about losing your own children and now I'm wondering if that was even true."

"Of course it was true!" Mrs Jones snapped and just for once she betrayed her emotions. She was angry. Two dark spots had appeared on her cheeks.

"Well, I'm sorry." Jack backed down. "But you lied to me about Alex. You said he'd be back home and he isn't. And now you don't even know where he is!"

"He escaped," Mrs Jones said. She took out a plastic box of peppermints and span it on the table in front of her. "He and Freddy Grey broke out together. We had no idea that was what they were going to do and the psychiatrist, Dr Flint, didn't tell us until it was too late. For what it's worth, I understand that it was Alex's idea."

"Why?" Jack was shocked. "Why would he do that?"

"Maybe he wanted to help me. Or maybe he thought it was the only way to save London. I don't know." Mrs Jones sighed. "You know Alex better than me, Jack. It's true that when he started working for us, we used him. We often had to force him to do what we wanted. But he was good at what he did. He knew that. And there were plenty of times when he was the one who made the decision. He went after Damian Cray without our knowledge. And Julia Rothman."

"And there was that business with the Grimaldi brothers," Crawley reminded her. "We actually tried to stop him getting involved."

"Do you really have no idea where he is?" Jack faltered.

"After he left Gibraltar, he was taken to Tangier." It was Crawley who provided the answer. "He was helped by a gang called La Máquina. He left Tangier the following day in a private plane which was last seen entering Greek airspace. We're assuming he's in Greece. We believe that was where Freddy Grey came from before his arrest."

"Are you looking for him?"

"Yes. But it's a huge country. And there are over a thousand Greek islands! We're in touch with the National Intelligence Service in Athens but our main hope is that Alex will somehow get a message to us."

"What if he doesn't?"

Jack had asked the question but before Mrs Jones or Crawley could answer, there was a burst of sirens outside the building, followed by the screech of tyres as not one but several cars pulled up.

"What's that?" Mrs Jones demanded.

Crawley was already on his feet, moving to the window. Looking out, he saw that the whole of Liverpool Street had been cut off and that there were a dozen police cars parked below, their lights flashing. Uniformed officers were rushing towards the entrance. More of them were setting up barriers, forcing pedestrians back. Moments later, an alarm went off in the building: not a siren or a bell but a soft, insistent bleeping like a Morse code machine that had got stuck on a single letter.

"John...?" Mrs Jones had stood up. She was shocked.

From outside the door came the sound of footsteps marching down the corridor.

"I don't know..." Crawley turned back from the window.

Mrs Jones looked urgently at Jack. "Whatever happens, say nothing. Don't give your name. Let me handle this."

The door burst open.

Dominic Royce walked in with Owen Andrews at his side. The Permanent Under-Secretary for Foreign Affairs looked furious. He was clutching a sheaf of papers. He was accompanied by four men in suits with dark glasses and radio earpieces, the wires curling under the collars of their shirts. They were MI5 or possibly Special Branch. They had to belong to some department of the police or secret service.

"May I ask what is going on?" Mrs Jones demanded. If she had been shocked a moment ago, her face now gave nothing away. If anything, she just seemed a little annoyed that a private meeting had been interrupted.

Royce ignored her. He was examining Jack. "Who are you?" he asked.

Mrs Jones interrupted. "You don't have to give him your name," she said to Jack, then to Royce: "She's one of our operatives. She's making a report..."

"That's a lie," Owen said. "She's Jack Starbright. She's Alex Rider's nanny."

Jack stared at the twenty-year-old with his slicked-back fair hair and pink cheeks. "I'm not his nanny," she snapped. "I'm his friend."

"Why are you here?" Royce asked her.

"I was about to ask you the same," Mrs Jones said.

Royce came to a decision. He turned to one of the security men. "Escort Ms Starbright off the premises. Make sure she talks to nobody. If she causes you any problems, have her arrested."

"Wait a minute..." Jack began.

But it was too late. Two men grabbed hold of her and marched her out of the room. The door slammed shut behind them.

"I hope you have an explanation for this," Mrs

Jones exclaimed. "You have absolutely no right—"

"I have every right," Royce interrupted her. He took out a sheet of paper and laid it on the table in front of her. "Can you explain this?"

Mrs Jones read the first line of the page then slid it towards her deputy. Crawley glanced at it. There was no need to do more. Both of them knew exactly what it was and where it had come from.

"This has been taken from my computer," Crawley said. He glanced at Owen Andrews with cold fury in his eyes. "Was it you who hacked into my system?" he asked.

"There's no need to answer that, Owen," Royce cut in. Taking his time, he sat down at the table and gestured for Mrs Jones to do the same. She hesitated, then lowered herself into her seat.

"A few weeks ago, Mrs Jones, you came to see me in my office at the FCO," Royce began. "As you will recall, I had just discovered that you had employed a minor by the name of Alex Rider. I was horrified. It seemed to me that you had been completely irresponsible and that he was a serious risk to security."

"That's rubbish," Crawley growled.

Royce turned to him. "If you say one more word, I'll have you removed." He glanced back at Mrs Jones. "I gave you strict instructions to have nothing more to do with him. But now I find..." He waved at the sheet of paper, "that you have deliberately disobeyed me. You have actually recruited him for a new mission and sent him abroad."

"Alex Rider is our only hope of preventing a major terrorist attack on London," Mrs Jones said.

"That's what you say. That's what you think. But for me, it only proves what I have suspected all along ... that you have completely taken leave of your senses and that you are no longer fit for command. Do you really believe that you can entrust the security of the entire country to a fifteen-year-old schoolboy? We are talking about one of the most dangerous terrorist organizations in the world – Nightshade – and you think he's the answer?"

"He's been successful before."

"You disobeyed me!" Royce slammed his hand down on the table. "You may not like it, Mrs Jones. Clearly, you do not like it. But I am your superior. You report to me and to my office! I have to say that I've been concerned about MI6 Special Operations for some time but it has now become obvious to me that you are a rogue operation. I can no longer trust you and, unfortunately, you leave me with only one choice."

Mrs Jones stared.

"I am closing you down with immediate effect. You and Crawley will return home. You will not communicate with each other or with anyone else on your staff. You will surrender your security passes, your ID cards and your computers. There will of course be a full inquiry but until that time you should consider yourself under house arrest."

"You can't do this!" Mrs Jones couldn't believe what she was hearing. "Alex Rider is still out there. He needs us!"

"If Alex Rider is in danger, it's entirely your fault. If he gets himself killed, you will have only yourselves to blame. I did warn you not to use him, Mrs Jones. The whole idea was madness from the beginning. It should never have been considered."

"But what about Nightshade?" Crawley exclaimed. "We know they're about to launch an attack on London. You may disagree with us, Royce, but you can't close us down. Not now!"

"You call me Mr Royce!" the Permanent Under-Secretary snapped and next to him Owen Andrews smiled. He was enjoying all this. "What have you learned about Nightshade? Do you know where they are? Do you know what their target is?"

There was silence in the room.

"Exactly. You sent a child to Gibraltar and then you managed to lose him. You know absolutely nothing. Well, I shall be taking charge of the investigation into Nightshade. I've already spoken to the Prime Minister. There are plenty of other departments within British intelligence that I am sure will prove more efficient and more reliable than you. The Security Service. The National Crime Agency. Joint Intelligence. I will be briefing them all this afternoon."

"You're making a mistake," Mrs Jones insisted.

"Alex is close to Nightshade. He'll get a message to us. We have to be there to take it."

"Alex Rider may already be dead," Dominic Royce replied. He nodded at his deputy. "You've done very well indeed, Owen. I want this whole building shut down. You can see to it for me. Make sure these two take absolutely nothing with them when they leave."

He got up and, with a brief nod, walked out of the room.

Crawley broke the silence. "There is something I want to make clear," he said. He was addressing Owen Andrews. "Not today, not tomorrow but one day, quite soon, I'm going to come and find you and I'm going to make sure you regret this for the rest of your life."

"I'm not scared of you," Owen replied. "There's a taxi waiting for you outside."

Mrs Jones said nothing. She was thinking of Alex Rider. Almost nobody – apart from herself and Crawley – knew of his mission and the danger that he was in. What would happen if he called for help and found she wasn't there?

He was all that stood between Nightshade and London. And now he was on his own.

TERMINAL VELOCITY

Alex Rider was not often afraid but thinking of what lay ahead of him, he could feel his stomach churning.

The Beechcraft King Air C90 that had brought him here was sitting on the runway just a few steps in front of him and he – along with Freddy, William and four others – was about to board. Alex watched the pilot climb into the cockpit. He was unsmiling, much of his face hidden by dark glasses, curly black hair and a beard. He was one of the so-called Cardinals. From what Alex could gather, they had all been recruited from prisons across Europe. They were being paid to work for Nightshade. They had no idea what was going on at Kavos Bay and they didn't really care.

Brother Mike had taken the Numbers through a last-minute briefing. The plane would take off in a few minutes. It would climb to thirteen thousand feet. A green light would illuminate in the back of the cabin.

And then they would jump out.

"Are you all right, Julius?" Brother Mike was sneering at him, as if daring him to say he was too nervous to make the jump.

Alex smiled. "Yeah – great. Thanks for asking."

"Remember to keep your knees together when you hit the ground. It would distress me greatly if you broke both your legs!"

There was at least one thing that none of the Teachers knew. Alex had actually been given intensive training by the SAS in the Brecon Beacons when he had first been recruited by MI6. He knew all the techniques – launching, tracking, turning and (thankfully) landing – even though his practice jump had been cancelled at the last minute. He just hoped he would remember what he had been taught when the moment came.

Even so, the thought of launching himself into the Greek sky made him sick. Everyone else on the plane had jumped dozens of times. They knew the conditions. They knew where to land. He would just have to follow them. And what if Brother Mike had followed through on his threat to pack Alex's chute? For all he knew, he could be stepping out to his certain death. He would only know when he was halfway down.

But standing here now in the morning sun, he knew he couldn't argue. Worse than that, he had to pretend he was delighted. Certainly, Freddy was pleased he was coming. "Isn't this fun?" he asked.

Alex nodded, unable to find the words to express what he was feeling. "How many jumps have you done?" he asked.

"Oh – about fifty. It's much harder at night. You can't see the ground until the last minute and it's easy to mess up."

"Are you going to be jumping in the dark when you do it in London?" Alex asked.

Freddy nodded, then stopped himself. "We're not meant to talk about it," he said.

He had made a mistake and Alex made a note of it. This was something new he had learned about Leap of Faith. It was happening at night.

"All right, you can board the aircraft," Brother Mike said. "Remember – use the blue circle to guide you ... aim for the red. And the critical time to start your manoeuvres is when you're three hundred and ten metres above the ground. You've got to be in position by then.

Alex had already been shown the target – two circles painted like a dartboard in a field inland from Kavos Bay. The outer, red circle was huge, at least thirty metres in diameter. The blue circle, inside it, was much smaller. Clearly, they represented a similar area in London ... but what? Piccadilly Circus perhaps? Or the Oval cricket ground? If Alex could find the answer to that question, he would know the real target.

And now he added another piece of information to the puzzle. Three hundred and ten metres. That must be higher than most of the skyscrapers in London. So why was it so important to the mission?

As Alex moved forward with the others, he could feel the straps pressing against his arms and chest and thought how strange it was that his life should depend on the piece of folded material that he was now carrying on his back. He had the main canopy – the parachute itself – but if that failed there was also a reserve. He put a hand up and felt the ripcord dangling over his left shoulder but he wasn't going to be using it. The parachutists were making a static-line exit with a strong cord attached to a metal pipe that ran along the roof of the cabin. The cord would pull out the canopy, ensuring that it would open correctly in the fast-flowing air. At least that was the idea. It was only after he had jumped that Alex would know if it had worked.

A miniature stepladder had been set beside the plane and one by one they climbed up into the cabin: three boys and three girls. Sofia – Number Six – wasn't with them but then, Alex remembered, she was going to reach the London target on some sort of coach. They sat in two rows, three on each side, packed tightly together in the narrow cabin, facing away from the pilot who was going through final checks, at the same time talking to the control centre through his headset.

The door was closed and sealed from outside.

"I bet you wimp out," William muttered as he took the seat next to Alex. The two of them were going to be the last to leave the plane. They were sitting next to each other, furthest from the door.

Freddy had overheard him. "You're just worried Julius will hit the target first time," he said. "You're scared he's better than you...!"

The pilot flicked switches and the propellers began to turn, picking up speed until they disappeared in a blur. With a jolt, they moved forward and began to taxi along the runway. Normally, a bunch of teenagers on a plane would be chattering with excitement, exchanging jokes – but the Numbers had fallen silent, utterly focused on what they were about to do. Alex didn't get the sense that any of them were scared or even slightly nervous. That was so typical of Nightshade. They lived only to do what they were told.

The engines had risen in pitch until they were drowning out all other sounds. Alex saw the pilot reach forward with one hand and the next moment they were racing down the runway, picking up speed until the sudden lack of bumps and vibration told him that they had left the ground. He felt his ears popping as they began a steep climb. Out of the corner of his eye, he could see the airstrip and the hillside falling away. He swallowed hard, trying to damp down his feelings of helplessness and fear. Two weeks ago he had been in London, on his way home from school. How had he got himself into this?

It seemed to take for ever but finally they reached thirteen thousand feet and levelled off. The entire cabin was vibrating, the plane bumping up and down on the air currents. The parachutists lowered their goggles and adjusted the altimeters which they all wore on their wrists. These would bleep when they reached three hundred and ten metres. The pilot raised a hand, giving a prearranged signal. Freddy leaned forward and opened the door.

Alex had flown often enough to know what to expect, looking down from the sky: the fields separated into bands of different colours, the glistening blue of the sea, the roads and houses made tiny, the whole world moving slowly or not at all. But there was something shocking about seeing it without a thick pane of glass to protect him. He could hear the wind rushing past. He could feel it buffeting his cheeks. His mouth was completely dry. What would happen if he refused to jump? He was very tempted to do exactly that. He could tell the others he wasn't well enough – even if nobody believed him. It was ridiculous anyway. There was absolutely no reason to do this.

Then the pilot flicked a switch and a red light came on at the very back of the cockpit. They had reached the drop zone! One of the girls threw something out: a brightly coloured streamer that unfurled in the air and fell towards the ground. The streamer was made of silk. It was a WDI, a wind drift indicator and Alex knew that it would show the parachutists the line they had to take to reach the target. He could see that too: the two circles, painted on the ground. The pilot shouted something, then flicked another switch. The light turned from red to green.

Freddy was the first to leave the plane. Without saying anything, without even noticing Alex, he got up and tumbled out of the door. The static line trailed briefly after him and then he was gone, falling into the void. The girls went next: Numbers Fifteen, Sixteen and Twenty-Two. Then it was Number Eleven's turn. He was the fair-haired boy Alex had met on his first night. The two of them had fought against each other in the karate class. Briefly, he paused in the doorway, enjoying the view. Then he threw himself out. Suddenly Alex was alone in the plane with William and the pilot. He steeled himself for what was coming next.

William glanced at him briefly as if daring him to chicken out. "See you down there!" he shouted and rolled lazily out of the door as if this was something he had done a hundred times before ... which he probably had. He was one of the best parachutists in the group and he was going to be Freddy's backup when they hit London. Alex waited for him to reappear in the jet stream, his canopy billowing open. He got ready himself.

It took him a few seconds to realize that William had disappeared.

Something had gone horribly wrong.

He and the pilot both saw it at the same moment. William's static line hadn't released his canopy. Somehow, it had got fouled and it was locked in place, still stretching out of the door with William dangling on the other end, just out of sight underneath the Beechcraft. Alex stared in horror, unsure what to do. Gritting his teeth, using both hands to keep himself steady, he edged forward to the door. He leaned out of the aircraft and felt the full force of the wind in his face. At first there was nothing. Then he saw William, about two or three metres below, twisting helplessly at the end of the line. His arms were hanging loose at his sides and Alex realized that the accident was even worse than he had first thought. The wind had caught William and dashed him against the side of the plane. He was not only trapped, dangling helplessly, he was unconscious.

Alex jerked himself back into the plane. "We have to free him!" he shouted. It was almost impossible to make himself heard against the sound of the propellers and the rush of the wind.

"We can't!" the pilot shouted back. "He has to free himself!"

"He's knocked himself out!"

The pilot sat where he was – but of course he couldn't leave the controls. They flew on, passing the circle and the other parachutists, dragging William with them. Now they were over the sea.

"What are we going to do?" Alex shouted.

The answer horrified him. The pilot reached down and produced a huge knife with a serrated edge. He passed it to Alex. "Cut him loose!" he commanded.

"But he's unconscious! He'll die!"

"Cut him loose!" the pilot repeated. "We can't pull him back in. And we can't land the plane – not if he's outside." His eyes were still hidden behind the glasses. His mouth was a snarl of rage. "Do it now!"

He was used to being obeyed. If it had been any one of the Numbers in the cockpit, William would already be dead. But Alex couldn't do it. This was Mrs Jones's son! If he ever made it back to London, was he going to tell her that he had found her lost child, only to be responsible for his death?

"No!" he shouted.

"Do it or we both die!"

There had to be another way. Alex made his decision and acted on it. Still holding the knife, he sat in the doorway with his legs hanging over the edge. He tried not to look down but even so he saw the curve of the world and the ground horribly far away. William was directly beneath him, a rag doll being thrown from side to side. The static line was stretching out through the open door. All he had to do was cut through it and it would all be over.

He let himself fall.

But he had hooked his arm and one leg around the line so that instead of being pulled away from the aircraft he was attached to it, climbing down inch by inch. It was incredibly painful. Alex felt as if the airstream was trying to tear him in half. He was holding the line with his left hand, using all his strength, fighting against the wind and the speed of the plane. At least the goggles protected his eyes but even so he could barely see. Now his face was level with the bottom of the door and his feet were almost touching William's head. He wondered if he could actually push William free, using the soles of his feet against the other boy's shoulders. No. It would be too dangerous. If the static line snapped and the parachute failed to open, it would kill him.

With his muscles screaming and his whole body rocking back and forwards, slammed by the wind, Alex lowered himself a little further, folding his legs round William's unconscious body so that the two of them were locked together, bouncing about under the plane. He was still holding the static line with his left hand. He had put the knife that he had been given between his teeth. He was beginning to spin. He was afraid he was going to black out himself. This was the moment of truth. He had to do it now.

He took the knife in his right hand and began to saw at William's static line. He had thought it would be easy – the blade was razor-sharp – but it was almost impossible to get any purchase without falling himself. Slowly, clumsily he drew it back and forth. He almost dropped it, felt it lose contact with the palm of his hand. But then, somehow, the blade cut through.

Everything happened at once. Alex and William suddenly fell, still locked together. Alex's legs were around William's chest and he was squeezing with all his strength, holding on to him. He knew that he had only a few seconds in which to save them both. They were both falling freely now but there was still one static line – Alex's – attached to the plane. It had already begun to draw out his canopy. He could see it, opening above him a blue and white explosion of lightweight nylon, shaped like a wing. There was no time left. He dropped the knife, letting it fall towards the earth, and reached down for William's ripcord. Somehow, he found it and pulled it. At exactly the same moment, his own chute deployed and he was ripped away, carried away by the airstream.

For a few brief seconds, Alex had no idea what was happening. He couldn't see William or the plane. Everything had become a blur. He twisted his neck and, to his relief, saw that his own parachute had worked perfectly. He would have been travelling at fifty-five metres per second – one hundred and twenty-five miles per hour – when he fell out of the Beechcraft. Terminal velocity. His chute had cut the speed by ninety per cent and now he was drifting down at a pleasant twelve miles per hour, around six metres per second. He might even have been able to enjoy the experience if his heart hadn't been beating at ten times its normal speed and with every nerve in his body screaming at him.

He saw William, not that far from him, falling at the same rate. He looked down and realized that they were nowhere near the other parachutists. In fact, they had left the edge of the island and were

over the Aegean Sea. It was going to be a wet landing – but fortunately the wind was blowing inland
and Alex guessed they'd end up not too far from
the beach. Even so, he had less than a minute to
get himself ready. He remembered what the SAS had
taught him. Turn into the wind. Wait until you're
twelve to fifteen feet above the land ... or sea. Flare
the parachute – pulling the toggles down to slow
the rate of descent. Look forward, not down. Legs
pressed together. Lean forward.

Perhaps the shock of what had happened had
somehow managed to wipe away his fear. Or perhaps it was simply that nothing could be worse than
those few seconds after he had exited the plane. But
he felt nothing but relief as his feet skimmed the
surface of the sea and then entered the warm water.
The parachute was trailing behind him, floating, and
he quickly released it, then swam over to William
who had landed a few seconds after him and who
was floundering about, going nowhere. The water
had evidently woken him up.

"What happened?" he asked as Alex reached him.

"Nothing," Alex said. "You had an accident."

"I missed the target!"

"You missed the whole island. But I wouldn't
worry too much about that. Can you swim?"

William was hurt. He rolled his shoulder and
winced. "I don't know..."

"I'll help you." Treading water, Alex unclipped the
shoulder harness and drew it away.

William didn't thank him. He just looked annoyed. "I've broken my arm," he said.

So that was it. This was one Number that wasn't going to be attacking London.

"Just be grateful it wasn't your neck," Alex said.

Together, they began to swim towards the shore.

NUMBER TWENTY-SIX

It was the evening before Leap of Faith and there was a celebration at Kavos Bay. The chef had driven down to meet the fishermen at Vai and had come back with fresh lobsters, mullet and sea bream, which he had barbecued over charcoal flames, serving them with great piles of chips and salad. This was a celebration for their hard work and also a special welcome for Number Twenty-Six.

It had been announced at church. Julius Grief was being given the ultimate honour. His name was being taken from him and from now on he would be known only as a number. Everyone knew what had happened on the Beechcraft King – even though the Teachers would have preferred to keep it from them. But Number Eleven had seen William trapped underneath the aircraft. Twisting round beneath his own parachute, he had watched as Alex began the rescue. Both boys had landed in the sea together and even Number Seven remembered enough to know that he was very lucky to be alive and that without the new Number Twenty-Six he wouldn't be.

The bad news was that Number Seven would no longer be able to take part in Leap of Faith. He was sitting at the table with his right arm in a sling: he had broken it when the wind had slammed him into the side of the plane. His place was going to be taken by Number Eleven, who would be flying out with Freddy and Sofia the following morning.

If Alex had hoped that he would find out more about the operation now that he had been accepted into Nightshade, he was disappointed. From the time that he had dragged William ashore, life at Kavos Bay had continued as normal. There had been several more parachute jumps but he hadn't even been invited back into the plane, as if the Teachers were actually angry with him for saving the life of one of their star pupils.

And now here he was sitting next to Freddy, dressed identically to him in the Nightshade uniform. It felt odd to be wearing a jacket again, particularly in the warmth of the Greek evening. As always, Sofia was on Freddy's other side. The Numbers never showed very much emotion but even they were unable to hide their excitement. A great many people were going to die the following day. It could be hundreds ... even thousands. Alex remembered the hazmat suits he had seen hanging outside the laboratory and the photographs in the operations room which had suggested that the whole of London might be the target. He remembered the conversation he had overheard in the conference room. Someone called the Doctor had paid Nightshade twenty million dollars. Leap of Faith wasn't going to be a minor incident. It was London's own 9/11.

There was still nothing Alex could do. That was the worst of it. He was writhing with frustration as he sat here but he had to pretend he was happy. Ever since the parachute accident, he felt that he had been more closely watched. There hadn't been a single opportunity to slip out of the compound, even assuming he could find a police station or a telephone somewhere down the hill. Worse, a Prime had been posted on the other side of the glass doors in the entrance hall of the Temple. Alex still had the latex glove but he couldn't use it. Part of him had hoped that he might be allowed to join the others on the journey to London. But although he had been given a number, nothing else had come with it.

He was in. But he was helpless.

Freddy had got to his feet. He was holding up his glass. The others fell silent. "I just want to welcome Number Twenty-Six," he announced. "And I think we should thank our Creator for sending him to us. We nearly lost Number Seven earlier today. We've already had two departures this year and he would have been the third."

Departures. Freddy meant deaths. Alex thought of the gravestones.

"What do you say, Number Seven?" he asked. He was looking accusingly at William Jones. There was a pause and then William stretched out his good hand. "Thank you, Number Twenty-Six," he muttered.

Alex took it. "Always glad to help."

Sitting two places away, Sofia smiled.

Then one of the guards approached the table. As a rule, the Greeks employed at Kavos Bay – the Primes – stayed well out of sight, but this man had been sent to find him. He leant down and spoke in an accent that almost made a nonsense of the words. "The Teachers send me. They want see you. Now. In the office."

He pointed in the direction of the Temple, which was lit up in the distance, the gold letters glowing. Alex was puzzled. Why should they need to see him now? It was a quarter past eight and very soon the church bell would ring, sending everyone to bed. There was, however, no question of disobeying. Alex got up and left the table. It occurred to him that this might be good news. They had made him a Number. Perhaps they were going to do something else to show their gratitude. In any event, he was being invited back into the very heart of the complex, which was exactly what he wanted. All he needed was two minutes on his own with an unguarded computer or telephone. This might be his chance.

He was still quite nervous as he sat in the electric buggy, being carried through the darkness, away from the other Numbers. Everything was silent apart from the whine of the engine beneath him. The buggy stopped. He got out and walked up to the glass doors, which opened to allow him in. A Prime stood waiting for him but said nothing. Together the two of them walked along to the conference room. The Prime opened the door.

On the other side, the four Teachers were at the wooden table, wearing their robes and their golden discs as usual. Of course, Alex knew that everything about them was fake. As soon as he had gone they would be smoking cigars and probably drinking spirits too. But for now they were silent, their heads lowered as if in prayer.

"Come in, Number Twenty-Six," Brother Lamar said. He sounded friendly enough. "Take a seat!"

Alex sat down opposite them.

"How was dinner?"

"It was good, thank you," Alex said.

"You'll have to forgive us for dragging you away before coffee."

"Here!" With a smile, Sister Krysten poured a small cup of Greek coffee from a silver jug. She brought it round for Alex, who took a sip. It was hot and very sweet. He wondered what this was all about.

"We want to talk to you about Leap of Faith." Sister Jeanne took over the conversation. She had added extra make-up to her cheeks, which looked very dark, like cooked meat. "What you did, saving Number Seven, I have to say that it revealed a side of you that we hadn't seen before. We didn't even know it was there."

"It was nothing," Alex said.

"No, no. It was really something. And as a result, we've been having a talk and we've decided that you may be able to help us in London. We'd like you to fly there with the others tomorrow morning. What do you say?"

Alex couldn't believe what he was hearing. The Teachers were offering him exactly what he most wanted. He took another sip of coffee. "Sure," he said, casually. "I told you before. I've got nothing else to do. I'm happy to help."

"You may be responsible for the deaths of a thousand or more of your fellow countrymen," Sister Krysten said.

A thousand or more! So he had been right.

Alex shrugged. "That doesn't bother me," he said. There was something wrong. What had the woman just said? Had she deliberately laid a trap? "Anyway, they're not my countrymen," he continued, smoothly. "I was born in France. And my dad was South African. I don't really belong anywhere." He drank some more of the coffee to cover the silence.

"That is true," Sister Jeanne said, approvingly.

"So what exactly is Leap of Faith?" Alex asked. "What do you guys want me to do?"

There was a brief silence. Then Brother Lamar began to speak. "We'll come to that in a minute," he said. "But actually, there's another reason we asked you to come here this evening." He paused. "We have a problem. The fact is that we're a bit concerned about Number Nine."

Freddy Grey! What had he done?

"What's wrong?" Alex asked.

"A couple of things. The first actually concerns you. He brought you here with him from Gibraltar. That was directly against our instructions."

Alex couldn't see where this was going. Should he defend Freddy? Or would it be better to pretend that he didn't care what they thought? "I don't see why you've got a problem," he said. "Number Nine knew I'd be useful to you. And I've already proved he was right."

Brother Lamar nodded. "That's true. But the fact still remains that he disobeyed us and by now you should have realized – that never happens. In fact, it's impossible. Do you get me? It can't be allowed!"

Alex fell silent. He waited for the next blow to fall.

"And then there's this..." Brother Mike reached under the table and Alex felt his stomach tighten as he produced the stuffed monkey that he himself had given Freddy in Gibraltar. "Do you know anything about this?" Brother Mike asked.

"Sure." Alex tried to sound uninterested, as if they were making a fuss about nothing. "The psychiatrist woman, Dr Flint, gave it to him. I don't know why. It's just a stupid toy. But he liked it."

"Numbers have no possessions," Sister Krysten said. "Possessions are part of your identity and Numbers have no identity. They all know that."

"He hid it under his mattress," Sister Jeanne added. "He tried to hide it from us."

"Well, it's my fault. I'll take the blame." Alex could feel the shadows closing in. He knew that there was danger in the room but he couldn't understand what it was or where it had come from. "I was the one who gave it to him. I didn't think it was any big deal."

"You said that the psychiatrist gave it to Number Nine," Brother Mike cut in. "Why are you lying to us?"

"I'm not. She gave it to me to give to him. It's the same thing." He paused, as if annoyed. "What is all this? I thought we were celebrating. You just made me a Number. Why are you so worried about Number Nine?"

"Because he's not the same. He's changed." Brother Lamar looked Alex straight in the eyes. "We've decided he's no longer any use to us, Number Twenty-Six. It's very unfortunate but at the end of the day no harm has been done. You will replace him."

"And what will happen to Number Nine?" Alex asked. He still had no idea what this was all about but none of it sounded good.

"That's why you're here," Sister Jeanne replied. She couldn't have sounded more reasonable. "We want you to kill him."

Alex stared. "What?"

"I think you heard me."

"When?"

"Right now."

Sister Jeanne must have pressed a communications button. The door opened a second time and

Freddy Grey walked in. He looked as surprised as Alex to be here but he sat down and said nothing.

"Use this," Brother Lamar said. He passed Alex a gun.

"What?"

"Shoot Number Nine. Once in the head will do it."

Alex took the weapon. He was feeling sick. What was he supposed to do? He couldn't kill Freddy. Even if he'd been his worst enemy, he wouldn't have been able to shoot him in cold blood. But he had just been told he was going to London, that he was taking part in Leap of Faith. It was his only chance to prevent it. If he didn't do what he was told, they would know he had been lying to them. He would have blown his cover and he would never get the chance to warn Mrs Jones what was happening. He would end up dead himself.

Meanwhile, Freddy was just sitting there. He had been told he was about to be shot but he didn't seem to care. He was making no move to protect himself.

"This is crazy!" Alex said in a voice that wasn't quite his own. "Number Nine is great. He's your number-one parachutist. You know that. He never misses! It's not his fault I gave him the toy..."

"We're waiting," Sister Krysten said in an icy voice.

"You can't be serious. Is this some kind of test?" Alex could feel the gun, weighing down his hand. Freddy would have known exactly how many bullets it contained. Was it possible that it was actually empty? That he would pull the trigger and nothing would happen? He didn't dare take the risk.

"You have three seconds..." Brother Lamar said.

"I won't do it!"

"Two seconds..."

Freddy didn't move. He had just been sentenced to death, but it was as if he hadn't noticed. His eyes were far away.

"One second..."

For a moment, Alex was tempted. He could bring the gun round on the Teachers. He could shoot all four of them.

And then?

"No!"

Alex had made his decision. He threw the gun down onto the table in a gesture of disgust. He could still bluff his way out of this. There had to be another way.

"Thank you, Number Nine," Brother Lamar said.

"Thank you, Brother Lamar." Freddy got up and left the room. He hadn't so much as glanced at Alex. He didn't even seem to know he was there. Somehow that worried Alex as much as anything.

The Teachers turned on Alex. Brother Mike picked up the gun. He smiled unpleasantly. "It's not loaded," he said.

Despite everything, Alex felt a sense of relief. "So it was a test," he said.

"That's right, Alex," Sister Jeanne said. "And you failed."

She had called him Alex.

He felt a chasm opening beneath his feet. "That's

not my name," he said and wondered why his voice sounded so distant from him. The room was beginning to bend out of shape.

"We know who you are," Brother Lamar said. "We have an agent in London who has told us everything. Your name is Alex Rider and you were sent by MI6 Special Operations to the Gibraltar prison to get close to Number Nine. You then persuaded him to bring you here. I feel I should congratulate you for getting so far. But there's something you need to know." He produced a cigar and lit it, his fat lips sucking greedily at the end. "MI6 Special Operations no longer exists," he went on. "They've been shut down ... permanently. Nobody cares about you any more, Alex. You've been cut loose."

"That's not true..." Alex spoke the words but they came out slurred. He wasn't sure what was happening to him. Suddenly his arms and legs were heavy. He felt as if he was being sucked into the chair.

"We could kill you right now. Mike has been urging me to do just that and I know he'd enjoy it. But if there's one thing that I've learned in this business it's that you don't waste an opportunity that's been given to you. The fact of the matter is that I can use you. You have a big part to play in tomorrow's operation even though you aren't going to be a willing participant. In fact, I'm pretty certain you won't survive it.

"You see, Alex, your organization is finished. Mrs Jones and John Crawley are under house arrest. They can't help you. But the problem for us is that there are other intelligence outfits in London and they seem to know that we have something targeted for tomorrow. Maybe that's down to you.

"And the terrorist alert level has just been raised from severe to critical, meaning that an attack is expected imminently. Everyone is on full alert. Five hundred extra police officers have been brought into the city. Nobody can prevent what we're about to do but they can make it a whole lot more difficult for us.

"So we're going to give them something else to think about. A diversion. Suppose one of the most dangerous criminals in the world suddenly turned up on the edge of London. Let's say he was seen at a railway station or on a park bench. What do you think would happen? Everyone would start looking for him. All those extra policemen would be diverted to find him. The press and the TV, they'd all be screaming for him. And nobody would notice us on the other side of town. We'd slip in through the back door while they were busy elsewhere."

"What have you done to me?" Alex muttered and his own voice no longer sounded like his own. The room was shrinking. The four Teachers were bending out of shape like spilled ink.

The coffee. He could taste it on his lips. He knew he had been drugged.

"And who do you think that criminal is?" the chairman asked – except he was no longer the chairman.

He was just a voice at the end of a long tunnel.

"No..." Alex tried once again to stand up.

"It's Julius Grief, Alex. It's you."

Alex pitched forward, just missing the edge of the table. He collapsed onto the wooden floor and lay still.

PART FOUR: REVELATION

RING OF STEEL

They had already started putting up the barriers around St Paul's Cathedral, although the service wasn't due to begin until half past seven that evening.

Altogether, a thousand officers were being deployed. They had been brought together from the Metropolitan Police, the British Transport Police and MI5 in an operation that had been planned weeks before. By two o'clock in the afternoon a "ring of steel" would have been constructed, with manned checkpoints forming a protective circle around the cathedral. Nobody would be able to get in or out without authorization. Every vehicle would be searched, the undercarriage examined, the registration numbers checked. Drivers could expect to have their steering wheels swabbed for explosive residue.

At midday, the cathedral had been closed to tourists as Scotland Yard anti-terrorist officers – accompanied by trained sniffer dogs brought in from the Dog Support Unit – began a search that took in every inch of the building. All the doors were being checked, one after another, to ensure they were locked. Metal detectors had been brought in and set up around the two public entrances that would be used for the service.

A few black-suited figures had started to appear, patrolling the area with Heckler & Koch machine guns and Glock 17 pistols. Dressed in black body armour, their faces almost completely concealed behind helmets, goggles and balaclava masks, they looked almost alien in this historical setting. The cathedral had been built in the seventeenth century. They could only have come from the twenty-first. Soon there would be more than fifty of them, drawn from the Specialist Firearms Command or SCO19 as it is known to the Metropolitan Police. They would be supported by EC145 Eurocopters, the twin-engine helicopters used by the National Police Air Service. They alone would enter the airspace above London. Planes heading for Heathrow or City would have to divert.

The event was a massive headache for everyone taking part – as well as for tourists, businessmen, Londoners … anyone finding their way blocked or their journey home delayed. But James Clifford had been a hugely popular Home Secretary and this was his memorial service, following his sudden death from a suspected heart attack three months before. It was only right that he should be given a decent send-off.

He was getting rather more than that. Two thousand people were expected for the service, which was going to be led by the Archbishop of Canterbury. A special choir, assembled from eight different schools around London, would be performing. A famous actor was reading the first lesson. The President of the United States was appearing on a giant video screen.

The Prime Minister of the United Kingdom was coming in person. So was the Leader of the Opposition. Almost every government minister would be joining them ... along with more than two hundred MPs from different political parties. Four members of the royal family were coming and as usual they would be accompanied by dukes, duchesses, earls, viscounts, lords, ladies and famous faces who always managed to turn up at funerals and weddings. The service would be filmed for the BBC News.

This was Nightshade's target.

There were just six hours until it began.

THE LAST DAY

Seagulls.

That was the first thing Alex Rider heard ... that and the breaking of waves. He was sitting on a shingle beach. He could feel the round stones underneath his legs and the palms of his hands. His back was resting against some sort of structure, a low wall. He was feeling sick.

He opened his eyes and saw the sea. He knew at once that he wasn't in Greece. It was too cold and the colour of the water – somewhere between grey and green – was a world away from the blue of the Aegean. He looked down and saw black shoes, grey trousers, a mauve shirt: the Nightshade uniform that he had been wearing when he was summoned to the Temple. Slowly, it all came back to him. Brother Lamar and the other Teachers had known who he was. Somehow they had found out. They had taunted him, daring him to shoot Number Nine, all the time knowing that he wouldn't. And they had drugged him. He could still taste the coffee in his mouth.

His arms were heavy. He wasn't sure if he could move.

Where was he and how long had he been here?

Brother Lamar had said that he was going to use him as a diversion. He was back in England. He was sure of it. This had to be the North Sea or the Channel in front of him. It had that feel. He looked across the water and saw a metal beam, breaking through the surface, the skeleton remains of some sort of building that had either fallen or burned down. How odd that it should have been left there to spoil the view. A few people walked past on the shingle. He was not alone. What time was it? From the position of the sun, he would have said midday.

Alex was trying not to panic. He still couldn't move and had no exact idea what had been done to him or how Nightshade were planning to use him. After he had been knocked out, they must have put him in a plane. It would have taken about five hours to fly to England. He thought back to the dinner, the celebration at Kavos Bay, and realized, with a shudder, that the operation called Leap of Faith had already begun.

This was the last day.

He turned his head and saw a structure that looked like an enormous tube, rising up, further down the beach. It was silver with a glass cabin wrapped around it. The whole thing had the feel of a fairground ride and Alex vaguely recognized it. A jumble of buildings stretched out behind it; blocks of flats, offices, hotels standing shoulder to shoulder, staring out at the sea.

It wasn't good enough. He had to move. Somehow he managed to jerk some life back into his arm and lifted his hand. He did the same with the other. He drew up a knee and clumsily got to his feet, fighting back his nausea and sense of exhaustion. He realized now that whoever had left him here had propped him up against a wooden breakwater. He used it to support himself and, twisting round, he saw a pier jutting out into the sea with a carousel, a helter-skelter and a bright yellow roller coaster at the far end and an amusement hall just above the beach.

BRIGHTON PIER. The words were written in huge coloured letters on the side of the building. So that was where he was. Brighton! He should have known the moment he saw the silver tube. It was an observation tower known as the British Airways i360 or the Brighton Needle.

It made sense. The plane from Greece must have landed at a private airport ... Shoreham perhaps. The Numbers – Nine and Eleven – would have continued by car to London. And he had been dumped here. For a few moments Alex stood where he was, waiting for his strength to return. He felt better standing on his own two feet. He tried to work out some sort of plan. The most important thing was to contact MI6. No. That wouldn't work. Unless Brother Lamar had been lying, MI6 had been shut down and Mrs Jones was under arrest. How was that even possible? But if he couldn't reach her, there was always Jack. Alex felt in his pockets, knowing that they would be empty. Of course, Nightshade had made sure he had no money. He would just have to ask someone to lend him a phone. He would phone Jack. She would know what to do.

Even as he made the decision, he saw a man walking towards him, swinging what looked like a vacuum cleaner over the shingle. It was a metal detector. He was searching for old coins in the shingle. Alex raised a hand and the man stopped and took off his headphones. He was elderly, well into his sixties, with tangled hair and stubble.

"Excuse me..." Alex began.

The man was staring at him and not in a friendly way. Before Alex could say another word, he stepped back, his feet crunching on the gravel, then turned and hurried off in the direction from which he'd come, cradling his metal detector in both arms.

Alex was suddenly uneasy. A very unpleasant thought had just come into his head and the one thing he didn't want to do was to hang around to find out if it was true. He felt very exposed out here on the beach. There was a road behind him. He headed towards it.

At first he moved like an old man but with every step he found his strength returning. He came to a row of shops built into a series of archways beneath the road: a snack bar, an art gallery, a tourist shop selling shells and stuffed toy seagulls. A ramp led up to the street and moving more quickly, he climbed up and found himself in front of a small, round building with an ornate roof and pictures of happy ice-cream cones – complete with eyes and waving hands – on the walls. It was a café. There were tables outside but only one was taken. A husband and wife were sitting, drinking tea, not talking to each other. The man was reading a newspaper. Alex saw the front page.

THE FACE OF EVIL

That was the headline above a large photograph. The face was his.

Alex stared at it, completely horrified. Neither the husband nor the wife had noticed him and he was able to move closer and read some of the text. "Julius Grief is believed to have returned to the UK after escaping from a maximum security prison abroad. Although he is only fifteen, he has killed many times ... considered to be extremely dangerous and possibly armed ... a senior officer from the National Counter Terrorism Security Office warned the public ... under no circumstances should he be approached ... if you see him call the police immediately."

Now Alex understood what Brother Lamar had meant. He had talked about a diversion and this was it. His picture was going to be in every newspaper, on TV, all over the internet. Everyone in England was looking for him. Whatever the real target was in London, it would be forgotten. Even as Alex stood there, the consequences of what Nightshade had done came crashing in on him like a multiple pile-up.

He had no money, no phone and no way of reaching London. To the whole world, he was Julius Grief and the only people who knew the truth about him had been put out of action. Apart from Jack, he had nobody to turn to. According to the newspaper report, he might be carrying a gun. Even if he tried to approach a policeman, there was a good chance that he would be shot down before he could utter a word.

He felt terribly exposed. First of all there were the people walking past him along the esplanade and the drivers in four lanes of traffic on the main road. It would only take one of them to make eye contact with him and he would be recognized. In fact it had already happened! The man with the metal detecting machine might be ringing the police even now. And it didn't matter where he went or where he tried to hide. There were cameras everywhere. He was probably being observed right now. He had to go somewhere, get out of sight while he worked out what to do.

But where? Brighton Pier was close by. There were crowds of people wandering in and out, playing the arcade machines in the Palace of Fun or heading for the rides that he had seen at the far end. Alex had heard that it was easy to hide in a crowd but he still couldn't bring himself to try it. He needed to be alone. He looked across the road at the various blocks of flats and hotels. There was a little park near by on the other side of a low wall with an aquarium contained in a small pavilion. It might be dark in there but he couldn't go in. How would he buy a ticket?

The man with the newspaper was staring at him. Fortunately, he hadn't recognized Alex, even though his photograph was actually in his hands. He was just annoyed that some weird school kid had been trying to read his newspaper. Alex turned away and hurried back down to the beach. He needed to think. Brighton Pier was jutting out above him. He had decided it was too dangerous to hide on the pier but nobody would see him in the shadows underneath it. That was where he headed now.

Alex fought his way over the shingle and didn't stop until the great bulk of the pier was above him. He found himself in a cool, damp world of stone and metal with the massive legs holding up the pier disappearing into the water and a network of steel cables and wire protruding at every angle. The beach sloped down steeply and he slumped onto it with the dark water lapping at his feet. Somewhere over his head, a nineties pop song was echoing out of the Palace of Fun but it seemed to belong to another world. He was alone with the breaking waves.

So.

What were his choices?

Alex was tired. Whatever drug he had been given was still in his system. And suddenly he was hungry and thirsty too. It wasn't easy to arrange his thoughts but he forced himself to focus. His first priority was to save London. But how was that possible when he still didn't know what was being targeted? If he went to the police and turned himself in – assuming they didn't shoot him the moment they saw him – what exactly could he tell them?

He had to go to London. He had to reach Jack. But that in itself wouldn't be easy. He didn't have any money to pay for a train and hitch-hiking was too dangerous. Anyway, it would take too long. Alex still didn't know the exact time. Leap of Faith was taking place in darkness ... but that could only be a few hours away.

And if he tried to get to the capital, wouldn't he be doing exactly what Nightshade wanted? He was the diversion. If he was seen approaching London, every policeman and woman would be sent after him. Maybe it would be better simply to stay out of sight.

He couldn't do that. He couldn't just sit there and wait for London to be hit. He made his decision. First he would have to do something about his appearance. He couldn't walk through Brighton looking like this. At the very least, he needed a hoodie or something that would hide his face. He had to borrow a telephone and contact ... not Jack. That was another nasty thought. It was Nightshade who had leaked the story to the press. They had told the world that he was Julius Grief. They knew everything about him, which probably meant that they knew about Jack too and they would be expecting him to call her. Alex had no doubt that they would be able to listen in on the call. He had seen the technology they had in the Temple ... the room with the microphones and the sound mixers, the sophisticated radio antennas on the roof.

Alex knew what he was up against. He had finally worked out how they had contacted Freddy Grey in Gibraltar. Nightshade had extraordinary technology on their side and they had been using it from the very start.

When Freddy had broken out of the prison, Nightshade had told him which way to take down the hill. They had known about the abandoned cinema and somehow they had given him the information ... right down to the door which had been broken open for him. They had hired La Máquina, and Freddy had known exactly when they were coming even though he hadn't spoken to them before they arrived. There could only be one explanation for all this and as impossible as it sounded, Alex was convinced he was right.

He got to his feet. It was time to go. There had to be a station in Brighton. He would find it and somehow he would slip onto a train. Alex slipped out from beneath the pier and was about to climb back up to the road when the sound of sirens caused him to step back. Three police cars shot past, heading towards the breakwater where he'd woken up. The man with the metal detector must have called them.

They were looking for him.

SMOKE AND FIRE

The police cars had stopped some distance away, further along the esplanade. Alex saw uniformed officers pouring out and hurrying down onto the beach. He didn't stand around watching them. He crossed the main road without waiting for the traffic to slow down, almost getting run over by a motor-cyclist who swerved round him at the last second, horn blaring. A smaller street led into the town centre and he dived into it, grateful for the shops and flats hemming him in on either side, hiding him from the manhunt going on behind.

It had to be early afternoon. The streets were fairly empty, suggesting that most people were at work. Even so, Alex still felt exposed. Walking past a newsagent, he saw his face staring out at him over and over again on the front page of every newspaper. THE FACE OF EVIL. TERROR BOY. THE FIFTEEN-YEAR-OLD KILLER. NO TEARS FOR GRIEF. The headlines were different but they all spelled out the same message. The security forces had put out an alert that Julius Grief had arrived in England. He was dangerous, probably armed. He had to be found. Glancing through an open door, he saw a television screen on the wall of a pub and there he was again, his face on Sky News with a banner running across the bottom: POLICE MOUNT NATIONWIDE SEARCH FOR TEENAGE TERROR SUSPECT. How could it have happened? Even if Special Operations had been disbanded, surely someone had to know the truth.

Alex had never been to Brighton before. He had no idea where he was going. He felt that the city had become a trap, drawing him in, and he knew that it would only take one person to recognize him and the cage doors would slam shut and he would never get out again. He walked quickly, trying not to draw attention to himself – but he still felt that everyone was watching him and every nerve in his body was waiting for the moment when some complete stranger would pounce on him and it would all be over. He had to hide his face. He looked for shops that sold hats or sunglasses even though he knew he didn't have the money to pay for them.

He came to a clothes shop. There was a rack of hoodies right next to the door. Cautiously, he looked inside. There was no security guard and he could only see two girls behind the counter, one serving a customer, the other texting on her phone. He took one step in and pretended to examine a dark green hoodie that looked about his size.

Neither of the girls had noticed him. He snatched it and ran.

Alex hated having to steal but he had no choice. This wasn't just about his own survival but the safety of an entire city. He had to get to London and he wasn't going to let anything get in his way. But he still took a note of the name of the shop. When this was all over, he would send them the money he owed them – always assuming he was still alive.

He ran down one street, then down an alleyway, finally emerging into a pretty square with a café on one side and an old-fashioned sweetshop on the other. Quickly, he took off the Nightshade jacket and stuffed it into a dustbin, then pulled the hoodie over his head, leaving the hood up so that his face was almost completely concealed. Now it was just a question of walking with his head down and his hands shoved into his pockets. Hoodies had been designed for teenagers who wanted their own space and that suited Alex fine. His whole body language would warn people to keep their distance and at the same time he could relax a little, knowing that he was finally anonymous.

He continued walking. This part of the city was quiet and attractive, much less commercial than the seafront. Cars weren't allowed in the streets, giving it the atmosphere of a traditional village with trees in pots and lots of wooden benches. Alex saw a signpost for Brighton station and hurried forward, the road leading him uphill. He was beginning to feel more hopeful. The man with the metal detector might have called the police but they couldn't be sure he was right. They would spend time searching the beach, asking questions of anyone who was there. With a bit of luck, it would be a while before they widened their search and by then he would have left.

A few minutes later, Alex reached the station and saw at once that he had been too optimistic. He still had no real idea how he'd arrived in Brighton. It was clear to him that it was going to be a lot more difficult to get out.

The entrance to Brighton station covered one side of a large square with a jumble of different buildings ... most of them quite ugly. There was a pub and a parade of shops on one side, a modern office and supermarket on the other, and a cluster of bus stops in the middle. Traffic was moving in every direction with buses lined up about to leave and a fleet of taxis waiting in a corner. The station was tucked away at the far end, quite hard to see with all the activity around it.

To add to the sense of confusion, a number of stalls had been allowed to set up near the entrance. Alex saw a stand selling home-made bread, another with fresh coffee. Further back, Brighton & Hove Buses had an information booth and there was a solitary man standing beside a coal brazier selling roast chestnuts.

None of this mattered to Alex. To get into the

station he would have to pass through one of five archways: three right next to each other in the middle or one on either side. And that was impossible. The police were taking no chances. Alex saw four of them in hi-vis jackets. They weren't carrying guns but they had everything else: Tasers, truncheons, handcuffs, radios. He had no doubt that they were looking out for him. If he tried to slip past, even with the hoodie pulled over his head, they would be sure to stop him. The moment he looked up, before he answered a single question, they would have him.

Part of him was close to despair. It was two twenty-nine in the afternoon. He could see the time on the station clock, which was set high up next to the roof, and even as he watched, the minute hand jerked round, completing the half-circle. Time was running out. Alex didn't know what to do. He couldn't take the train but what other way was there to get to London? Was trying to reach London still the best idea? Perhaps it would be better to turn himself into the police after all. But how could he warn them about a terrorist attack when he still didn't know where or when it was taking place?

He realized that he was standing still and with everyone else on their way to catch a train or just coming off one, that was one sure way to draw attention to himself. He turned his back on the policemen and walked over to the supermarket as if he meant to buy something. He passed close to the man selling chestnuts and felt the heat of the coal fire on the side of his arm. Briefly, he heard him chatting to a woman ... someone he knew.

"I don't know, Charlie," she was saying. "How can he be so dangerous? He's only fifteen years old and those pictures of him ... he looks nice enough!"

"There's no smoke without fire," Charlie replied. "If it wasn't true, it wouldn't be in the papers. And don't you be fooled by appearances, Bess. The prisons are full of handsome crooks!"

They were talking about him!

But it was what Charlie had just said, the mention of smoke and the fire, that gave Alex an idea. He was right next to a supermarket and he would find what he needed there. He hated stealing again and it would be a lot more risky this time with security guards and CCTV. On the other hand, what he was looking for wouldn't be something that anyone would normally want to take: it wasn't chocolate or alcohol or anything expensive. And it was too late for scruples. He had made his decision. One way or another he had to get this over with.

He went into the supermarket and made his way to the section selling women's hair products. He went past brushes, shampoos and conditioners, finally coming to a whole shelf stacked with different cans of hairspray. He picked up the smallest of them, examined the label and pretended to put it back in its place. Instead, he used his middle finger to slide it up his sleeve. He did everything very carefully, not hurrying, trying to look completely innocent. Even now, with the can safely tucked out of sight, he stood where he was, examining the other products. He noticed a security guard glance his way, then go past him. Showing no emotion, he tucked his hands into his pockets and left the shop.

Only when he was in the open air did he move more quickly, slipping behind a parked van, making sure nobody had followed him. The hairspray was pressed against his arm. He freed it from his sleeve and held it in the palm of his hand. It had a white plastic lid which he took off. That made it smaller. Now it was all just a matter of luck and timing.

He walked over to the chestnut seller. "Are you Charlie?" he asked.

"Yes."

Alex was being careful not to show too much of his face. He pointed at one of the bus drivers, standing on the other side of the information booth. "My dad wants to talk to you."

"What about?"

"He wants to buy six bags of chestnuts. For him and his mates."

"So why doesn't he come over?"

"He's working. He's not allowed."

The chestnut seller was puzzled. Why would a bus driver send his son over to buy his product? All the same, six bags was six bags – better business than he'd had all morning – and anyway the kid seemed to know his name so perhaps his dad did too.

"I'll wait here if you like," Alex added.

That made sense. "All right." The man moved away.

Alex watched him go. The man called Charlie turned round as if he was about to change his mind and Alex waved, assuring him that everything was under control. Charlie smiled and continued on his way. Alex took one last look in his direction, then slipped the aerosol onto the blazing coals, underneath the chestnuts.

Charlie was about ten paces away, moving towards a bus driver who had probably never met him before and certainly didn't want any chestnuts. Alex hurried in the opposite direction, heading for the archway on the far left of the station, closest to the shops. One of the policemen was standing directly in front of him, blocking the way, and he slowed down, not daring to get too close. At the same time, he glanced back at the chestnut seller who was talking to the bus driver. Even at this distance, Alex got a sense of their confusion. The chestnut seller turned round, looking for him, then began to move back towards his brazier, worried now that the boy in the hoodie might have stolen from him.

How long would it take him to notice the aerosol spray resting in the flames? And how long would it be before it exploded?

It was something he had learned in school. Everyone knew that you never put an aerosol can anywhere near a fire. The reason is simple. The can that Alex had taken was made of thin metal sheeting and contained two products. One was the hairspray – which was itself highly flammable. That was why he had chosen it. The other was a propel-lant ... the gas that would force the spray out when the nozzle was pressed. The gas was already highly pressurized but the heat of the burning coals would rapidly increase the pressure, turning the can, effec-tively, into a small bomb.

The idea was to create a diversion but it didn't seem to have worked and suddenly Alex was sweat-ing. The chestnut seller was already halfway back to his brazier. If he saw the can he would yank it out immediately. And now Alex had another, even more unpleasant thought. Charlie mustn't get too close. Suppose the can exploded as he leaned over the flames? He could get badly hurt or even killed. That wasn't what he wanted at all and he wished he'd had more time to come up with a less danger-ous plan.

It was too late. The can exploded. Alex heard a huge bang and saw the entire brazier disappear in a ball of fire. For a moment, the chestnut seller was invisible but then the flames shrank again and Alex was relieved to see that he was all right. The hood of the brazier had protected him from the worst of the blast. But all around him there were people screaming, running away. Blazing coals had been thrown in every direction. One man had been hit and the sleeve of his coat was on fire. There was a woman smothering her children in her arms, desperately trying to protect them. The bus drivers were panicking. There must have been oil or petrol on the road and a pool of fire had rippled under one of their vehicles, setting off its alarm. Smoke was pouring out from beneath it.

The police officers had been told to guard the station but how could they simply stand there while all this was happening? They didn't know if they had just witnessed a terrible accident or a terrorist attack but it didn't matter either way. Their first instinct was to help and, forgetting everything else, they ran forward – all four of them – into the crowd even as a column of fire ripped up inside the bus, shattering the windows and sending fragments of glass whirling over the crowd. Suddenly Brighton station had become a scene out of a war film. Miraculously, nobody had been hurt. But the smoke was billowing into the sky and everyone was screaming as they ran for cover.

Alex had slipped through the archway the moment it had been left unguarded. He was inside the station now, on the forecourt with a great glass and steel roof curving overhead. He was confronted by a long row of modern barriers with the platforms and the trains on the other side. He saw at once that there was no way he was going to get through without a ticket. If there had been any police inside the station they had rushed out to see if they could help. But there were plenty of uniformed railway guards manning the barriers. They had heard the commotion but they had been sensible enough to stay where they were. Nobody was going to get past them without being seen.

The train times were clearly signalled. Alex saw that a train for London was leaving Platform One at 14.46. It was now 14.44. Platform One was right in front of him. He couldn't get through the barrier but over to his left, a flight of metal steps led up to a staff office on the first floor, above an Indian food stall. He could see the door, set in the wall, high above. The staircase zigzagged up, slanting over the platform before folding back on itself to reach the door.

Alex didn't think twice. He ran up the stairs, hoping he wouldn't meet a guard or a driver. He reached a platform about halfway up and hoisted himself over the other railings, dropping about five metres to the platform below. He landed like a cat, both feet flat, his hands stretching in front of him. The train was leaving. He actually heard the hiss of the closing doors. Straightening up, he hurled himself into the nearest carriage. The door shut behind him.

Had anyone seen him? If they had, they would stop the train and come and arrest him. The next few seconds seemed to stretch out endlessly. He was aware of the other passengers examining him, wondering what was wrong. Perhaps they had heard the explosions too. Alex didn't breathe until the train jerked forward and began to move. With a sigh of relief, he slipped into a seat and watched Brighton station slide away behind him. Nobody came running out after the train. Gradually, it picked up speed.

It would take one hour and ten minutes to reach London. But he was on his way.

ACROSS LONDON

The train was delayed outside Preston Park.

They had only been moving a few minutes when they ground to a halt and a voice came over the speakers. It was a signal failure. "We'll hopefully be on our way as soon as possible," the driver announced, cheerfully.

Alex could only sit there, silently screaming. It was almost as if Nightshade had deliberately reached him and sabotaged the railway in order to delay him. He tried to work out how much time he had. They had left at a quarter to three. One hour ten minutes to London. When would the sun set? Around five o'clock. That meant there wouldn't be long until...

What? He still didn't know.

Alex was really hungry, but even if there had been a buffet car on the train, he had no money to buy food. To make matters worse, two women sitting opposite him had taken out sandwiches and crisps and were tucking in while they chatted. He was tempted to beg something from them but didn't dare draw attention to himself.

Finally, after what felt like hours, the train started again and he sat back and watched the empty fields and the grey sky crawl past as the train rolled – painfully slowly, it seemed to him – through the English countryside. He knew he couldn't even call Jack. He was too concerned that her phone would be tapped. Was there any other way he could reach her? Yes. Alex had an idea about that, although it wouldn't be possible for another hour when school ended. At least there didn't seem to be a ticket collector on board. Alex was worn out. He could still feel the drug in his system. And looking down the long, empty carriages with their plain, modern seating and glass shelves, there was definitely nowhere to hide.

Sitting by the window with his head resting against the glass, he managed to doze off and the next thing he knew, he was at Blackfriars Bridge the largest station in London. The platform stretched all the way across the River Thames and, looking out of the window, Alex could see fabulous views of the city with the Gherkin and the Shard right in front of him. It reminded him of the photographs he had seen on the first floor of the Temple.

Somebody had left a copy of *Metro*, the free London newspaper, on the floor. Alex leaned forward and picked it up. Sure enough, he found himself – or rather, Julius Grief – on the front cover with another headline warning the public not to come near. He was about to fold it away when he noticed a second, smaller headline on the same page.

LORD CLIFFORD MEMORIAL

He had seen the name before. Where? Of course – he remembered – it had been inside the Temple along with all the photographs and weather charts. The train was still idling at the platform, refusing to move, and Alex quickly read the story. James Clifford, a former Home Secretary, was having a memorial service this evening at seven-thirty in St Paul's Cathedral. Staring through the enormous plate-glass windows that ran along the edge of the station, he could actually see the golden cross on the dome of the cathedral poking up above the other buildings. It was on one side of the Thames with the Shard on the other.

Everything came together at that moment. Suddenly he knew the target, the time, the method ... all of it.

Snatching up the newspaper, he launched himself out of his seat and onto the platform, reaching it just as the doors closed behind him. The train moved away, disappearing into a tunnel. Alex stood there, catching his breath. Different thoughts were racing through his head, fighting for his attention. Number Six approaching the target on a coach. Number Nine and Eleven coming in by parachute. Nightshade communicating with them the same way they had communicated with Freddy when he escaped from Gibraltar. It was all mad and yet somehow, it made complete sense. The question was – how did he stop it?

He spotted what he was looking for further down the platform. A man with a guide dog had appeared, coming up the escalator. Alex hurried over to him.

"Excuse me, sir," he said. He was trying to sound as young as possible.

"Yes?"

"I'm really sorry to trouble you, but I've lost my phone and I need to call my mum. I wonder if you'd have one I could borrow."

"Of course." The man didn't even sound surprised. He reached into his pocket and took out an iPhone.

"I'll pay you for the call," Alex said.

"There's absolutely no need. Just make sure you're finished before the next train arrives."

Alex had chosen the one man in the station who wouldn't be able to identify him – even though he hated taking advantage of him and lying to him. But the entire panorama of London was right in front of him. He tried to imagine the ambulances, fire engines and police cars screaming across the city, everything at a standstill, people panicking. All this would happen in just a few hours if he was unable to prevent what Nightshade planned.

He quickly dialled – not Jack's number but Tom's. School would have finished at Brookland and by now Tom should be back home. He just hoped that Tom had remembered to charge his battery and that he hadn't had his phone confiscated for texting in class. Tom was Alex's closest friend but he was also remarkably unreliable.

The phone rang three times before it was answered. "Hello?" It was Tom's voice. He was puzzled because he didn't recognize the number that was calling him.

"Hi – this is Darklight," Alex said.

He didn't want to say his name. He had rung Tom rather than Jack because he thought it less likely that Nightshade would have intercepted his mobile phone. But it was still possible that they were listening out and even mentioning his name might trigger some sort of recognition software. Darklight was the main character in Deadmaster, the computer game that he and Tom had been working on.

"Darklight?" There was a long pause. Then – "Where the hell are you? What's going on? Have you seen the newspapers?"

"Tom – don't say anything. People may be listening."

"Why? What are you talking about?" There was another silence as Tom brought himself back under control. "What do you want me to do?"

Alex heaved a sigh of relief. That was Tom for you. He wasn't going to ask any more questions. He just wanted to help. "Listen to me," he said. "I need you to drop whatever you're doing and go round to my best friend...."

"I thought I was your best friend."

"My other best friend. You know who I mean. Tell her to meet me as soon as she can at the place we went to together. Where we saw the dolls. She'll know what I mean."

"I hope so. Because I don't."

"Tell her to meet me there. But warn her to be careful. There's a chance that she's being followed. And you take care too. This is really dangerous. I'm sorry to have to involve you."

"Don't worry. I was about to do chemistry home-work. I'm be happy to be involved."

"Thanks, Tom."

Alex rang off and handed the phone back to the blind man. "Thank you, sir," he said.

"That wasn't your mother," the man remarked. He didn't sound angry.

"It wasn't. I'm sorry. I lied to you."

The man nodded. "You sounded scared."

Alex thought for a moment. "I am."

"Then I hope you manage to find your friends. Good luck."

"Thank you."

Another train drew in and Alex took it. The station clock was showing 4.48 p.m. The sun had already begun to set.

Jack was in the kitchen, trying to concentrate on a book – *Learning the Law* – when the doorbell rang. There were newspapers scattered around her, all of them showing Alex's face. She had drunk half a dozen cups of coffee since the news had broken. She looked a wreck and she knew it. She had no idea what was happening and the worst of it was that there was nobody she could call, nothing she could do.

Puzzled, she got up and went to the hall. She opened the door and saw Tom Harris, dressed in his school uniform, standing on the other side. His shirt was untucked and he was sweating ... clearly he had cycled here at speed. The bike was lying on its side next to the front gate.

She was about to speak but, frantically, he brought his finger up to his lips, his eyes pleading with him.

"What?" She mouthed the word without saying it.

Tom pointed upstairs. Baffled, Jack let him in.

Tom took one last look over his shoulder, then piled into the house, closing the door behind him. He still didn't say anything but went straight upstairs into Alex's bedroom. He didn't need to ask the way ... he had been there a hundred times before. Jack had followed him and watched, astonished, as he went into the bathroom and turned on the shower.

"Tom? What on earth do you think you're doing?" she demanded as the water came cascading down.

"That's what they do in spy films," Tom said. "When they don't want to be overheard."

"There's nobody here."

"There may be microphones." He stepped closer to her, lowering his voice. "I had a phone call from Alex."

"Alex?" It was the one word Jack most wanted to hear and she almost shouted it out. Tom had to gesture at her with both hands, warning her to keep quiet. "Where is he?" she whispered.

"I don't know. He didn't tell me. And he was using someone's borrowed phone. He wants you to meet him. He said to go to the place with the drills. That's where he'll be."

"Drills? What was he talking about?"

"I don't have the faintest idea. He said you'd know."

Jack's mind was in a whirl. When was the last time she had seen Alex? She remembered. "Are you sure he said drills?" she asked. "Could it have been dolls?"

Tom frowned. "It could have been. He didn't have much signal and it was quite difficult to hear."

"The House of Dolls. That was the last place we met."

"That must have been it, then. He said it was where you saw the dolls. But he also said that you had to be careful. He said you might be being followed."

That made sense. Jack remembered her last moments at MI6, the police cars pulling in outside. She had known that something had gone seriously wrong and the news headlines had only confirmed it. The media had managed to get Alex confused with Julius Grief and part of her knew that it must have happened on purpose. Nightshade wanted him stopped and to do that they had turned him into a moving target.

"When does he want to meet?" Jack asked.

"He said as soon as you can."

Jack nodded. "I'm leaving now. Thanks, Tom – you can go back home."

"Forget that!" Tom looked offended. "He's my best mate and he called me. I'm coming too."

Jack was about to argue but she could see that Tom was determined and there was no time to waste. "All right," she said. "Let's go."

Two minutes later, they left the house, strolling out as if they were in no particular hurry to be anywhere else. They were both aware that they might be being watched and it was almost impossible to behave normally. They were pretending to be normal, which wasn't the same at all. The important thing was not to give the game away, not to let anyone know that they were suspicious. If there was someone following them, they would hopefully spot them and then take evasive action. And that would be easier if they kept the element of surprise on their side.

The road outside seemed to be pretty deserted. It was still too early for people returning from work and although Jack noticed a couple of cars parked a short distance away, she couldn't see anyone inside them. The house was in a quiet part of Chelsea, off the King's Road, and very few people ever went past. There was a woman walking her dog and while Jack didn't know her, she recognized the dog. A council worker was on his way home, pushing a cart with a collection of brooms. Otherwise, they were alone.

"Where has Alex been?" Tom asked.

"The last time I heard, he was in Gibraltar. To be honest with you, I've got no idea what's been going on." She sighed. "I really hoped this was all over."

"Being a spy?"

Jack nodded.

"So how come his face is in all the newspapers? And why are they calling him Julian Grief?"

"It's Julius Grief. And it's a long story, Tom. You'll have to ask Alex."

"I don't know how he's going to explain it all when he gets back to school."

They had turned onto the King's Road and walked down to the nearest bus stop. Jack glanced behind her as if looking for a bus and checked that there was nobody following them. In fact, a bus was just approaching and they jumped onto it, taking a seat at the back.

Jack looked out of the window and frowned. "That car..." she said.

Tom followed her eyes. "The black Nissan?"

"Yes."

"What about it?"

"There was a black Nissan parked near the house. I thought it was empty – but it had the same number plate."

"Are you sure?"

"RAY. It spells a word. That's how I noticed."

Tom twisted round, uncomfortably. "There are two men inside."

"Don't look!" Jack was sitting bolt upright, wondering what to do. She might be wrong. It might have been a different car at the house – but she couldn't take any chances. If there was someone following her, she couldn't lead them to Alex.

The evening rush hour had just begun and there was already a lot of traffic. The bus turned off the main road and came to South Kensington tube station. Jack got up. "We're getting off here," she said. "Just walk slowly. Don't look back. We have to pretend that everything's OK."

"Whatever you say." Tom got up too.

The bus stopped and they climbed down, then walked slowly to the station entrance. Out of the corner of her eye, Jack noticed the black Nissan pull in to the side of the road. The entrance to the station was right in front of her and she pointed as if explaining something to Tom. If the driver and the other man were watching her, they would assume that the bus was too slow and they had decided to take the Tube.

She turned the corner and immediately broke into a run. The entrance to the station was unusual in that there was an arcade with shops that connected two streets. The platforms and ticket office were reached down a flight of steps halfway along. Jack and Tom hurried past the steps and emerged on the other side. A taxi with a yellow light passed at exactly the right moment and she hailed it and jumped in.

"The British Museum!" She called out the destination and sat down breathlessly. Even as they set off, she was looking out of the back window. The man who was following her must have assumed she had gone down to the Tube. He hadn't come out of the station. She searched the cars that were closing in behind them and saw no sign of the Nissan. She was fairly sure they were safe.

"That wasn't bad," Tom said. "Almost as good as Alex."

"You've got to be kidding," Jack growled. "Alex would have blown them up or forced them off the road. Just a shame I forgot my hand grenade."

"Next time," Tom said.

They passed through a traffic light, which turned red behind them. Nobody followed.

Alex examined the House of Dolls from across the road. John Crawley had told him that this was an MI6 safe house but there was one question he had to ask himself. How safe was it? If it was true that MI6 had been shut down and that Mrs Jones and Crawley were both under arrest, then anyone could be waiting for him inside. His hope was that it was empty. It might be that very few people even knew about it. If so, it would provide him with exactly what he needed. It was also a perfect place to hide.

A taxi went past, followed by a couple of cars. Alex crossed the road, watched by the single teddy bear that had been left behind, sitting in the window.

He came to the door and examined the electronic keypad. When Alex had been brought here the first time, he watched the driver punch in a code. The six digits – 753159 – had formed the shape of a letter X and that had made it easy to remember. Of course, it was always possible that MI6 had changed the code. It might set off an alarm. Alex pressed the buttons. He heard a buzz and the door clicked open.

A hand grabbed hold of him.

Alex pivoted round, his fist lashing out – and only managed to stop himself at the last second. It was Jack! Tom was with her. He fell into her arms feeling all the weight in the world lifting off his shoulders.

"Where have you been?" Jack demanded. "I've been so worried about you!"

"Yeah," Tom added. "And do you know every policeman in the country is looking for you ... like you're sort of public enemy number one?"

"Let's talk inside," Alex said.

They went in. The door swung shut behind them.

LEAP OF FAITH

"What is this place?" Tom asked.

"It's an MI6 safe house," Alex said. "It's somewhere they bring their agents."

"It's creepy."

"You haven't seen it yet." Even as Alex talked, he was fiddling with one of the dolls ... the clown with orange hair. He jerked one leg, then another. Finally, he twisted the head and was rewarded with a click and a faint hum as an entire section of one wall, complete with dolls and teddy bears, slid into the floor revealing the gleaming new passageway behind.

"Wow!" Tom was impressed.

"Alex ... why have we come here?" Jack asked.

"I couldn't think of anywhere else to go and there's something I need."

"Are we being watched?"

Alex looked up for CCTV cameras. "I hope not."

Ahead of them was the conference room where Alex and Jack had met Crawley. The jamming equipment was still on the table but the hologram on the other side of the French windows had been switched off so there was no garden, only a bare brick yard. Alex quickly explored the rest of the safe house. Another door led into a dining room with a kitchen leading off and to his relief there was a well-stocked fridge and shelves full of tinned fruit, bread, biscuits, coffee, tea and slabs of chocolate ... enough to survive for several weeks.

On the other side of the corridor, Alex found an office with phones and computers but these all seemed to have been disconnected. A metal cabinet stood against one wall and it looked as if it might have been used to store guns or other weapons but unfortunately it was locked. Clocks on the wall showed the time in six different zones. A view of the street outside was being relayed to a giant screen.

Otherwise, there were several bedrooms with bathrooms and toilets. None of the beds had been made. The safe house wasn't just empty. It felt forgotten.

"So what now?" Jack asked.

"I need something to eat," Alex said. He hadn't had any food for almost twenty-four hours.

They made themselves ham sandwiches with fruit and yogurt. The house must have been restocked very recently as everything was fresh and that made Alex worry that someone might look in during the evening. It was just one more risk he would have to take. While they ate, he explained everything that had happened to him: the escape from the prison,

Tangier, Crete. He talked about Mrs Jones's children: Sofia was now in London, while William had been left behind. Finally, he told them about Leap of Faith.

"They're going to hit St Paul's tonight. As far as I can see, they're going to take out half the British government and hundreds of other people too."

"Why?" Jack asked.

"I don't know. But they've got the VX nerve agent Mrs Jones told us about. I saw biochemical suits when I was on the island."

"They're mad!" Tom said. "They're all mad!"

"But we can stop it," Jack cut in. "You've done all the work, Alex. All we have to do is call the police and the whole thing will be over."

"I wish it was that easy," Alex said. Before Jack could stop him, he went on. "First of all, we'd have to make them believe us. Are we sure we can even trust them? Pablo told Mr Crawley what was going to happen and he got killed. Mrs Jones tried to stop it and she was arrested. And somehow Nightshade found out who I was. They said they had an agent working for them in London. I didn't make any mistakes ... so somebody must have told them! My face is in all the newspapers and they're saying I'm Julius Grief. Nightshade must have planted the story – which means they could have people working for them all over London. In the newspapers, in the police, maybe even in MI6."

He looked across at the clocks. It was now six o'clock. "We don't have time to get the police involved. The service at St Paul's begins in ninety minutes."

"Then what are we going to do?" Jack asked.

"There's only one thing we can do."

"No..." Jack began.

"We're going to have to stop them ourselves."

The coaches bringing the different choirs to St Paul's Cathedral had already begun to draw in. They were pulling up in an area below street level, at the back of the building. A single door led into the crypt, directly beneath the space where the service would take place. Eight schools were being represented and over a hundred children would be singing. Because of all the extra security, it took a long time for each coach to arrive.

First the coaches were stopped on the approach road which sloped down underneath the cathedral. The road led to an enclosed yard, concealed from the general public with a glass-fronted office on one side. A number of policemen and police dogs were waiting for them. The drivers had to show ID and authorization, and only then were the coach doors opened and the passengers let out. Everyone had to walk through metal detectors before they were allowed into the building itself, and although they didn't know it, they had also passed through an SPO-NX screening system which scanned the natural radiation coming from their bodies and searched for "cold" spots. If they had been carrying anything made of metal, plastic or ceramic, it would have shown up and they would have been stopped at once. Nobody entering the cathedral was allowed to carry anything, not even a hymn book or Bible.

The children did not need to carry ID themselves but all their names had been written down, they were accompanied by their teachers and there was a headcount as they went in. Despite all these precautions, the police had to fight against the fact that it was getting dark and, inevitably, there was a lot of confusion with so many people arriving. Also, the children were excited to be performing at such a huge event and refused to stand still. Nightshade had expected all this. They had used it.

Nobody had noticed the extra passenger travelling on the second coach, which had stopped off at three schools during its journey, picking up forty-five choirboys and girls. Sofia Jones, Number Six, had been hiding in the toilet when the coach left its depot and had quietly slipped out once it was full. It is possible to spend a million pounds on security and still make very basic mistakes. In this case, the children were not wearing uniforms and it was impossible to tell who had come from which school. Nobody recognized Sofia. But they all assumed that she must belong to one of the other schools.

She passed through the various scanners for the simple reason that she was not carrying anything. When she arrived at the entrance, a security guard with a clipboard asked her name and she smiled and pointed at the list of names. "Lucy Wilson." The name was there but the guard had already ticked it. "You've already done me," she explained. "I went back out to find my friend."

The guard shouldn't have believed her. He should have pulled all the children out again and demanded a new headcount. This was the moment of truth and Nightshade had calculated exactly what would happen. The guard was young and new to the job. He was nervous about causing a long delay for no good reason. The girl was about fourteen years old and looked completely innocent! She had arrived here with all the others and wasn't carrying anything dangerous ... or anything at all. If he stopped her and questioned her, he was afraid he might even make her cry.

He smiled. "All right, Lucy!"

Number Six went in with the other children. Inside, officials from the cathedral were separating the boys from the girls – steering them towards the areas where they would change into their cassocks and surpluses. There were people everywhere: officials, priests, teachers, police, performers and journalists. A BBC television crew was covering the event and had set up a camera in front of the altar.

They didn't, however, notice the single girl who made her way across the chapel to a small, arched door in the corner, where a spiral staircase led upwards. From here, she made her way to the dome.

* * *

On the southern side of London Bridge, about a mile and a half from St Paul's, a van was drawing into an empty street. This part of London, on the other side of the River Thames, was surprisingly empty, as if everyone had gone home early to avoid all the noise and disruption. It was already getting dark. The sun had set long ago but it had left a glow in the sky and the clouds were reflecting the electric lights of the city below.

The van stopped and its engine was turned off. It had parked underneath the Shard, one of the most famous and certainly the tallest building in London. The Shard was a monster, an invader that had begun to dominate both the city and the sky from the moment it opened. It had seventy-two floors that were occupied and fifteen more above them. Forty-four lifts and three hundred and six flights of stairs kept everything connected. Eleven thousand glass panels had been used in its construction.

Alex, Jack and Tom had been standing on the other side of the street for more than an hour, waiting for something to happen. Alex was convinced that the Shard had to be the answer – the way into St Paul's. The so-called Teachers had put the children through intensive parachute training. He had taken part in it himself. But at the same time, he knew that all the newspapers had reported that the airspace over London was closed. There was no way a private plane would be able to get anywhere near. So how else could they reach the dome? He remembered Brother

Mike briefing the parachutists. *"When you're three hundred and ten metres above the ground. You've got to be in position by then."* Jack had checked it on her phone. The Shard was 309.7 metres high. That was where the challenge began.

The red circle painted on the ground at Kavos Bay had to represent the dome of St Paul's. The smaller, blue circle was the tower on top of the dome with a walkway going all the way round the ball and cross. It was known as the Golden Gallery. This was where they were supposed to land.

Alex felt his pulse quicken as a door in the side of the van slid open and two figures got out, both dressed in black jeans and combat jackets. They were carrying large nylon containers that looked like backpacks but he knew they must be the rigs for their parachutes. Each of them had a helmet looped over one arm and a pair of goggles hanging around their neck. Freddy went first, with Number Eleven a few steps behind him. Neither of them hesitated. A door had been left open for them at the back of the Shard. They walked towards it.

"That was them," Alex said. "We've got to move..."

"And when you catch up with them?" Jack asked.

Alex said nothing. He answered her by drawing a knife out of his pocket. He had taken it from the kitchen at the safe house.

Tom stared. "You're going to kill them?" he muttered.

"Why do you always think I'm going to kill people?"

Alex shook his head. "Of course I'm not. All I have to do is cut one cord of their parachutes and the whole thing is over. If they can't jump, they can't get anywhere near St Paul's." He turned to Jack. "Call the police now. Tell them where I am." Suddenly he was deadly serious. "Tell them about the VX. They must have it with them. This whole area's going to have to be cordoned off."

"You're not going after them on your own!"

"I'm coming with you," Tom insisted.

"No." Alex shook his head. "I was trained for this all my life. I'm used to it. You've helped me enough just by being here. Thanks, both of you. This won't take long. I'll be right back."

Before there could be any more argument, he slipped the knife back into his pocket and hurried towards the open door.

Leaving the street, he found himself in a service corridor that seemed to run the full length of the building although it was hard to be sure. The Shard was so huge and rose so far into the sky that it was unclear where it actually began and ended. Everything was silent apart from the faint hum of machinery in the air. It was obvious though that this entrance was not meant to be open to the public. Someone must have been bribed to unlock it from inside. Alex walked past a trolley loaded with cleaning equipment, piles of boxes and shelves with tool boxes, industrial torches, spare light bulbs and files. There was a lift at the far end. It was intended for maintenance engineers rather than visitors. There was nothing fancy about the lift doors – two sheets of metal that had just slid shut. The walls were bare, covered with white tiles.

He approached the lift doors, knowing that he had missed Freddy Grey and Number Eleven, who were already on their way up to the roof. Alex could see a blinking arrow in a panel, marking their progress. It didn't matter. His plan had always been to confront them on the roof, while they were distracted, preparing for the jump. Sabotage the parachutes and the whole thing would be over. It was as simple as that. He just had to get close enough before they saw him.

The lift had arrived at the top. He punched the button, calling it back down again.

"Who are you? What are you doing here?"

The voice came from directly behind him. Alex whirled round to find himself facing a huge bearded man, all muscle, dressed in brown overalls. He was built like a gorilla with massive arms and hands hanging below his waist. He wasn't security. He looked like a maintenance engineer. Perhaps he was the man who had been paid to leave the door open. He was carrying an oversized monkey wrench in his right hand. He might have been using it to mend something in the building but it looked suspiciously like a weapon.

"I'm with them." Alex pointed vaguely towards the elevator and the roof.

"No. You're not."

"Nightshade sent me."

"I've never heard of them." Was he lying? He was gazing at Alex with naked violence smouldering in his eyes.

"Maybe you should call the police." Alex said the first thing that came into his head. He was trying to work out what he was going to do. The corridor was too narrow for any karate strikes and anyway the man was twice as big as him. Would a single punch or kick even take him down? He thought about the knife in his pocket. He hoped he wouldn't have to use it.

"I don't need the police." The man tightened his grip on the monkey wrench. His words confirmed what Alex had suspected. If he was just a maintenance engineer, he wouldn't have hesitated to call in the authorities. He must have been paid by Nightshade. His job was to let the two parachutists in and to protect them while they made their way to the roof.

Alex tensed himself, waiting for the attack that he knew was about to come.

But then there was a dull thud and the man grunted, his eyes widening in surprise. Slowly, he turned round and Alex saw a figure standing behind him. Tom Harris had followed him into the building. He was holding one of the heavy torches that he had picked up from the trolley. He had crept up on the man and brought it crashing down on the back of his neck. Even so, it hadn't been enough to knock him out. Tom swung the torch a second time, smashing it into the side of his head. The man spun on his feet and collapsed onto the floor.

The two friends were left staring at each other. Tom looked amazed. "I've never done that before," he said. He grimaced. "Do you think I've killed him?"

"No." The man's chest was rising and falling and Alex could hear his breath. "You shouldn't have come in," he said.

"I was worried about you. Jack's outside, talking to the police."

"Do they believe her?"

"It didn't sound like it."

The lift had come back down. The doors slid open. "You'd better get out of here before he wakes up," Alex said, glancing at the figure on the floor.

Alex stepped into the lift and pressed the button for the top floor. Nothing happened. He pressed it twice more, then noticed the glass pad next to the controls and realized that the lift needed an electronic key. He silently swore. That was something he had never considered. Of course, every lift in the Shard would have been programmed for authorized users. After everything that he had been through since he had woken up on the beach at Brighton, he might not even be able to reach the roof!

Tom had realized what was wrong and was already kneeling beside the unconscious maintenance man, searching his pockets. "Help me turn him over!" he called out.

Alex hurried over to him and between them they managed to turn the man onto his back. He weighed a ton. Now they had access to the front pockets of his overalls and Tom pulled out a bunch of keys attached to a card. He handed them to Alex. "Here you are!"

"Thanks."

The maintenance man groaned. Tom picked up the torch and hit him again.

That was the last thing Alex saw as he pressed the card against the pad and the lift doors slid shut. He hit the top button and at last the lift began the journey up. He had wasted a lot of time – dealing with the maintenance man and then finding the key. The lift was moving swiftly between the floors – he could feel his stomach sinking – but still it seemed to be taking an age to reach the top. Was he going to arrive in time?

Finally, the doors opened again and Alex stepped out into an arena he would never forget.

The lift had taken Alex to the very top of the building, far above the observation platform on the seventy-second platform. The extraordinary design of the skyscraper had left the upper floors open to the elements. The glass windows fell away as if they had been cut with a giant knife and walls made of criss-crossing steel girders rose up on all sides, so it was as if the actual building had somehow faded away. The walls were transparent. He could see all the way through them to the night sky and the twinkling lights of the city which were scattered for miles around. At the same time, he was hit by the full force of the wind. At ground level, everything was calm. Up here, he was in a gale.

Freddy Grey was standing on the very edge of the platform with his back to Alex. He was wearing his helmet and goggles and his parachute was already out of the rig and open, dangling over the edge of the building, connected to two metal rings on either side of his chest. Number Eleven was kneeling behind him, preparing his own parachute the same way. Alex knew at once what they were doing and he felt his heart lurch at the thought of it. It had been explained to him by the SAS – the technique known as the "Rollover McConkey" launch. In a few moments, Freddy would dive forward head first off the edge of the building, throwing himself over his canopy. The reason was simple. The difference in height between the Shard and St Paul's was just two hundred metres. Freddy couldn't afford to plunge down too far if he was going to jump from one to the other. So the parachute had to be open; deployed from the very start.

Alex started forward but before he had taken more than a single pace, Freddy leapt. He gave no warning. He didn't even look round – as if even he, who feared nothing, didn't dare think about what he had to do. He stepped off the edge and dived forward in a somersault, dragging the cords with him. Within seconds, he was underneath the parachute and airborne. The canopy had inflated and the wind was carrying him safely away from the Shard. Alex might even have admired him for his daring and for the success of the manoeuvre. Instead, he had to fight back a sense of failure that drained all the strength out of him.

He had arrived too late. Freddy Grey was on his way to St Paul's, doubtless carrying the nerve agent with him. Alex had thought he could end the operation here. He had been wrong.

He knew what he had to do without even thinking about it. It was impossible to hear anything out here at the top of the Shard, and Number Eleven, still preparing his rig, was unaware that Alex had come out of the lift. Alex continued towards him and put all his strength into a palm heel strike which slammed into the side of the other boy's head, knocking him off his feet. It was the first time he had ever deliberately used a karate move against someone his own age and he hated doing it – but he knew he had no choice and no time to consider the alternatives.

Moving very quickly, trying not to imagine what lay ahead, he dragged off the other boy's jacket and put it on himself. He and Number Eleven were about the same size but it was a snug fit. He added the helmet and the goggles, then examined the rig. There was a square pocket at the back with something inside. He opened it and drew out an odd-looking container, the same shape as a rugby ball though about half the size. It was made out of some sort of strengthened plastic with a metal stud at one end and narrow fins at the other. It didn't weigh very much. When he tilted it, he could feel some sort of liquid moving inside.

Alex felt sick. It was obvious what he was holding. He had the deaths of a thousand people in his hands, for this had to be the missile that contained the VX nerve agent. Presumably, there was some sort of detonator concealed inside the nozzle. Number Eleven would drop it and it would explode when it hit the ground. The nerve agent would be dispersed. Everyone it touched would die.

Freddy Grey would be carrying a second missile. Alex had no doubt about it. Nightshade had taken out insurance. If one boy failed to reach St Paul's, the plan could still go ahead. If both boys made it, the attack would be twice as deadly.

There was nothing Alex could do with this first missile now and he needed the pocket for something else. Very carefully, he carried it over to the edge of the roof and concealed it in a gutter. With a bit of luck, the police would arrive before Number Eleven recovered consciousness and they would find it and ensure it was neutralized. But he couldn't hang around here waiting for them. Freddy Grey could already have reached St Paul's. He had vanished into the night sky and now there was no sign of him.

Everything had gone wrong. Alex had to follow him.

Leap of Faith. Now he knew how it had got its name.

He strapped the rig onto his back, then draped the parachute over the edge of the Shard so that it hung below him. There were two cords that clipped into the metal rings on his chest. He didn't want to look at London but he couldn't stop himself. There it was, horribly far below him, the Thames a twist of steel reflecting the light of a moon that had slithered out from behind the clouds as if to watch the boy who might be about to die. He saw cars crossing the different bridges, lights blazing white in one direction, glowing red in the other. And thousands more lights gleaming behind the windows of offices, hotels, flats, houses. London stretched all the way to the horizon. Even there it didn't seem to end.

Alex felt the wind tugging at him, urging him to do it.

He jumped.

THE ORNAMENTAL GALLERY

They were the most terrifying two seconds of Alex's life. Everything was confused. The sky, the Shard and the city had dissolved into each other, and he had no way of knowing what was up and what was down. He was a spinning ball, falling, out of control, and there was a part of him that wondered if he hadn't just committed suicide. But then he heard the flap of material opening above his head and at the same time the two cords pulled at either side of his chest as they became taut. Suddenly he was hanging, not falling, and, looking up, he saw a wing of grey nylon stretching out over his head ... not a parachute but an aerofoil, specially designed to cut sideways through the air.

He couldn't think straight but instinct made him reach up and find the two toggles that would allow him to steer. That was the easy bit. Pull the left toggle to turn left and the right toggle to turn right. Except that the wind was blowing him all over London and there were all sorts of thermals – air currents – being thrown at him because of the different heights of the skyscrapers below. Right now, Alex's life depended on a stretch of "ripstop" nylon that measured about ten metres from tip to tip. If the air currents were too violent, the whole thing would crumple and that would be the end of it: he would plunge to his death.

Alex looked down and saw the glittering train tracks that snaked out of London Bridge station. There were so many of them! For just a brief moment he felt a sense of wonderment; the city was so huge, a home to eight million people, with thousands and thousands of roads and buildings and buses, cars and trains, everything in constant motion twenty-four hours a day. How could anything so vast have been created? How did it even work? He saw the moon beaming down on him and almost laughed, finding himself suspended in a sort of no man's land between the city and the universe.

Then he was hit by a sudden gust and the terror returned. He could see St Paul's directly in front of him on the other side of the river and knew that he had to approach it from exactly the right angle and at exactly the right speed, or he would miss it altogether and everything he had done would have been for nothing. At least the wind was behind him, carrying him over the city at about twenty miles per hour. Somewhere in his head he tried to work out his glide ratio. Gravity was pulling him down. The wind was carrying him across. He had to work things out so that he was still high enough by the time he reached St Paul's – and it also flashed through his mind that he would have to circle the cathedral in order to land into the wind. His target was the smaller gallery that ran in a circle beneath the ball and cross. Somehow he would have to grab on to it. He would actually be above the dome ... at least that was the plan. If he missed his target or smashed into it, he would end up a very long way below it. And in several pieces.

St Paul's seemed to be coming towards him terribly fast. He pulled with both hands. This lowered the edge of the aerofoil, which in turn had two effects. It slowed him down and allowed him to rise slightly in the air. He was close enough to the cathedral to see the TV vans and the police cars parked outside, and although it might have been his imagination, he thought he heard a brief burst of organ music. Well, that was suitable. This might, after all, turn out to be his own funeral. He was flying to the right of the building, over the south transept and then the choir. This was where he had to make his turn.

He pulled with his left hand and felt the air currents move. He was freezing cold, suspended high over London, but the sweat was pouring off him. He was too low! He could see the circular railing that enclosed the gallery, the archways and the door behind it, the columns holding up the next part of Sir Christopher Wren's glorious construction. He was still falling diagonally, swooping out of the night sky. He twisted round into the wind and felt it slowing him down. The railing was right in front of him, filling his vision. Now! He reached out and grabbed hold of it. His arms shuddered as they took the weight of his body and his spine jerked as if it was going to snap in half. His thigh smashed into stone and his shoulder into metal. He almost let go and fell. He could feel the parachute whipping in the wind, trying to tear him away from the edge. For the last sixty seconds it had saved his life. Now it was as if it had changed its mind and wanted to kill him. With a groan, Alex reached for the release handle which was hanging on the right-hand side of his harness. He pulled and the aerofoil was torn away, disappearing in the wind. Alex clung there for a moment, regaining his strength. Then he pulled himself over the railing, collapsing on the other side. He had made it! He was safe.

The thought was no sooner in his mind than he remembered Freddy Grey, the second VX canister and the audience of two thousand people below. This was far from over. In some ways it had only just begun.

He moved towards the door, noticing that the bolts had been drawn from the inside. That must have been Sofia's work. There had been a ton of security surrounding the cathedral. It would have been impossible to carry the nerve agent through the main door. But in the growing darkness, nobody would have noticed two parachutists dropping out of the sky, high above the electric lights in the streets and office buildings, and it had been Sofia's job to let them in.

But where was Freddy now and where exactly was he heading? Alex remembered a school visit to St Paul's. After they had looked around the cathedral floor, they had climbed about two hundred and fifty steps to the famous Whispering Gallery. It had got the name because if you whispered against the wall on one side, you could be heard thirty-three metres away on the other. That had to be it!

In fact, Freddy was waiting with Sofia for him one level down. He had taken off his helmet and goggles but the rig was still on his back. Sofia was with him.

"What took you so long?" Freddy called out. There was no chance of their being overheard. They were inside the dome; a strange world of curving walls, spiral staircases, metal girders and empty spaces which seemed both cramped and endless at the same time. Alex remembered now the photographs that he had seen inside the Temple. As he climbed down, his own footsteps echoed all around him, but otherwise everything was silent.

He had to answer but didn't want to give himself away. He was lucky that Number Eleven had been chosen as Freddy's backup. Alex and Number Eleven looked similar. They both had fair hair. Alex's face was largely hidden by his helmet and goggles, and he was high above both Freddy and Sofia. Even so, his voice could still give him away and he answered with nothing more than a grunt, as if the question had annoyed him.

It was enough for Freddy. "Wait for us here," he said, turning to Sofia. "You need to make sure no one comes up."

"I know what I have to do," Sofia replied, coldly.

"We'll be five minutes."

He was already on the move, making his way down the next flight of stairs. Alex followed, brushing past Sofia and being careful to keep his face turned away from her. Freddy had come to a wall painted olive green and, set in the middle of it, there was a door of the same colour with no obvious handle. He prised it open and at once Alex heard organ music and singing that welled up from below. The memorial service for Lord Clifford had begun. A steep flight of steps, almost a ladder, led down to a narrow walkway that ran in a complete circle with a curving wall on one side and a railing, chest-high, on the other. Alex reached the bottom and caught his breath.

Finally it was just the two of them ... just as it had been in Gibraltar when Freddy had been in prison and Alex had been sent to get close to him. They were in an extraordinary place tucked high up inside the dome of St Paul's Cathedral, somewhere that no member of the public ever came. Circular windows, like portholes, had been placed at intervals in the wall and the doorway that they had just come through was itself circular, giving the impression that they were inside a ship or a submarine.

The Ornamental Gallery. That was what the Teachers had called it when he had overheard them talking in Crete. This had to be it.

Alex looked over the railing and saw a white and grey marble chessboard far, far below. About two or three hundred chairs had been arranged in sections. They occupied the space between the north and south transepts, the nave and the high altar, and were presumably reserved for special guests. Despite what he had thought earlier, Alex realized that he was high above the Whispering Gallery. Nobody would see him, even if they happened to look up. And when Freddy dropped the VX missile, it would explode in the very heart of the congregation. Not a single person in St Paul's would escape.

He already had it in his hands! Alex had been too slow. Just as he had guessed, the missile was exactly the same as the one that Number Eleven had been carrying and which he had left on the roof of the Shard. He wondered if the police had arrived there yet. They certainly hadn't come to St Paul's. The service was continuing, uninterrupted. The school choirs were singing a hymn: "*There's a wideness in God's mercy*". The music was beautiful and he could clearly make out the words. It occurred to him that Nightshade were showing no mercy at all and that their own, fake religion had nothing to do with what was being celebrated here.

The police didn't know that anything was wrong. Nobody was going to help him. If he was going to stop this from happening, he had to do it on his own.

"Freddy!" he called out.

Freddy looked up, startled. Alex took off his helmet and goggles. "Julius?" He couldn't believe what he was seeing.

"My name isn't Julius. It's Alex."

"How did you get here? What are you doing?" Freddy sounded almost amused, as if the whole thing was an enormous surprise that had been arranged for his benefit.

"I've been sent to tell you. It's all over. Leap of Faith has been cancelled."

"No." Freddy shook his head. He was holding the missile close to his chest. "That's not true."

"It is, Freddy." Alex took a step towards him. "If you drop that missile, you'll kill thousands of people. Some of them are children. Do you hear those voices? They're school choirs! Why would you want to kill children?"

"I do what the Creator tells me!"

"You mean you do what he tells the Teachers. But the Teachers have been lying to you. Everything they ever told you was a lie."

"You don't know. You don't know anything!"

"Yes, I do. I'm your friend..." Alex took another step. Four more steps and he would be close enough to reach the missile.

"You were sent to Gibraltar to trick me." Freddy was angry. "It was you who lied to me."

"No. Those people you met in London, they were your parents. The Teachers stole you before you were old enough to remember. They've taught you that it's a good thing to kill people. But it's not. Nobody in their right mind would believe that. Trust me. Or if you don't trust me, look into yourself. Do you enjoy killing? Have you ever enjoyed it?"

"I do what I'm told!"

"Then ask the Creator now. Ask the Teachers. You hear their voices! If I'm lying to you, they'll tell you ... like they always do. They spoke to you in Gibraltar, didn't they! And I heard them when we were going to bed in Kavos Bay. They talk to you all the time. But if I'm lying to you, why aren't they telling you that now?"

Freddy cocked his head as if trying to hear something and Alex took another step forward. Far below, the hymn was nearing the end. "For the love of God is broader than the measure of our mind..."

"Ask them!" Alex urged.

Another step.

"I don't need to ask them!"

"They've gone, haven't they, Freddy! They're not in your head any more."

Three steps away from him, Alex knew that he had got it right and that the huge gamble he had taken had paid off.

The voices.

All along he had been aware that Freddy was somehow in contact with the Teachers. How else had he been able to find his way down the Rock of Gibraltar at night without ever having been there before? When they had reached a fence, Freddy had known, without doubt, which direction to take and he had led them to the abandoned cinema, the one place on the peninsula which the authorities hadn't thought of searching. It was supposed to be locked, of course, but Nightshade had arranged for the door to be smashed in, just as they had arranged for La Máquina to arrive the next day. Alex remembered that too. Two men – Matiás and Sebastián – had come to the cinema and Freddy had known they were there before there was any sound of them. Someone had told him.

Alex had puzzled about it all along and then, inside the dormitory at Kavos Bay, he had actually heard the voices himself. He had searched for microphones in the room but had been unable to find them, and in the end he had come to the obvious conclusion. The voices had to be inside Freddy's head. Somehow, using some sort of technology that he could only guess at, the Teachers were talking directly to the Numbers.

He remembered two things. First, there was the strange scar on the side of Freddy's neck. Alex had seen an identical scar on William when the two of them had been made to fight in the gymnasium. And then there was the recording studio inside the Temple with a bank of audio mixer numbers from one to twenty-three. Only it wasn't a recording studio: it was a radio-transmitting room. This was where the

Teachers came to contact the Numbers. It had to be.

But nobody was talking to Freddy now and there was a reason for that too.

When Alex had first been taken to the conference room inside the House of Dolls, Mr Crawley had shown him a machine sitting in the middle of the table. *"It's a portable RF inhibitor. It'll jam every radio frequency..."* MI6 had used it as a security device, to make sure they weren't being overheard. It was the same size as a small book and Alex had gone back to the House of Dolls to steal it. He was carrying it now, in the pocket of his parachute rig. He had turned it on before he made the jump and knew that Freddy wouldn't be able to receive any signal at all. He could pray all he liked. But for once, neither his Creator nor his Teachers would reply.

"Ask them!" Alex insisted. "Am I your enemy?"

Freddy stared at him. Alex moved forward. Two steps away.

"If our love were but more simple..." The last verse of the hymn had begun.

"They're not saying anything because they know I'm right." Alex held out a hand. "Give me the VX. You're not a bad person, Freddy. You don't want to kill anyone. This is all over now. You can go home and have your old life back again. Your mum and dad are waiting for you. You have no idea how much they've missed you."

"No..."

"Yes!" Another step. "That's why I was sent to you.

Not to hurt you but to help you. Please..."

Alex had reached Freddy. Gently, he reached out and took hold of the missile, his fingers closing around the plastic frame. He knew that Freddy had the power to hurt him; to kill him even. But without the voices to guide him, he was unsure of himself and perhaps the child he had once been was still there, lurking somewhere inside.

Alex had the missile. He could feel the liquid moving inside. But Freddy still hadn't let go of it. It was between them.

"...*our lives would be illumined...*"

"I promise you, Freddy! No-one's going to hurt you any more."

Alex pulled gently. Now he alone held the missile.

"No!" This time it was a shout. Freddy had been fighting with himself – the boy he had been against the Number he had become. But it was the Number who had won and Alex saw that he had only a few seconds to act. Freddy was furious. He would kill Alex as quickly and as cold-bloodedly as he had murdered the four armed policemen in Rio de Janeiro. Then he would drop the missile on the congregation inside St Paul's.

Alex couldn't allow him to do that. He jerked backwards and sideways, hurling himself over the steel railing and into the air, taking the VX with him, cradling it in his stomach.

The fall would have killed him, of course. The missile would have detonated and in the end he would have done Freddy's work for him. But he hadn't taken off his harness and although he'd used the main canopy, that still left the reserve. Even as he toppled backwards, clutching the missile with one hand, Alex used the other to reach for the handle on the left side of his chest and pulled. This activated a spring-fired mechanism which sent the smaller chute hurtling out behind him. A second later he had left Freddy far above him and he was falling, far too quickly, plunging towards the congregation seated in the crossing of the nave. There was a snapping sound above him and he saw, in the middle of the blur, that the cathedral had become a bright red square of nylon that had suddenly snapped open above him. The music had stopped. People were screaming as the figure – a terrorist or a lunatic – plunged towards them. He saw chairs toppling as the congregation scattered. The floor was rushing up towards him. There was no way he was going to land on his feet. He couldn't manoeuvre. He couldn't do anything except pray and even in the last seconds it occurred to him that at least he had chosen the right place for that.

He hit the ground on his back and once again he was lucky. In the last few seconds he had slowed down enough to survive and the rig on his back had acted as a cushion, softening the impact. Even so, all the breath was knocked out of him and he felt as if every bone in his body had been smashed to pieces. He wondered if the missile had detonated

and somehow found enough movement in his neck
to look down and examine it. It was in one piece.
Nothing was hissing or spilling out. It was intact.

Gradually the sound of screaming and stamping feet made its way into his consciousness. Out
of the corner of his eye he saw the Prime Minister
being hurried to safety. Priests and choristers were
running for cover, their cloaks flying while a dozen
armed police officers had appeared from nowhere,
forming a circle that closed around him. Even if
he'd wanted to, Alex wouldn't have been able to get
up. He found himself staring down the muzzles of
a dozen automatic machine guns.

"Oh my God!" somebody shouted. "It's Julius
Grief!"

"No. I'm Alex..."

But Alex had passed out before he could complete
his own name.

A FEW LOOSE ENDS

Three days later, Mrs Jones found herself once again crossing the splendid entrance hall of the Foreign Office in Westminster, on her way to see Dominic Royce. A great many things had changed since the last time she had been here. First of all, she had been reinstated as head of MI6 Special Operations. London had come within inches of being hit by a devastating terrorist attack which would have left thousands dead and it was thanks to her that it hadn't happened. It was she, after all, who had recruited the fifteen-year-old agent who had prevented it.

Mrs Jones had not forgotten what Royce had done. First, he had ordered her to get rid of Alex Rider. When she had refused, he had closed her down and put her under house arrest. Well, she was back now. She was coming to this meeting straight from Downing Street, where she had spent half an hour with a Prime Minister who would never forget the sight of a teenage boy falling out of the air in

419

St Paul's. As winter drew closer, the weather had turned colder and that seemed to suit her mood. She was angry, in no mood to forgive as she strode towards the great staircase.

And there was another difference. She was on her own. Owen Andrews, Royce's assistant, had not been there to greet her.

She didn't need him. She knew the way. She climbed to the second floor and continued to the door at the end. The secretary who had met her before was waiting for her but if she had been unwelcoming on that first visit, this time she was all smiles.

"Good morning, Mrs Jones. Mr Royce is expecting you. You're to go right in. Can I get you a cup of coffee – and maybe a biscuit?"

"No, thank you. And could you please make sure we're not disturbed?"

"Whatever you say, Mrs Jones."

Dominic Royce was waiting for her, sitting behind his desk with his hands folded and a notepad in front of him. He had never been a physically large man but he seemed to have shrunk since the attack on St Paul's, as if the room was swallowing him whole. There was a sheen of sweat on his forehead and although he smiled, the eyes behind the wire-frame glasses were definitely nervous.

"Good morning, Mrs Jones," he said. "Please sit down."

Mrs Jones said nothing. She took her place opposite him.

"I want to begin this meeting by making a few things clear." The Permanent Under-Secretary was doing his best to sound forceful. "I am not going to apologize for removing you from your role and for briefly closing down Special Operations. I had given you direct orders. When you employed Alex Rider, you were acting against the law of this country and you were taking a risk which I considered to be unacceptable. I had every right to put an end to it. And you were in no position to argue."

"I wasn't expecting an apology," Mrs Jones said.

"You weren't? Well, that's good. At least we agree on something."

Royce took off his glasses and polished them with a handkerchief. This was the difficult bit. He put them on again.

"As things turned out, Alex Rider did a remarkable job. He located Nightshade. He worked out what they were planning. And, single-handedly, he managed to prevent it. I've sent a note to the Prime Minister. It's been suggested that he should get a medal for what he did."

"Alex has been offered medals before," Mrs Jones said. "But I'm afraid our agents don't go in for that sort of thing so, although I'm sure he's very grateful, I'll be turning it down on his behalf."

"Well, of course you must do what you think is right." Mrs Jones had referred to Alex as her agent and this time Royce hadn't argued. "I'm sure we both agree that we need to draw a line under all this and move forward," he went on. "I'm willing to forget that you disobeyed me. I see no reason why we shouldn't be able to continue working together as we did before."

"You're very kind," Mrs Jones said. Her voice was still cold.

"There are quite a few loose ends that need to be cleared up." Royce reached into his double-breasted jacket and took out a fountain pen. "Let me start with Alex Rider," he said. He was trying to be more friendly. "How is he?"

"Alex is back at school," Mrs Jones replied. "He's lucky to be alive. He base-jumped into the middle of St Paul's carrying a missile filled with a deadly nerve agent. His face was all over the news: he had been identified as Julius Grief and at that moment he was probably the most wanted man – or boy – in the country. There were thirty armed police officers inside and around the cathedral, and any one of them could have shot him. It was only because he was surrounded by priests and senior politicians that they held fire. He was also lying on his back and he had the good sense to put his hands out, palms up. He was clearly in no position to do anyone any harm.

"Even so, he was treated extremely roughly and he had several more bruises to show when he got back to Brookland. They took him to Paddington Green, which is exactly where we held Freddy Grey when he first entered the country. Two officers from Counter Terrorism interviewed him and of course he told them a story it was almost impossible to believe. However, they reported back to Sir Graham Adair in the Cabinet Office. Sir Graham happens to know Alex and after that, things happened very quickly. First of all, they contacted me. You'd put me under house arrest but that was immediately lifted. I went to Paddington Green and identified Alex and he went straight home."

"I'm glad to hear it. And what about the other boy? Frederick Grey?"

"Freddy was arrested trying to leave St Paul's. It's interesting that following his last encounter with Alex in the Ornamental Gallery – the highest gallery in St Paul's – he didn't offer any resistance. It's just as well because the police didn't know what they were dealing with and he could have killed quite a few of them before they found out."

"I understand there was a young girl with him."

"That's right. We haven't yet been able to find out her name. She refers to herself as Number Six. The plan was that she and Freddy would be picked up by an air ambulance belonging to Nightshade which would fly in as soon as the VX had been dropped. Nobody would have noticed it in all the panic. But since there was no attack, the helicopter never arrived and anyway the police were already on their way because they had been alerted by Jack Starbright. The two of them are now being held at a secure location outside London."

Mrs Jones was not going to tell Royce the truth,

that Number Six was her own daughter, Sofia. Apart from Alex, Jack and John Crawley, nobody knew that.

"You have to understand that although both children are extremely dangerous, they are themselves victims," she went on. "Nightshade had stolen them from their parents and had brainwashed them using a variety of techniques."

She paused.

"It's the most monstrous thing I've ever heard," she said. "First of all their names were taken from them, turned into numbers. Then they were drawn into a fake religion where they believed that their kidnappers were Teachers and that what they were doing would somehow make the world a better place. But the worst of it was that, all the time, they heard voices. Not imaginary ones. Real ones.

"Nightshade had operated on them and inserted radio transmitters inside their heads. That may sound impossible but the technology had been in use for some time. The Americans used it with their forces in Afghanistan. It's called a Molar Mic and it's basically a microphone and a speaker that has been drilled into the tooth. The sound is transmitted directly through the teeth and skull to the inner ear. They also had a radio loop which had been inserted into their necks. Alex noticed that several of the Numbers had the same scar which had been left over from the operation. He guessed what had been done to them even though he had no understanding of the science.

"Can you imagine what it must have been like for these poor children? From a young age they were isolated, taken away from their parents and given a view of the world that was totally false. Worse than that, they grew up hearing voices in their heads and they believed that it was some sort of creator telling them what to do. As soon as they were old enough, they were sent out on Nightshade's deadly missions. We've spoken to Alex about the four Teachers he met. One of them was called Sister Krysten. From his description, we believe that she may be Professor Krysten Schultz who worked as a director at the Harvard School of Engineering in America until she disappeared twelve years ago. She was at the forefront of a new technology, creating microscopic radio receivers by using the atomic imperfections in diamonds. It seems she left Harvard to join Nightshade and she, as much as any of them, helped create the Numbers."

Royce had listened to all this in silence. He looked shocked. "What about Nightshade?" he asked. "Have you managed to find them? Presumably Alex was able to tell you where they were."

"Yes. They'd taken over a military camp on the eastern tip of Crete. We sent an SAS team out there as soon as we'd heard from Alex but unfortunately we were too late. When the nerve agent wasn't released in St Paul's, they must have guessed their plans had gone wrong and that they might be in danger. So they evacuated. Kavos Bay was empty when we got there. We've got our forensic teams going over the place now but they seem to have taken great care to leave no clues behind. All the computers were gone. And the other children – there were twenty of them – had vanished too."

Mrs Jones took a deep breath. Again, she wasn't going to tell Dominic Royce, but the twenty children had included her son, William. She had got her daughter back but he was still missing.

"We still hope to find them," she said. "Two of the Nightshade children had died. They had been buried outside the church and we've dug up the bodies. We should be able to identify them from dental records and we'll be able to let their parents know. But as far as this business with Nightshade is concerned, it's far from over. I will track them to the ends of the earth. I do not use the word 'evil' very often but I think it perfectly applies to them. I will find them and bring them to justice."

"You can be assured that you have my full support," Dominic Royce said.

"Thank you."

"Have you managed to identify any of these other so-called Teachers?"

"Yes. As a matter of fact, we have. Again, the descriptions given to us by Alex were very helpful."

"I'm sure."

"The leader of the pack called himself Brother Lamar. We believe he is almost certainly Lamar Jensen, the former chairman of LJ Weapons Systems.

You'll probably remember that it was one of the biggest weapons manufacturing systems in the world, based in Hampton, Virginia. He was selling guns and missiles to every major government, including, America, India and Saudi Arabia.

"But then they found out he was also selling weapons to a number of terrorist organizations. Islamic State, the Taliban, Boko Haram ... they were just some of his customers and all the money they paid went straight into his back pocket. Anyway, he was arrested and he'd still be in jail except for the fact that he managed to escape and disappeared. That was fifteen years ago."

"And he set up Nightshade."

"Yes. In a way, it was a brilliant idea. He realized that the most effective weapon in the world is the human being who doesn't care if he lives or dies. He may have got his inspiration from the Japanese kamikaze pilots in the Second World War. He chose parents who were fit, active, connected to intelligence or the military and he stole their children. They were the raw material. Then he twisted their minds and sent them out into the world. And the fact that they were still children – or teenagers – helped. A boy and a girl playing with a radio-controlled plane in a park. Two Girl Guides with a tray of cakes. A choirgirl entering St Paul's Cathedral. Nobody would look at them twice. They were invisible, obedient and ready to die."

"What about the other two Teachers?"

"Brother Mike and Sister Jeanne. We're still working on them."

The Permanent Under-Secretary was beginning to relax. The meeting had gone better than he had expected. "Well, Mrs Jones," he said. "Once again, you have my thanks. You've done a brilliant job and I'm very glad we were able to iron out the little difficulties between us." He hesitated. "There is just one more thing."

"And what is that?"

Royce opened a drawer and took out a sheet of paper, a copy of an email that he had received that morning. "It concerns my assistant, Owen Andrews."

Mrs Jones said nothing, waiting for him to go on.

"I gave him a week's holiday to thank him for his hard work and he went to Costa Rica." He passed the email across. "I just received this from our ambassador in San José. It seems that Owen has been arrested. He was found unconscious on the beach. He was dressed in a Batman costume. And they found five hundred grams of cocaine concealed in a plastic bag..." Royce coughed. "...under his cape."

"Yes?" Mrs Jones didn't sound interested. She hadn't even glanced at the email.

"It's quite serious. The authorities there take a very dim view of drug smuggling. He could go to prison for ten years!"

"I'm afraid there's nothing I can do," Mrs Jones said.

"Well, I was just wondering..."

"How it happened? I can tell you that." She gave him the thinnest of smiles. "John Crawley arranged it."

"I'm sorry?"

"You won't be surprised to learn that Crawley was very upset by what happened. Owen hacked into our computers and Crawley told him that he would make him regret it for the rest of his life."

Royce's face darkened. "You're not saying that you support this sort of behaviour?" he demanded.

"I most certainly do support it," Mrs Jones said. "I thought it was well-deserved."

"This is outrageous." Royce was back to his old self. And he was furious. "You must be out of your mind if you think—"

"You can stop right there, Mr Royce." She waited until he had calmed down a little. "I know the truth," she said.

"I'm sorry?"

Mrs Jones took out a little plastic box of peppermints and slipped one into her mouth. It was something she always did when she had something unpleasant to say.

"This all began in Rio de Janeiro," she said. "Our agent, Pablo, knew that there had been a leak. "Nightshade was waiting for him and he was almost killed. Then, when he met Crawley in Flamengo Park, two children were there. We know now that they were Numbers Six and Nine. They had been sent to intercept Pablo's meeting with

John Crawley and this time they were successful. They killed Pablo with a remote-controlled plane.

"But how did they know he'd be there? Only four people in the entire world knew when and where that meeting was taking place. Pablo himself, Crawley, me..." She paused. "And you."

Dominic Royce stared at her. "I hope you're not suggesting that I told anyone about it," he stammered.

"No. I'm not suggesting it. I am saying it ... with certainty. You told Nightshade about Pablo. You also told them about Alex Rider. It was only after your assistant, Owen Andrews, found out that we had sent Alex to Gibraltar, disguised as Julius Grief, that Nightshade learned about it too. They drugged him and tried to use him as a diversion, and I have no doubt that they hoped he would be killed by our own forces."

Royce smiled. "Mrs Jones, I know you're annoyed with me but do you really think you can sit there and make these fantastic accusations?"

"And then there's the question of who tipped off the newspapers about Julius Grief." It was as if she hadn't heard him. "They were publishing their warnings about him before he arrived in the country. We've spoken to the editors and of course they protect their sources but we know that the information came from the Foreign Office."

"If we believed that Grief was returning to the UK, it was our duty to warn the public..."

"No. You knew it was Alex, not Julius Grief." Mrs Jones hadn't raised her voice but she sounded ferocious. "There's no point in your denying it. You're not the only one who knows how to hack computers. We've looked at yours. We've managed to pick up your email trail ... heavily encrypted, of course. But we have a record of all your correspondence with Nightshade.

"And there's something else. When Alex was at Kavos Bay, he overheard the Teachers talking about their client. They referred to him as the Doctor."

"I'm not a doctor."

"I know. But your initials are DR. They were talking about you. We've traced the payment of twenty million dollars that you paid to a bank in Geneva. You arranged for Lord Clifford to be killed at his home in Cookham so that there would be a memorial service. And you planned to kill everyone who attended, including the Prime Minister and the entire cabinet. There's only one thing we don't know and I'd be grateful if you'd tell me. And that is – why? What were you hoping to gain?"

There was a long silence. Dominic Royce sat where he was but it was as if part of him had left the room. He was hollowed out, empty. He knew there was no point arguing with this terrifying woman from MI6 Special Operations. She had beaten him. She knew everything.

"It was a wake-up call," he said. "You probably won't understand, Mrs Jones, but I was doing it for the good of the country."

"You're right. I don't understand."

"Then let me explain." He took out the handkerchief again and wiped it across his forehead. "Our politicians are completely useless!" He screwed the handkerchief in his fist and pounded down on the desk. "We have a government that doesn't know how to govern and an opposition that is mean, stupid and vile. Every day, when I look at Parliament, I see grown-ups behaving like children. They shout at each other. They're vain and self-interested. There are huge issues facing the world – global warming, plastic in the oceans, poverty, famine – but they behave as if it's actually them and their careers that are more important!

"I don't know where they all came from or how they got into power. But they have to go. It's been my dream! Wipe the lot of them out and start again. The average age of an MP in this country is fifty, Mrs Jones. *Fifty!* There's a whole generation out there who can make the world a better place but before they can do that we have to get rid of the people who stand in their way. And that was why I reached out to Nightshade.

"I would have liked to have put a canister of VX into Parliament. But that's impossible. It's too well protected. Somehow I had to get all the politicians out into the open. I had to persuade them to go somewhere I could reach them more easily. And then I had an idea for a memorial service. Lord Clifford was hugely popular. If he was dead, all the MPs would come to his memorial service, giving me the chance to get every one of them. Can you imagine how wonderful it would be if we could start afresh?"

"It wasn't just politicians in St Paul's," Mrs Jones said. It had been a long time since she had spoken. "You'd have killed thousands of innocent people."

"I was sorry about that. But it would have been the biggest attack on Great Britain since the Blitz. It would have brought us all together. It would have reminded us that we need to fight for our future." Royce was close to tears. "All I wanted to do was to make Britain great again."

"You don't make anything great by killing people," Mrs Jones said.

There was another silence.

"And what happens to me?" Royce asked.

Mrs Jones considered. "I think you should take a long holiday," she said.

Royce nodded. "That might be a good idea. Do you have anywhere in mind?"

Mrs Jones smiled, but without a trace of humour. "I'm told that Gibraltar is nice at this time of year. As you know, we have a facility there and I've reserved a room for you. I think you'll find yourself in good company."

Royce stared. All the colour had drained out of his face.

Mrs Jones got to her feet. "There's a car waiting for you outside. No need to pack."

She turned and left the room.

DELHI STATION

Alex Rider and Freddy Grey were sitting in the quiet, airy room. Everything was white: the curtains, the bedspread, the walls, even the morning light. They were not close together. Alex had been warned to keep his distance and there was a guard outside the door, just in case. But Freddy did not seem to be dangerous. He had been glad to see Alex. The two of them could almost have been friends.

The compound was just outside the town of Tidworth in south-east Wiltshire, on the edge of Salisbury Plain. This is an area that has long had a close association with the British armed forces. The Ministry of Defence owns thirty square miles of the Plain and local residents are well used to the sound of gunfire and mortar explosions during training exercises. Tidworth Camp was established as long ago as 1905 and to this day has a large number of barracks – all of them named after battles that took place in India including Delhi, Lucknow and Jellalabad. A sophisticated and very private hospital was completed in 2014. It came to be known as Delhi Station. This was where Freddy was being held.

It was a Saturday in November, a cold, bright day with a real bite in the air. Three weeks had passed since the service at St Paul's Cathedral and this was the first time that Alex had seen Freddy. Alex had asked Mrs Jones if he could make the visit and to his surprise she had agreed at once. She had even sent a car for him. Jack had offered to go with him but Alex had refused. He needed to be here on his own.

A smiling matron, also in white, had shown him into Freddy's room.

"How is he?" Alex had asked.

"Well, don't expect too much from him. These things take time. But we'll get there eventually." She spoke with a Scottish accent and Alex liked her at once. "We told him you were coming and he was very pleased."

"Really?"

"Oh yes. He's looking forward to seeing you."

In fact, Freddy said very little during the meeting. He was wearing grey track pants and a sweatshirt. As well as a bed, the room had a desk, a television and a shelf full of books and other things that his parents had brought for him. The two of them had rented a house not far away in Marlborough and visited him every day. Alex noticed a stuffed toy sitting on a chair with its arms dangling and its legs apart. The MI6 forensic team had found Benjamin in Crete and brought him back. It was stupid but Alex was glad that the monkey had made it out.

"Have you been on Salisbury Plain?" he asked. It was difficult making conversation with Freddy, who answered every question politely but who offered nothing to fill the silences.

"No. I'm not allowed to leave the hospital grounds."

"But you've seen your parents?"

"I've seen Sir Christopher and Lady Grey. They've been very kind to me."

He still hadn't accepted who they were.

"How about Sofia?" Alex asked.

"She's here too. We've seen each other a few times."

Alex had been here for half an hour but it felt longer and he knew it was time to go. He and Freddy had been through so much together that he had thought there might be some connection between them but he had to admit that he had been wrong. Even so, there was something he wanted to say before he left.

"Freddy..." he began. Then: "Can I call you that?"

"Yes. It's my name."

"I came down to see you because there's something I want you to understand. I don't know what you think of me. You probably think I'm your worst enemy ... that I lied to you. I'm responsible for you being here. But I want you to know that I'm on your side. And if there's anything I can ever do for you – well, you can call me."

"I'm not allowed a phone."

"One day they'll give you a phone. And you can always ask your ... you can ask Sir Christopher if you want to reach me."

Freddy said nothing so Alex got up and went over to the door. He knocked and the guard opened it.

"You're not my enemy," Freddy said.

Alex turned. He hadn't expected to hear anything more.

"I'd like it if you came again."

Alex nodded. "I will. I promise."

The door closed behind him.

Alex walked down the corridor and back into the reception area, a comfortable space with modern furniture and windows with a view of Sidbury Hill. There was a woman sitting in an armchair, her legs crossed, waiting for him.

"Good morning, Mrs Jones." Alex sat down next to her. "Have you seen Sofia?" he asked.

Mrs Jones nodded. "She hasn't recognized me yet," she said but there was no sadness in her voice. In fact, to Alex, she had never looked happier. "The doctors tell me it could take months or even years," she went on. "But we have the best people working here. We'll get there in the end."

"I'm sorry I left William behind," Alex said.

"You saw him. You saved his life! The fact that I know he's alive means that I can actually hope." She reached out and laid a hand on Alex's arm. "I don't know how to thank you, Alex. It feels like so long ago that you and I first met and I know we were wrong to use you the way we did. But what you've done ... not just for London and for the country but for me! There are no words to express how I feel."

"I'm glad I was able to help." Alex glanced out of the window and saw the car waiting for him. He needed to get back to London. He and Tom were going to see Chelsea play at home and that evening he had dinner with Jack. "Can I ask you something?" he said.

"Of course. You can ask me anything you like."

"I'd like to help you find Nightshade. I don't want to miss any more school. I'm miles behind anyway. I'm getting double homework and Jack's looking for a tutor for Saturdays. But Nightshade were horrible. What they did was horrible. I really would like to meet Brother Lamar and Brother Mike. I'd like to find all of them and make sure they never hurt anyone again. And I want to help find William. He and I weren't exactly friends but I liked him. I like Sofia too."

Mrs Jones smiled. "We're still searching Kavos Bay," she said. "We know who they are now and every single intelligence agency in the world is looking for them. We'll find the other children, including William. You need to concentrate on your GCSEs. We might want to recruit you properly one day and we can't do it if you haven't passed your exams."

"Well, let me know if there's any news."

"I will."

Alex got up and left the building. The front door slid aside to let him pass. The driver of the car started the engine.

What neither Mrs Jones nor Alex knew was that, on the other side of the world, thousands of miles away, the four Teachers were sitting around a table, each one examining the file that they had been given. Alex's photograph was on the front cover and inside there was information about his age, his address, the school he went to, his friends, his hobbies, even the football club he supported.

Leap of Faith had been a colossal failure. They had lost two more Numbers in London and their client had disappeared. It had been their biggest operation ever and they had been defeated by a fifteen-year-old boy. The Teachers had already made up their minds. What had happened was intolerable. They were not going to let the matter rest.

Driving out of Tidworth Camp on his way home, Alex had no need to go looking for Nightshade. They had decided to come for him.

ACKNOWLEDGEMENTS

There are two people without whose help this book would really have been impossible to write.

The first is Oliver Caroe, the Surveyor to the Fabric of St Paul's, who took me on an unforgettable tour of the cathedral from St Faith's Chapel – also known as the OBE chapel – all the way up to the very top (and inside) of the dome. The Ornamental Gallery, where Alex confronts Freddy in the final part of the book, really does exist and I feel very privileged to have visited it. Oliver's enthusiasm and historical knowledge really did inspire my writing.

I am also very grateful to Ray Armstrong, a skydiver who first parachuted solo when he was sixteen and who helped mastermind the amazing skydive in *Mission Impossible: Fallout*. He gave me the information I needed to create Leap of Faith although, sadly, I was unable to experience it for myself.

I have been brilliant supported by the team at Walker Books, led by Jane Winterbotham, my long-suffering editor. I would also like to thank Sarah Handley, who oversaw the entire editorial process and my publicity manager, Rosi Crawley, who makes sure that readers know the book actually exists. The book was copy-edited by the eagle-eyed Clare Baalham, who can spot two repeated words even when they're four hundred pages apart.

Thanks to everyone who has contacted me on Twitter. It's very encouraging to know that there are people who look forward to and enjoy my books.

And, as ever, I'm so lucky to be supported by my family. Jill Green, my brilliant wife, first read the manuscript (and has just made the Alex Rider TV series). My sons, Nick and Cass, are still my most ferocious critics.

READ OTHER GREAT BOOKS BY
ANTHONY HOROWITZ...

ACTION
ADRENALINE
ADVENTURE

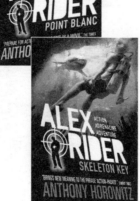

Alex Rider – you're
never too young
to die…

Alex Rider has 90
minutes to save
the world.

High in the Alps,
death waits for
Alex Rider…

Once stung, twice as
deadly. Alex Rider
wants revenge.

Sharks. Assassins.
Nuclear bombs.
Alex Rider's in
deep water.

He's back –
and this time
there are no limits.

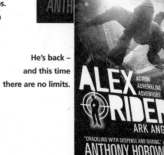

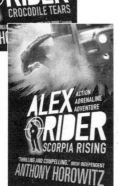

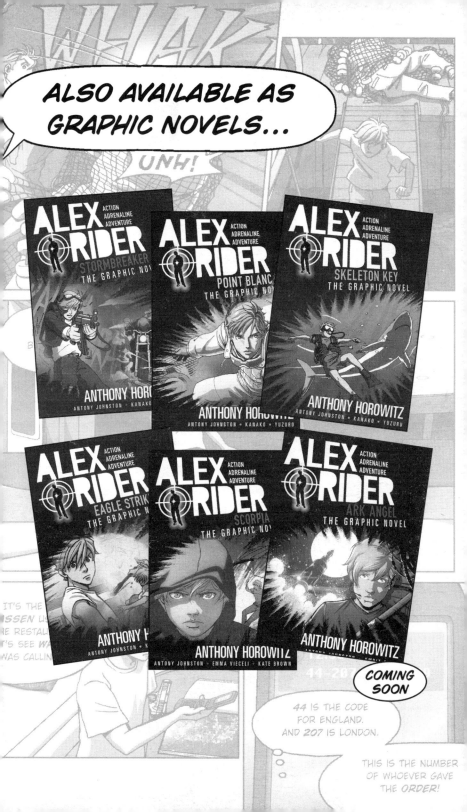

Photograph © Jon Cartwright

Anthony Horowitz is the author of the number one bestselling Alex Rider books and the Power of Five series. He enjoys huge international acclaim as a writer for both children and adults. After the success of his first James Bond novel, *Trigger Mortis*, he was invited back by the Ian Fleming Estate to write a second, *Forever and a Day*. His latest crime novel, *The Sentence is Death*, featuring Detective Daniel Hawthorne, was a bestseller. Anthony has won numerous awards, including the Bookseller Association/Nielsen Author of the Year Award, the Children's Book of the Year Award at the British Book Awards, and the Red House Children's Book Award. He has also created and written many major television series, including *Collision*, *New Blood* and the BAFTA-winning *Foyle's War*. He lives in London with his wife, two sons and his dog, Boss.

You can find out more about Anthony and his work at:
www.alexrider.com
@AnthonyHorowitz